Gypsy

GYPSY

J. Robert Janes

Constable · London

First published in Great Britain 1997
by Constable & Company Ltd
3 The Lanchesters, 162 Fulham Palace Road, London W6 9ER
Copyright © 1997 by J. Robert Janes
The right of J. Robert Janes to be
identified as the author of this work
has been asserted by him in accordance
with the Copyright, Designs and Patents Act 1988
ISBN 0 09 477150 2
Set in 10pt Palatino by
CentraCet, Cambridge
Printed and bound in Great Britain by
Hartnolls Ltd, Bodmin

A CIP catalogue record for this book
is available from the British Library

Gypsy: Brownish to white European moth which flits from place to place causing much damage. A serious pest.

Member of a scattered, nomadic people with a mind-set of its own.

Author's Note

Gypsy is a work of fiction in which actual places and times are used but altered as appropriate. Occasionally the name of a real person appears for historical authenticity, though all are deceased and the story makes of them what it demands. I do not condone what happened during these times, I abhor it. But during the Occupation of France the everyday crimes of murder and arson continued to be committed, and I merely ask, by whom and how were they solved?

Acknowledgement

All the novels in the St-Cyr-Kohler series incorporate a few words and brief passages of French or German. Dr Dennis Essar of Brock University very kindly assisted with the French, as did the artist Pierrette Laroche, while Ms Bodil Little of the German Department at Brock helped with the German. Should there be any errors, they are my own and for these I apologize but hope there are none.

For Steele Curry whose inherent kindness
and boundless enthusiasm are much appreciated.

1

At last the dust began to settle, and all about the room things began to change colour.

Grey grew on the gold and crimson of an Aubusson carpet. Grey gathered on the Generalmajor's dressing-table. It was on the mirror that had split into shards just waiting to fall. It was on his jackboots that were set so neatly to one side, and on the silver and cobalt blue dish of Russian caviar, on the black of those exquisite little pearls not tasted in years, yes, years.

The spoon had been tossed aside to fling a fortune on to the floor. A fortune Herr Max of the Berlin Kriminalpolizei and the IKPK had injudiciously put a shabby brown brogue squarely and uncaringly over. Squish. All gone. Ah *merde*, the stain, and dry cleaning was so expensive these days. Impossible for most.

Shattered flutes stood where once they had held champagne. The Taittinger 1934, a great year, was being soaked up by the settling dust, and the sight of its bottle on ice parched the throat and made one swallow.

As if to mock their panic, the door to the old black iron-studded safe suddenly relaxed and slowly turned inwards, allowing yet another of its firebricks to fall. An avalanche of rubble carelessly accompanied the brick, causing Hermann to blurt dumbfoundedly, 'Has the fire alarm finally stopped?'

The bang had been deafening. Herr Max had only just stepped into the suite and now ruefully wiped the dust from his face. 'So, *und* where is he? *Verdammt, dummköpfe*, is he still in the hotel?'

The Gypsy, the international safe-cracker. The Ritz Hotel, the place Vendôme – Paris and the Occupation; 18 January 1943 at precisely 10.59 p.m. Berlin Time. Monday evening, one hour and one minute before curfew.

'The hotel?' demanded Herr Max.

'He can't be,' breathed Louis in *deutsch*.

'*What is this you are saying*?' shrieked the visiting *Detektiv Inspektor*.

'The safe. It's empty, but as the Gypsy was not in the suite when it blew, how could he have emptied it then?'

'Then?'

Kohler could hear Louis sighing inwardly before his partner said resignedly, 'The Gypsy must have emptied it earlier, Herr Max. His little pleasure was to blow it for our enjoyment. When the door knob was turned – it was yourself who did so, wasn't it? – the circuit was completed and an electrical current passed through the blasting cap. Those *are* bits of electrical wire, are they not? Those *are* the remains of at least two dry-cell batteries?'

'Nitro, Louis. The fumes are giving me a headache.'

'Me also.'

'He has used beeswax to seal the seam between the door and the walls of the safe. He has poured the nitroglycerine in at the top and has used too much.'

'Ah now, has he really, Herr Max?'

Kohler swore under his breath but said loudly, 'Louis, our visitor is absolutely correct.'

'That is exactly what I said.'

'Don't be difficult.'

'Then, Hermann, please inform all those who have come running to put their fire-extinguishers away and to calm themselves. Perhaps one of us – yourself, Herr Max – could summon the Generalmajor? Try any of the bars in the hotel or perhaps the main foyer? Who's to say, really, where a high-ranking officer of the Third Reich will meet a woman he has asked to share a little repast in his quarters?'

'A woman?'

'There are or, rather, there were two glasses. I am of course assuming *une affaire de coeur, n'est-ce pas? Une liaison dangereuse peut-être.*'

'Speak clearly. You know I can't understand you.'

'*Pardonnez-moi.* An affair of the heart, a dangerous liaison perhaps.'

Max Engelmann grunted disparagingly. 'We will let the General-major return when he chooses. For now it is sufficient for us to examine the scene of the robbery. Please do not disturb a thing.'

'Of course. There's nothing left to . . .'

'*Louis, shut up!*'

St-Cyr grabbed his partner by an elbow and hustled Kohler

10

into the bedroom to violently hiss in French, 'What would you have me do, idiot? Let that Büroklammer put his big feet on top of everything? Why is he here, Hermann? Who invited him and how, please, did he know "this" safe was the one to be robbed and by the Gypsy? Why not any other?'

'Those are all good questions but they'll have to keep. For now, hold your temper. That's an order.'

'You know I don't like taking orders from you!'

'Then just back off. He's from Berlin, eh? That can mean many things. Besides, he's no paperclip and you damned well know it!'

'Ah yes, Berlin. I had thought the IKPK fini. Kaput! Disbanded at the outset of the war.'

The International Police Commission had been based in Vienna, linking many of the major police services in Europe and around the world, but then the Anschluss had come, the takeover of Austria in 1938, and in '39, the war.

'Quite obviously I should have remained far more alert to its continued existence,' confessed St-Cyr sourly.

'Me too.'

Though much coveted by Reinhard Heydrich before his assassination by Czech Freedom Fighters in May of 1942, most had felt the IKPK had simply ceased to function, but why should it have? Pimps, prostitutes, pickpockets, con artists, forgers and safe-crackers could still migrate like gypsies. And of course the SS would not only want to keep track of them but to use them whenever necessary. Ah merde, wondered St-Cyr, was that how Herr Max had obtained word of this job?

'The IKPK's card-index files, Hermann. The SS will have them. Every international criminal, every safe-cracker . . .'

'Come on,' said Kohler softly. 'Hey, we'd better get back to him.'

'Of course.'

The fight against common crime had always been difficult, only the more so now under the Nazis, for one never quite knew exactly what the SS and the Gestapo might be up to. A robbery such as this could well have been engineered by them for purposes quite unrelated even to the loot.

In the interlude Engelmann had relighted the butt of a small cigar and was savouring its rich blend of tobaccos, straight from

Rotterdam and budgeted to the very end. 'So, *meine Kameraden der Kriminalpolizei*, are we ready to work together?'

Louis threw him a dark look. Kohler simply grinned and said of his partner, 'He's a Chief Inspector of the Sûreté Nationale who's used to handling things himself. Once you've got that under your belt, the rest is easy.'

'Easy or not, just see that he behaves.'

Max Engelmann took them both in at a glance. These two *Schweine Bullen* from Gestapo Paris-Central and the Sûreté would soon find he'd been a policeman under the Kaiser and that his father had been a Swabian woodcutter, his mother a laundress, himself once a poacher who had betrayed others. Friends, yes, and fellow countrymen but no matter.

Kohler was giving the *en suite* washroom a good going over. St-Cyr was at the Generalmajor's dressing-table but was watching his *Büroklammer* in the shattered mirror. *Und* what do you see, my friend? grunted Engelmann inwardly. A giant like your partner, but one whose gut is far more prominent? Of course I need a shave and haircut but the scruffy, ten-day-old, grey-black beard is my usual – a skin condition, you wonder? Please don't trouble yourself. The poorly clipped beard and moustache simply enhance a natural fierceness that is deliberate, as is the shabby trench coat. *Und ja, mein lieber Franzose*, the spectacles are large and thinly gold-rimmed, the bifocals to correct the near-sightedness of grey-blue little eyes my mother's youngest half-sister shared with me. *Unfug* a *Detektiv* such as yourself might wonder about, so I will not elaborate.

Mischief . . .

Miraculously a crystal vase had escaped the blast, though the hothouse roses were coated with dust. The Baccarat or whatever went over, sending its little flood across the inlaid fruitwood of the King Louis-Whatever table the Ritz had felt suitable.

Startled, the Frenchman stiffened, and just for good measure the mirror relaxed, letting its shards rain on to the dressing-table.

Perfect! sighed Engelmann, grinning inwardly. 'We must question the Generalmajor, Herr St-Cyr, and then his guest. Perhaps if you were the first to do so, I could come in at the end for another spin of the wheel.'

'That safe was first opened using its combination lock.'

'Did the woman the Generalmajor was expecting to entertain give it to another?'

'Or did he foolishly write the combination down somewhere as so many often do?'

'Perhaps we should look.'

'I am and I have.'

There was a desk, ornate and gilded, but the Frenchman had already been over it. Still, the challenge was out and one had best have a look.

'You will find it on his memo pad beside the photo of his children,' said St-Cyr drolly. '"Erika's birthday, 23/5/35; Johann's is 18/1/40."'

'Did you try it?' asked Engelmann.

Was the discovery such a surprise? 'Alas, our Gypsy friend also used beeswax around the mechanism and blew the dial off. Only a check with the manufacturer will settle the issue if our victim remains silent on such an oversight, but I leave that to you since the safe is from Mannheim, from the firm of Leinweber *und* Friesen. They went out of business in 1908.'

'He should have used something newer.'

'It's the shortages,' interjected Kohler passionately as he rejoined them. 'Everyone has to make do.'

They set to work. They fussed, they probed. Did the Generalmajor swim or dine in his absence? Did the woman? Just what the hell had been in the safe and how had the Gypsy gained entrance and known the victim would be absent?

Everything pointed to the woman, but why had someone let Engelmann know of the job in the first place so that they would arrive after the fact?

'Why prepare that little surprise for us and yourself, Herr Max?' asked Louis.

'Why, indeed,' grimaced the visitor distastefully.

'Who told you about it, and when?' asked Kohler.

Engelmann drew in a tired breath, taking the time to size them up again before saying, 'A little bird sang like a nightingale but unfortunately forgot to get the words straight. I received a telephone call at my hotel this evening from her conductor at 10.17, telling me the time and location of the robbery. He then contacted Sturmbannführer Boemelburg, who then notified yourselves.'

'And this little bird?' asked Louis.

'Will now have to answer for the mistake she has made in not letting us know sooner and in not warning us.'

Oh-oh. 'Can't you put a name to her?' bleated Kohler.

'That's just not possible.'

'Then who the hell is her "conductor"?'

'That I cannot tell you either.'

Verdammt! 'Perhaps she didn't know the Gypsy would leave this little surprise for us, perhaps he lied to her about the timing,' muttered Kohler, lost to it.

The visitor tossed his head as if struck. 'Lighten her punishment – is this what you are suggesting?'

Ah damn. 'Something like that, yes.'

Engelmann thumbed dust from his glasses. 'Then please realize that when the cage is opened, the bird tastes freedom and rejoices. It is only understandable. But soon it realizes that if it fails to return, the hand that scatters grain will set snares and pluck its feathers.'

A *mouton*, then. Not a little bird at all. A prison informer who had been told what to do by her 'conductor'.

When the Generalmajor Hans-Albrecht Wehrle arrived in grey flannels, shirt and tennis sweater with a towel still about his neck and badminton racket in hand, they were ready for him. He took one look at the safe, let his lower jaw drop and fought for words as his dark blue eyes flicked in panic over the carnage.

At last a dry whisper was heard. 'The diamonds ... Berlin ... Berlin have been expecting them.'

Wehrle fought to comprehend the future, was sickened by the thought, blanched, gripped his forehead in distress and swore at last and loudly, '*Mein Gott*, it's happened. I've been operating for over two years without a hitch. I wasn't careless – one can't afford to be, but ...'

Louis plucked at Engelmann's trench-coat sleeve to ask if he might begin. 'Of course. It's as we agreed, *ja*? You first *und* then myself.'

'Generalmajor, you were expecting a guest?'

'She has nothing to do with this.'

'That's what they all say. Her name, please?'

Ah damn the man! 'Nana ... Mademoiselle Thélème. She's ... she's having her hair done. The hairdressers all work such odd

14

hours due to the power outages. She ... she'll be along in a few minutes.'

'We hope so,' said the Sûreté flatly. As if on cue, the lift down the corridor sounded and they waited but the wretched thing went on and up to the second floor and then to the third.

'Look, I ... I can explain about her. It's ... it's *not* what you think.'

'*Gut.*'

Herr Max had grunted this. Sourly he indicated the dust-covered chairs and sofas, the small bar – all the comforts of home away from home – even to helping himself to the cigarettes and being greedy about it.

'Oh, sorry. I'm forgetting myself.' A bent cigarette was offered. Kohler took it, then on impulse just to drive the message of consideration for others home, broke the thing in half and gave one part to Louis. Herr Max didn't even bother to notice.

They lit up and sat waiting and watching the victim. Hans-Albrecht Wehrle was fifty-six years old, a businessman who had made himself useful and had been granted the cover of a commission. The brow was high and deeply furrowed, the greying dark hair thin, well-trimmed and receding rapidly, the expression masked now that the reality of what had happened had fully registered.

Had he already found himself a window of escape? wondered Engelmann. Such people usually did. The look became grave, the blue eyes wary. How was it they had arrived so soon? – he could see Wehrle thinking this and then, yes, had his guest betrayed him to the thief?

The cheeks and chin were cleanly shaven, the chin dimpled. Deep cleavages slanted inwards emphasizing the bridge of a distinctly Roman nose. The build was good. A not unhandsome husband for his second wife and his mistress also, or was his association with this Nana Thélème really as he had claimed?

Herr Kohler had read those troubled eyes and had found them wanting, as had his partner but both would keep their counsel until prodded.

'So, Herr Generalmajor, the contents of the safe. Let us begin with that,' said Engelmann disregarding entirely that St-Cyr was to conduct the first interview.

'The diamonds were both rough and finished. Some were

gems but small and not very good, though all would have made cutting and bearing stones when the flaws had been removed. The industrials were for similar uses, others of them to be crushed and ground into grinding and polishing powders.'

'And your task, your position?' asked Louis, having been prodded well enough.

Nervously Wehrle gave a brief, self-conscious smile. 'As a special attaché to the Ministry of Production, my task is to find the diamonds without which our armaments industry would come to a halt.'

Diamonds were essential for cutting and grinding the hardest of materials but was he still worrying about his guest being involved in the robbery? 'About how many diamonds – the weight?' asked St-Cyr, favouring the bushy, dark brown moustache he had taken to wearing long before the Führer had come to power.

'Four kilos. In value perhaps between 35,000,000 and 50,000,000 francs. It's illegal to sell them, of course, except through the official channels. They should all have been declared long ago.'

'Yet you could still buy them, even though "unofficially"?'

'That's understood.'

The lift began its upward traverse again. Hermann had purposely left the door to the suite open so that they might hear it.

Again they listened and again it passed beyond the first floor. Crestfallen, Wehrle fidgeted uncomfortably, even to muttering, 'She'll come. You'll see she will. She had nothing to do with this. I'm certain of it.'

Never one to sit still for long, Kohler got up suddenly. 'Sure she will. Hey, that's 1,750,000 to 2,500,000 *Reichskassenscheine*.' (The Occupation marks, about £175,000 to £250,000.) 'Was there anything else?' he demanded, taking a last drag. 'Or was that enough for her and the Gypsy to share?'

The bullet graze across Kohler's brow was fading, the scar down the left cheek from eye to chin surely not the work of duelling? wondered Wehrle. Even for a Bavarian and a detective, Herr Kohler was formidable. A Fritz-haired, greying giant with shrapnel scars about the face as well as a storm-trooper's lower jaw and build and faded blue eyes – were they always so lifeless?

The nose was pugnacious, the age perhaps fifty-five years, so a good three years older than the blocky, shorter, somewhat portly Frenchman, and perhaps the same amount younger than the grizzled one who was fresh in from the Reich and smelling of old cabbage.

Wehrle tried not to avoid their gazes. 'There were some napoleons in my money belt. Fifteen, I think, but I can't be precise. I buy when I can, you understand.'

Kohler pulled down a lower left eyelid in mock surprise. 'And?' he asked.

Must they all be at him? 'Some sovereigns in a cloth bag, some American gold eagles and ... and my stamps. These last are a hobby, at least they ... they were unless I can get them back.'

It was time for a little sweetness. 'Can you supply us with a list?' asked Engelmann, using a pocket-knife to ream a thumbnail.

'Of course. It's in my desk. There was also the office postage and petty cash. Would you like a record of those as well?'

'Where is the office?' asked St-Cyr swiftly.

'The Hotel Majestic, naturally.'

St-Cyr tossed his head in acknowledgement. When the Germans had marched into Paris on 14 June 1940, the Wehrmacht had taken over the Majestic and other such places. Lots of them, with sentries at the entrances and *ausweise* needed to come and go, but why had the safe not been housed there?

Again the sound of the lift interrupted things but now it seemed to hesitate, putting them all on edge. But then it went away and for a moment there was silence. 'She's not coming,' grunted Engelmann. 'Perhaps after all, you had best tell us about her.'

'Look, we know how it is,' said Kohler companionably. 'Paris is a long way from home. Leave is something your superiors, if they're anything like mine, feel irrelevant. A man does need a little female company now and then.'

How utterly pious! snorted St-Cyr inwardly. Just recently divorced but long married, Hermann *lived* with two women he had rescued. Giselle was a former prostitute, a very intelligent, purposeful and beautiful girl with jet black hair and violet eyes; Oona, a Dutch alien without proper papers, was beautiful also – blonde, blue-eyed, about forty years of age and nearly *twice* the age of the first. God's little dilemma.

17

Nervously Wehrle got up and went over to the bar then thought better of it and sought out the champagne only to hold the bottle up to them as evidence. 'He opened it. Neither of us were in the room. He filled the two glasses – even I can see that – but he *couldn't* have had more than a sip.'

As the Sûreté watched, Herr Max's dispassionate gaze lifted to settle on the victim. 'And what, please, makes you so certain your mistress did not let the thief into these rooms?'

'Nana's not my mistress, damn you! She *works* for me and I pay her well. She has an ear for things and is often in the right place at the right time. As a diamond buyer I *can't* be too obvious, can I? Discretion allows the timid to come forward without fear of arrest. No names are necessary or recorded. I pay in cash and there are no questions asked.'

Perfect, then, if one had robbery in mind.

It was Louis who said, 'But ... but if in cash, were there not also bundles of banknotes in your safe? And why, please, was the safe not housed in your office at the Majestic?'

Again there was that nervous, self-conscious little smile as if still clawing at thoughts of his Nana's having betrayed him.

'We had just closed a deal and were to celebrate. That's why there wasn't much cash in the safe. That's why the champagne.'

'And the caviar.' He was just too wary, too full of doubts about her, felt Kohler. Louis sensed it too, and so did Herr Max.

'The caviar, yes. It was a promise, a little treat. Nana loves it. And as for the safe being here, I travel a lot. Mostly I work away from the office. I always have.'

Again they heard the lift, again they waited, breaths held, hearts pounding now perhaps.

The damned thing stopped. The gate came open. Every step the woman took was muffled by the carpet but they each knew when she would appear in the open doorway and then, there she was.

Kohler swallowed hard. Louis, he knew would be intrigued. Herr Max apparently took but a moment to imagine flinging her into a chair before switching on the spotlight to shine it into her eyes. Slap, *slap*! and blood on her beautiful lips ...

'Nana ...'

'Hans, what has happened? Who are these men?'

18

'Ihere Papiere. Bitte, Fräulein. Bitte.'

'Hans . . . ?'

'Fräulein, he can do nothing for you now. Just give me your papers,' grunted Engelmann impatiently snapping his fingers.

Reluctantly Louis translated, and as he watched her, Kohler thought he detected an all but imperceptible wince. A handsome woman. Tall, proud – haughty even. Andalusian? he wondered. Spanish certainly. Part Moor? She was making him think of hot sun, lolling cattle nearby and midday silence. An abandoned hacienda among ancient olive groves. Two horses, no blanket on the ground. Just the sun high above and seen through the dusty grey of the leaves.

Her hair was jet black and thick, worn loose and long beneath the stylish hat of Arctic fox. Her eyebrows were dark and wide and served only to enhance eyes that did not flash in anger but could, though now they remained as if looking well into the distance to something other than themselves. They were large, dark olive eyes with deep touches of the Moor, the Carthaginian perhaps, or Phoenician – Louis would have run back through the gamut of her ancestry and perhaps this was what she was seeing in the distance.

The chin was proud, the lips not compressed, just wide and very firm in resolve. A touch of lipstick. No wrinkles yet at the age of what? he asked and told himself, thirty-eight. No powder, no rouge, her skin not white, not coffee brown but of the softest shade of hazel. Perfume . . . Was she wearing any?

She didn't flinch under his scrutiny nor that of his partner but remained immobile as Herr Max thumbed her papers, grunting from time to time as a pig would at its swill.

At last Kohler thought he detected a quivering nostril as she waited, not looking to either side but straight at her Generalmajor with . . . Was it hatred, he wondered; was it, I will kill you for this if you do not defend me?

The white cashmere gloves would be soft. The off-white overcoat was of alpaca, a fabulous thing cut so that it brought out the tallness of her, the shoulders.

'Herr Kohler, don't take too great an interest in our guest. Fetch some coffee. While you're at it, call your superior officer. As Sturmbannführer Boemelburg is Head of the Gestapo in France, and has taken a definite interest in our Gypsy, he will be waiting in his office for just such a call. Inform him of the details. An all-points alert for our friend. Every rail station and road. A sweep of what remains of the gypsy haunts – please include the ... Ah, what was it?' he asked himself and peered again at her papers, even to lifting his specs out of the way and squinting myopically.

She got the hint. 'The Club Monseigneur,' she said and swallowed tightly. 'The Schéhérazade also, but only sometimes.'

He tossed his head in acknowledgement but let her say, 'They're in Montmartre, on the rue d'Amsterdam and the rue de Liège, but tonight is my night off.'

'Everyone needs a break,' he said, scratching a scruffy cheek and nodding sagely.

Again Louis, his brown ox-eyes still intrigued, was forced into the reluctant role of translator.

'A sweep of what's left of the gypsy warrens, as I was saying,' went on Engelmann. 'Montmartre, near the railway yards and the Gare Saint-Lazare. Belleville, too, eh, Herr St-Cyr – that is where you live, isn't it? Those little streets where the tenements are so close, the rats can get across the gaps without hitting the paving stones below or getting tangled in the laundry lines after fucking someone else's wife, with her consent, of course.'

My wife, monsieur? Is that it, eh? raged St-Cyr inwardly. How *could* the bastard say such a thing? 'The Gare du Nord and Gare de l'Est – the Canal Saint-Martin and Bassin de la Villette,' came the cold retort, 'but if I were you, I would look further afield. Saint-Ouen perhaps, and Saint-Gervais.'

The whole of Paris perhaps, and St-Cyr still touchy about a pretty wife – his second and much younger than himself – who had made love repeatedly to the Hauptmann Steiner, the couple's naked antics secretly recorded by Gestapo Paris's Watchers and kept on file for posterity. Steiner's uncle, the General von Schaumburg, was still Kommandant von Gross Paris – that was why they'd been watching the nephew – and everyone knew the Gestapo didn't exactly hit it off with the Wehrmacht. 'The industrial suburbs, I think, and the flea markets,' grunted Engelmann. 'Bagneux as well. There are Russian exiles in those high-rise pigsties the thirties brought.'

Ah damn, thought Kohler. The two of them were really at each other's throats and some son of a bitch down at Gestapo Paris-

Central had let Herr Max know all about Louis's wife. Had the visitor from the IKPK viewed the films? He must have. Then he would also know that the Hauptmann had been sent to Russia by his uncle, and that he had later died there. Marianne St-Cyr had been coming home with Louis's little son when she had tripped over a wire, a Resistance bomb that had been meant for Louis. Not two months ago and a mistake if ever there was one – he was no collabo but like many, had been forced to work for the Occupier. One would never know how she had felt, repentant or otherwise, least of all poor Louis who had forgiven her *and* the Resistance, and had been trying ever since to get back the films he had never seen, thank God.

Herr Max tossed the woman's papers on to the coffee table, glanced at his wrist-watch and said, 'The *métro* and the buses. Have them shut down.'

'They've already stopped. It's 2333. They grind to a halt at 2300. No diamond bearings, I guess,' quipped Kohler to lighten things and get her back her papers.

'VERDAMMT! *Don't you ever do that again. You and this* Teich-froch *of yours are under my orders. Mine, Kohler. Orders, do you understand?'*

This pond-frog . . . 'Okay, I'll call the Chief.'

'And you will ask him, *ja*? to define for you just what I have said.'

Though the woman, like each of them, had been startled and had leapt at the shrillness of Herr Max, she had somehow calmed herself only to be unsettled again by the whispered exchange that had followed.

Without waiting for her to recover, Engelmann grabbed her by the wrist, hustled her to a chair, and told her to take off her coat, hat and gloves. 'You won't be needing them. It's warm enough.'

'*Und in den Zellen, mein Herr?*' she asked defiantly.

Startled, poor Louis took a step forward only to think better of it. Herr Max was only too aware of him and now grinning, since she had betrayed a knowledge of the language she would rather have kept to herself.

'In the prison cells, Fräulein?' breathed Engelmann softly. 'But . . . but what is this you are saying? Have you been in prison before?'

She took a little breath. Her *deutsch*, when it came, was cold and fluent. 'Never. Now am I to be placed under arrest for assisting the Third Reich? Hans, do something.'

That icy contempt would have to be shattered. 'He can't, Fräulein,' said Engelmann. 'He mustn't. You see, your diamond buyer has just realized it would be imprudent. He has, *meine gute Dame*, cast you to the wolves, to me.'

To the Gestapo . . .

'That's not true! Nana, these people . . . One has to be patient. Things take a little time. Questions are only natural. You've nothing to hide.'

Or have you? wondered St-Cyr with a sinking feeling that would not go away.

'*Und* now we begin it, Fräulein,' sighed Engelmann. 'You let the Gypsy into these quarters. You either left the lock off or gave him a key. You told him where your lover had written down the combination, and then you went to have your . . . Was it washed and dried? Please, I must touch it.'

'*Don't*! I know nothing. I've done nothing.'

Her hair was soft. He let it fall. 'Then you have nothing to fear.'

'Herr Max . . .' began Louis only to see the visitor glowering at him and hear him saying, 'Please, she is all yours. You first with the questions as agreed, and then myself.'

Once away from them, Kohler took a moment to steady himself. *Verdammt!* Max Engelmann reeked of trouble. The IKPK? and now here it was resurrected and squatting on their doorstep, especially on Louis. Poor Louis.

The Gypsy, ah *merde*. A plague in the late twenties and the thirties but then someone had given him away – betrayal and jail in Oslo, 17 May 1938. Seven years of hard labour on a diet of cold *hardfiskur*,* no mayonnaise, and torn chunks of *ruqbraud*,* only to turn up as free as a bird in Occupied Paris.

The cable from Heinrich Himmler via Gestapo Mueller in Berlin via Gestapo Boemelburg in Paris had been terse. MOST URGENT. REPEAT URGENT. IKPK HQ BERLIN REPORTS INTER-

* dried fish and rye bread

22

NATIONAL SAFE-CRACKER GYPSY REPEAT GYPSY HAS REPORTEDLY SURFACED. LAST SEEN TOURS 1030 HOURS 14 JANUARY HEADING FOR PARIS. APPREHEND AT ONCE. HEIL HITLER.

Like most of the Sûreté, Louis had heard of the Gypsy, but why bring in Engelmann, why put them *under* that bastard's orders when he couldn't even speak French and couldn't know the city or the country for that matter, or did he? And why, please, had he deliberately insulted Louis with that crap about unfaithful wives?

Was someone playing with them? Were their loyalties being 'investigated' again? Louis was a patriot; himself a conscientious doubter and objector of Nazi infallibility, brutality and all else. Everyone knew both Louis and himself were kept on by Boemelburg simply because they produced results. One hundred per cent.

In an age of officially sanctioned crime, they were virtually the only honest cops left to fight common crime. But as sure as that God of Louis's had made safes to crack, there was an IKPK card-index file with the Gypsy's profile for the SS in Berlin to peruse at their leisure. Were they using the Gypsy? Was it all a sham?

Deeply troubled by the thought, Kohler went along the corridor, round a corner and up a small flight of stairs until he had what he wanted.

She was sitting in her little cupboard, waiting patiently to clean up the dust. She had her shoes and black stockings off, and was soaking her bunions and corns in a basin of salt water to which she had added a small handful of rose petals – red ones, ah yes.

'God, they're a bugger, aren't they?' he said of the shoes these days. 'Mine are killing me.' And from a tattered pocket, he rescued a forgotten cigarette and broke it in half.

Lighting them, he handed her one and said congenially, 'Hey, don't worry, eh? No one will see us, and if I have to, I'll tell them it's business.'

Business? She swallowed and began to do up the belt and buttons she had released to give a tired waist a little room.

'The robbery,' he said. She ducked her eyes away and cringed – knew he had seen the rose petals, knew he'd noticed the two tickets she had found for the Opéra, the magazines and the

23

newspapers, all in German he would know only too well she could not understand.

'The pictures,' she managed. 'I look at them.'

'That's what the Propaganda Staffel count on, but like I said, don't worry. I simply want to ask you a few small questions. Nothing difficult.'

Her bunions were swollen, the corns aflame. The toenails had been painted but some time ago. The uniform, a dress of thin black cotton with a starched white lace cap and an apron, needed attention. The shoes had been made of ersatz leather and cardboard, their soles of softwood.

At the age of sixty-seven, life had been unkind. Bony in places, sagging in others, she had been a girl of the streets and brothels until married to the night shift at the Ritz and to cleaning up after others.

'So, the robbery,' he said again and she didn't know whether to fear him or to be beguiled, for he was formidable with that slash down his face and the other one across his brow, but there was laughter in his faded blue eyes and it was not unkind, or was it?

'I saw nothing. I heard nothing. I was occupied in another part of the hotel.'

'Don't be stubborn. The rose petals came from room 13. It's the Opéra tickets that worry me.'

'They're no good now. The performance will be . . .'

'Your name? Papers . . . Papers, *bitte*, eh?' He snapped his fingers just like Engelmann had done and hated himself for doing so but it was no time for her to be stubborn.

'Mademoiselle Georgette Bernard,' he breathed, scanning the ID photo and glancing at the guilt-ridden, swimming brown eyes.

Self-consciously she touched a curl and then her cap. 'Monsieur . . .'

'It's Inspector and hey, I really do want us to co-operate.'

'I found the tickets on the carpet in the corridor outside room 13.'

'When?'

'Sometime after . . . after the Generalmajor had left to play with the birds.'

'And the rose petals?'

24

'A rose with its stem had fallen and was lying between the tickets. I . . .'

Had the Gypsy a sense of humour? Had the bastard left them in the hall as some sort of calling card or a reminder for Nana Thélème? 'Now start by telling me if that's your master key up there on the hook, then why is there another hanging from your belt?'

Things would not go well. 'That is Mariette's key. She's the day-girl. When she leaves at six, she changes out of her uniform and hangs it up, the key also.'

'Good. And when you come on to change and get your key, do you leave the door to this cupboard locked?'

She crossed herself and silently said a small prayer. 'The door is never locked. I . . . I am away from here for some time – the carpets, you understand. The mirrors, the endless dusting – I can see that you appreciate my absences and that, the back, it was often turned and I could not possibly have known always that . . . that Mariette's key had remained constantly in its place.'

'And would anyone else have known of this?'

'The Mademoiselle Thélème? Ah no. No, Monsieur l'inspecteur. It's impossible. That one comes only by the lift. Never the stairs and certainly not the ones you have climbed, since they are only for the staff and the notice forbids entry to all others.'

She was really doing well. 'When did the Generalmajor leave to play badminton?'

'At about ten minutes before eight. Always when he is in Paris and not out for dinner, he does so. Always after the little birds, he has the shower bath and then takes to the pool, and then . . . well, whatever suits him. Who am I to say?'

Ah now . . . 'Pardon?' he asked.

She tossed her head. 'Mademoiselle Thélème always comes by the side entrance, the one that is on the rue Cambon and reached by way of the garden-restaurant. After he's done with her, she leaves by the same route, sometimes happy and light of step, sometimes wounded. Who's to say what makes the heart beat faster than at other times. An hour or two – Mariette is the one you should talk to. She has to clean up and make the bed in the morning. That is not my duty.'

'Okay, so the Generalmajor went out at about eight this evening. Your back was turned and the day-girl's master key was up there on the wall. Did you see anyone in the halls, anyone who was not of the usual?'

'I saw many. They come and go. Most wear the uniform and I must continue working and duck the eyes away so that they will not notice me. Several carry the attaché cases. All are very important, and some do take their women with them to their rooms. Yes, I have seen such things. Others live here with them. It's allowed.'

'But number 13 is at the end of the corridor and therefore a little out of the way. Was there anything else? *Think*. Please try to remember. It's important.'

In dismay, she sadly shook her head but her deceitful toes were playing with each other in the swimming pool of their basin. 'Okay,' he breathed, and taking out a thin roll of bank-notes, unsnapped the elastic band and gave her 200 francs.

'A night's wages,' she sighed pityingly. 'You do not tip?'

500 more were found. 'There was a captain, a general – they are all the same to me, you understand. Oh *mais certainement*, he was fair-haired and blue-eyed but a Dutchman, I think. The Dutch are even more conceited and arrogant than *les Allemands*. He carried himself well. A man of forty years. Tall, handsome, very sure of himself and quick of step. Ah! to pass unnoticed, it is only necessary to let others see you living normally.'

The song of their times.

'The scars on the face like yourself, though not so terrible. Three of them – both cheeks and the nose. The chin, it was sharp; the lips, those of a teenaged boy like the one I once knew. The eyes with laughter, yes, but also the gaze that constantly searches, the heart most especially.'

'But . . . but you just said you were not to look at the guests?'

'Ah! this I could not help since the mirror I was polishing faced him and I could not stop him from pausing to straighten his tie. He was very smartly dressed, wore the pistol in its holster and had the Iron Cross at his throat. The attaché case . . . ah, now. Could there have been explosives in it, Inspector? *L'eau de vie de nitroglycérine*? He has set the case very delicately on the table before straightening his tie and looking at me.'

'At about what time?'

'I cannot tell you. The watch, it is in for repairs.'

'The *mont-de-piété*?'

26

The pawnshop. 'Yes.'

He sighed as another 500 francs were found. 'That's to get your watch back.'

The Boches were such fools! 'At 8.15 he has gone along the corridor towards room 13. I have had to dust the spare suite that is always kept for the Reichsmarschall Goering, even though that one has a villa in Paris. My back, it was turned for some time.'

'At 8.15.'

'Yes. And then, Inspector, at 8.47 he has taken the lift. This I have also seen.'

Verdammt, and so much for her not having had a watch!

'Henri will tell you what I have just said, but to grease the elevator operator's memory you will need much more. 2000 at least.'

A bargain, then. He was half-way down the narrow staircase when she hesitantly called after him. 'Monsieur, has Mademoiselle Thélème been detained? It . . . it is only that she could not possibly be involved. You see, she has a little boy who is the light of her life. She would do nothing to endanger him. A mother's love is beyond all loves. This I know though the heart, it has been broken now for more than forty years.'

'She's okay. She's in good hands. My partner's looking after her.'

The suit was very much in vogue, yet sensible, thought St-Cyr. Four stag-horn buttons complemented the finely woven, soft, grey-blue mohair, while a chain of gold links caused the jacket to flare over the hips, emphasizing the slender waist and long and shapely legs beneath the midcalf-length skirt.

The ribbing of the wool ran the length of Mademoiselle Thélème. The high-heeled shoes were of glossy blue leather – Italian and pre-war but perfectly kept.

A woman, then, who knew how to dress and was proud of it, even to following his scrutiny, not denying herself that little pleasure yet keeping her mind acutely alert to everything else.

It was disconcerting to have to question her in front of Engelmann while the Generalmajor flitted nervously about in the background, uncertain still of her responses and of where things were heading.

Hans Wehrle definitely didn't like the attention he was getting but that could simply mean he understood only too well the sort of things that could happen. Ruefully St-Cyr wished his partner was with them, but Hermann had chosen to forget about the coffee and was, no doubt, engaged in other matters.

'So tell me, please, about the Gypsy?'

She shrugged. 'I know nothing of gypsies. Who cares about them?' She tossed a dismissive hand. 'They've all been arrested and sent away, haven't they? Pah! We don't see any of those people any more and if we did, we would have to report them.'

Or worry that they were working for the Occupier – he could see her thinking this and acknowledged it with a curt nod. Safe . . . she had been so very safe and cautious in what she had said.

'But you sing at two of the gypsy places?' he hazarded.

'Fiercely loyal White Russians, Czech and Hungarian balalaika and fiddle players. Sentimental songs that have been around for ages. They aren't *real* gypsies. Oh *mein Gott, Inspektor*, they couldn't be, could they?'

And the Occupier does enjoy slumming from club to club until forced to leave before curfew or risk being locked in for the rest of the night, getting drunker and drunker until the sentimental tears came, or sleep.

'I have a friend who sings,' he offered and she knew he was watching her closely for the slightest suggestion of alarm. 'A chanteuse. The Club Mirage.'

'That's nice. It's over in Montparnasse, isn't it?'

'Yes. The rue Delambre and eight hundred war-weary men a night. It's quite a crowd.'

'But a living, I think,' she said so softly her voice was like a caress.

'I thought, perhaps, you might have met. You wear the same perfume. *Mirage.*'

She didn't drop her eyes or give a hint of disquietude but steadily returned his gaze. 'It's very expensive. A general gave it to me. Not Hans, another.'

'And you've not met her?'

'No. No, six nights a week allows too little time to socialize. I've a son, also, and whatever free time I have is devoted entirely to him.'

'But not on evenings like this.'

Touché, was that it? she wondered, cursing his questions but giving no hint of this. Herr Engelmann had expectantly sat up at the exchange. Hans had stopped fiddling about and was waiting anxiously for her response ... 'My son understands that occasionally his mother must visit with a friend for an hour or two.'

'But he isn't aware of the nature of those visits?'

And just *what* do you think was the nature of this visit? she wanted to demand of him but looked, instead, into the distance, perhaps to the welcome of a long-lost camp-fire.

'My Jani understands that sometimes mummy has to sing at private dinner parties and that she cannot always refuse.'

Not these days.

Her breath was held for just a split second. St-Cyr knew that tough exterior had at last been truly dented but she recovered so quickly, he had nothing but admiration for her.

Herr Max's scrutiny was now hard and penetrating. Hans Wehrle found himself lost in doubt and forced to sit down.

'These private dinner parties, Inspector ...' grunted Engelmann sourly.

'It's Chief Inspector.'

'If you insist.'

'I do.'

There was a nod and then the firmness of, 'Please ask her to tell us about them. The most recent, I think.'

'Hans, is this necessary?'

The look she gave was swift, hard and damning.

'Nana, I can do nothing. It's up to them. Please try to understand it's not me who has been robbed but the Reich.'

Engelmann cleared his throat and, focusing on the gaping maw of the safe, let her have it. 'Nothing you may well know, Fräulein, but someone made the Gypsy aware of the contents and the vulnerability of that safe, and someone alerted the authorities not only to a robbery by him but ...' He paused. '... also the timing of it. Not quite, however, thus his apprehension has unfortunately eluded us for the moment.'

There was dust everywhere, still the stench of bitter almonds, of nitroglycerine.

'Nana, *mein Gott*, don't be so stubborn. *Tell* them!' leapt Wehrle.

She shrugged. 'It was nothing – how could it have been? The villa is mine but it has been requisitioned for the duration, so I had the opportunity to see at first hand if it was being properly cared for. One does wonder, isn't that so? And, yes, many of the guests were in uniform – the men, that is. And, yes, I took some of my little orchestra with me and we sang a few "gypsy" songs for them.'

'When?' breathed Hermann who had slid so quietly into the room none had noticed him and all wondered how long he'd been there.

'Last Monday.'

A week ago . . . 'SS, Gestapo and friends of friends?' he asked, pleasantly enough.

'Collaborators, yes. Some of the big boys.'

'In the butter-eggs-and-cheese racket?' went on Kohler.

The black market. 'Perhaps. I really wouldn't know about those types.'

'The rue Lauriston?' he asked.

The French Gestapo. 'Yes, perhaps those also.'

The Gypsy had been seen in Tours heading for Paris at 1030 hours, 14 January. The dinner party had been on the eleventh. 'Where's the villa?' he demanded.

'In Saint-Cloud.'

'*Pas mal, pas mal*, mademoiselle. Saved up your *sous*, did you, to buy it?'

'*Yes!*'

'Present address?'

'It's on my papers.'

'Just give it to me.'

'Above the Club Monseigneur, on the rue d'Amsterdam.'

The quartier de l'Europe and perhaps the dullest, noisiest, ugliest of neighbourhoods in Paris. 'That's quite a comedown.'

'But a lot closer to work.'

'Were there any other singers present at the dinner party?'

Ah *maudit*! why could he not have left it alone? 'No. No, there were no others. Not that I knew of.'

Kohler saw her throw him a look so poignant he winced and felt a fool. There *had* been others, and now she knew he was as aware of it as she and so was everyone else. 'The coffee's here,' he said. 'I thought a little brandy might help, Herr Max, and found they had a bottle of Asbach Uralt tucked away for connoisseurs like ourselves. There's some Beck's *Bier* in case the dust has made you really thirsty.'

The Ritz was full of high-ranking German officers on leave or stationed in Paris, and had been since the Defeat, hence the availability of the refreshments, among other things.

'You think of everything.'

'We try to, my partner and I. It's a habit we've grown accustomed to.'

Not one to waste time, Engelmann closed with Nana Thélème and was soon getting his turn at the wheel. The Generalmajor remained agitated – Wehrle knew Berlin weren't going to like the loss. Would he be held responsible? Would restitution be demanded in hugely increased requests? Absolutely! But ... but was there something else ...? Only time would tell. 'Louis, our visitor from Berlin is trouble. He's not happy. Something has upset him.'

'A robbery he was told of but not quite!' snorted the Sûreté.

Kohler offered a cigarette, cadged from the Generalmajor. 'Berlin are never happy. Hey, we'll sort the son of a bitch out before things get heavy.'

There was a sigh that, after working with Louis since September 1940, Kohler knew only too well.

'Let us hope there is time, *mon vieux*. The cigarette is perfect with real coffee, real sugar and milk. You're learning.'

Kohler humbled himself. Sometimes Louis needed this. 'A key was available, Chief. Probable entry was witnessed at 8.15 p.m., exit at 8.47. Our Gypsy knew the Generalmajor would be playing shuttlecocks, but he took the trouble to find the pistol, uniform and attaché case of a Wehrmacht Hauptmann.'

The coffee was spilled as the cigarette was stubbed out. 'Why didn't you say so *before* you gave me a moment to myself? Have we a body on our hands, Hermann? A German body?'

If so, reprisals would have to be made by the Kommandant von Gross Paris and others, namely Hermann's boss. Three, five ... ten would be taken from the cells or streets and shot.

'It's too early to say, but the son of a bitch must have got the uniform somewhere.'

'Was he tall, blue-eyed, blond and forty years old? Handsome, distinguished, and very much the ladies' man?'

31

'It was him all right. The whip scars on the face are much tidier than mine. A Dutchman, the *femme de chambre* thought.'

One could nearly always count on Hermann. 'He earned the scars as a boy. In the spring of 1914, at the age of eleven, he left home in Rotterdam to wander with the gypsies. The parents were very understanding – the threat of war was imminent, I think you will recall. The father was a writer of historical romances, the mother an artist, whose paintings Berlin will no doubt have trashed and burned if aware of them. Bohemians at heart, so they knew their son was doing what he thought best and that he would come home a much wiser boy.'

St-Cyr finished the coffee so as not to waste it. 'Of course, he didn't return until after the war but even then his stays with the Rom extended into months. He had learned the language. He fitted right in, Hermann. They will have imparted to him everything he needs to know in order to survive in times like this, and to take advantage of them.'

Oh-oh.

Though persecuted terribly and classed with others by the Nazis as *Rassenverfolgte* (racially undesirable), the life style tended to make the gypsies much harder to locate and arrest. They were scattered widely into small groups and nearly always had been on the move from country to country. Evading capture better than most, they had, centuries before this lousy war, learned how to disperse at a moment's notice. Even so, countless tens of thousands had already been deported, a tragedy.

But the war had increasingly brought changes to them. No longer did their women thieve a few chickens and geese for the pot from hard-labouring peasants, thus engendering further hatred and reprisals from the local gendarmes. No longer were potatoes or laundry lifted to be carried hidden in voluminous skirts or fortunes told and coins begged.

Instead, the men hid their women and children, travelled much less and, in a cruel winter like this, would have sought refuge in far corners.

'Some have even turned to working with the Resistance, Hermann, with *Gaje** and unheard of before. In the south, they

---

* all those other than gypsies.

almost totally control the supply of forged ration cards. IDs are a sideline and they're good, among the best.'

'Then he'll head south and join up with a *kumpania*.'

An alliance of caravans, a 'family' which could be broken down and scattered at a moment's notice. 'Perhaps.'

Louis tossed off the last of his coffee, filled his cup with good German brandy to deny the Occupier that portion – one had to do little things like that – and, relighting the cigarette for the same reason, no doubt, drifted off to single out the victim and engage him in a quiet word the Generalmajor wanted no part of.

Kohler looked about the room, wondering what it all must mean for them, wondering, too, just where the Gypsy would hole up and if this would be his only target. The industrial diamonds were nothing to a man who travelled light but he had taken them anyway which hinted at a Resistance motive. Sabotage the enemy where it would hurt the most, get him right in the balls.

The gem diamonds were, of course, another matter, so, too, the gold coins and the stamps – the Resistance were always short of funds – but had the Gypsy suddenly got religion or something? And had the woman really been a part of it?

She threw him a brief glance that left only the impression of wariness. He knew he'd have to get her alone and he hoped Herr Max wouldn't insist on arresting her. Such things were always a bind once started. If a reinforced interrogation was required, she'd be beaten to a pulp. Louis and himself would try to stop it from happening. They weren't torturers, weren't sadists, but because of this and their never failing to point the finger where deserved, they were not welcome in certain circles, and were under a constant cloud of suspicion even from Berlin.

Those other types would make her talk. Few could resist them and hadn't Herr Max said a *mouton* had informed on the Gypsy and that a conductor had passed the word along?

'Generalmajor, where were you last Monday evening?'

The eleventh, the dinner party in Saint-Cloud. 'Not with Nana, if that's what you're thinking.'

When no comment was made by St-Cyr, Wehrle fussed and finally passed a worried hand over a deeply furrowed brow.

'Look, I was here in Paris. I can't be seen with her, can I, even at a function like that? How could I be? Word would soon get around and the clients would only become suspicious of the SS or the Gestapo, or those of the rue Lauriston interfering. The people I have to deal with are nervous enough as it is.'

The rue Lauriston, the French Gestapo . . . 'How long has your association with her been going on?'

'Two years. She . . .' Wehrle threw Mademoiselle Thélème a look of anguish the woman could not fail to notice. This caused her to pause in her response to Max Engelmann and the Berliner turned swiftly to glare suspiciously at them.

'She . . .?' asked St-Cyr, dragging the victim back to things.

'She'd had word at last from a source she had been trying to secure for some time. Nana's not just a singer. She and her mother run a very successful school of popular dance. You'd be surprised how many lonely men want to learn to dance or to just be with someone for an hour or two. These days more than ever.'

And so much for her working six nights a week at two clubs and spending all the rest of her time with her son.

'Nana's patient and yes, because of the villa in Saint-Cloud and her life in Paris before the war, she knows a great many people. Even prospectors want to learn to dance and listen to gypsy music when on infrequent visits.'

'Prospectors?'

'A former prospector of the Congo, South Africa and the Niger. Illegal stones then, in the thirties, illegal now. Nearly a full kilo of crushing boart – superb in itself. Samples from a prospect he still remains excited about. But . . .' Wehrle took a moment to nervously run a finger through the dust on the coffee table. 'But 1800 carats of mixed stones, mostly industrials suitable for cutting tools but among them, 657 carats of *Jagers*, Top Capes and Capes. The first of these are good, clear white stones with a bluish tinge due to fluorescence; the latter two are also flawless, but with faint yellowish tints. It was an exceptional haul and well worth the trip.'

The truth at last. 'And when was this trip made?' hazarded the Sûreté.

'Nana *can't* have been involved. Damn you, how many times must I say it?'

'The trip, please?'

34

'Last Tuesday. To Tours.'

'Pardon?'

'To Tours, damn it!'

'Name and address?'

Wehrle sighed. 'Émile Jacqmain, a Belgian, a Walloon who has lived in France since 1930 when not abroad in Africa.'

The brandy and the cigarette were savoured, the Sûreté waiting expectantly like a bullfrog for its dragonfly.

'The house is on place Plumereau. The flat is right above a butcher shop. Jacqmain *can't* have had anything to do with this. It's ridiculous you should think he could. I checked him out thoroughly. I *don't* as a rule walk into any of these arrangements carrying a million or so francs and *not* examine the credentials well beforehand and, I might add, discreetly.'

'Good.'

'Good? Is that all you have to say?'

Cigarette ash was tipped into an empty coffee cup. 'Did Mademoiselle Thélème travel to Tours on Tuesday so as to pave the way for you?'

'She'd have needed a *laissez-passer*. I'd have had to sign for her.'

'And did you?'

'Yes but . . . but we couldn't celebrate until this evening.'

'But I thought you said you couldn't be seen together?'

'We can't, but he insisted nothing would go through unless she spoke to him first on that Tuesday. My hands were tied.'

'Did you travel together?'

Wehrle was frantic. 'How could we have? We didn't even see each other except briefly at the station. She went into his flat at about 2 p.m., I didn't meet with him until seven that evening. As it was, I had to stay over.'

'And keep everything in your hotel room, not in the safe?'

'Yes! Now are you satisfied?'

'Generalmajor, forgive a poor detective. One questions everything but is never satisfied. Always there are so many things to remember.'

'Such as?'

'That this deal was not only a big one, *n'est-ce pas?* but also apparently quite different.'

St-Cyr took a moment. Longing for another cigarette, he

borrowed two. 'That safe was full but how full, please, in terms of your usual collections?'

Ah *Gott im Himmel*, the bastard! *'Very.* It . . . it was a superb shipment. One of the best, if not the best so far.'

The truth again. 'And eagerly anticipated in Berlin?'

'That is correct.'

'And you had paid Jacqmain how much, please?'

Would this infernal idiot from the Sûreté look for dirt under everything? '850,000 francs. About a tenth of their value. Usually I offer a little more but one always starts low.'

'Yet Jacqmain accepted this?'

It was not a question. A faint smile would therefore be best. 'Could he really have argued, since his name was known to me? He was afraid for his life, Inspector. The diamonds had become a liability.'

Soon after the Defeat of 1940, all items of personal property in excess of a value of 100,000 francs had had to be declared and lists submitted to the authorities. Failure to report such valuables carried an automatic penalty of confiscation and, if serious enough, a lengthy jail sentence or forced labour in the Reich.

No doubt Nana Thélème had reminded Jacqmain of this but, still, for him to have been afraid for his life could well imply something more serious.

'Louis . . .?'

Hermann was looking like death. 'Well, what is it?'

'The son of a bitch knocked off Cartier's in the rue de la Paix.'

2

Shadows fell on bejewelled finches in locked little cages of gilded wire. When torchlight found them, their encrusted emeralds, topazes and other precious and semiprecious stones suddenly lit up as if, now awakened, the birds would begin to sing. It was curious.

The cages were a window-dressing, their padlocks of gold perhaps a statement to the Occupier that some things would not be sold. And to be fair, the shop would have been lost had it not been kept open. Yet business had been extremely good, the temple of *haute joaillerie* booming, as were all the exclusive shops of the rue de la Paix.

'The Reichsmarschall Goering purchased an 8,000,000 franc necklace here,' said St-Cyr, letting the black-out curtain fall back in place. 'Diamonds and thumb-sized sapphires perhaps, and for his wife, his Emmy.'

The conquering hero. Head of the Luftwaffe. 'Louis . . .'

'Hermann, I am merely trying to get a fix on things. Unlike our Generalmajor's suite, this place has locks upon locks and the best of burglar alarms.'

An iron grille guarded the door during off-hours; steel shutters the display windows. 'Every two hours, and at random, a patrol goes along the street and, as is his custom, the Feldwebel in charge checks every door to see that it is locked just in case the *flics* should miss such a thing.'

'Impregnable,' offered Kohler lamely.

Black, velvet-lined boxes littered the floor. At the far end of the shop, every one of the floor-to-counter individual safes had been opened and their trays pulled out for perusal. The little dressing-tables at which only the wealthy would sit looked decidedly lonely.

'The bastard's moving too fast for us,' said Kohler grimly. 'What's next, eh?'

'He must have got in somehow.'

Cartier's were famous for their art deco approach and the mingling of precious and semiprecious stones. The style was simple, the lines straight, the pieces often one of a kind, exquisitely worked and fabulously priced.

'He can certainly pick his places,' offered the Sûreté, hands jammed into the deep pockets of the decidedly shabby overcoat the Occupation and frugality had allowed, the brown fedora much damaged. 'Please tell the boys in blue to wait outside in the cold.'

Herr Max was grumpy – the lack of sleep perhaps, or still smarting from the Ritz, thought Kohler. 'So, what is missing, *ja*?' asked the visitor from Berlin, distastefully taking it all in.

There were travel cases, combs to fix the hair in place, beaded handbags and watches, and all had that decidedly bright, sharp, angular look. Frivolity in wartime, was that what was bothering Herr Max?

'The sous-directeur and his assistants are trying to tally things,' said Kohler.

'*Und* who reported the break-in?'

'A *flic* found the front door open at 0127 hours.'

'Did he help himself before notifying others?'

'I'll check.'

'You do that. He's blown a hole in things, hasn't he, our Gypsy? Here we were believing the woman had let him into the Generalmajor's suite and had told him where the combination of that safe was kept, and now this. What are we to think?'

Brushing the dribbled sparklers from a chair, Engelmann sat down to moodily soak up what had happened and to relight the stub of the cheroot that had steadfastly clung to his lips ever since leaving the Ritz at a run. Hell, the shop was just down the street anyway.

'*Sonderbehandlung*, Kohler. That is what my superiors have insisted, and since they are also your superiors, you and that French fart will take note of it.'

Special treatment ... *Verdammt!* 'I *knew* there had to be something to bring the IKPK out of hibernation. What's he done then, our Gypsy? Decided on an agenda of his own?'

'This we do not know. We only know that he was sighted in Tours on the fourteenth, boarding the train to Paris. He "surfaced", Kohler, and my superiors want to know why he did so, how he got there, and what he has in mind.'

'And you can't tell us who reported seeing him?'

Must Kohler always be such a nuisance? 'The same as notified us of the Ritz but failed entirely to warn us of this.'

The *mouton* then, the informer. A woman the Gypsy obviously must know.

The office was spacious, the desk immaculate. The cigarette case was of platinum, with an oblong, octagonally shaped plaque of Baltic amber raised at its centre and from which incised rays sparkled as if the amber was some sort of strange sun and the entrapped fly its prisoner.

38

'"Tshaya",' said St-Cyr softly of the inscription. '"*Vadni ratsa*".
The first is a woman's name; the second means the gift is from
the wild goose of Romani legend.'

Agitated, the clerk blurted, 'The client came in on Saturday,
Inspector. He *insisted* it be ready for today – ah! for Monday,
yes? It is now Tuesday. It's not *easy* to acquire amber like that.
We *worked* all day Sunday and half of Monday. Enslaved, that's
what we are. *Enslaved*.'

'Yes, yes, of course. A Hauptmann – you're certain of this?'

'Herr Oberlammers. He . . . he has signed for it, yes? Everyone
has to these days. It's the rule.'

'And he was to pick it up yesterday afternoon?'

'That is correct.'

'At what time, please, did he come into the shop on Saturday?'

The salesman's expression grew pained. 'At just before
closing.'

'And were there any other customers?'

'Seven. We're short-handed. I . . .'

A breath was taken and held in anticipation of further questions not long in coming.

'Do you mean to say you left him alone while you served
others? You took your eyes from him?' demanded the Sûreté
accusingly.

'Inspector, how was I to know he was looking the place over?
He was in uniform. He asked if he might use the telephone so as
to get the inscription correct.'

Kohler gave his partner a nudge. 'The burglar alarm, Louis.
The bastard recircuited the wires so that the alarm remained off
but the light came on when the switch was thrown.'

The control box was in the office, on a wall. 'Entry?' asked St-
Cyr of his partner.

'A rear door. A tradesman's entrance – grilled, but no problem.
Forced with an iron bar, muffled with a horse blanket.'

'And the safes out front?'

'All drilled and punched. Bang on each time, Louis. First the
hole to locate and expose the cam of the locking bolt, then the
hammer and chisel.'

'He came equipped but did he come alone?'

'Apparently, but he couldn't have carried the tools in that
attaché case he walked into the Ritz with.'

'Then did he knock this place off first, Hermann, before leaving his little surprise at the Ritz, or vice versa?'

'He would have had to come back here to open the front door for the *flics* to find.'

There was a nod. 'Then he did the Ritz job first, and while we were brushing the dust off ourselves, he took his time with this, having prepared the way well beforehand.'

Clément Laviolette was sous-directeur, a far different person from his sales clerk. Clearly he didn't want the Kripo and the Sûreté asking too many questions. 'Inspectors, it's nothing – *nothing*, I assure you. Those little safes we have out front are merely for show. Our vault in the cellars is inviolable. Please . . . a few trinkets are missing. Mere baubles.'

He was positively beaming, and when he sat down in an Empire *fauteuil* to benevolently fold his hands in his lap, he said, 'Two millions at most when he could have had thirty. The rectangular, chain-linked diamond necklace with matching bracelets. Two rings with step-cut, rectangular, *blanc exceptionnel* stones of 31.98 and 19.53 carats respectively. A wider diamond bracelet than the others – stronger, yes. More distinctive, more of a statement. The latent *pugiliste* in the female perhaps? A pair of ear-rings – single droplets those – he could have had the proper ones to go with the chain-links but passed them up. A ruby pendant, a diamond brooch, an epidote-and-diamond necklace which was exquisite for the delicacy of its platinum lacework and for the warm and enticing combination of its soft green and pale yellow tints.'

He sucked in a breath, never letting his eyes leave them. 'But it is as if this *perceur de coffre-fort* was searching for something he had had in mind for a long time yet couldn't quite make up his mind when presented with the *confiserie* of our establishment.'

The *bonbon* shop, ah yes. 'Seven years between sheet metal in Oslo, Louis, the sentence commuted by our friends in Berlin for all we know, but time enough to dream. Then one empty safe and a fortune left behind.'

'One empty safe . . .? Ah! messieurs, the vault in the cellars was not touched, as I have only just informed you.'

Kohler let him have it – St-Cyr knew he would. 'Then why weren't the little safes out front emptied and their contents locked away below? Isn't that the normal procedure at the close of each day?'

There wasn't a ruffle of discomposure. 'The pressures of business. The shortages of suitable staff. It's understandable, is it not?'

'Five millions,' grunted Louis.

'Perhaps a little more,' conceded Laviolette. 'When we have the final figure we will, of course, be quite willing to divulge it.'

How good of him. 'Ten at least, Louis.'

'The insurance, Hermann.'

They turned to leave the office. 'Messieurs . . .' bleated the sales clerk. 'The cigarette case . . . It . . . it has only had the deposit.'

'Tack it on to the rest, eh? Lose it if you have to.' Kohler slid the thing deeply into the left pocket of the greatcoat that, had he worn a helmet instead of a broad-brimmed grey fedora, would have made his appearance all the more formidable.

Touching a forefinger lightly to his lips and shaking his head, he whispered, 'Don't even mention it to the detective out front. It would only upset him.'

The vault was indeed inviolable. Even tunnelling under it would have been of no use. 'He had to have known the staff had become complacent, Hermann, and that things were being carelessly left overnight in the safes upstairs.'

'Someone has to have looked the place over for him. A woman, no doubt. One who could have made several visits. This piece, that piece . . .'

'See if there's a record of the clientele. Try for a singer, for Mademoiselle Thélème. The shop is on her way to the Ritz.'

'Done, but why did the son of a bitch leave the cigarette case behind? He must have known they'd have it ready? He'd have had access to the office and to the sous-directeur's desk during the robbery.'

'Perhaps our Gypsy was too busy. Perhaps it was only a means to his looking the place over and to hot-wiring the burglar alarm.'

'Perhaps he simply forgot it in the rush,' said Kohler, lost to it.

'Then why have it inscribed in such a manner?'

'That's what I'm asking myself, Louis. Why did he deliberately go out of his way to identify himself with the Rom while wearing the uniform of those who must at least officially hate them?'

The house at 3 rue Laurence-Savart was in Belleville, on a street so narrow, the canyon of it threw up the sound of the retreating Citroën.

As Hermann reached the corner of the rue des Pyrénées, the tyres screeched and that splendid *traction avant* grabbed icy paving stones. Then the car shot deeply into the city St-Cyr loved, and he heard it approach the Seine – yes, yes, there it was – after which it reached place Saint-André-des-Arts and coasted quietly up to the house on the rue Suger. Five minutes flat, from here to there. No traffic. There seldom was at any time of day or night, and in ten minutes one could cross the city from suburb to suburb. The cars all gone. 350,000 of them reduced to 4500 or less; 60,000 cubic metres of gasoline a month reduced to an allocation of less than 600.

As one of the Occupier, control of the Citroën had passed instantly into Hermann's hands. They were capable, of course, and occasionally Hermann did let him drive his own car just so that he wouldn't forget how to. And yes, they had become friends in spite of it and of everything else. Two lost souls from opposite sides of the war, thrown together by the never-ending battle against common crime.

'War does things like that,' he said aloud and to no one but the darkness of the street. 'We're like a horseshoe magnet whose opposing poles agree to sweep up the iron filings. All of them.'

The city proper held about 2,300,000; the suburbs perhaps another 500,000 and yet, even with 300,000 or so of the Occupier, on any night at this hour or just after curfew it was so quiet it was uncomfortable. And at 4.47 Berlin Time, it was all but ready for the first sounds of those departing for work. Not a light showed, and the time in winter was one ungodly hour earlier than the old time; in summer it was *two*.

Boots would soon squeak in the twenty degrees of frost. The open-toed, wooden-heeled shoes of the salesgirls, usherettes and secretaries would click-clack harshly, though most had long since lost interest in how they looked or in trying to find a husband, what with so many of the young men either dead or locked up in POW camps in the Reich.

After more than two and a half years of Occupation, nearly three and a half of war, hunger was on everyone's mind unless some fiddle had been worked, or one slept with the enemy or had one living in the house. The system of rationing had never worked and had been open to so much abuse, most existed on less than 1500 calories a day.

Yet they had to get up at 4 a.m. the old time, six days a week.

He turned his back on the city. He went into the stone-cold house, saying softly, 'Marianne, it's me . . .' only to stop himself, to remember that she was not asleep upstairs but dead. 'Ah *merde*, I've got to watch myself,' he said. Fortunately there were still a few splintered boards left from the explosion that had killed her and their little son. Hermann had had the Todt Organization repair the damage. With pages torn from About's *The King of the Mountains* – a tragedy to destroy it – he lit a fire in the kitchen stove.

And searching the barren cupboards found, at last, one forgotten cube of bouillon.

'Things like this build character – isn't that what you always said, *maman*?' he cried out for it was *her* house. It had always been hers even after she had passed away, and hadn't that been part of the trouble with the first wife *and* with the second?

'No. It was the long absences. The work. The profession, and I was determined to succeed, but if one does not climb the ladder, one soon slides down it.'

Flames lit up the room and, cursing himself, he ran to draw the black-out curtains Madame Courbet across the street had thoughtfully left open to brighten the place while cleaning it.

The Gypsy had done the Ritz robbery between 8.15 and 8.47 p.m., Monday, but the *flic* who had found Cartier's front door open had not done so until today at 0127 hours. Lots of time, then, for the Gypsy to have been as thorough as possible, yet he had left things behind, had definitely *not* taken all he could have.

'And that', breathed St-Cyr, 'is a puzzle, unless he was trying to tell us something.'

The bouillon cube was old and so dry he had to remove a shoe to smash it with the heel, only to worry about damaging the

43

footwear. Scraping the crumbs into a hand with the blade of a dinner knife, he fed them to the pot from the surface of whose cup of water rose the first tendrils of steam.

More wood was added to the stove, and from his pockets, guiltily now, the half-dozen lumps of coal Hermann had pilfered unseen from the cellars of the building that housed Cartier's.

Hermann had kept six for himself – he was like that. He wouldn't take what was his right as one of the Occupier, the Citroën excepted, and certain of his meals. He would go without but 'borrow' from those who had.

Idly St-Cyr wondered if his partner had picked up a little bauble or two for Giselle and Oona. Underwear, yes – silk stockings if they could be spared and the victim found in such a state only one pair would be necessary for the funeral if the coffin was to be left open. If.

'But why Cartier's?' he asked himself, removing his overcoat at last but keeping the scarf tightly wrapped around his throat, the chest covered thickly. The flu ... one never relaxed one's vigilance for it was serious. So many had died of it last winter.

Cartier's was close to the Ritz but Van Cleef and Arpels was on place Vendôme and much closer, other world-famous jewellers too, yet the Gypsy had settled on that one.

He had left the cigarette case for them to find – St-Cyr was certain of this but as yet had no proof. 'Tshaya,' he said, and blowing on the cup of bouillon, '*Vadni ratsa.*'

Kohler heard the telephone ringing its heart out in the hall downstairs. The sound rose up the stairwell floor by Christly floor until, tearing himself out of bed, he ran to stop it. Down, down the stairs, he pitching through the darkness rather than have Madame Clicquot bitch at him any more. The rent, the lack of coal – 'Why will you not see that we receive our proper share?' Et cetera.

They collided. The candle stub flew out of her hands; the stench of garlic, onions and positively no bathing was ripe with fortitude. 'Monsieur ...' she exhaled.

'Madame, forgive me. *Allô ... Allô ...* Operator, put the bastard on. Gestapo ... yes, I'm Gestapo, eh? so don't take offence and hang up.'

'Louis . . . Louis, what the *hell* is it this time?'

A moment was taken. And then, 'Cartier's, Hermann. The Opéra, June of 1910 and Diaghilev's Ballets Russes. The Schéhérazade. The Thousand and One Nights, The Arabian Nights.'

'I'm listening.'

'I was there with my parents. It was magnificent!'

'I'm still listening.'

'Bakst put such colours into the décor. Nijinsky was the black slave.'

'Continue.'

'Louis Cartier, the grandson, was so impressed he revolutionized Cartier's style and the way we see gems and semiprecious stones. He and his assistant, Charles Jacqueau, began to create what were then very daring combinations of onyx, jet or pearl and diamond, with malachite, jade and amethyst or lapis lazuli. That's why he hit Cartier's.'

'You're not serious.'

'The Club Schéhérazade, idiot! Tshaya, Hermann. Nana Thélème. She was wearing a dress with stag-horn buttons and a belt of gold links. Those are gypsy things. Their most powerful talismans are not man-made but natural. A polished bit of antler, a beach pebble bearing its tiny fossil . . .'

'A plaque of amber with its entrapped fly, eh? Hey, *mon vieux*, I'm going back to bed. Your French logic is just too much for me!'

Tshaya was Nana Thélème? Ah! Louis was crazy. Too tired, too overwrought.

The flat was freezing. Giselle wore three sweaters and two pairs of woollen trousers, kneesocks, gloves and a toque. Oona also.

There was no room for him in the bed – there hadn't been when he had arrived home. Ah! the three of them didn't share the same bed. Those two would never have put up with anything like that! not even in this weather . . .

Oona's bed was freezing and when he had settled back into it, he knew Giselle would accuse him of favouritism and that she wouldn't listen to his protests even though her bed had been fully occupied.

He was just drifting off to the tolling of the Bibliothèque Nationale's five o'clock bell some distance across the river, when

Oona slid in beside him to fan the flames of jealousy into a little fire of their own.

'Kiss me,' she said. 'Hold me. I'm worried.'

'Can't it wait?'

'Another seven and a half months? Perhaps. It all depends on Giselle, doesn't it?'

'What do you mean by that?'

'Only that she's the one who's expecting, not me. You were thoughtless, Hermann. You got carried away and did not take precautions.'

'It's the war. It's those lousy *capotes anglaises* they hand out. Someone's been sabotaging them.'

The condoms. Long ago in Paris the Englishmen had worn rubber coats with hoods, and the French had given the name to that most necessary of garments.

'Perhaps you are right,' she murmured, snuggling closely for comfort, 'but, then, perhaps not.'

When she awakened, he was sitting on the edge of the bed, wrapped in his greatcoat, gloves and fedora, smoking a cigarette, and she knew he'd been like that ever since. Unfortunately he had had to be told things and, yes, unfortunately she had had to be the one to have to tell him. 'A woman notices such things, Hermann. I'm sorry.'

'Don't be. Hey, you were right to tell me. Giselle wouldn't have.'

11 rue des Saussaies was bleak at any hour but especially so in winter as the sun struggled to rise. Its grey stone walls and iron grilles were webbed with frost. The courtyard's snow had been packed hard by the traffic of the previous night.

Gestapo plain clothes came and went in a hurry always. A *panier à salade* languished, the salad shaker,* having emptied its guts at 3 or 4 a.m. A wireless tracking van drew in to report after a hard night's trying to get a fix on a clandestine transceiver. Had they zeroed in on someone? wondered Kohler. Those boys didn't work out of here, so their presence had to mean something was up.

* the Black Maria

46

Black Citroëns were in a row with black Renaults, Fords and Peugeots, black everything and hated, too, because like the trench coats and the briefcases of the plain clothes, they were a symbol of what this place had become.

Once the Headquarters of the Sûreté Nationale, it was now that of the Gestapo in France yet had retained all of the attributes and successes of the former, particularly a records section which was second to none, even to that of the Sicherheitsdienst in Berlin.

Kohler coughed. Louis hunched his shoulders and pulled up his overcoat collar before saying, 'To business then, and stop worrying, eh? Everyone knows that without sufficient food, the female body loses its ability to menstruate. Treat Giselle to some good black-market meals. Include Oona. Stop being so pious. See if it doesn't help. Load the larder. Use your privileges and your head, and suit-up *before* you have another go at either of them!'

Father Time and no patience, no sympathy at all! Louis had always gone on about Giselle's returning to her former profession, to the house of Madame Chabot on the rue Danton, which was just around the corner from the flat and a constant reminder. 'Oona's positive.'

Ah, *pour l'amour de Dieu*! what was one to do? Drag along this worried papa-to-be who was old enough to have been the girl's grandfather? 'I *can't* have you distracted, Hermann. Not with the Gypsy. Besides, Pharand wants to see me. He's insisting.'

'Then quit fussing. Hey, I'll take care of that little *Croix de feu* for you. Just watch my dust!'

The *Croix de feu* were one of the notorious right-wing, fascist groups from the thirties. Kohler went in first, Louis followed, but when they reached the Major's office, the Bavarian left his partner out of sight in the corridor and shot in to ask, 'Have you seen St-Cyr?'

The secretary spilled her boss's coffee. A Chinese porcelain vase went over – a priceless thing – and she cried out in dismay even as he righted it only to hear Pharand hiss from his inner sanctum, 'Not in, eh? and at 0900 hours! It's *les hirondelles* for him.'

The swallows . . . the bicycle patrols in their capes and *képis*. 'Why not the pussy patrol?' sang out Kohler.

Louis's boss came to stand in the doorway. 'Enough of your shit, Hauptsturmführer. Where is he?'

'That's what I'm asking.'

The carefully trimmed black pencil of the Major's moustache twitched. The rounded cheeks were sallow and unhealthy in winter, though they'd always been like that. The short black hair of this little fascist was glued in place with scented pomade and splashes of *Joli Soir*, the dark brown eyes were alive with barely controlled fury.

'He was to see me first. A report is forthcoming. Orders are orders, is that not right, Hauptsturmführer? The Ritz, then Cartier's and now ... why now ... Ah! you did not know of it, did you?'

The bastard ...

The pudgy hands came together as if squeezing the joy out of his little triumph. At fifty-eight years of age, Osias Pharand still had his friends in the upper echelons and hadn't wasted them. Readily he had moved out of his plush office – had given it up to Gestapo Boemelburg and had willingly shifted his ass down the hall. Taken his lumps because he had known the French would run things anyway, and had cluttered the den with the trivia of his years in Indochina and other places.

A stint as director of the Sûreté's *Deuxième bureau des nomades* had been a big step to the top – you'd think he'd have come to appreciate the gypsies for having provided so many rungs in the ladder but no, he hated them as much as he hated the Jews. But for the Resistance, for the so-called 'terrorists', he reserved an unequalled passion.

'Bring St-Cyr in here now,' he said.

The air was full of trouble but Kohler couldn't resist taunting him. 'He's probably with Boemelburg already. The IKPK, eh? Hey, the two of them worked together before the war. They're old friends, or had you forgotten?'

'*Never*! Not for a moment. It's the only thing that saves him but with this ...' Pharand toyed with the fish. 'With this, I do not think even that will be enough. The matter demands special treatment – *Sonderbehandlung*, or had you forgotten?'

'Maître Pharand ...'

'Ah! I've got your attention at last. Another robbery. A big one, eh? Now piss off. Go on. Get out. Leave this sort of work to those best suited for it. Let me live with my secrets until they become your partner's demise. Perhaps then he will understand that it is to me that he owes his loyalty and his job. I could have helped you both.'

Boemelburg was not happy. 'The Gare Saint-Lazare. The ticket-agent's office. That idiot of an agent-directeur didn't bother to deposit last week's receipts or those of the week before. Apparently he does it only once a month.'

'But ... but there are always those on duty, Walter? A station so huge ... Traffic never stops ...' insisted St-Cyr.

A stumpy forefinger was raised. 'Passenger traffic does stop, as you well know. Those arriving must wait until the curfew is over; those departing must purchase their tickets before it begins. The wickets are then closed, the receipts tallied and put away in the safe, and the office locked.'

'How much did he get?' asked Kohler, dismayed by the speed with which the Gypsy was working.

The rheum-filled Nordic eyes seemed saddened, as if in assessing them, Boemelburg was cognizant of certain truths. A flagrant patriotism in St-Cyr, questionable friends, a rebellious nature in Kohler, among other things. '682,000 francs in 100 and 500 franc notes. He left the rest.'

It had to be asked. 'What else, Walter? I've seen it before,' said St-Cyr. 'You always drop your eyes when you want to tell us something but are uncertain of how to put it.'

A big man, with the blunt head and all-but-shaven, bristly iron grey hair of a *Polizeikommissar* of long experience, Boemelburg had seen nearly everything the criminal milieu could offer but he was also Head of SIPO-Section IV, the Gestapo in France.

'Three Lebels, the 1873 *Modèle d'ordonnance*, and one hundred and twenty rounds, the black-powder cartridges. Forgotten during the Defeat and subsequent ordinance to turn in all firearms. Overlooked in the hunt for delinquent guns. Left in their boxes and brand-new, Louis. Good *Gott im Himmel*, the imbeciles!'

'From 1873?' managed the Sûreté. 'But that is ...'

49

'Yes, yes, only two years after the Franco-Prussian War. Look, I don't know how long they were in that safe. No one does. Each agent-directeur simply thought it best to leave those damned boxes alone.'

'It's serious,' said Kohler lamely.

'Are the Resistance involved in this matter?' shouted the Chief.

Ah no ... thought St-Cyr, dismayed at the sudden turn. Counter-terrorism, subversion, tracking down Jews, gypsies and all others of the Reich's so-called undesirables were Walter's responsibility, not just combating common crime. But then, too, in one of those paradoxes of the war, he ran gangs of known criminals who did the Gestapo's bidding when they, themselves, wanted to remain at arm's length.

A cop, and now a thug too, he unfortunately knew the city well, having worked here in his youth as a heating and ventilating engineer. He spoke French as good as any Parisian, even to the *argot* of Montmartre.

That grim, grey look passed over them. 'I'm warning you. I want no trouble with this. Berlin are adamant. The Gypsy is to be apprehended at all costs. Taken alive if possible – there are things we need to know from him – but dead will do. That's what they want and I must insist on it.'

'And Herr Engelmann ... why is he here?' asked Kohler.

'Why not? The IKPK have card indexes on all such people.'

'Then it didn't stop functioning at the onslaught of hostilities. Heydrich kept it going?' asked Louis.

'As the Gruppenführer knew he should have. Herr Engelmann is not just with their robberies division. He holds a cross-appointment with the Berlin Kripo. In the course of his duties in '38, and then in '40 and '41, he went to Oslo several times to interview our friend, and has come to know him intimately, if anyone can ever do so.'

'Then why is he being so difficult? Why doesn't he take us fully into his confidence?' asked Kohler.

Security allowed only so much to be said. 'That is precisely what I have asked him to do. Full co-operation. A concerted effort to bring this safe-cracker in and quickly before he does us all an injury from which we cannot recover.'

Boemelburg was clearly worried. Leaning forward, he hurriedly shoved things out of the way, and lowered his voice.

'Whose agenda is he following? What are his next targets? Where will he hole up and exactly who is helping him?'

Nana Thélème or someone else?

The set of fingerprints was very clear, the head-and-shoulders photographs sharp, but to St-Cyr the file card – the top in a bundle of perhaps thirty – was like one of those from the past. It evoked memories of Vienna and the IKPK and worries about the distinct possibility of another high-level assassination, the then impending visit of King George VI to France in July of 1938. Boemelburg and he had worked together on it, a last occasion before the war.

The IKPK had sent such cards to all its member countries, requesting whatever they had on a certain criminal or type of crime. These cards were then stored in rotatable drum-cabinets and a detective such as Boemelburg or himself, or Engelmann, could in a few moments collate data from cities in France with that from Britain, the Netherlands, Turkey, Italy, Greece and, at last count in 1938, some twenty-eight other countries around the world.

Lists of stolen property were painstakingly spelled out where possible. Missing persons, unidentified cadavers, murder, arson, counterfeiting, fraud, drug trafficking and prostitution – all were there at the turn of the drum and yes, very early on, even in 1932 and '33, there had been concerns about a Nazi takeover, yet the service had offered immense possibilities. A radio network in 1935 linked many of the major cities, allowing policemen to talk directly and informally to colleagues in other countries, very quickly forming professional liaisons that were of benefit to all.

Special cards were tinted to denote *les Bohémiens*, though keeping track of their wanderings often proved exceedingly difficult. But in any case, the Gypsy was not one of the Rom, so his cards were like all others, if more numerous than most.

'Janwillem De Vries,' grumbled a disgruntled Herr Max who didn't like being told to co-operate with the present company. 'Father, Hendrick, no known criminal activities but a socialist do-gooder when not pouring out historical pap to stuff the teat of it into the eager mouths of bored Dutch *Hausfrauen*. Mother, Marina, no suggestions of anything there either. Vivacious,

51

quick-minded, deft with the brush but impulsive and given to wandering off for days on her bicycle, or to working in her studio night after night. A flirt – *mein Gott*, there is ample evidence of it, given that she often posed in the nude as a statue for her photographer friends. Orpheus and her lute, but that one was a boy, wasn't he? Died, unhappily, 18 June 1929 of a drowning accident on the Linge near Geldermalsen while trying to reach some lilies she wanted to paint, though to see her sketches is to see nothing but the confused and flighty mind of the avant-garde who should have been trussed up with her apron strings and taught a few lessons!'

Naked? wondered Kohler idly – was this what Herr Max had meant?

The visitor lit a cheroot, he looking as if he'd just got out of bed and hadn't quite had time to dress properly.

'Apprehended 20 April 1938 – caught with his hands in the wall safe of one Magnus Erlendsson, a prominent shipping magnate who should have known better than to keep such things at home and to tell others how clever he was. The tax authorities were most interested and Herr Erlendsson quickly found himself going from one theft to another!'

Engelmann gave a throaty chuckle – work did have its compensations. 'Oostende,' he coughed. 'Coffee . . . is there a little, Sturmbannführer? A brandy also *und* a raw egg, I think.'

Tears moistened the hard little eyes behind their gold-rimmed specs. He took a breath, then remembered the cheroot.

'Oostende . . .?' hazarded Kohler.

The visitor let his gaze linger on the Bavarian before clearing his throat of its blockage. 'First, don't ask until you're told to. Second, rely on me to lead this little discussion.'

The matter of the uniform the Gypsy had acquired in Tours was brought up. 'He didn't kill him, did he?' blurted Kohler only to feel Louis kick him under the table to shut him up.

'Reprisals . . . is this what you are worrying about, Kohler? Hostages to be shot. How many, I wonder?' asked Herr Max.

He gave it a moment. Boemelburg's look was grim and it said, Kohler, how dare you worry about such things? You, too, St-Cyr.

'To say nothing of his embarrassment and the reticence of his tongue,' went on Herr Max, allowing what appeared to be a smile, 'our Hauptmann Dietrich Oberlammers is alive and well but he fell prey to the oldest of gypsy tricks, which leads us right back to that villa in the hills overlooking Oslo.'

'A woman,' breathed Louis, 'but was it the same one?'

'She rubbed herself against the Hauptmann in the half-light of a corridor or room,' sighed Kohler. 'She offered everything she had but gave him nothing more than deep glimpses of bare flesh and sweet caresses, then let him strip off in some *maison de passe* before heisting his papers and uniform.'

'The wallet of Herr Erlendsson also, and news of the Oslo safe's location and contents,' added St-Cyr, his mind leaping back in time to the spring of 1938.

'The combination also,' grunted Herr Max. 'Erlendsson was fool enough to have given it to her in a moment of drunken bravado while she was in his hotel room. Oostende and Oslo were worlds apart, so what could it have mattered eh? But it did! Oh my, yes, but it did!'

'Is she now your *mouton*?' asked St-Cyr.

A little more co-operation could not hurt. 'That is correct. She betrayed the Gypsy to us in Tours, and she was with him back then in Oostende and in Oslo in April of 1938.'

'But she didn't tell you everything, did she?' sighed St-Cyr, taking an apprehensive guess at things.

There was no answer. They waited for her file cards – the Gestapo's on her too – but Herr Max didn't produce any. He simply said, 'Find her,' and gave them time to swallow this while he had his egg and brandy.

Then he pulled the elastic band from the stack of cards and thrust the top one at Kohler. '*Read it!*'

Hermann's face fell. 'Mecklenburg, Louis. 20 November 1932. The estate of Magda Goebbels's ex-husband. An unknown quantity of gold bars and jewellery. How can anyone have an "unknown" quantity in a safe?'

'That is none of your business,' countered the visitor.

'The manager's office, the Kaiserhof Hotel in the Wilhelmstrasse, 17 March 1934. "Cash in the amount of 25,000 marks but also 8000 American dollars and one gold pocket-watch. Property of . . ." Ah *verdammt*, Louis, der Führer!'

'Read on,' sighed Engelmann. 'It can't get worse but then . . .'

'The residence and office of the Köln banker, Kurt von Schroeder, 5 May 1935, a strong supporter of the Party, I think,' said

Kohler lamely. 'Jewellery to the value of 7,000,000 marks; cash to that of 28,000,000. Do you want me to keep going?'

'Of course,' grunted Engelmann.

'The villa of Alfred Rosenburg in the Tiergarten, 15 December 1937. Documents . . .?'

Again they were told it was none of their business, but there had been some loose diamonds, gold coins and banknotes, though no values were given.

'The residence of Prinz Viktor zo Wied – Berlin, too, the Kurfürstenstrasse, 17 January 1938, then Joachim von Ribbentrop's villa in the suburb of Dahlem, 18 January, the same year.'

Von Ribbentrop had been made foreign minister of the Reich on 4 February, just seventeen days after the robbery. Kohler felt quite ill. How had the Gypsy pulled off those jobs in a police state? Why had the idiot taken on the *Nazis*, for God's sake? None of the robberies would have been mentioned even to the IKPK's member countries, let alone the press, yet the hunt must have gone on in earnest.

'And in Oslo we finally had him,' sighed Herr Max. 'That's when all the pieces came together for us.'

'Correction,' said Louis. 'The Norwegians had him.'

'But soon we had Norway.'

Not until 9 June 1940. 'Then why didn't you have him extradited? Surely there was room enough in the Moabit?'

Berlin's most notorious prison. 'Because his willingness to co-operate was absent. Because we had other matters to concern us.'

'You finally made a deal with him,' snorted Kohler. 'You let that son of a bitch out of jail but he didn't keep his word and now you want him back.'

'Correction,' interjected Boemelburg. 'We have to have him back.'

'Ah *nom de Jésus-Christ*, Louis, why us?'

The stairwell resounded with their taking two and three steps at a time. 'Because we're common crime. Because the quartier de l'Europe, that favoured haunt of *les Gitans*, was once my beat long before I was fool enough to become a detective.' St-Cyr caught a breath as they reached a landing. 'And because, *mon vieux* . . . because, why *sacré, idiot*! they're up to something.'

Kohler stopped so suddenly they collided. *'What?'* he demanded, looking his partner over.

Louis's heart was racing. 'Either to rob for them or to set a little *souricière* for someone.'

A mousetrap . . . 'But he's decided to rob for himself – is this what you're saying?'

'Perhaps, but then . . . ah *mais alors, alors*, Hermann, is it not too early for us to say?'

Unsettled by the thought, they went up the stairs more slowly. Hermann wouldn't use the lifts, not even in a place like this. Caught once and left hanging by a thread, nothing would change his mind, not even the most modern and best maintained of elevators.

When they reached the sixth floor, the only sounds they heard were those of their shoes. No longer was there that din of hammering typewriters, telexes and the constant ringing of telephones. No one hurried past. No one shouted in German or French. Even from the cellars, there were no sudden screams of terror.

Records occupied the whole of the top floor. Its grey labyrinth of steel filing cabinets, card-index drums, shelves and mountains of dossiers was separated from all outsiders by the brown and unfeeling plateau of the linoleum-topped counter all such governmental edifices held.

Turcotte and every one of his clerk-detectives, all thirty or so of the day shift, were standing rigidly to attention, grim-faced, some with tears.

'What the hell has happened?' breathed Kohler – he couldn't believe it. Usually Turcotte fiercely guarded his domain and acidly fought off all requests to hurry.

The intercom brought answer via Radio-Vichy and the shaky voice of the aged Maréchal Pétain, now in his eighty-seventh year. 'Mesdames et messieurs, it is with deep regret that I must report the nine-hundred-day siege of Leningrad has been lifted. Though the population has been dying at the rate of twenty thousand a day, this is expected to lessen in the weeks ahead.'

'Effort brings its own reward,' whispered Kohler, giving a

well-known phrase of the Maréchal's. '*Les Russes* are no longer food for the fish of the Neva and the Teutonic generals of this war are being taught a damned good lesson.'

Hermann was still bitter but seldom showed it. He had just recently lost both of his sons at Stalingrad where von Paulus was about to surrender the last remnants of the Sixth. He had tried to convince the boys to emigrate in '38 to Argentina but being young, they had replied, 'You fought in the last one; let us finish it in this one.'

The moment of silence following the broadcast was rigidly observed. Not a one of the clerks would have broken it. They were all terrified of their boss and afraid of being sent into forced labour or worse. 'A far different response than last Wednesday, Thursday or Friday, eh, Louis?' he whispered. 'They're not patting each other on the back and saying, "I told you so."'

The Wehrmacht, on a violent whim of the Führer, had dynamited the whole of the Vieux Port of Marseille, evicting thirty thousand souls with but a two-hour notice, and sending most of them to camps at Fréjus and Compiègne. An altercation in a whorehouse had started it all, the Resistance shooting up the place and others paying for it. So many, no one could have predicted it.

'Well?' demanded Turcotte, lord of his empire.

Kohler winced. 'We're having trouble, Émile, and need a little help.'

'Such subservience is rewarding but we can do nothing for you today.'

'Oh, sorry. Berlin were asking. It was Berlin, wasn't it, Louis?'

The little ferret got the message, but when the wheels were turned, the index cards of most gypsies had been stamped with one big black word and Turcotte had his little triumph. '*Déporté ou fusillé, c'est la même chose.*'

Deported or shot, it's the same thing.

'We're looking for a *mouton*,' said St-Cyr, hauling him out of harm's way. 'A female. Last seen in Tours, Thursday the fourteenth, but also a regular of the Santé or the Petite Roquette or the cells here and over on the ave' Foch if her conductor feels she needs a change of air.'

The SS or the Gestapo ... The lark-eyed gaze flew evasively over the warren. 'I know nothing of this.'

'We didn't think you would,' came the soft response, 'but of course when one has been seen buying sugar and white flour from the green beans to flog it to the butter-eggs-and-cheese boys, one must be careful, isn't that so?'

The German soldiers in their grey-green uniforms, the black marketeers . . .

St-Cyr the cuckold. St-Cyr the friend of the Resistance who had mistakenly put him on their hit lists but had blown up his wife and son instead.

'Start talking, Émile, or what I have to tell those same people you are thinking of will include the denunciations of old enemies.'

'You bastard . . .'

'Just give us what we want. It will save us all time.'

The drum was spun, the card turned up and accidentally ripped from its wheel of fortune to be then spat upon in fury and thrust at them.

'*Une roulure rumaine. Une fille de la duperie, la superchérie et escroquerie!*'

A Rumanian slut. A daughter of deception, trickery and swindling.

'Now leave us,' said St-Cyr. 'Go back to your weeping.'

'The end's coming, Émile,' breathed Kohler, giving him a parting shot. 'You had better prepare yourself for the worst by sealing your lips. Hey, maybe if you behave, Louis could fix it so that you'll get the Médaille Militaire and Croix de Guerre with palms.'

'Up against the post,' muttered St-Cyr under his breath.

'Not until we've had breakfast.'

The file card Turcotte had torn from the drum was replete with entries which went right back to when the Gestapo's *mouton* had been ten years old. A charge of stealing two chickens and a round of goat's cheese had been compounded by the laying on of curses. Sentenced to six months in Bucharest, she had escaped in less than two weeks. A guard was found to have been fooling around with her. Even then she had known how to convince men she was ripe for plucking only to deceive them.

The name on the card, which had been updated in August

1941, was Lucie-Marie Doucette but St-Cyr knew that such a name could well have meant nothing to the gypsies. A mere formality the *Gaje* authorities insisted on to control border crossings, entry visas and issue identity papers and passports.

She was, as Turcotte had so viciously stated, of Rumanian descent – at least, it would have been thought by those in authority that she had been born there. She'd have let them think what they wanted, knowing only that she had again fooled them.

Her real name was Tshaya. She was dark-haired, strongly featured and quite striking, but in the expression she had last given the police camera, there was deceitfulness, wilfulness, hatred ... ah! so many things, and a depth of sadness which went well beyond her years.

The hair was parted in the middle, blue-black, long and glossy. Loosened strands trailed provocatively across the forehead, enhancing allure and all but hiding the ears which would have held gold rings or coins, though these must have been taken from her.

The eyes were large and dark beneath strong brows. The nose was full and prominent, the lips not parted. The face was what one would call a medium oval, the chin not pointed but determined, the throat full.

They had put her age at twenty-eight in August 1941. She would not have argued. Again such *Gaje* things meant little. For the gypsies, life was of the present, not of the past or of the future, alas.

Someone – her conductor perhaps – had tersely written in: *Of the Lowara tribe. Daughter of the horse trader, Tshurkina la Marako, deported to Buchenwald 14 September 1941.*

She had stayed behind and they had had their reasons for keeping her. Perhaps she had escaped for a time – there was no record of it. But they had used her.

Colour of skin: dark brown. Height: 1 metre, 68 centimetres. Weight: 62 kilos. Length of arms, length of legs, bust measurement, waist, that of the hips, the wrists and ankles – all such things were given in the tiniest of handwriting, especially the shape and size of the ears, for like fingerprints, the ears remained the same throughout life.

Signes particuliers: whipmarks on rear of thighs, buttocks, back, shoulders and upper arms, all dating from the summer of 1928

58

when she'd have been fifteen years old, if the age of twenty-eight was correct, which it probably wasn't.

Her father? he wondered but thought it highly unlikely. Banishment for a time, perhaps, if the offence, such as stealing the gold of another, warranted it, not a savage beating.

But someone had tied her wrists to a post or tree and had let the whip do the rest.

Hermann was no stranger to this sort of thing and his mood darkened when told of it. Instinctively he gingerly felt his left cheek. That scar was the measure of truth over loyalty to one's peers, and it ran from just below the eye to his lower jaw.

The SS had done that to him. What had begun as a 'nothing' murder in Fontainebleau Forest, a commonplace murder, had ended at a château near Vouvray as a far different matter not two months ago. The scar was more than matched by the one that ran beneath his shirt from the right shoulder to the left hip. They were still being held accountable for pointing the finger, still reviled, distrusted and held suspect by both the SS of the avenue Foch and the Gestapo of the rue des Saussaies.

'She's *e gajo rom*, Hermann – married to a non-gypsy, Henri Doucette. There's a notation at the bottom of the card.'

'Not the Spade?'

'The same. Once touted as our answer to the Americans' Gene Tunney. A major contender for the heavyweight championship in 1928 though no fight was held that year, and still, I think, the work-out man at the Avia Club Gym over behind the Porte Saint-Martin unless he's found more lucrative things to do.'

The rue Lauriston perhaps? The notorious French Gestapo that was made up of gangsters the SS had let out of jail immediately after the Defeat to make 'collections' among other things.

'Let's go and have a word with him. Let's stuff a rawhide whip down his throat before we cut off his balls.'

'There's no mention of his being responsible for this.'

'Then he'll tell us, right? and he'll have nothing to worry about.'

Chez Rudi's was just across the Champs-Élysées from the Lido. Everyone knew of it, and those who could not eat here or anywhere else would linger beyond the front windows watching those inside.

It being mid-morning, no meals were being served because

lunch was being prepared, but all around them the Occupier came and went, many in uniform, most with their newspapers. *Pariser Zeitung*, the *Völkischer Beobachter* – Hitler's own paper, or *Signal*, his picture magazine. *Le Matin*, too, and others. All controlled because that was the way things were.

The *café filtre* was black and strong and excellent when taken with two lumps of sugar. *Real* sugar and *twice* in the same day!

'I saw that, Louis. You slid four of those sugars into your pocket. You know Rudi doesn't like the customers when they take things. Put them back.'

A nod would suffice. Hermann turned to look over a shoulder, as indicated. There were four of them with their faces pressed to the glass. 'Why aren't they in school?' he blurted.

'Perhaps the schools are closed due to the lack of coal.'

'It's not my fault.'

'No it isn't but if you expect me to eat in a place like this, try to understand that it is difficult for me.'

Kohler grabbed four thick slices of bread. Butter, honey and plum jam were added, some cheese also, he piling the slices up on a napkin and calling out to the kitchen, 'Rudi, I've got to do this!'

The kids took the bread and ran, and he stood in the grey light with the snow swirling around him as he watched in despair, his feelings hurt because they hadn't even thanked him.

'They called me a dirty *Kraut*, Louis. They spat at me and said spring would come but that it was taking a long time.'

Parisians the city over were saying this, spring being the end of the Occupation and of the Occupier.

'I was thinking of my boys,' he said, looking at the jam on his fingers.

'And I wasn't thinking. Forgive me.'

A shadow fell over them. 'It's such a small world, isn't it?' fluted Rudi Sturmbacher, noting the file card beside St-Cyr and then comparing the scars with the largest of those on the cheek of the Kripo's most errant *Detektiv*. 'They say hers glisten when oiled and that, by the time the Spade was done with her, the dress and blouse were in shreds yet she remained defiant.'

The Spade . . .

At 166 kilos, Rudi was the centre of all gossip, Chez Rudi's a minefield of it. The flaxen hair was so fine it blew about every time he moved and was therefore closely trimmed. The florid cheeks were smooth and round and netted with the blue-black veins of too much good living, the pale blue eyes wary, sharp and swift to greed, sex or larceny.

'Who's oiling her?' asked Kohler blithely.

The puffy eyelids widened beneath their thick thatches of ripened flax. 'No one at the moment but there are those who are so fascinated by her scars, they want her back.'

'Sit down,' said Kohler. 'Hey, rest a while and tell us what the airwaves are saying about the Ritz, Cartier's and the Gare Saint-Lazare.'

The big lips were compressed. A floury hand was wiped on an apron that had seen use since well before dawn, though Rudi often changed them and it must be due to the shortages that he hadn't.

'Well?' asked Kohler.

'The airwaves . . .' A steaming bowl of sauerkraut and sausage was brought, a little mid-morning sustenance.

Rudi cut off a slice of sausage and examined it. These two could be useful. 'Information for information, are we agreed?'

'Of course,' said Louis.

They were desperate, then, and still very much on the run, and that could be good or bad depending on the whereabouts and accessibility of the loot, all 50–70,000,000 of it and taken in one night. The talk of the town.

St-Cyr would never agree to anything in spite of his having said, 'Of course.' Rudi fed the slice of sausage to Hermann. 'That sous-directeur of Cartier's overlooked a sapphire-bead-and-cabochon necklace with oriental pearls and South African diamonds to the value of 250,000 *Reichskassenscheine.*'

5,000,000 francs. 'Anything else?' managed the sausage-eater.

'A sapphire and diamond bracelet with five rows of square-cut, deep blue sapphires, then a row of clear white diamonds on either side. Three hundred and seventy-five blue ones, each exactly the same; one hundred and fifty of the white. One of a kind.'

They waited. Hermann was fed another bit of sausage and then a forkful of sauerkraut, the juice running down his chin and Rudi dabbing at it with a napkin so as not to mess the tablecloth.

'100,000 *Reichskassenscheine*,' said the mountain. 'Ear-rings to match – that was another 50,000. And a ring, the stone set in platinum. Another 30,000.'

'That sous-directeur is just inflating the loss for insurance purposes,' grumbled St-Cyr.

No sausage was offered, not even the sauerkraut.

'He wishes he was,' said Rudi, watching them both as one would two frogs before spearing them for their legs. 'But apparently a woman had been in on several occasions to try on the sapphires. Tall, blonde, statuesque and with eyes not unlike your little Giselle's, my Hermann. That perfect shade of violet. A chanteuse who couldn't quite make up her mind.'

'Ah no, not Gabrielle . . .?' blurted St-Cyr, aghast at the implications.

A bit of sausage was cut off and savoured, Rudi judging the smoke-curing to have been as perfect as the times and the constant demand for sausage had allowed. 'The same,' he said. 'Maybe she has some explaining to do, maybe she hasn't. Like I said, it's a small world.'

Louis leapt from his chair to grab his coat and hat and then to head for the street and the car. Rudi nailed Kohler's wrist to the table with a grip of iron. 'The fence or fences, Hermann. The loot, *mein lieber Detektiv*. I want a part of it.'

'For the future?'

'Who knows what might happen but it's wisest, I think, to be prepared for all eventualities, is it not?'

'Leningrad is only a city. It means nothing.'

'Nor, then, does Stalingrad or the machine-gun nests the Wehrmacht are installing around town.'

'Still no snipers on the roof?'

'Not yet.'

Rudi had wanted the snipers up there in case the citizens of Paris should take a notion to revolt.

'Information, my Hermann.'

'I'll see what I can do.'

'*Gut*. Oh, I almost forgot. A cigar, *ja*? for the proud papa to be. Take care of your little *Liebling*. I hope it's a son to replace one of those you lost. Twin boys, perhaps, who knows? But watch over her. Don't let them pick her up just because you weren't co-operating. Your visitor is straight from Berlin and doesn't trust either of you. He smells a rat. Don't disappoint him. Give him one.'

'Louis . . .? Do you mean *Louis*?'

Kohler threw a tortured look towards the street. The cigar was crumbled in a fist and fell to the floor, a waste.

Rudi patted him on the shoulder. 'But first the Gypsy, *mein Schatz*,* and his woman, his Tshaya.'

3

The rue de la Paix was an unexpected sea of traffic. The snow came steadily. A misery for the drivers, the weather was a joy to the passengers who laughed, stood up precariously in their hacked-off bathtub seats, settees, and ancient *fauteuils* to throw snowballs at one another. The girls wore thin overcoats, wavy hair and pillbox hats with nets of veiling or snap-brim fedoras and upturned collars, the boys were in grey-green, blue or black uniforms. There was no language barrier, not today.

A circus. Cartier's wore a banner: *Fermé pour les altérations*.

Every newspaper had seized on the robberies and had raised the hue and cry with: HEISTS IN THE MILLIONS. WHAT WILL BE NEXT?

First one enterprising *vélo-taxi* driver and then another had conceived the brilliant idea of a Robbery Tour. And since no two of those crazy rickshawlike contraptions were the same, colours, shapes and sizes clashed as the din rose to attic garrets five and six storeys above the fashionable shops.

Angered, dismayed – terrified, yes, damn it! by what Rudi Sturmbacher had just said, Kohler threw up his big hands in despair and said, '*Merde*! Let's leave this bucket of bolts in the middle of the street.'

This beautiful Citroën . . . 'They'll only scratch the paint. They're already doing so.'

Kohler got out to hold up his badge and part the waves. An onslaught of snowballs drove him back behind the wheel.

* my treasure.

'I could have told you so,' grumbled the Sûreté and, looking well along the street, nodded towards place Vendôme. 'They pulled it down. The city's like that, Hermann. Once the people get the fever of an idea nothing can stop them. That's Paris.'

'Pulled *what* down?' They'd work to do and Louis was in a huff and sensing trouble. 'Make it short, *mein Kamerad. Don't* give me any of your fucking *Quatsch*.* Not today.'

Hermann's conscience was troubling him. 'The column, idiot. After our defeat in the Franco-Prussian War, the citizens got to hating what it represented – all those deaths and failures in Napoleon's Russian Campaign. They set up a government here in opposition to that of Versailles and one of the first things they did was to pull that thing down.'

'They didn't? Hell, the damned thing's the height of a blast-furnace stack. It must weigh tonnes.'

'It does. Thousands watched as it broke into three pieces before hitting the ground, and then into at least thirty. There were clouds of dust.'

'Yet it was put back.'

Louis gave the Gallic shrug Kohler knew he would. 'They were bound to, but that's another matter. What's important for you people to grasp, Hermann, is that they *did* pull it down, and in one day. 1 May 1871, a Monday at 5.40 p.m.'

You people . . . 'Rudi only asked me if I had a source for him. Some cheese.'

How lame of Hermann. 'And did you?'

'You don't trust me.'

'I'm your partner. I have to.'

And I'm your friend, aren't' I? – Kohler could sense this in the tone of voice. Crises they had had before but never anything like this. Giselle would be yanked from the flat or the street and thrown into a cell – beaten probably. She'd lose the kid. And Oona . . .? Oona would be deported and never heard of again. Shit!

Kohler gazed well down the street over the jostling sea that all but imperceptibly flowed towards them. He saw Oona in rags, her eyes bluer still and gaunt with hunger. She'd be worrying about Giselle. 'All right, Rudi warned me. Herr Max is after your head.'

* crap.

Twelve hundred Russian and Austrian cannons had been taken at Austerlitz in 1805 by blood, tears and sweat and hauled all the way back to Paris to be melted down and cast into the bronze sheathing of that first column. In 1875 that sheathing had been recast using moulds still kept from the time of the First Empire. 'It's a small world, as your countryman has only just informed us, Hermann. Moscow and Russia were Napoleon's nemesis. Stalingrad, Leningrad and Russia will be Hitler's.'

'I'll help you.'

'But that might not help us.'

'Gabrielle can't be involved in this business, Louis.'

'That's what we must endeavour to determine.'

Gabrielle Arcuri was Louis's chanteuse, the new love of his life, though that affair had remained unconsummated – Kohler was certain of this, certain, too, that Louis was still missing Marianne and Philippe and blaming himself for what had happened to them.

He had met Gabrielle not two months ago while on that nothing murder in Fontainebleau Forest. She'd been a suspect then, was she a suspect now too? Ah *verdammt*! lamented Kohler silently. Why did the Occupier have to be such bastards?

Leaving the car in the centre of the street, they managed to lock the doors, then thread their way to the pavement and along to Cartier's.

Gabrielle was involved with the Resistance – a tiny cell, a nothing cell. They both knew it of her, knew also, as did she, that Gestapo Paris's Listeners had recently bugged her dressing-room at the Club Mirage, so the matter, it was serious.

'Is her group hiding the Gypsy, Hermann?'

'*Merde alors*, I wish I knew. The idiots! Don't they know what Gestapo Paris will do to them? Boemelburg, Louis. *Boemelburg*!'

The post, the shots at dawn if still alive.

Clément Laviolette, the sous-directeur, was distraught. 'A tragedy,' he lamented, on seeing them enter the shop. 'Irreplaceable, Inspectors. Twelve cushion-shaped sapphire beads of a depth of blue and clarity I have never seen before. *Never*! Years ... it has taken years to accumulate such stones. Each bead has a round diamond brilliant of two carats in its centre. There are thirty-two matching sapphire cabochons graded as to size and linked so as to drape from the neckline of cushions. Each cabochon is separated from the next by a pearl of such exquisiteness, they, too, have taken years to accumulate.'

'There was a bracelet,' said St-Cyr.

'Ear-rings, too, and a ring. Matching stones. Ah *mon Dieu*, Inspectors, what are we to do? The pieces had been paid for, you understand. 8,600,000 francs up front, the receipt for which I myself have signed.'

A tragedy, like he'd said, thought Kohler. 'You didn't lose the cash, too, did you?'

'Unfortunately, yes.'

'Yet you did not inform us of these items last night?' exclaimed St-Cyr. 'Surely you must have known . . .'

'They weren't in the vault, were they?' bleated his partner.

Vehemently the sous-directeur shook his head. 'They were in my private safe. It's in my office behind the painting. We . . . we did not think . . . Ah! the door to it was securely closed and the dial turned to the number 47 just as I myself would have left it.'

Believing the worst, Kohler sighed, 'So, when was the payment made, eh?'

'On Saturday. There had been a few minor adjustments to make – nothing much. Mademoiselle Arcuri was really very pleased. A little something new, to go with the dress that is her trademark. We've been trying for some time to get just the right pieces together for her. She was ecstatic.'

I'll bet she was, thought Kohler ruefully. Five numbers to the combination – would there have been that many for her to have memorized?

It was Louis who said bluntly, 'Please show us your copy of the receipt.'

Dated the sixteenth, the same day as the Gypsy had ordered the cigarette case, it was clear enough.

'She came in at about eleven for a fitting. As with our other special clients, this was done in the dressing-room that is just off the office. There it is very private, and if the client chooses, why the door can be closed so as to dress or undress as much as one wishes.'

'Left alone, was she?' demanded Kohler.

Again Laviolette vehemently shook his head. 'There was only one tiny alteration for us to do – she had hoped to take everything with her and to wear the pieces that evening, but could not wait while it was done. One of the linkages had to be shortened a half-millimetre.'

A nothing business. 'And she paid in cash?' he asked.

'In 500 franc notes.'

It wasn't good, thought St-Cyr, but the receipt might just save her since it offered an alibi of its own, she having made a substantial investment and placed great trust in the firm. And as for carrying around that sort of cash, some did it these days. Her take at the Club Mirage was ten per cent of the gross, kept in an old trunk perhaps to avoid taxes – he was going to have to speak to her about this. It couldn't go on. 'Monsieur le sous-directeur, think back, please. At any time was Mademoiselle Arcuri or any customer other than the Gypsy left alone in that office while the wall safe was uncovered?'

'No. No, of course not. We're most careful.'

'Yet you didn't bank the cash,' snorted Kohler. 'Why was that, eh?'

'Such a large sum,' hazarded the Sûreté, grimly gesticulating. 'One would have thought a little caution perhaps? Oh *bien sûr*, business is booming, but even so . . .'

'Noontime had come upon us. The bank was closed for two hours. I myself had to eat.'

'Yet you had all day Monday to make the deposit,' countered St-Cyr softly.

They had best be told something. 'With such a sum, and with such pieces, we always want to know absolutely that the sale has gone through.'

'So the money was in the safe, along with the necklace and other pieces?' said Kohler.

'That is correct.'

'Then why, please, did she not pick up the jewellery yesterday?' asked Louis

Ah damn these two. 'She . . . she said she wished to argue with herself a little more. It was, she said, a great deal for her to spend. The authorities . . . she was worried someone might question such an expense. It would have to be declared, of course. That is the law.'

The careful shopper, thought Kohler, raking the sous-directeur with the look he reserved for duplicity. 'Anything else, eh? Just what the hell did he really get from that "private" safe of yours?'

'Nothing else. Apart from those items, that safe was empty.'

Kohler took out the cigarette case to run a thumb over its amber in doubt. 'He's lying, Louis. They'd have kept the accounts ledgers in that safe, in case of fire.'

St-Cyr took the cigarette case from him, nodding at Laviolette to indicate that he should accompany them to the office at the back of the shop.

'Inspectors . . . a little oversight, yes? These days one has to watch what one says.'

'Of course. Now the truth about that safe of yours,' said the Sûreté, stopping him in the corridor to tap him on the chest with the cigarette case the Gypsy had ordered.

His back to the wall, Laviolette frantically threw a glance into the shop to where anxious clerks were trying to pick up the pieces of their little lives but had stopped to gape at the front entrance.

'Herr Max, Louis.'

The crowd on the street had not diminished but now a gate-crasher was forcing his way through.

'The truth, monsieur, and quickly before that one sinks his teeth into you,' hissed St-Cyr.

'The blanket *laissez-passer* I have which allows me to travel anywhere outside of Paris except for the *zone interdite*.'

The Forbidden Zone next to coastal areas and along the Swiss and Italian frontiers.

'My first-class railway pass. My spare pocket-watch and . . .' He licked his upper lip and tried to hastily tidy his moustache. 'And four packets of *capotes anglaises*, two bottles of Ricard pastis, one of vermouth and . . . and the keys and deeds to a little house I have in . . . in the fifth.' Ah *maudit*! would God help him in this moment of crisis?

'Booze and a woman, and wouldn't you know it, eh?' snorted Kohler, blocking the way, thus hiding them from Herr Max who was making noises about the crowd. 'Is that all?' asked the Kripo.

68

'*Oui. Positive.*'

'No it isn't,' said the Sûreté. 'We want the name of the woman and the address of that little nest for which he has taken the keys.'

'My wife . . . My daughters . . .'

Laviolette was sweating.

'Hey, they won't even hear of it if you behave and keep all this between the three of us. Silence, eh?' said Kohler.

'*Numéro trente-cinq,* rue Poliveau.'

'The quartier Saint-Marcel,' said Louis.

'Suzanne-Cécilia Lemaire, veterinary surgeon and zoo-keeper – zebras, hyenas, jackals, wolves, wild boar and foxes at . . . at the Jardin des Plantes.'

How the hell had they met? wondered Kohler, pulling down a lower left eyelid in disbelief. 'Age?' he demanded. It took all types, and when Laviolette said, 'Thirty-two', patted him on the shoulder, all sixty-two years of it, and said, 'Don't get bitten. Women in their thirties are even more dangerous than those in their early twenties.'

'Now go and entertain our visitor from Berlin while we lock ourselves in your private office to have a look for ourselves,' said St-Cyr. 'Let this be a warning to you.' The Jardin des Plantes . . . ah *merde.*

They were moving swiftly. 'The back door, Louis. The cellars.'

'Get the car. Meet me in the rue Volney! Fire some shots in the air if you have to, but get it, Hermann, and hurry!'

There was just a chance the Gypsy might have holed up in that house. If so, he was a gambler and was prepared to take risks but had thought the sous-directeur would not have said a thing.

The safe was open, and from the door to the private dressing-room, there was more than a clear enough view of the dial but not of the numbers. Gabrielle could easily have stood here, waiting for Laviolette to bring her the pieces but . . .

Pulling open the dressing-table drawers, St-Cyr soon had what he wanted, and closing the door to the wall safe, set the vanity mirror with its little stand on top of one of the filing cabinets. Tilting it until he had the dial in view, he retreated to the dressing-room. It was no good. She would have had to stand much nearer the desk but from there, with the use of the mirror, she could have watched the dial and, after several visits, have had the combination or close to it, but had she done so?

They might never know.

And why, please, he asked, would Laviolette not have noticed the subterfuge and put a stop to it?

No, then. She must have done it some other way or not at all. But if she had, then that, too, implied she had known of the Gypsy and had made a thorough survey of the target for him.

The quartier Saint-Marcel had been going downhill for years. Built mainly in the first half of the 1800s, its houses of two and three storeys still held that sense of a small provincial town or village. The slanting roofs were often cut off and at odd angles with the sky but also with a towering wall of dirty yellow brick which represented 'redevelopment' into a monotony of identical flats.

'It's unprotected,' said Louis of the district. 'Ripe, sadly, for tearing down. That thing', he indicated the apartment building, 'was built in the 1920s.'

Still a stronghold of *le petit commerce* and of retired shop-keepers, sales clerks and maids of all work, its shops were small, its ateliers struggling, the narrow courtyards far too long and far too handy.

Neither of them liked the look of the place. The doorway to number 35 hadn't been used in years. The black paint was peeling, the monogrammed ironwork over the curved bottle green light above was First Empire but badly rusted.

They had left the car around the corner but even so, two plain-clothed detectives, no matter how casually they kept their hands in the pockets of their overcoats, could not fail to attract attention.

A lace curtain fell in a first-storey window across the street. Stares were given from behind the window of the *café-bar* below.

'Louis, you watch the street, I'll take the courtyard.'

'That door has been sealed with iron spikes as long as my hand. He's not Hercules is he, our Gypsy?'

The courtyard was close, the stucco walls mildewed, the house separated from others by yet another courtyard behind it.

Lines of grey washing were frozen stiff. There were clouds of breath not just from the neighbours but from the ateliers of a mender of cooking pots and a scavenger of roofing slates and floor tiles.

Steps pitted by frost and worn into hollows by long use led up to a side entrance. Unattractively the number 35B in cardboard was pinned to a door that had been left off the latch.

Cautiously, St-Cyr took the Lebel from his overcoat pocket and, pulling back the hammer, gave the door a quiet nudge. Hermann was right behind him and had drawn his Walther P38. 'Louis ...?' he softly said and in that one word there was consternation and terror – ah! so many things.

They had both smelled it. They hesitated when they ought really to have run. The shutters were all closed, the cast-iron stove was cold, the air ripe with the stench of bitter almonds. *'The kitchen!'* managed Hermann, removing his hand from the stove; they were moving quickly now, delicately.

The aluminium stew-pot on the hotplate was still boiling, the fumes were thick and white and acrid ... 'Ah *nom de Jésus-Christ*, be careful!' hissed St-Cyr.

Both of them looked questioningly at the ceiling above. Both looked to the pot where the remains of several broken-up sticks of dynamite in water bubbled thickly beneath an oily, pale yellow scum, the nitro.

Two eye-dropper bottles had already been skimmed. A small glass funnel lay on its side. There was a ladle, a long-handled wooden spoon. Absolutely no friction could be tolerated, no sudden shocks, no sparks, no matches or cigarettes. Both bottle and funnel would have been tilted during the filling so that the nitroglycerine would trickle smoothly down the inside of the glass. A master of self-control, a fearless idiot but desperate.

They left the kitchen and took the steep, narrow staircase on and up – they didn't want to. He's armed and dangerous, they would have said if they could have found the words. Their heads were buzzing so hard from the fumes and the dizziness, it was all they could do not to bolt and run, to gag and clear the street.

The Empire bed was huge and sturdy and heaped with rumpled covers. No one hid in the massive Breton armoire that held the woman's clothing. No one was in the spare room, a

71

nursery perhaps in bygone days or a tiny sitting-room, but now jammed with suitcases and the bits and pieces from the mistress's former flat.

The bathtub on its four cast-iron legs had been painted green too many years ago. The geraniums were wilted, the towels cold.

Kohler nodded towards a shuttered door. Louis saw him do so in the gilded mirror above the tub.

Shots would be exchanged out on that roof – there was no hope of preventing them. Hermann ducked out on to the little porch where in summer the veterinary surgeon and zoo-keeper would have sunned herself or cooled herself after a bath, her lover too. He slipped and fell, went down hard, the Walther P38 banging off two rounds as he rolled aside and threw himself behind a low railing that was lined with stone planters.

Nothing ... there was no answering fire. 'I thought ...' he blurted.

'You thought incorrectly, so did I.'

They heard the Citroën start up – hell, there were so few cars in Paris that wasn't hard to do – and when it left the street where they had parked it, they knew he had taken it.

'The keys,' swore Kohler. 'I put them under the driver's seat when I got our guns.'

'*Idiot! Now what?*'

'We find us a telephone and call the bomb-disposal boys, but first we turn off that hotplate before the soup boils dry.'

Suzanne-Cécilia Lemaire lay under the covers, bound hand and foot and gagged. A not unpleasant-looking young woman, she was furious at what had happened to her and embarrassed that anyone should see her wearing four heavy flannelette nightgowns, two sweaters, three pairs of thick woollen kneesocks and gloves, her auburn hair put up in *papillotes* for the night, her eyes weeping from the fumes.

'*Bâtards!*' she shrilled when released. '*Who the hell are you, and who the hell was he?*'

The hands of caution were raised and she was told the street would have to do for the moment, and quickly.

Hermann almost kicked over one of the little bottles. It had been left for them on the doorstep. Sickened, he watched as the woman paled and sucked in a breath. Tears streamed from her.

A lower lip quivered. 'No one told me this would happen,' she blurted. 'He's *crazy*! He said that if I knew what was good for me, I should lie very still.'

The quartier Saint-Marcel had been cleared of every living soul but those of the Wehrmacht's bomb-disposal unit. The Café of the Deceiving Cat, on the avenue des Gobelins, was teeming with disenchanted residents and merchants all shouting about Sûreté incompetence and loss of income. The Gestapo never got publicly blamed. *Never*!

'By five o'clock it'll be in all the newspapers,' sighed Kohler ruefully. 'Hero boils it up. Shots exchanged. Sûreté car stolen in getaway.'

'They'll make a living legend of him,' said Suzanne-Cécilia Lemaire, her soft brown eyes clouded with worry, hesitantly cradling her *'café au lait'*, no milk, no sugar, no coffee but hot. With the paper curlers removed and her hair combed, she looked a little better but was far from sure of things.

'Why not go and find the car, Hermann? Try the quartier de l'Europe. He may have friends there. He can't drive around, not for long.'

Louis wanted to be alone with the woman. 'And if not there?'

The woman threw Louis an apprehensive glance, was watching everything.

'The Avia Club Gym but I would prefer to be with you for any interviews.'

She took this in.

'The Spade, ah yes. Okay, Chief. I'll find you back at the house on the rue Poliveau?'

As if on cue, the thud of a massive explosion several blocks away brought dust from the ceiling and everyone to a crouch.

Silence followed. It was as if the rain of rubble was still up in the sky and had yet to come down.

'Ah Christ, Louis. Widows and orphans!'

Everyone began to move. A hand shot out and grabbed Suzanne-Cécilia by the arm; she threw the Sûreté a look of panic, more tears springing from her.

'*Sit down!*' he ordered. 'Hermann, go and find the car. Neither of us can do anything for them. It's impossible, *mon vieux*.'

'Boemelburg, Louis. He'll demand hostages. He'll say it was a Resistance plot. Ah, hell!'

'Calm down. We can only take it as it comes.'

'That's what I'm afraid of.'

He left them then and they had a last glimpse of him agonizing over things on the boulevard. Like the soldier he had been, Hermann began to run towards the disaster knowing exactly what he'd find because he'd seen it all before.

'My partner was a bomb-disposal expert, among other things, in the last war.'

Filled with despair, she darted her eyes away, and for a moment could not find her voice, then said abjectly, 'You must know each other very well. What one thinks, the other is aware of.'

'Usually, but not always, and he's the stubborn one. Now please, mademoiselle . . .'

She pulled her shoulders inwards to wrap the bathrobe about herself more tightly. Terrified by this new development, she said hollowly, 'It's Madame Lemaire. My husband was killed in 1940 at Sedan. A woman has needs, Inspector. My Honoré left me no money but the widow's pension and, as we have no children and I'm too young to stay that way, I have to think of the future.'

'Laviolette . . .' he muttered, passing her his handkerchief which she took with a faint, '*Merci*.' 'It seems an odd choice. Your lives are so different, your interests . . . Do you share *anything* in common?'

Ah *Jésus, Jésus*, she said to herself, why must he ask a thing like that at a time like this? The house in pieces – had it really been the house? How many dead, and she the only tenant? The Gestapo would come for her – they would have to, yet here he was trying to distract her. 'We . . . we met in the zoo. Clément would come to feed the animals – he knew we had little to give them and for him, it took him away from his wife on a Sunday afternoon and allowed him to exercise a kindness. I found him one day with oats he had gathered handful by handful in Normandy – can you imagine him doing such a thing?' Quickly she dried her eyes. 'My zebras loved it, Inspector, and he genuinely loved them and was not at all like most who come to see them. And to think,' she sighed and shrugged and tried

74

desperately to smile faintly, 'he had brought the oats from far away. Not for himself, you understand, but for my animals.'

'*Bon*. Compassion's rare these days. You met when, exactly?'

'Inspector, is my private life suspect?'

'Ah no. No of course not. I merely wish to establish why Monsieur Laviolette should leave the keys to that house in his private safe.'

Again she threw an anxious glance towards the street as if expecting the Gestapo momentarily.

'They ... the keys were with the deeds. For this, you must understand that Madame Laviolette holds him constantly under suspicion and frequently includes his private office and desk among her searchings.'

'Henpecked, is he?'

'The roots of your suspicions are deep, Inspector. Why is this, please?'

'Just answer the questions.'

'Or you will get angry with me, eh? Hey, monsieur, you're perturbed enough when it is *I* who have been subjected to such indignities, I ...'

He wasn't having any of it. '*Yes*, then. He *is* henpecked and not just by that wife of his, by his four daughters, two of whom are married. They constantly examine every aspect of his life and criticize him amongst themselves.' She blew her nose.

Creases framed the frown she gave. Her lips were parted slightly as if she wondered, still, what he was thinking of her answers. The nose was not big or small but decidedly impish. The thick, auburn hair was a little less than shoulder length, in waves and curls, masses of them, and worn over the brow with only a part in the middle to all but hide her frown and emphasize her eyes.

'Life on the sly with a thirty-two-year-old zoo-keeper and veterinary surgeon must be better,' he grunted. 'Should they ever discover the affair, your Monsieur Laviolette will immediately blame his wife and daughters to their faces for having caused him to stray!'

Taken aback, she said softly, 'He's not vindictive. Oh *bien sûr*, the house, it was an investment and not much – he wouldn't let me spend a sou fixing it. He always said she would only find out if he did. But . . .' She clutched the robe about her throat and tossed her head. 'But he has made his promises and I believe he'll keep them.'

New laundry for the old and she beginning to distance herself from the explosion. 'You're far too intelligent to believe it, Madame Lemaire. So when, please, did the two of you first meet?'

Ah damn him. 'Last summer. 13 June.'

'And he was feeding oats he had gathered in early summer to the zebras?'

Merde! how could she have been so stupid? 'He had purchased a small sack of last year's harvest from a farmer. I thought . . .' She shrugged. 'Well, that you would understand that's what I meant.'

'And when, exactly, did the affair begin?'

Laviolette would be questioned closely, therefore she had best answer as truthfully as possible. 'The end of June,' she said. 'I . . . I only make 650 a day, Inspector. It's not so much for a woman who does a man's job, is it? That's when we decided on our little arrangement. He wanted someone to live in the house, otherwise the authorities would have taken it over, isn't that so? It was close to my work. In a few minutes by bicycle, a little longer on foot, I could be there without the expense of the *métro* or *autobus* but now . . . now I don't know what I'll do. His wife is bound to find out. The press . . . Ah *nom de Dieu*, I had not thought of them.'

A study in contrasts, the expressions she gave in quick succession changed from firmness of resolve to doubt, hesitation and despair as she realized they had already mentioned the press.

'The bolts on your side door, madame?' he said.

'Pardon?' she managed, startled by this new direction.

'Why were they left open? Ah *certainement*, the Gypsy had the key but there were two other bolts, one at the top, the other at the bottom. The owners of those old houses felt they never could take chances. The *cambrioleurs* of those days were tougher than they are today.'

The housebreakers . . . 'The bolts stick in winter because the cold freezes the dampness in the wood, so I . . .' She shrugged. 'I left them open, otherwise it would have been a window for me and those are – were, I should say – stuck tightly and shuttered also.'

She'd try to have an answer for everything. 'Then only the key was necessary. The Gypsy entered at about 4 or 5 a.m. Did he have two suitcases or a rucksack – what, please?'

She drew back, and again threw a frantic look towards the street. 'I . . . I wouldn't have known, would I? He wouldn't have carried all that loot upstairs. He'd have needed his hands, his wits . . .' Why was the Sûreté so suspicious of her? *Why?* she wondered anxiously. 'I awoke to find a gun pressed under my chin and a hand clamped over my mouth. He was lying on top of me, Inspector. *Me!* Can you imagine what I thought? Ah! a woman's worst nightmare. He assured me that wasn't the case, and since he had the gun, I did not resist.'

The Inspector fiddled with the pipe he had taken out but had yet to pack with tobacco. He was waiting for her to add to what she'd just said and she knew that if she did, it would not be wise of her, but if she didn't, he'd believe her evasive. 'He lit the candle I have beside my bed – or had, I should say. It's necessary to have such things due to the frequent electricity outages, is it not? He let me see him. He was tall and thin and blond and had the sharpest blue eyes of any man I've ever met. Swift, calculating – far ahead of my thoughts or anyone else's, I must think, and very sure of himself with women – with men, too, I suspect, though I cannot say for certain. The nicest smile, the gentlest hands. *Très caressant*, you understand, even when tying a vulnerable woman and gagging her.'

'Yet he warned you to lie still.'

'*Yes!*'

'And when we left the house together, madame, you said on the doorstep . . .' St-Cyr flipped open his little black notebook. '"No one told me this would happen."'

'I . . . I didn't know what I was saying. I was angry. I was scared. I'd been put upon.'

'*Who* was it that failed to warn you?'

'No one. I'm not lying, Inspector. I've no reason to. How could I have?'

Ashen, she threw another glance at the street. He couldn't let her go. He had to keep an eye on her and keep her from the

Gestapo. 'And now you have no house or clothing beyond what you wear. Permit me, please, to offer the use of my house until you're settled once again.'

'Is it that you wish to keep me a prisoner?'

'Ah! of course not. The house is empty. There are two bedrooms and if I am ever there, you may lock your door and leave the key in the lock though, as a detective, I would not advise this elsewhere.'

'Why is that, please?'

'Because as every experienced housebreaker knows, such a key can easily be manipulated.'

'And your partner?'

'Lives with two women and at the moment, has his hands and flat full.'

'And you have no one?' she asked, fiddling with her robe.

'A chanteuse, but she's very understanding and works nearly every night. Besides, she has her own place.'

'Then perhaps I could stay with her. Would this be possible?'

'Perhaps, but you will need clothing, and this I have plenty of – my dead wife's. I ... I haven't had time yet to pack up her things. You're about her size, I think, though she was a little younger than yourself.'

'Ah!' she tossed her head in acknowledgement. 'And how, please, did that one die?'

There seemed nothing else for him to do but to tell her, and she knew then that he had deliberately manoeuvred her into accepting and that he had not yet wanted to let go of her.

And his partner? she wondered. Would that one reinforce the Sûreté's doubts or merely treat them with impatience?

And why, please, had the Gestapo not come for her, not yet? Were they leaving it to this one and his friend? Was he offering the house to keep them from her?

'All right, I accept. It's very decent of you but I should warn you I sometimes have to work late and for this, I must stay overnight in my surgery. Just so that you understand and don't come looking for me.'

'Of course.'

*

78

The look Boemelburg gave would have broken glass. Grabbed by two strong-arm boys while frantically clearing rubble, Kohler had been hustled into a black Renault and hurtled across town at 180 kilometres an hour.

'Four men, Hermann. *Dead*, do you understand? Two others so injured they will not recover. Did you *think* von Schaumburg wouldn't shriek at me to find and arrest those responsible immediately?'

Old Shatter Hand ... Rock of Bronze, the Kommandant von Gross Paris under whose authority the ordering out of the bomb-disposal boys had fallen. An old friend from previous investigations. Well, sort of.

'Sturmbannführer, we didn't know the Gypsy would be doing a boil-up. He's moving far too fast even for us. He's also leaving surprises.'

'And the dynamite?'

'We don't know how he got it. We're working on it.'

'You're "working on it". *Ja, das ist gut*, Hermann. You disobey my orders. You lock Herr Max out when it is he who is in charge. *Verdammt!* could you not have gone up with the mortar dust to save the lives of those men?'

Furious with him, Boemelburg seized and hurled a Chinese porcelain figurine, a leftover from the days when Louis's boss had occupied the office.

10,000 *Reichskassenscheine* went everywhere and even Pharand down the hall would have heard it and leapt.

'I'm warning you, Kohler. This matter is to be handled delicately. Berlin, you idiot. SONDERBEHANDLUNG, JA?'

'Chief, your heart.'

'Fuck my heart. It's your balls we have to worry about *und* your neck. Mine too.'

'We know so little,' bleated Kohler. 'We're not being told everything.'

'Sit. Light up if you wish and wipe the dust and blood from your face and hands. There ... over there, idiot. My basin of water and towel.'

Kohler would see death when he looked in the shaving mirror. He would realize he looked ninety. Damned worried. Too much Messerschmitt benzedrine in his blood and too little sleep.

Everyone knew he was popping those pills the fighter pilots took to stay awake and alive.

'Don't get careless with this, Hermann. We all have to make sacrifices.'

And wasn't Louis to be one of those sacrifices – wasn't that what Rudi Sturmbacher had said? thought Kohler. Had the gossip started here?

His big hands shook when he lighted a cigarette – the aftershock of the rue Poliveau.

'A brandy, I think, and then some coffee,' grunted the boss.

A *mouton* had let Gestapo-Paris know about the job at the Ritz but had failed to get the timing right or mention Cartier's or the Gare Saint-Lazare. Kohler fished about in his pockets for the cigarette case only to remember Louis had it. 'Lucie-Marie Doucette. Tshaya,' he said, 'daughter of a horse trader. We're to find her – is that all Gestapo Paris-Central can give us, Chief?'

'Herr Max can, perhaps, tell you more.'

'Like who's her conductor? Is it the Spade?'

The boxer, Henri Doucette. 'Perhaps. I really wouldn't know.'

Kohler sighed inwardly with disbelief and said, 'Herr Max obtained an agreement from the Gypsy in writing, Sturmbannführer. De Vries was then released from the Mollergaten-19 and taken to Tours so that this Tshaya could make contact with him and let her conductor know what was up.'

'That is correct.'

'Then her conductor was told by Herr Max what to feed her. She must have believed the Gypsy had escaped from prison. She'd have rejoiced in this and would have lied about the timing of the Ritz robbery in order to save him.'

'You're beginning to understand, Hermann. She's well known to De Vries. They travelled in the same *kumpania* during the war years and every summer for years afterwards. She's the daughter of the family that, on seeing how well the boy had come to learn their ways and language and to respect them, took him in and treated him almost as one of their own, even though he was a *Gajo* and *marhime.*'

And polluted, as were all *Gaje*. 'Is she helping him now?'

'This we do not know but suspect.'

'Someone must be.'

'That's what we want you to find out.'

80

'And never mind her conductor?'
'You'll find him too. I'm sure you will.'

The Club Monseigneur's neon sign was out because all such things had been forbidden. In the greyness of swirling snow and fast-fading light, the rue d'Amsterdam was busy. There were uniforms everywhere among the pedestrians, *Vélo-taxis* and *gazogène* lorries, and one lonely Citroën parked where it ought not to have been.

The only *flic* in sight was writing up a traffic ticket for the only car in sight. Enraged, Kohler said loudly, 'Piss off! Go on, beat it, eh? There may be a bomb under that thing.'

The Führerlike moustache twitched. 'A bomb . . .?'

'That's what I said. Now don't try my patience.'

'But . . . but the car is not where it should be? It was stolen.'

'So you're writing up a parking ticket?'

'*Certainement*! The law is very clear in the matter, monsieur.'

Ah *putain de bordel*! a stickler. 'Then write it up but don't touch the car. Not until I'm done with it.'

Reluctantly Kohler got down on all fours to peer under the car, only to find it better if flat on his back. He strained to look up into the engine, got his hands all greasy and had to wipe them on his overcoat. Oona would be furious. She was always trying to keep him tidy. Giselle would back up every word, if not in tears over the baby . . .

When he lifted the bonnet, he found three sticks of dynamite wrapped with black electrical tape and wired to the ignition. Sickened, he took his time. There was verdigris on the bloody blasting cap. It was too delicate to touch . . . too delicate . . .

The cold weather didn't help. It made the wires stiff. Carefully he tucked the sticks into his overcoat pockets and then dropped the cap down a sewer only to realize he ought really not to have done this.

The *flic* handed him the traffic ticket and Kohler took it without a word, the injustice of it all building silently within him. The bonnet was gently closed. The keys were under the seat just where he had left them.

He was still counting but there was no nitro lying around loosely in its little bottle, though there had been two of those bottles at least, and the Gypsy had left only one of them on the doorstep of that house in the rue Poliveau.

The *flic* glared at him from the pavement and Kohler was tempted to say, Why not get in and give it a try? but it was his responsibility, no one else's.

Though he didn't want to, he got in behind the wheel and when the engine suddenly came to life, he let it run for a moment while the tears trickled freely down his ragged cheeks.

Switching the ignition off, he locked all four doors and put the keys in a trouser pocket. Then he looked uncertainly up to the Louis XIV wrought-iron balusters of the narrow balconies above the club. He tried to pick out Nana Thélème's flat.

'Aren't you going to move the car?'

The Paris *flics* could be almost as obnoxious as the waiters.

When Louis found him, Kohler said, 'Is that bastard up there with her or long gone?'

Hermann was a wreck. 'He wouldn't have hung around. He would have known this was one of the first places we would look but if we ask any of the locals, none of them will have seen a thing.'

'*Merde*! I've got to pee. Hang on. It can't wait.'

Electrified by his refusal to move the car, the *flic* yanked out his truncheon and started for them only to ignore the ice.

Louis helped him up and brushed him off. 'Forget about all this talk of arrest, eh? That one is Gestapo and dangerous.'

'*Asshole, I don't give a damn if you both are dangerous!*'

The left knee bent a little as Louis feinted that way but then the right fist came up and hard. There was a crack.

Unconscious, the *flic* was put in the back seat and handcuffed.

'He won't freeze, will he?' asked Kohler.

'Not with the farts he's been letting off.'

'Make sure he can breathe. We don't want him puking all over the place.'

'Shall I awaken him?'

'He'll only start shrieking again.'

They took the lift. Hermann seemed too tired to care. He didn't even wince when they had to stop at the third floor. But on the fourth, he did look back in surprise as the gate was closed and only then realized he'd been in the lift.

'I'm still shaking, Louis. That bastard is out to get us. Three boulder-breakers and so nicely wired, I couldn't have done it better myself, but he's like a hop-head. That blasting cap he used was so corroded it could have blown his fingers off.'

The sticks of dynamite were old and at their ends, an oily, pale yellowish fluid had formed little beads that were sticky. Lint from Herr Kohler's overcoat pockets clung to them as the sticks lay on the end table beneath the foyer's mirror.

Terrified by what he was now seeing, Herr Kohler seemed unable to say anything.

Nana Thélème threw her eyes up to questioningly look at him in the mirror as he stared down at those things. 'Louis ...' he finally said.

'Ah *nom du ciel*, idiot! What have you done?'

'Carried them. Thought nothing of it. That blasting cap ... I guess I was concentrating too hard on freeing it and didn't really notice.'

St-Cyr was swift. 'Is there a telephone, mademoiselle?'

She found her voice. 'Downstairs. On the concierge's floor, near her *loge* or in the club, by the bar.'

'Stay here, Hermann. Don't let her touch them. *Don't* drop anything.'

'Just call the bomb boys and have them bring one of their little boxes, Louis. Tell them this one's for real too.'

Still they stood before the mirror, and still Herr Kohler stared at those things.

'Taken from the magazine of an abandoned quarry,' he said at last and the emptiness of his voice matched that of the faded blue eyes. 'The French ... the Resistance, eh? How could the silly sons of bitches have carried it at all without killing themselves? Nitroglycerine with sawdust or gelatine as the filler. That's all dynamite is. Fifty per cent strength – you can just make out the number on the side. Velocity better than 5300 metres a second. Sends a powerful shock wave which creates a tremendous shattering effect even when unconfined.'

She waited and he tonelessly continued. 'Extremely useful for wrecking old machinery or blowing apart the car of unwanted detectives, preferably with them in or near it.'

She winced. 'I ... I know nothing of this.'

'Nothing? Then why the hell did that bastard park the car directly under your windows?'

The stench of the nitroglycerine was so powerful, she gagged and turned away only to have him yank her back. 'Ah no, Mademoiselle Thélème. If I'm to die because of you, I'll need your company. One good knock, eh? That's all it needs when the sticks are like that. Shock or friction, and to think I was so lucky down on that street of yours not to have blown myself to kingdom come.'

Still they waited. A little later he said, 'When breaking railway lines, bridge abutments or gun emplacements we used to put down a patty of wet clay first. A good daub of it. Then the sticks lying side by side but never ones like those, and only one would have the cap and fuse, or cap and wires if we were to use electrical blasting. It's all really very simple once you get the hang of it and quit being afraid. More clay covers the charge – a thicker layer. Works every time. Defused them too, the other side's. Had to. Orders were orders. I want the truth, mademoiselle, 'cause you and those damned things are scaring the hell out of me.'

'He's the father of my son, my Jani.'

'Janwillem De Vries, the Gypsy.'

'Yes, but we never married. He was arrested in Oslo and was sent to prison.'

'That why he hates you?'

'I . . . I don't understand what you mean?'

'Then I'll make it plainer. Did you tip off the authorities in Oslo so that they could put him behind bars?'

'No, I didn't. I hadn't seen him in ages by then. Nearly two years. I thought . . . why, that he'd gone completely out of my life.'

He hated to correct her. 'When was your son born?'

Ah damn! '5 November 1938.'

Kohler didn't say anything. He let her think what she would, but as sure as that God of Louis's had made birds to sing, the Gypsy and this one had been together in late January or early February of 1938. De Vries had been arrested 20 April of that year. Would the news of fatherhood have pleased him? he wondered, then thought briefly of Giselle and looked again at the dynamite.

'So, now he's turned up in Paris again and he's aware you've moved from Saint-Cloud to here.'

'Yes, but . . . but don't ask me how he became aware of it.'

'Tours,' he said. 'Was he the reason you went there last Tuesday?'

'No! I went there because of the diamonds. Monsieur Jacqmain, the prospector, would not sell them to Hans unless I . . . I personally guaranteed his safety by making yet another visit.'

'You're a busy woman. You go to a party on the previous night. You sing your heart out for the SS who are occupying your villa, then you catch the 5 a.m. express to Tours.'

'Not quite. The train did not leave until eight.'

'Tell me something, mademoiselle. Who attended the party and why was it given?'

'Now listen, I've already told you at the Ritz all I know about who was there. As to why the party was given, those kinds of people don't tell people like me anything. We played and sang for them, that is all.'

But was it? he wondered. 'And on Thursday the fourteenth the Gypsy is seen in Tours boarding the train for Paris.'

'Look, I'm sorry those men were killed at the house in the rue Poliveau and I'm sorry he tried to kill you but . . .'

'"The" house – you said "the", mademoiselle? That implies you knew of it.'

Ah no . . . 'I didn't.'

'But maybe you did, and when my partner gets back we're going to sort you out. Oh by the way, in case you were wondering, Jean-Louis St-Cyr's name is still on some of the Resistance's hit lists. Could that be why your Gypsy's trying to put paid to us?'

'I . . . I wouldn't know. The Resistance . . . ? Please, what the hell do I have to do with those people?'

'That's what I'm asking myself.'

The two detectives spoke quietly, and Nana Thélème wished with all her heart she could hear what they said. The bomb-disposal unit were packing things up. The car on the street below

85

was being given another going over. The sewer had been opened to find the blasting cap.

They'd trace the dynamite – this would cause them some delay but she really didn't know how she could possibly stop them from doing so. She still could not understand why Janwillem had left such a device below the apartment of his son, the little boy he'd never seen.

Had the bomb gone off, it would, at the least, have sent flying glass inwards, perhaps killing Jani and herself.

Letting the edge of the velvet drape fall from her hand, she stood a moment undecided – wished then that she had not been trying on the loose-fitting, rose-coloured, striped silk chiffon trousers with their long waistcoat of rose and gold lamé and the outer one that came to just below her waist but was of many vibrant colours and much fine needlework. She wished she had not had her dancing shoes on. The heavy, black high-heels with their sturdy straps gave her height, strength and that overt alertness and suppleness of body she did not want at the moment.

St-Cyr was studying her. He'd remember that her hair was still loose and that there was the look of the gypsy about her. He'd see the gold ear-rings, the heavy gold bracelets and rings. He'd think there was more to her than met the eye.

Tshaya ... A fly in amber. *Vadni ratsa*. Why had Janwillem asked for such a thing as that cigarette case? Was it to have been her final insult?

No. No that was the bomb in the car below.

'Louis, the Resistance have to be involved. They're the only idiots desperate enough to fool around with stuff like that. We've got to find the quarry and quickly, and then trace the stuff to whoever took it.'

The Resistance and Gabrielle, and was this not the reason Herr Max wanted a certain Sûreté's head? 'Perhaps but ... ah *mais alors, mon vieux*, is it that others wish simply to make it appear as if the terrorists are involved?'

The SS of the avenue Foch, the Gestapo of the rue des Saussaies, or the French Gestapo of the rue Lauriston. Louis couldn't know he had talked to Boemelburg. Not yet. 'I've thought of that too. Engineer a crisis, eh? so that you can then have all the authority you want to stamp it out.'

86

The relief of Leningrad, the defeat at Stalingrad were excuses enough but so, too, were increasing acts of 'terrorism' and related evasions of the forced labour draft, the hated *Service de Travail Obligatoire* which was sending so many workers to the Reich but also driving the young men to swell the ranks of the *maquis*.

'Knock off a few places to make sure the loot taken more than compensates for the effort, eh? since if the plan works,' said St-Cyr, 'all those involved in it will be handsomely rewarded with a lot left over for the bosses.'

'But it isn't working, is it?' said Kohler sadly. 'He's buggered off on them.'

'And now they have to have him back.'

Louis dragged out his pipe, only to ruefully examine the meagre contents of his tobacco pouch and, momentarily furious with life, put both away. 'There's no denying his parking the car outside her flat can do nothing but cause her trouble.'

'He can't be happy with her but is he with anyone?'

'Someone's been helping him and not just with that uniform and ID he got in Tours,' muttered St-Cyr. 'He knew Wehrle's safe would be loaded. He knew all about Cartier's, knew the Gare Saint-Lazare kept its receipts too long, and knew enough of the house on the rue Poliveau to take the keys to it.'

'He had to have help getting from the Gare to that house. Two suitcases, a large rucksack ... The patrols, the risk of being stopped ... He was carting dynamite too, wasn't he?'

'A bicycle would have been sufficient, Hermann. He has all the recklessness and nerve needed to ride one when fully loaded and on ice. No problem.'

Louis was just evading things. 'A car,' breathed Kohler sadly. 'Who do we know in the Resistance who has one?'

Hermann had finally got to it. 'I was hoping you wouldn't ask, but even Gabrielle can't drive about after the curfew without a *laissez-passer*.'

'I'll check it out. I'm going to have to, Louis. Someone had to haul that dynamite around. Someone had to find it first and then store it. Boemelburg and Herr Max will expect it of me. I'm sorry, but I have no other choice.'

'Tshaya ... we have to find her too.'

*

87

'Lucie-Marie Doucette. I know nothing of her,' said Nana Thélème. 'The name, it is unfamiliar to me.'

The flat grew still.

Herr Max had arrived at the departure of the bomb squad. Furious with her, and with Kohler and St-Cyr, he said quietly, 'Nothing, Fräulein?'

Louis started forward. Kohler grabbed him. Still she stood defiantly in those all-but-Ali-Baba trousers – that was the way Engelmann would see her – with arms tightly folded across her chest. And all around her, the Turkish and Afghani leavings of the Marché aux Puces, the flea-market stalls in Saint-Ouen, threw back their throw-rug colours and kilim-patterns. Dark reds, blues, greens and yellows, the geometry of their patterns and the pseudo-mid-Eastern attire so foreign and repulsive to him, they could only bring anger at her obstinacy.

'Nothing,' she said.

The hammered brasses glinted. Gilded, carved neo-Gothic chairs were caught in wall-mirrors that must have come from some circus, the beautifully sculpted head and shoulders of a gypsy patriarch too, a *Rom Baro*, a 'big man', a leader with a fiercely bushy moustache that drooped at its ends. The *Rassenverfolgte*, the racially undesirable and here she was keeping images of them.

Herr Max removed his bifocals, letting his gaze pass myopically down over her. Untidy wisps of hair fell across his brow. 'Tshaya?' he asked again.

All around the room, watercolours gave scenes of gypsy encampments and caravans. Portraits too. The smoke, the scent of camp fires, of women and young girls washing clothes in a stream, of an ancient matriarch pouring Turkish coffee from a superb brass *jezbeh*, of another wearing heavy necklaces and earrings of gold coins. Holland, Belgium, Normandy, the Auvergne ... Provence, Spain and Andalusia, where hadn't Janwillem De Vries travelled with them?

The paintings were exceptional and St-Cyr realized then that De Vries could so easily have become an artist of a far different sort but . . . she had got the message.

'All right, I . . . I did know of her once,' she said sharply.

Engelmann gripped her by the chin. She yanked her head

away. 'But ... but your former lover slept with her, Fräulein, with this *marhime lubnyi* you hate so much? That unclean whore took him from you, yes *you*! She could have had any man she wanted, but chose instead that which was forbidden by gypsy law. A *Gajo*. Always it was your Gypsy she wanted right from when she was seven years old and he but a boy of eleven. When marriage to De Vries was refused absolutely by her father and all the others of the *kumpania*, she ran away to Paris to find him. Age fifteen then, in 1922.'

Her nostrils pinched. The smile she gave was swift and cruel. 'She found she had a sudden likeness for muscles, for the smell of male sweat and the thrill of being splashed by blood during a fight!'

Oh-oh, thought Kohler.

'Henri Doucette,' sighed Herr Max, pleased that he had got her to respond with such acrimony. 'The Spade, Fräulein, a guest at that party in your villa a week ago Monday. Her husband, her conductor. She was his *mouton*, his informer. Tell me, please, did he applaud your singing?'

Dear Blessed Jesus, help me, she said silently and then acidly, 'He was too drunk and loud to have noticed.'

'But had brought her along?'

'Yes.'

'And she knew who you were?'

'Yes.'

'And you were forced to sing gypsy songs in front of her, knowing you were no gypsy yourself but that she had taken the father of your son from you?'

Her voice leapt. '*What would you have had me do? Refuse those loudmouthed, arrogant pigs?*'

His eyebrows arched. 'The SS? The Gestapo and the French Gestapo who were their guests?'

'It was *my* house! Doucette deliberately tried to humiliate me. They thought it a great joke. They were drunk. There was food everywhere. On the walls, the ceiling, the carpets – my carpets! They threw it. They encouraged their whores to do so and when one of them tried to dance naked on the table, they clapped and roared and slapped her behind.'

'No. No that is not quite correct. Tshaya danced for them fully

89

clothed as a gypsy. While you remained silent, your little orchestra played for her. She showed you how it was really done. If anyone humiliated you, it was her.'

'He ... he had sex with her on the table afterwards while they all shouted encouragement. He ... he stripped her naked and she ... she spat in my face when I tried to cover her.'

Ah *Gott im Himmel*, swore Kohler silently. Louis was thinking the same. Debauchery – her villa, everything she had once owned and had taken pride in but for these few things, the paintings ...

'I don't know where either of them are, nor do I know if they are hiding together or who, if anyone, is helping them.'

'Then why the tears?' asked Engelmann. 'Is it that you are afraid for them?'

She clasped her mouth to stop herself from vomiting and turned away. '*Because you can't control a man like that! Because wandering is not just a way of life, it is life!* Lock him up and he'll go crazy. *Crazy!* do you understand? *That* is what you have to deal with now.'

'And is she helping him?' said Herr Max.

'*She must be!*'

'But ... but you were the only one other than the Generalmajor Wehrle who knew the contents of his safe?'

Stung, she turned back to face him. '*No!* that is incorrect. Everyone who sold diamonds to Hans knew those things were in his safe. Others, I don't know who, would have known he made his shipments to the Reich once a month or even once every two or three months. It all depended on how much there was.'

'Where will she go?'

When Nana Thélème shrugged, Engelmann hit her. Shocked, dazed and bleeding from the nose and mouth, she stumbled back and fell to the floor.

He stepped between her legs and she waited defiantly for the kick he would give.

Doucement! 'Now just a minute, Herr Max,' swore St-Cyr. 'Janwillem De Vries has at least one bottle of nitroglycerine. If we waste any more time here, Berlin will be certain to question the delay.'

'The Spade, Louis. Let's go and have a talk with the son of a bitch!'

'Yes, yes,' said Herr Max, grinning at them for having given him exactly what he had wanted from them. 'Perhaps she should join us. Then if Doucette says something she disagrees with, she can clarify the matter.'

'I'll have to change,' she said, sucking in a breath while silently cursing him.

'No you won't. You'll come just as you are. It'll do you good. It's never warm in the camps in winter.'

'Buchenwald . . . is it that you are going to send me there?' she blurted.

He did not answer. Shattered, she found she could not move.

Louis took her gently by the arm and quietly confided, 'For now we must do as he says. Here, be sure to put on your overcoat and boots, a scarf and hat. Mittens . . . have you no mittens?'

'I've done nothing.'

'That won't matter.'

Buchenwald . . . Why not any of the other camps? Why had she said it if not knowing, too, that Tshaya's father had been sent there?

Déporté 14 September 1941.

4

The silhouette on the unwashed wall threw a right that would have killed a man. The Spade ducked and weaved. A right, a left, an uppercut. Murderous that one too. Then back, moving always lightly on the balls of his feet. Another left. A left, a left. Feinting, weaving, now a drop to the right to block the punch.

Sweat poured from the tattooed shoulders and grizzled Fritzhead. The muscles glistened, tightened. Doucette didn't let up. The shadow of him threw a punch. He ducked, went in on himself hammering hard. At the age of forty, he was still far better than most. An army, a battering ram. *'Il a le style armoire à glâce,'* snorted Kohler. He has the build of an icebox.

Crisscrosses of sticking plaster had come away from the back of the swarthy neck to reveal two gigantic boils, flame red and hard against the sweat. Another was in the small of his back where the skin was pink from exertion and glistened. There was pus in the crater of that one and it, too, was ready to burst.

'Erysipelas in the offing,' said St-Cyr drolly. 'An acute streptococcal infection if not careful. A very high fever. Nothing to eat for four days. Champagne is the only thing. One tosses and turns in delirium. Five weeks for a full recovery if nothing intervenes, namely death. It's highly contagious.'

'*He's* contagious,' hissed Nana Thélème softly under her breath, her dark eyes filled with hatred in spite of all her anxiety.

Herr Max good-humouredly lit a cheroot and, pausing to unbutton his overcoat, dropped the spent matchstick into a waiting bucket of sand and announced, 'Henri, some visitors.'

The black satin shorts were tight over the muscle-hard buttocks. Unwashed, the webbed elastic band of the *boxeur's* athletic support absorbed the constant sweat. The gym was busy, noisy, hot and heavy with body odour. Here a Wehrmacht sergeant pounded a punching bag, there another. An SS-Obersturmführer skipped to beat hell in competition with two of the local toughs. The girls watched. The girls oohed and aahed and laughed or threw kisses.

A fight was in progress in the ring, two middleweights were working each other over. No referee.

'Henri . . . Henri . . .' The bells rang.

The punching bags came to a stop. The skipping was silenced. The match ceased. Towels were grabbed, faces wiped, wine or water taken and mouths rinsed before spitting it on the floor. Perhaps thirty were in training. Others sat or stood around. Spectators mostly.

Rushed in by laughing SS in uniform, two teenagers were dragged up into the ring – mauled until their overcoats, sweaters, shirts, shoes and trousers were off.

Given gloves and shorts, they were forced to wait as Henri Doucette, ignoring his visitors, climbed dutifully into the ring.

'The bicycle pumps,' sighed St-Cyr ruefully, and when Nana Thélème threw him a questioning glance, he said, 'Surely you've seen the SS and other officers remove their ceremonial daggers to hang them up in the coat-check rooms of the clubs and restaurants? Having followed them in, the kids haven't daggers, so they hang up their bicycle pumps to enrage the Occupier. This, apparently, is to be their punishment.'

'*Tant pis pour eux*,' she said softly. Too bad for them.

Teeth-guards were lifted, dripping from a bucket of water, to be crammed into reluctant mouths. Afraid, confused – uncertain still of what was to happen – they listened as the Spade began to give them lessons.

They were to fight each other and he'd take on the winner. It had to be a good fight. 'Ten rounds!' cried one of the SS. There was laughter, cheering, clapping from delighted females.

The kids tried not to hurt each other, and when no blood was produced, Henri stepped in. 'Hey, I'll show you how.'

'They're too little, Henri,' cried one laughing blonde with sparkling eyes. 'Make men of them. It'll save me the trouble.'

'I don't think I can watch this,' said St-Cyr, and pulling off his overcoat and fedora, thrust them at Hermann before climbing into the ring.

He took the boys aside. He said, 'You must avoid his right and always try for the left side. He's partly blind in that eye – a fight he lost in 1928 perhaps because the gypsy wife who hated him fiercely by then had come back briefly to sap his strength. He tries to hide it. Shame him. It'll anger him. Then dance away and *don't* let him hit you.'

They came together, their manager and the Spade. They spoke, but what was said could not be heard.

Then Louis turned away only to turn back so swiftly his left connected hard. There was a crack.

Poleaxed, Doucette tried to shake his head and Louis let him have it with a right.

He dropped like a stone.

There were boos, there were cries of anger but the kids were allowed to leave the ring and to get themselves dressed, the Sûreté saying to them as a father would, 'Now, no more of that, do you understand?'

A hush descended over the gym. Tension crackled. Kohler knew he'd have to defuse it somehow. Firing two shots into the sand, he yelled, '*Clear the place! We're on a murder investigation.*'

'Who's been murdered?' asked the *pugiliste* from the Sûreté and once champion of the police academy, but years ago.

'You, unless I can prevent it.'

The *ventouses*, the suction cups, were of plain glass and red hot, and each time one was applied, Henri Doucette shrilled and wept like a baby. Flat on his stomach in the dressing-room without a stitch to cover him, he clenched his still-taped fists as the boils burst, and so much for the Gestapo of the rue Lauriston and one of its key members.

'I'm saving you from agony, Henri,' said the Sûreté. 'One day you'll thank me. We can't have you ill when we need you.'

There was another in a very tender place and this the surgeon had left to the last.

'Hold him, Hermann. Take him by the wrists. You, the ankles, Herr Engelmann. It's all in a detective's work.'

The scream filled the room and brought the latest pigeon to gape in panic from the doorway. She was all dressed up in plunging green velvet and emeralds to match her wounded eyes and breasts.

'*Petit*, I'm here,' she said. '*Chéri*, don't cry. It's for the best and when we're alone, your Nathalie will comfort you.'

'*Piss off*, Putain! *Can't you see I'm busy?*'

She leapt and turned away in tears. 'You're always saying things like that. A whore . . . I love you, Henri. I *want* you!'

'*We're finished! It's over. Over, do you understand? Slash your wrists if you must but don't come crying to me if you mess up! Make a good job of it this time.* Complet, eh? Fini *and* au revoir.'

Nana Thélème took charge, urging the girl to leave. 'Give him time. They won't be long.'

'He means it,' the poor thing wept. 'He's been so cruel to me. Always it is like I am a dog at his feet!'

'Then why not give him up?'

The sea green eyes that were so large and innocent blinked their tears away with candour. 'I have to eat. I have to have a place to stay. He buys me things and yes, I love him. I like it. Can you understand that? I can't.' She shrugged her slender shoulders. 'I've tried but always the inner self, it fails to answer me except with temptation.'

94

There were stares from the others in the gym, looks that were not nice. The SS who had brought the teenagers still hung around, spoiling for a fight.

'Sit down. Here, have a cigarette.'

'I've plenty. Let me give you one.'

Her fingers shook. Grabbing the hand, Nana steadied it. 'Inhale. Fill your lungs. Count to ten and then exhale.'

Calmed a little, the girl sat back on the bench but shrank into herself. 'I hate this place. Every time I come here I feel as if they are going to rape me. All of them and all at once in the ring. I want that too, don't you understand? Secretly I'm so afraid of it and this . . . why this gives me great pleasure.'

'Relax. They're nothing.'

'You were at the party. You were the one who came to sing.'

Though the eyes were dark brown, the left one was cloudy, and when Doucette looked directly at a person, it was not quite on a level with the right eye, but tilted up a little.

'*What do you want with me?*'

He had never liked the police but was from Belleville. 'A few questions. Nothing difficult,' said the Sûreté.

The Spade threw the visitor from Berlin a questioning look only to see that one nod curtly in agreement.

'*What about you putting me down like that, eh? Why should I do* anything *to help you?*'

'Ah! easy, Henri. Easy,' soothed St-Cyr. 'Forget it, *mon ami*. Be magnanimous. Everyone will know it wasn't fair. They'll say I tricked you. It's me they'll blame, not yourself.'

Again the visitor nodded.

'Okay. Shoot. Let's have it.'

'*Bon*. Take us back to last Thursday, the fourteenth. You and your wife went to Tours.'

'She's not my wife. I disowned the slut the day I used her father's whip on her, since he wasn't man enough to do it. She'd been running away from me all the time. Weeks, months . . . She deserved it.'

'But you're her conductor now?'

Again he looked to Herr Max for guidance. 'Okay, so I took her to Tours. It was all laid on. She was to bump into the Gypsy.

Perhaps he was suspicious, perhaps not, who's to say? She was to call in on a regular basis. She was to tell me everything he planned and did, and who he met, but she's buggered off with him and I haven't heard from her since Monday when she called in to warn us of the robbery at the Ritz.'

Hermann was translating for Herr Max. 'But is she with him now?' asked St-Cyr.

Dumbfounded, Doucette threw Engelmann another look, and wiping sweat from his chest, asked, 'With who the hell else could she hide?'

'That's what we want to know.'

'Then think again, cow. Her family's gone. She has no one else she can trust, no friends, eh? She knows no one and yet she still evades us? How can this be?'

The Gestapo and the French Gestapo of the rue Lauriston had people out looking for her, then. A city-wide search in addition to that of the police and the Wehrmacht. 'You do the thinking, Henri. You took her to a party on the eleventh. She danced.'

'That one was there.' He pointed to the door beyond which were the gym and Nana Thélème. 'You brought her here. Why did you bring her?'

Nervous now, Doucette used both hands to grip the towel that was draped over his shoulders. He was sitting on the edge of the table, dangling his feet into space, and looked evasively down at his boots.

'Why did we bring her, Henri?' said Louis. 'You tell us. I think you'd better.'

'Her . . . her *bonne à tout faire* was . . .' He threw Max a tortured look.

Engelmann understood enough of what had gone on to help him out. 'On 15 December last, her maid of all work was arrested. It was nothing. A week in the women's cells of the Santé.'

The Santé . . . Paris's largest and most overcrowded prison. Population 12,000 normally but now about 18,500, since it varied from day to day and there was always a desperate need for space.

'She wept most of the time,' said Doucette. 'The others had to beat her to shut her up. Two of them fell in love with her and wouldn't leave her alone except to fight over her.'

96

Ah *merde* . . . 'And what, please, did this girl tell your ex-wife a month ago?'

'That her mistress was mixed up in something and that she was afraid she had been arrested because of it.'

'Henri knows a lot about you,' confided Nathalie. 'There are things he hasn't told that one in there from Berlin, things he is keeping quiet even from his friends at the rue Lauriston.'

Sitting before Nana Thélème on the bench, the girl in green velvet paused. The noises of the gym grew. The skippings, the punchings . . .

'What things?' asked Nana warily.

'Things a *petite oiseau* told him. Well, actually, it was a *mouton*.'

'*Tell* me, damn you!'

The girl looked up. Her cleavage dropped to reveal bruises, scratches and bite marks. 'Tshaya. The one he . . . Well, you know,' she shrugged.

'Am I the reason she was invited to that disgusting party?'

'*She* was the reason *you* were invited.'

Nana Thélème looked away in despair. '*Tshaya can't know anything!*'

'She does.'

The dark eyes leapt with fierceness. 'Such as?'

'A prospector.'

'Ah no . . .'

No, mademoiselle? Despair now, was that it, eh? and Henri knowing secrets which must not be revealed to anyone. 'You made several visits to the prospector's house in Tours. He wrote letters to you. He had something he wanted you to do for him.'

'Tshaya can't have met him recently. She *can't*! Not in years.'

Sweat poured from the *pugilistes* in the ring. A nose was bloodied. A tooth was spat . . .

'She *has* met him recently.'

'Pardon?'

How shrill of this beautiful Andalusian who had had the Gypsy's bastard and had just recently had her face bashed. 'A place, a very special place. His favourite *bordel*.'

'*The fool!*'

97

Would Henri beat this Nana Thélème? Would he fuck her, torture her? Between 50,000,000 and 70,000,000 francs were missing. A fortune. Diamonds ... lots and lots of those and sapphires too. Pretty things Henri wanted for himself, well, some of them, for his little retirement. 'A *lupanar* with a *chambre de divertissements détachés.*'

'The house on the rue de la Bourde in Tours.'

The street of the blunder, the heart sinking at the news. Was all now lost? Was that it, Mademoiselle Thélème? 'The same. The House of the Hesitant Touch.'

'*What?*' demanded Kohler, only to see Louis raise a cautioning hand.

The atmosphere in the dressing-room was tense. They were still discussing Nana Thélème's maid giving secrets away in a prison cell.

'Something about a prospector,' muttered the Spade, wiping sweat from his face.

'The diamonds,' breathed Kohler.

'No, not those,' insisted Doucette, resigned to telling them. 'That was almost settled. It was something she had to take to a place near Senlis, the girl thought. Something bad the Mademoiselle Thélème could then get from there if she wanted.'

The dynamite – was that it? wondered St-Cyr. There were stone quarries nearby.

Herr Max reached out to hand Henri a clean towel. 'Go *und* have a *Brausebad. Ja, ja, mein lieber boxer,* you have said all that is necessary for now.'

'Where is she? I want her,' said the Spade.

'Tshaya?' asked Engelmann.

'No other woman can fuck like her. No other.'

Frantic, Kohler stopped the Spade on the way to the shower-baths. 'Which *lupanar* did you find her in, eh?'

'*Le bordel de la touche hésitante* in Tours. *La grille de la treillis indochinois.* She was the one behind it.'

'Louis, we're going to have to go to Tours.'

'Of course, but first there are things we must do.'

Nana Thélème sat in the front seat between the two of them. Engelmann had released her into their custody. It was to be their necks against hers and she knew they were trying to get her to tell them everything but she couldn't do that. She mustn't.

'Four women,' mused the Sûreté, scraping frost from his side window to stare out into the pitch darkness Paris had become at nine o'clock in the evening. 'One a gypsy herself. One a singer of their songs. One a veterinary surgeon and zoo-keeper, the mistress, if we are to believe it, of the sous-directeur of Cartier's.'

'And the last one?' she asked.

'That is the one who most concerns me, mademoiselle. You see, when we first met, you said you did not know of her yet she has a little car and is allowed that privilege.'

'And sings to eight hundred war-weary men a night, you said. The Club Mirage is in Montparnasse on the rue Delambre. All right, I do know Gabrielle Arcuri and she did drive me to Senlis to visit the dying mother of Monsieur Jacqmain, the prospector. That was one of his conditions. He and his mother had not spoken in years. He had received a letter from the woman's housekeeper, but by the time we got there, Madame Jacqmain had passed away.'

'And when was this trip to Senlis?'

Ah damn him! 'Right after I went to Tours. On ... on the following day, on Wednesday, the ... the thirteenth.'

'Then why did you lie to me about not knowing Gabrielle?'

She gave a nonchalant shrug he would be certain to feel since their shoulders were touching. 'One lies these days. It's an age of them, is it not?'

'But to lie successfully one must be consistent.'

She sighed. She said, 'Chance plays such a part in life. You have heard, perhaps, of the arrest of my little Juliette, my *bonne à tout faire*. Who would have thought of her saying anything to anyone? What did those women do to her in that prison, Inspector? She's tender. She's pretty. She's a very gentle creature and very loyal, but now ... now she says so little. She's not been herself since.'

'Did you tell Janwillem De Vries of the contents of that safe of the Generalmajor Wehrle's?'

99

'I didn't, but it was not necessary for me to do so, not if the Gestapo of the rue Lauriston had been keeping an eye on things and smelling a fortune. If only they could get their filthy hands on it before Hans did. If only they could get at those people through me. My maid, my Juliette, knew *nothing* of what I was doing for Hans, *nothing* of the diamonds or of that safe.'

'But knew of the prospector?'

'Unfortunately.'

'Do you know Madame Suzanne-Cécilia Lemaire?'

They would check with Céci. 'My Jani loves to visit the zoo. Madame Lemaire was most kind and let him help her feed the wolves. He's only a little boy. Don't ask me why he is so fascinated by such animals. The fables Juliette tells him at bedtime, the nightmares, I suppose.'

She grew silent, but then said sadly, 'A mother has to be present at all times when a child is young, yet when she has to earn a living, such a duty is not possible.'

'Gabrielle's son lives at the château near Vouvray with his grandmother, the Countess.'

'Yes. I've been there too. Once or twice. I can't remember.'

And what of the dynamite? he wanted so much to ask but thought it best to go carefully.

On the way up in the lift, in its privacy, he said, 'Mademoiselle, it's the silhouettes that so often defeat a boxer for he can't hide behind them. They reveal his every weakness.'

'And mine?' she asked.

Her expression was tragic but she would have to be told. 'The SS or the Gestapo won't use the guillotine. They'll use an axe, so if you wish to confide in me, please do so now before it's too late.'

'It already is. Janwillem saw to that when he parked your car below my windows.'

'But why did he do so? That is the question?'

'Ask him when you find him. Ask him why he wanted to kill the son he has never seen. Only he can give you the answer.'

The caviar was *malossal*, the Russian for slightly salted, and it was to be eaten with the little pancakes those courageous people called *blini*. Wedges of fresh lemon were provided – all but unheard of these days; also a small dish of finely chopped fresh green chives.

The vodka was crystal clear and so cold, the bottle still wore its coat of frost. The dressing-room at the Club Mirage was tiny and bugged by Gestapo Paris's Listeners and yet Gabrielle would use her voice.

'So, *mon amour*, you have come to see me and as you can surmise, I've been expecting you and have prepared myself for your questions. Once again I am suspected of something? These robberies, Jean-Louis, that terrible explosion, have been in all the newspapers. Don't keep me in suspense a moment longer.'

'Gabrielle, *please*! It's difficult enough. A few small questions just to help the investigation along.'

'Nothing difficult?' she arched, catching him unawares.

He winced. 'Not difficult. No.'

'And Hermann, where is he, please?'

'Gone to see Giselle and Oona, and then to have a look into the Gare Saint-Lazare robbery.'

'Cartier's ... my sapphire necklace ... the bracelet, ear-rings and ring. The 8,600,000 francs they will have to return now that this ... this Gypsy has stolen them from me, *yes from me*! Jean-Louis. How could you even *think* I had anything to do with that business?'

'We *don't*! Hermann and I are both convinced of this but others must be satisfied. It's the way things are. Berlin are insisting.'

'Berlin ...?'

She blanched. He reached out to comfort her. 'The Reichsführer Himmler,' he said. 'The Führer himself, perhaps.'

'Those poor boys who were killed ... What will become of their families and loved ones? I must hold a benefit – yes, yes, that's what I'll do. Please, a moment, my fans will see the need and we can send the money off tomorrow morning. Wreaths for the funerals, condolences and then ... then some lasting financial help for the old ones. It's the least we can do, isn't that so? and I must do it now! 100 francs from you. 500 ... No, 1000, I think. *Merci*.'

She left him, she with his wallet in hand and soon he could hear the crowd shouting for her and, when the tumult had subsided, her saying, '*Mes chers amis* ...' And the hush was so great, not a breath stirred. 'We must open our hearts to the families of those brave boys who have so valiantly given their lives in the rue Poliveau so that the safety and homes of others could be spared.'

When she sang 'Lilli Marlene', tears fell and St-Cyr could imagine the men spellbound even as his own eyes moistened, for it was a soldier's song, and he'd been one himself. She had a voice that transcended everything. Clear, pure, bell-toned and soul-searching, but for how much longer would it be allowed to continue?

He remembered an ancient grist mill on the Loire close to the Château Thériault, not two months ago. The Resistance had sent her one of the little black coffins they reserved for those they thought were collaborators who should become examples to others. He, himself, had received one. She'd got the drop on him with an ancient double-barrelled fowling piece in that mill of her mother-in-law's and ever since then, he'd borne her a healthy respect.

A White Russian who had fled the Revolution with her family, she had, having lost them, arrived alone in Paris at the age of fourteen and had been a chanteuse ever since. She was a widow whose husband had been badly wounded at Sedan in May of 1940 and had then died in the late summer of that year. And, yes, she was suspected by the Gestapo but not yet sufficiently to drag her in for questioning or to put her under constant surveillance. Or perhaps it was simply that she was known to too many high-ranking Germans who adored her and therefore extreme care had to be taken.

Sonderbehandlung here, too, he wondered. Sickened by the thought, he opened one of the small vials of her perfume. Its twists of cobalt blue crystal poignantly reminded him of that nothing murder in Fontainebleau Forest, that small murder which had led to Hermann and himself being reviled by many at Gestapo Paris-Central and in the SS, but which had brought Gabrielle and himself together.

There was civet, a little too much jasmine he had thought then and still did. Angelica, vetiverol and bergamot. Lavender of course . . . *Mirage* it was called and he had known the creators of it, old friends.

The Club Mirage had been named after the perfume.

Though he wanted desperately to make certain there was

nothing incriminating the Gestapo might find, he forced himself not to search through her things. The perfume and the sky blue, shimmering silk sleeveless sheath were among her trademarks, the dress electric with thousands of tiny seed pearls arranged in vertical rows from ankle to diamond choker. Her hair was not blonde but the colour of a very fine brandy, her eyes were the shade of violets, matched only by those of Hermann's Giselle.

'So,' she said on catching him out once more, and he could see by her delight how successful the fund-raising had been but also how pleased she was at finding the vial of perfume in his hand. 'A few questions, Inspector. Nothing difficult.'

'It's Chief Inspector. Hermann is always reminding me of this.'

'He's going to be a father again. Isn't it splendid? A baby, Jean-Louis. *A baby!*'

'Oona . . .? Giselle . . .?'

The flat on the rue Suger was empty, freezing as usual but in complete darkness too. And when Kohler found the black-out curtains wide open, he saw a lamp on the table in front of the windows and panicked. Had Giselle been arrested? Had Oona been taken with her? It had been deliberate, this placing of the lamp. The stub of an unlighted candle was beside it with a box of matches in case of a power outage.

Arrest would have been guaranteed. Three months in the women's cells of the Santé, the Petite Rouquette or Fresnes were the usual, any of which would have sufficed if she had hoped to lose the baby.

The bored *flic* behind the desk at the quartier Saint-Germain-des-Prés's Commissariat de Police on the rue de l'Abbaye thought he was out of his skull. She wasn't in the emergency room at the Hôpital Laennec on the rue des Sèvres though everyone agreed that when young girls get pregnant they might well do crazy things.

She and Oona were sitting spellbound beneath the smoke-hazed, garlic-and-onions beam of the projector at the Cluny on the boulevard Saint-Germain, her favourite cinema. Hats on, hats off . . . The place was packed. Couples were making out

103

here, there, it didn't matter where so long as they had the chance ... The screen was filled with a shabby Marseille flat. An abortionist ... ah *verdammt*! One so evil, the camera zoomed in on the ingrained dirt of the bastard's cracked fingernails. A terrible eye was clouded by cataracts. A shrew of a wife was railing at him from behind beaded curtains, and at his fresh innocent, his most recent victim.

Helpless, the young would-be virgin looked about the room with abject dismay. There'd be a catheter, a pair of surgical tongs and a length of rubber tubing whose syringe would suck soapy water from a bucket as the bulb was squeezed. Then it'd be down with the underpants, up with the knees ... 'Wider ... a little wider, mademoiselle.' Right in past the cervix, deeply ... 'Up ... I must get it up a little more.' Squish! A massive shock, the girl probably dead in a split second as air entered her bloodstream. A pretty thing, a hell of a waste ... '*Giselle! Oona!*'

Kohler stopped himself, his heart racing. He and Louis had seen it all not a week ago. A maker of little angels and a flea-bitten tenement across the river in Courbevoie and definitely *not* the figment of celluloid.

'Come with me. *Please*! I ... I couldn't find you. I was worried. Hey, I've got to go over to the Gare Saint-Lazare and need a bit of company. Louis ... Louis is busy with other things.'

Still in the dressing-room at the Club Mirage, St-Cyr touched a finger to his lips, and taking out some scraps of paper and a pencil, quickly wrote, *Cartier's. The Gypsy knew the combination of the sous-directeur's safe.*

Questioningly Gabrielle raised her eyebrows.

Did you tell him of it? he demanded in pencil, thrusting the paper at her.

Out in the club, the audience were now clamouring for her. 'How can you think such a thing?' she asked aloud. 'At least let us give the happy couple a bassinet and a few baby blankets. Giselle will need so many things.'

Gestapo Paris's Listeners could make what they would of that. *Someone is helping the Gypsy. The robbery at the Ritz for sure; Cartier's for sure, and probably the Gare Saint-Lazare.*

'Not us,' she said, a whisper but given too quickly – she could see him thinking this and dreaded his response for she hadn't said *Not me* and should have.

Patently ignoring the mistake but filing it away, he wrote, *Please tell me where you were on Tuesday the twelfth.*

'I . . .' she began, only to stop herself. He'd check. He wouldn't hold back, even though he loved her – did he really love her? She wanted to believe this but they had been alone together so seldom. *I had to go to Tours,* she quickly wrote. *There, does that satisfy you?*

'A little,' he said and wrote, *Did you meet Nana Thélème in Tours?*

'A rattle . . . ? Is it that you wish to give the baby a rattle?' she asked aloud and, saddened by his insistence on pursuing the matter, answered, *Yes!* in writing, *but quite by accident. We had a cup of coffee in a small café.*

And did she ask you to drive her to Senlis on the following day?

Gabrielle flinched in despair.

The dynamite, he wrote. *Someone is supplying the Gypsy with it.*

From Senlis? she asked, writing it out for him and listening for the Gestapo – waiting tensely for them to barge in and shriek, *'Hände hoch!'*

She lighted a candle and burned all the scraps of paper.

'Giselle must want this baby very badly, Jean-Louis, but will your partner make an honest woman of her now that his wife has gained her divorce and has found another?'

Back home in Wasserburg, ex-wife Gerda had married an indentured French farm labourer, a humiliation Hermann had yet to complain about and probably never would.

St-Cyr waited for Giselle's answer about the dynamite but she refused. Tears began to mist her lovely eyes. *The stone quarries,* he harshly wrote. *The prospector Nana went to Tours to meet. Monsieur Jacqmain asked her to go to Senlis.*

To see his dying mother! That was all. I swear it. I could not refuse, she wrote and burst into tears.

In dismay, he saw before him what he'd seen when they'd first met: a determined evasiveness, lies and half-lies and every possible female ruse.

There had been some rough but beautifully coloured diamonds then; there were diamonds now.

Do you still belong to the Society of Those Who Have Been Left Behind?

The war widows. 'Why should I not?' she demanded aloud.

His nod was curt, his whole being the detective she had first encountered. 'My friends are clamouring for me. Will you come and listen?'

Neither of them had touched the vodka or the caviar. 'Of course. But first . . .'

There was silence as he took from a pocket the crystal of clear quartz they both had been given last Saturday – his last investigation; a child of eleven, an heiress. Had she been a clairvoyant, that child? 'It is magic,' she had said so seriously. 'You will need it, I'm afraid, for the cards are not good. A visitor is to come into your lives who will pit you against each other with terrible consequences. Please do not forget this. Remember to be true to each other.'

The crystal was one of those 'diamonds' of the curious stone and mineral trade, a dipyramid perhaps two centimetres by one and a half, six-sided and pointed at both ends but grown lopsidedly and full of internal fractures. They had gone to meet the child at a villa in Neuilly on the far side of the Bois de Boulogne. On the way, Jean-Louis had received a telex that had been meant for Hermann, since all such messages were directed to his partner. MOST URGENT. REPEAT URGENT. IKPK HQ BERLIN REPORTS INTERNATIONAL SAFE-CRACKER GYPSY REPEAT GYPSY HAS REPORTEDLY SURFACED. LAST SEEN TOURS 1030 HOURS 14 JANUARY HEADING FOR PARIS. APPREHEND AT ONCE. HEIL HITLER.

Jean-Louis did not know the *réseau* to which she belonged had received a wireless message tacked on to what the British had sent regarding the child's parents.

GYPSY . . . REPEAT GYPSY DROPPED TOURS NIGHT OF 13 JANUARY. PROVIDE EVERY ASSISTANCE. MOST URGENT. REPEAT URGENT. WILL HAVE EXPLOSIVES. GIVE FULL PRIORITY. CODE NAME ZEBRA.

The Gypsy hadn't had any explosives even though London had said he would have them. He had denied it to their faces, but of course they had already taken care of the matter on the thirteenth, during the trip to Senlis.

Three women. Nana, Suzanne-Cécilia and herself. Dynamite. Code name Disaster.

Nitroglycerine also, and plenty of blasting caps and fuse. Ah *Jésus, Jésus*, what were they to do?

The Gare Saint-Lazare was the world's third largest railway station. Gargantuan, it was divided into two long arrival-and-departure sections by an immense hall, every one of whose panes of glass, high up there above, had been crisscrossed by strips of brown sticking paper and given a thick and repulsive wash of laundry bluing.

The resulting gloom was only increased by the paucity of blue-washed lamps, the whole having a distinctly other-world feeling. Breath steamed. People spoke quietly. Though they hurried to and fro, the cumulative hush was broken only by stifled coughs, sneezes and the clack-clacking of wooden-soled high-heels. 'Giselle . . .'

The girl kicked off her shoes and Oona gathered them in. Kohler knew he was in trouble. The two of them had given him the silent treatment all the way across town. 'Look, I'm sorry, eh? Hey, I'll take you both to the pictures tomorrow night. I swear it. The same ones if you want.'

'*It's not what I want!*' hissed Giselle, meaning an abortion. '*I'll kill myself first!*'

'Oona, talk some sense into her.'

'*Me*? Haven't I done enough? Didn't I find her sitting in front of that window debating arrest? Didn't I convince her to see that film? Pah! why should I say anything? It's *your* job. *You're* the father!'

'*Verdammt*! I want her to have the kid.'

There, he had got that out at last. 'And what about me?' she demanded.

Ah *merde*, where the hell was he to find the chef de gare or the sous-chef? he wondered. Pedestrians became travellers of the deep under clocks whose Roman numerals registered an alien time. 10.57 p.m. Tattered, picked-at posters advertised excursions to Deauville. Sun, sea and sand, and wouldn't that be lovely except for it being the fiercest winter on record?

Condensation had frozen on the inside of walls and windows. Furtive sparrows sought warmth up there, pigeons too. The floor was spattered with their droppings.

107

Achtung! Achtung! Avertissement: Peine de mort contre les sabo-teurs. Warning: Death to saboteurs.

Beneath the notice someone had scratched: *Les dés sont jetés en Russe.* The dice have been cast in Russia.

For a moment time was transfixed and one saw clearly the shabby suitcases and the clothing people wore, the made-overs, cast-offs and hand-me-downs, the things rescued from the thirties and from the trunks of long-dead relatives.

A girl tried to straighten her grandmother's black lisle stockings, another was checking the seams of the paint job she had given her bare legs.

Soldier boys came and went. *Les filles de la nuit* plied their trade but could only wait to be asked, since here the law prevailed and the place was thick with cops of all kinds.

Kohler knew only too well that if one wanted to hide, as the Gypsy must, the city was by far the best of places.

There was a Wehrmacht soup kitchen for the boys that had come from the bunkers of the north. Soup with potatoes in it and maybe a bit of meat. Black bread and margarine.

He managed two servings and led Giselle and Oona to a bench. 'Now wait here, please,' he begged. 'I've got a little job to do.'

'And me ... what about me, Hermann?' demanded Oona. 'You have not answered my question.'

'Later, eh? I'm busy.'

Croissants, baguettes, brioches and pâtisseries were all banned and had been for nearly two years now. The daily bread ration, *if* one could get it, had been reduced to two 25 gram slices. A notice advertised that a reward of 100,000 francs would be paid for information leading to the arrest of terrorists or those assisting them. There were soldier-warnings about syphilis, tuberculosis and cancer – Berlin believed the French were rife with these diseases. Others warned the citizenry of the dangers of eating cats – the rat population would explode and bring on the bubonic plague.

Giselle chewed a doubtful morsel then decided to discreetly drop it under the bench. When she found a much-thumbed, tattered notice for the restaurant La Potinière at the Hôtel Normandy in Deauville, she stared at it for the longest time.

'*Potage normand*,' she said with longing. '*Huîtres au gratin.*
Darnes de saumon à la crème ou tripe à la mode de Caen. Poulet à la
Vallée d'Auge, salade Cauchoise, soufflé surprise et ... et Puits
d'amour.'

One longed for the past but also for the simplest things. Far
from menus like that, Giselle had spoken repeatedly of late of
poached eggs and glasses of milk. 'Don't worry so much, *chérie*,'
soothed Oona. 'You'll be all right. I'll see you through. I promise.'

'You're so good to me. If there wasn't this Occupation, would
it be the same?' She tossed her pretty head.

The short, jet black hair, clear, rosy cheeks and stunning violet
eyes were lovely. 'You'd still need a *nounou*.'

A nanny. 'I've no training in having babies. I'm not the
mothering kind.'

'Wait till she nurses, then you'll know for sure where you
stand. Now come on, finish your soup and bread. Dream of
Deauville, eh? and of better times. Cream puffs.'

'"Wells of Love".'

'Oysters au gratin. Salmon steaks in cream . . .'

'"She" . . .? Why is it, please, that you feel it will be a girl?'

'Ah! why would you ask me that? I hate this lousy war. My
two children gone from me, my husband too!' Oona threw her
tin cup away and tore her hair in anguish.

Kohler hurried back to comfort her, saying, 'Hey now, I'm
going to take care of you both.'

Blonde, blue-eyed, tall, graceful and about forty years of age,
Oona had lost her children during the blitzkrieg, her husband, a
Jew, to the French Gestapo of the rue Lauriston and not so long
ago . . .

When he found the safe, it was waiting for him and Kohler
knew at once that here was trouble of a far different sort. It was
huge. It was ancient. Its door was closed and locked but there
was something sinister about this and when he asked the sous-
chef de gare, he discovered the door had been left open by the
Gypsy, but had been later closed and locked and only then had
they discovered that the wheel-pack had been reset. Now no one
dared to try to open the damned thing.

It was as if the Gypsy was tempting him. It was as if he
shouldn't weaken and yield to the challenge.

'Louis, this guy's playing with us all the time,' he said, but Louis wasn't here.

The vodka had remained untouched, the caviar too, but they were again writing notes to each other in the dressing-room.

The dynamite, Gabrielle. I must insist that if you know of it, you tell me how the Gypsy came by it.

She couldn't tell him the truth. She mustn't! *Perhaps he had it with him – have you thought of this?*

She was still being evasive. *Are you suggesting he first extracted the nitro he used at the Ritz and then found he needed more?*

Two boil-ups, the last at the house on the rue Poliveau ... *Mon Dieu, how could you possibly think I would know anything of such?*

The Resistance, your little réseau?

We don't do things like that! We're women. We have no such experience.

Was the *réseau* composed only of women? he wondered. *He tried to kill us, Gabrielle! He booby-trapped our car!*

She was visibly shaken and stammered, 'I ... I didn't know of this. Forgive me.'

Fine. He'd be firm now and give the next question aloud. 'Tell me why on Monday last you did not pick up the jewellery you had ordered at Cartier's?'

So, they were back to that again and Jean-Louis wanted the Gestapo to listen in, but why had the Gypsy tried to kill them? They hadn't told Janwillem to do so. They had only warned him to be careful of them, that if anyone could stop him, it was them. 'I was too busy.'

'A moment, please. Ah! I have it here in my notebook. Laviolette, the sous-directeur, said that you wished to argue with yourself a little more. It was a great deal of money. The authorities ... someone might question such an expense. It would have to be declared.'

'That is correct.'

'Then why, please, did you just tell me you were too busy?' He nodded for her to speak aloud.

'Now that you have reminded me, I do remember. He was most distressed. Certainly I promised to collect the pieces first thing on Tuesday but by then, it . . . well, it was too late, wasn't it?'

'Please don't distress yourself.' *It doesn't become you*! he wrote. 'Someone told the Gypsy of the contents of the safe and gave him the combination.'

Again their were tears. 'Have you questioned everyone at Cartier's?' she blurted.

'Not yet.'

'Then perhaps, Inspector, you will find among them the accomplice if such a one exists!'

She was still not co-operating! He raised his voice. 'There was a blanket *laissez-passer* in that safe and a first-class railway pass. The Gypsy can have those altered – a difficulty, yes, since he's on the run but whoever is helping him could take care of it.'

Did the Gestapo suspect her of this too? she wondered but said softly, 'Tshaya . . . the newspapers are saying a gypsy girl is with him.'

'I've not had time to read them.'

'They say she was married to a boxer but that he whipped her savagely.'

'What else do they say?'

'That she's the Gypsy's lover and that the two of them will turn the city upside down before they leave. That only then will the memory of them be left to last the centuries.'

Will they be apprehended?

Never! Of this I can guarantee.

You?

The press. I meant to say the press. Ah damn . . .

St-Cyr knew he had to warn her that the Germans had released the Gypsy from the Mollergaten-19 in Oslo but if she was taken in for questioning, this would be the first thing Herr Max would ask.

Look after yourself.

You also.

'Do you have your receipt from Cartier's for the 8,600,000 francs?'

'Yes, it's in my purse.'

He snapped his fingers. She smiled faintly and when she handed him the beaded silk purse, which was another of her trademarks, he looked questioningly at her.

111

The purse had been left at the scene of that nothing murder. 'I thought it appropriate,' she said, looking steadily at him.

Without a word St-Cyr put the receipt into his wallet. Then he reached for his glass, and raising it, said grimly, '*À ta santé*, Gabrielle.'

She took hers up and, though it was foolish and proud of her, gave him good health in Russian. '*Za vashe zdorov'e*, Jean-Louis.'

The door closed and he was gone from her, the caviar untouched, a waste yet she had no desire for it and, sitting down at her dressing-table, picked up the quartz crystal he had deliberately left for her.

Very thin slices of such crystals, if clear of fractures and inclusions, were used in shortwave wireless transceivers. Each thickness let in or out wavelengths of only a very narrow band. Their set had two such 'crystals': one for daytime use, which they never used but kept for emergencies only; and one for the small hours of the night which were best for transmitting and receiving.

Jean-Louis could not know that a British aircraft had dropped the Gypsy by parachute near Tours on the night of the thirteenth. He could not know that weeks of planning had gone into this and that they had received a message from England telling them to help this safe-cracker, nor could he know that the Gypsy had very quickly proven himself to be far too difficult to handle. They and the British had trusted Janwillem De Vries and he had broken that trust.

The house on the rue Poliveau was gone – six dead Boches, a terrible complication no one could have foreseen. Hostages would have to be taken. Berlin would insist on nothing but the truth and in the process, their little *réseau* would be smashed and Jean-Louis and Hermann would be caught up in things and held responsible.

'*Alles ist Schicksal*,' she whispered bitterly, borrowing the saying from the German. Everything is controlled by fate. Janwillem De Vries had taken one flask of nitro and a dozen sticks of dynamite. More he couldn't have carried and was to have come back but had buggered off on them and had severed all contact.

*

112

In the dank blue haze of the Gare Saint-Lazare the clock on the four-cornered tower registered 11.27 p.m. Giselle wondered what was keeping Hermann. He had gone into the ticket office hours ago, it seemed. Oona was watching him through the grating of one of the wickets.

People hurried, for the curfew was fast approaching and soon everything here would be closed up tightly, the wicket gates slamming down, the doors shutting while Hermann, he . . . he took his time.

She studied a faded poster that was behind wire mesh. Waving, sunburnt, big-breasted *Rheinmädels* smiled at marching soldier boys who lustily sang, '*Wir fahren gegen England*'.

We're going to England.

'Don't believe a word of it,' said someone in French. Startled, she turned to look up and into the bluest of eyes.

'Where have you been all my life?' he said. Those eyes of his danced over her, he taking in each feature to linger on her lips, her chin, her eyes and hair. '*Enchanté*,' he said, and he had the nicest of smiles and yes, it was good for a woman to hear such things.

'Monsieur . . .?' she began.

He was tall and thin – quite distinguished-looking, very handsome, about forty years of age, and the Hauptmann's uniform he wore carried combat medals and ribbons on its breast.

'Can I give you a lift?' he asked.

'Ah, no,' she answered. 'I . . . I'm waiting for someone.'

'I thought so,' he said and sadly shook his head. 'Another time perhaps.'

She could not place his accent. Was he a Fleming? There were scars on his face, little slashes where the skin had been parted and left to heal unstitched. He set the fine leather suitcase down, the canvas rucksack too, and began to put on his greatcoat. 'The Claridge,' he said. 'You can reach me there, or is it at the Ritz? I can never remember.'

He found a scrap of paper in a pocket and nodded as he read it. The hair was blond and closely trimmed, the nose was long but made his expression all the more engaging. A man, a little boy. Mischievous, serious – ah! there was laughter in his eyes as he watched her scrutiny deepen.

113

'Your name?' he asked. 'At least allow me that.'

'Giselle le Roy.'

'Must you really wait for him?' He nodded towards the ticket office and she realized he had known all along that Hermann was in there.

Two of the scars were high up on the cheekbones and equally placed. The third one was on the bridge of that nose. For a moment the hands of the clock stood still. Giselle tore her eyes away to the ticket office, to Oona who was starting towards them. Oona . . . she tried to cry out. The blast erupted. Flames, debris, dust and smoke flew at her, she shrieking, '*Oona! Oona!*' as she felt herself being dragged to cover, to hit the floor and be buried under him . . . him . . . *Bang* . . . a deafening BANG!

No one came running. Dazed, some bleeding, people picked themselves up. A large piece of glass shattered at her feet. Another and another. Pigeons scattered. Sparrows grew silent.

Three of their number fell, and when their little bodies hit the floor, they bounced.

'Hermann . . .?' began Giselle. '*Hermann!*'

A hand caught her and dragged her back. She fought to pull away. She shrieked, '*Let go of me!*' and he did, but did not smile.

The house at 3 rue Laurence-Savart was occupied and St-Cyr knew it right away. The perfume of smouldering animal dung was pungent. 'We dry it first,' said a female voice.

Startled, he looked questioningly at the century-old cast-iron stove in the kitchen where the last pages of About's *The King of the Mountains* had disappeared. The smell reminded him of films he had seen of darkest Africa, of slaves and villages and King Solomon's mines.

Madame Suzanne-Cécilia Lemaire, the veterinary surgeon and zoo-keeper from the Jardin des Plantes and the rue Poliveau, had moved in.

'Hermann won't believe it of the dung,' he said. 'He has the curiosity of a small boy towards all things French but this . . .'

'Aren't you going to try the soup?' she asked and only then did he see her curled up on the floor beside the stove. 'It's warmer here.'

The soup was thick and of onions and garlic, yet the dung had purged the air of its aroma. 'You'll get used to it,' she said. 'One gets used to lots of things. This Occupation of ours teaches us that humility and ingenuity are blood brothers to survival.'

'It has simply broken down a lexicon of social customs which should have been cast aside long ago,' he said tartly. 'Did Madame Courbet give you any trouble?'

The housekeeper who lived across the street and had a spare key ... 'She looked me over, tossed her head and clucked her tongue before raking me with that voice of hers. "Men, all they think about is rutting with a woman! Old enough to be your father, madame. A Chief Inspector of the Sûreté, for shame! His wife hasn't been dead two months. The period of mourning must be respected!"'

'For Madame Courbet it has to last an eternity,' he sighed. 'She questions everything. A pair of high-heeled shoes I brought home once. A heel was broken – did she tell you that? They were the shoes of a girl I had met on a street after curfew. She was avoiding the patrol and her feet were freezing.'

'But you didn't bring her home like me. Only her shoes.' And so much for 'social customs which should have been cast aside long ago'.

'What else did the street's most virulent gossip tell you?'

'That you have been seeing another woman, but that this chanteuse comes seldom and only in the small hours at curfew's end, and sometimes with a general as her companion. That you desperately need looking after. That you are a hero to her son Antoine and the other boys of the street but that they are saying you were never home and that your poor wife – Ah! she was all but a virgin after five and a half years of marriage and, like the first wife, just couldn't stand the stress of not having sex, so ran off, this one with a German officer who gave her a lot of it but ... but she had to come home when he was sent away to Russia to die.'

A mouthful, and thank you, Madame Courbet! 'Hermann had the house repaired. The bomb smashed the front wall and every pane of glass on the street.'

'And now?' she asked.

'He's at the Gare Saint-Lazare, I think. Looking into that robbery. Late, of course. One of us should have been on the scene as soon as we had word of it but ...'

'But the Gypsy kept you on the run.'

'He tried to kill us again.'

Hurriedly she got out of the nest she had made for herself, dragging blankets she wrapped around herself.

'Build up the fire. Open the draught. Buffalo is better but zebra will have to do.'

The snow was terrible, the quai Saint-Bernard an impasse into which the tiny slits of blue-shaded headlamps fought for visibility.

Gabrielle knew it was crazy of her to have come out on a night like this without a *laissez-passer* and so close to curfew, but Céci had to be warned.

No lights shone in the Jardin des Plantes. Only by feeling its way, did the little Peugeot two-door sedan finally manage the gates, which were locked, of course.

Leaving the engine running – cursing herself again and all that had gone wrong – she struggled out. Snow rose to her ankles. Her silk stockings would be ruined. The engine didn't sound too good either. Was there water in the gasoline again?

She rang the bell. Old Letouche, the concierge, was almost stone deaf. He'd be asleep. Had he died in his sleep?

Shivering, railing at herself, she blew on gloved fingers and stamped her high-heels to pack the snow down a little. 'Monsieur,' she called out. 'It's me, Gabrielle. Is Suzanne-Cécilia here?'

'Not here,' came the frayed, wind-tattered voice.

'But she had nowhere else to go? I was worried about her?'

'Not here. Gone to the detective's house.'

'The detective's . . .?'

'He offered, she accepted. I gave her my share of the dung to help her along. It's freezing in here without a fire.'

'Which detective?'

'The one with the house, of course. "The difficult one", she said.'

Dismayed, she looked away in the direction of Belleville. She couldn't go to the house, not until the curfew was over. 'And by then,' she asked herself, retreating to the car, 'will it be too late?'

What had begun with so much promise had fast become a nightmare. The Gypsy had proved himself far too difficult to handle. They had lined up the robberies for him but he had gone his own way and had done nearly all of them in one night! They didn't even know where he was hiding.

'And as for this Tshaya of his, if the Gestapo get their hands on her, she'll be only too willing to betray us and already must know far too much.'

It was a mess – it was worse than that. It was a catastrophe! '*Zèbre*,' she said from behind the wheel now. Why but for the intrusion of fate – 'Yes, fate!' – had the British chosen to use such a code name?

They couldn't have known the wireless set was hidden in the zebra house. Direction-finding at such long distances was simply too inaccurate. Even the German direction-finding vans had to get in really close.

The Wehrmacht's Funkabwehr unit and now, also, the Gestapo's Listeners constantly monitored the airwaves for clandestine transmissions. They used three widely spaced listening sets and, drawing lines from each of these to the source, triangulated the approximate location. Then, by repeatedly smaller triangulations as they moved in with their listening vans, they narrowed things down until, at the last, a house or flat could be singled out.

But so far the *réseau* had seen no sign of any such activity. Suzanne-Cécilia had been very, very careful. Transmissions were kept to a bare minimum and were always given at the same time and on the same frequency. Now only once a week and on Fridays at 0150 hours Berlin time.

It had to have been coincidence, the British using Zebra as the code name. It had to have been!

'I must do something,' she said. 'I *can't* just sit idly by and let De Vries destroy everything we've worked so hard for!'

Single-handedly, and over nearly eighteen months, Suzanne-Cécilia had painstakingly assembled the wireless transceiver from parts she had gathered. Oh for sure they had talked of doing something – anything – but the times had not been right, the Occupation so very difficult.

But then on a cold, clear night in October of last year, and well before she had met Jean-Louis and Hermann, Céci's faint tappings into the ether had finally brought a response, NOUS VOUS LISONS. We read you.

Cécilia had used, and still did, her modification of the French

117

Army code of her husband's unit – one of many, and yes, the Germans would be aware of it, but what else could she have done? By some quirk of – yes, fate again – the code book had been sandwiched among the bloodstained letters that had been returned to her along with her dead husband's boots.

Lieutenant Honoré Lemaire had been in the same unit as her own dead husband, and it wouldn't take Jean-Louis long to discover this. 'The Society of Those Who Have Been Left Behind, eh?' she said bitterly. 'Of course we are working together!'

Tasks had been assigned by London. The constant comings and goings of generals and other high-ranking officers – the troops too. Ah! she herself did this. It was easy for her. The audience at the Club Mirage changed constantly. The boys all loved her, trusted her. She was their loyal friend.

The sales of major international works of art at the Jeu de Paume – stolen, many of them. Could a list be provided? Of course! She was known to frequent the sales, often on the arm of a German general or other high-ranking official.

The sales of priceless antiques too, in the rooms of the Hôtel Drouot, the Paris auction house.

So many things and all of it had been working so well but then Jean-Louis and Hermann had solved the Sandman murders. The child, the heiress, had lost her only friends and her parents too, and had been left all alone in the world.

Would London help? The child's father had been a noted designer of weapons. The couple had gone to England just before the blitzkrieg and had not been able to return, had supposedly died in the bombing of Coventry.

On 15 January at 0150 hours London had sent its answer. It hadn't helped. They couldn't have sent over things like that.

Right after the message there had been a distinct break of several seconds – end of transmission – but then, suddenly, the green light had come on again and another message had come in. A message she could not have revealed to Jean-Louis and still could not do so.

The Gypsy had been dropped near Tours on the night of the thirteenth. Code name Zebra, but by then, of course, Nana and Suzanne-Cécilia and herself had known he was in Paris because he had arrived on the fourteenth.

Puzzled as to why there should have been that break in the

transmission, Gabrielle took out the quartz crystal the child had given them. She looked away into the darkness and the falling snow to where she knew the zebra paddock and house must lie. Céci's surgery and laboratory of physiology were very convenient to the zebra house, and it had been perfect. It really had. As veterinary surgeon, she could legitimately spend nights here tending sick animals. No one would have thought to question this.

'But now?' she asked herself. 'What now?'

The dust had settled in the Gare Saint-Lazare but the ringing in the ears would probably never go away.

Kohler tried to get his bearings. The ticket office was a shambles. The massive door to the old iron safe was off its hinges, bent, ripped apart and still disgorging sand and bricks, and half embedded in the floor.

'I told you not to tamper with that dial, Inspector. I warned you the safe had a booby trap built into its locking mechanism!'

The sous-chef de gare was livid. 'Then why didn't it blow off the Gypsy's hands?'

'The portrait, yes? The Maréchal, you idiot! Have you forgotten this?'

Tattered, dust-covered and furious, the little twerp blinked and apprehensively licked the dust from his lips when he saw the Kripo take a step towards him.

On the wall above the safe, Pétain, and before him legions of former presidents, had looked sternly out at ticket agent and buyer. Nearly one hundred years of thumbprints had greased the lower left corner of that picture frame and wall. The damned thing had been slid aside enough times for the world to have seen the marks from any three of the wickets.

The combination had been written in pencil on the wall but the Gypsy had changed the settings. He'd written the new combination above the old one, the numerals so perfect one had to wonder about the severity of his schooling as a boy, but no one had wanted to try the numbers.

The booby trap ... A travelling salesman fresh off the boat from Buffalo, New York, in 1903, had installed the bloody thing on a trial basis and had never come back for it. *The Badger Safe*

Protector. Two little vials of fulminate of mercury probably, but those hadn't blown the door off and wrecked the room.

For that De Vries had used the fulminate to detonate a charge of nitro or dynamite. Three or four sticks at least.

'The bomb boys can pick up the pieces and tell us all about it. How many dead?'

'I do not know. None so far.'

In the pandemonium of injured and rescuer, cop, stretcher-bearer and nurse, there was no sign of Oona or Giselle. Oona had been at one of the wickets. He, himself, had taken shelter before using a length of cord to pull the handle open. He had called out to her to leave and she had ... *'Oona!'* he cried out, startling several. A *flic* started for him, a Feldgendarm also ...

Desperately he searched the hall. Both of their backs were to him. She was standing beside Giselle who had an arm about Oona's waist. There were no cuts, no abrasions. She must have tripped and fallen to the floor. They were staring at a poster ... a poster!

DANCE

TANGO, WALTZ ETC AND ALL THE LATEST BALLROOM DANCES

LESSONS AND CLASSES

Madame Jeséquel, Professeur Diplômé, et Mademoiselle
Nana Thélème, danseuse électrique de flamenco.
Studio Pleyel No. 6
252 rue du Faubourg-Saint-Honoré, Paris
Téléphone: Carnot 33.56

Deutsch spoken   *se habla espanol*

5

The revolver weighed at least a kilogram when loaded. The build was grim, the grip firm, and when Nana Thélème pulled the hammer back, it made two clicks, at half-cock and the full.

She knew it was madness to have such a thing. The box had been wrapped in newspaper but tied with a red silk rose and left with the coat-check girl downstairs in the club but now ...

She pulled the trigger. The click, as the firing pin struck an empty chamber, was louder still. There were six packets of cartridges, one hundred and twenty rounds, the two other revolvers. All had been cleaned of the grease that had protected them from rust over the years in that safe at the Gare Saint-Lazare. They looked brand-new.

'The 1873 *Modèle d'ordonnance*,' she said, a whisper. Why had Janwillem sent them to her? She had loved him. She would have done anything for him. 'I didn't betray you in Oslo!' she swore softly and clenched a fist. 'Tshaya must have but you . . . you are still blaming me. She's a Gestapo informer, Jani. A betrayer of others too!'

Picking up the card that had been inside the box, she hurriedly reread it. *Pour toi, chérie, et pour tes amies de l'armée secrète. Bonne chance.*

Bâtard! she silently cried. He had told them he had escaped during the battle for Norway in the spring of 1940. A trawler to England, and bravo! She had wished it with all her heart. But had the British then found him such a nuisance they had been only too willing to get rid of him, or had he simply lied enough to convince them of his usefulness in France?

And what missions had the British assigned him, in addition to their own targets? The safes of the SS at *numéro* 84 avenue Foch? Those of the Abwehr at the Hotel Lutétia, or those of von Stülpnagel, the Military Governor of France?

Three revolvers. One for herself, one for Suzanne-Cécilia, and the last for Gabrielle.

He had had no need of them and had never used a gun during all of the robberies he had committed. 'I prefer explosives,' he had once said and had given her that smile of his which had warmed her heart with its gentleness and yet had been so full of gypsy mischief. 'They're much better, but like a good woman, you have to know how far you can go with them.'

He had gone too far with her, had promised marriage early in 1938 but had then taken up again with Tshaya and had left for Oostende at that one's beckoning.

And from there, the two of them had gone to Oslo.

Mollergaten-19, prisoner 3266, cell D2. Seven long months of solitary confinement for one who had always been free, and then cell C27. Three other convicts for constant company, the space shared being no more than 8 square metres. Four bunks to a cell, and a tiny, grilled window too high to look out of and forbidden in any case.

Had he told Tshaya he couldn't stay with her any more, that he was to have a son? Had he said he was going to marry her arch rival?

Prison would have been enough to have made him hate her instead of Tshaya. None of her letters to him before the war had been opened. All had been returned. Only sketchy details of his existence had been provided by the prison authorities.

And now he was giving not just herself but the others a last chance. Three revolvers against those of the Gestapo, the SS and the Wehrmacht.

The soup had been excellent, the Chief Inspector St-Cyr more than content. No matter the lateness of the hour, and she but a perfect stranger, he liked to have a woman about the house at 3 rue Laurence-Savart. He was pleased the clothing of his dead wife had fitted so well. The long and heavy white flannelette nightgown from Brittany was warm enough perhaps. The black lisle stockings could not be seen but for a slice of ankle above the low-heeled black leather pumps. Grey flannel trousers had been rolled up out of sight but were ready in case she needed to escape a Gestapo visit.

Suzanne-Cécilia was glad she had taken the time to ruffle her hair so that it would constantly remind him of her awakening.

'Madame,' he said, having given up all thought of rationing the last of his emergency pipe tobacco, 'let me ask again if you know Mademoiselle Nana Thélème?'

'The chanteuse at the Club Monseigneur and also sometimes at the Schéhérazade?'

'Yes, that's the one.'

Her soft brown eyes would not duck away as some might have done but would gaze steadfastly at him with complete candour. 'Does she have a little boy?'

Merde, why must she continue to avoid things? 'There's no perhaps about it. He's the Gypsy's son.'

She tossed her auburn curls at his gruffness. 'It's a family matter then. No. No, I cannot say that I have made her acquaint-

...any people come and go at the Jardin. Saturday ...s and Sundays are busiest, even in winter. My work ...t allow me close contact with any of them.'

...t you became the mistress of one.'

...Clément Laviolette, of Cartier's, yes. It's a puzzle, isn't it?'

Did he think it a tragedy? she wondered.

Neither Gabrielle nor Nana Thélème could possibly have been recently in touch with her, thought St-Cyr. The risk of using the telephone would have been too great but, still, she must be very aware of Gestapo interest in herself because of the house on the rue Poliveau if nothing else. 'Tell me then,' he asked, 'why is it that Mademoiselle Thélème said you let her son feed the wolves?'

'I can only tell you what I know to be true, Inspector. If this ... this singer of gypsy songs says she has met me, well ... what can I say but that the chance meeting so often leaves no memory.'

He sighed in despair. He looked at her steadily as if in judgement and, yes, Gabrielle had said he was persistent but why had he suddenly taken to using his matchbox as if it were a wireless key? Gabi had told him about having access to a transceiver – yes, of course – but not about herself. Never that!

The message came to an end. It had read: SOS GESTAPO, and she thought he had tapped that out because of listening devices in the house and this sickened her, but then he said, 'Your husband, madame. Please tell me a little about him.'

He slid the matchbox across the table. She winced. She knew her fingers were trembling and that he could feel this as she took the box from him.

Trapped, her answer was perfect. HE WAS THE WIRELESS OPERATOR FOR HIS UNIT. HE DIED AT SEDAN DURING THE INVASION AS I HAVE ALREADY TOLD YOU.

St-Cyr took the matchbox from her. I TOO WAS A SIGNALS OPERATOR BUT IN THE WAR BEFORE THIS ONE.

Ah! she silently said and tossed that pretty head of hers.

SO MADAME LET US NOW GET DOWN TO BUSINESS BEFORE IT IS TOO LATE FOR ALL OF US.

*

At 2.47 a.m. tobacco smoke filled the air, the lights were low on hanging carpets, cushions, brasses, samovars and plush red-velvet drapes. Kohler let his gaze sift over the Club Monseigneur's tables, Giselle and Oona did too, looking always for the Gypsy.

Gestapo, SS and Wehrmacht officers, teary-eyed and homesick, most of them – *Mein Gott* what sentimentalists! – sat with their women or unaccompanied except for black-market big shots and gangsters, all lost, it seemed, to the haunting melancholy of a clear and soft serenity that carried yet a sense of restlessness all found slightly disturbing. It was as if unsatisfied, the chanteuse – the gypsy woman in the red dress and through her, her audience – sought constantly for the unattainable. Long pauses accompanied repeated phrases. Rhythm drove her more and more to seek the release she wanted. Tune after tune followed but now a vigorousness crept in, the orchestra in their black corduroy trousers, white blouses, tasselled felt caps, sashes at the waist and high, brown leather boots, straining with her, racing ... racing until ... until, with a whirlwind of violins, cimbaloms and tambourines, that voice of hers lifted the audience out of their melancholy. It raced away with them in rushes. Its volume swelled. She shouted. They stood. They clapped. They cheered. And as she continued to throw her hair, to sing, to clash those heels of hers on the stage and bash her tambourine, the violinists dispersed among the tables, playing here, there, their cap-tassels jerking, the music electric, fierce, fast, the piece exploding again and again as individual violinists competed against each other until ... until the woman in red with the earrings of gold coins, her linked belt of them and bracelets too, had raised her long, lithe arms.

With a crash! the song came to an end. Exhausted, she bowed her head and for an instant her eyes were closed, each feature fixed in memory: the long, jet black hair that was parted in the middle but allowed tonight to fall loosely to her shoulders, the sharpness of dark black eyebrows against the soft hazel of her skin, the cheekbones high, the nose and chin proud and undefeated. The rising and falling of her chest was half hidden by the neckline of her dress whose shade had faded with the lights and now was matt red, warm, deep and like the embers of a fire just waiting to be fanned into flame.

124

This was Nana Thélème. Kohler shook his head in admiration – he'd hate to have to arrest her for anything, would hate to let the Gestapo or Herr Max get their hands on her. '*Formidable*!' he croaked. 'Louis should have heard her.'

He marvelled that she could sing at all. The split in her lower lip had been well disguised, the swollen cheek hidden under rouge. But to sing as well as that, knowing what she must, and to such company had required an immense strength of will.

When she found them, and the introductions had been made, she said softly and regretfully, 'Tshaya would have sung it far better than myself. Whereas I can only dream of living it, she has done so.'

It was a confession of sorts, a reason perhaps why Janwillem De Vries had gone back to the boyhood love of his gypsy days.

They sipped Tokay. The orchestra played more quietly – little tunes she called birdsongs, with improvised trills and flourishes the audience half listened to. Kohler confided what had happened. Oona and Giselle both said earnestly, 'We saw him, mademoiselle.' 'He spoke to me,' added Giselle. 'He saved my baby from the force of the blast, my face, my eyes . . . By doing so, Oona saw him and understood enough to hit the floor before she was killed.'

Everything was going wrong. Janwillem had changed so much.

'Three women,' said Kohler. 'Yourself, Gabrielle Arcuri and Suzanne-Cécilia Lemaire. Are there others?'

Was it to be a time of reckoning?

'Tell me which of you lined up again and again until you knew exactly what the banking schedule of that ticket office was and where the combination to that safe had been written down.'

'Which of us . . .? Please, Inspector, I don't understand. It's all a mistake.'

Verdammt! why must she be so difficult when surely she must know the end was near? 'Look, which of you is hiding him, where's he being hidden, and what's his next target?'

It would do no good to lie and hadn't Gabrielle said Herr Kohler could be trusted if necessary? 'We . . . we don't know where he is. None of us. He's . . . he's simply not co-operating.'

'Gone off on his own, has he?'

'Yes, and obviously with Tshaya, though this we did not anticipate and ... and had had no inclination of. How could we have?'

He'd best get it clear. 'But you met with him on the fourteenth when he arrived in Paris. How the hell did you even know he'd be on that train?'

'We *didn't* know anything, Inspector! Jani ... The first I knew of his arrival was his knock at my door. He said ... All right, he said he'd escaped to England in 1940 and that ... that the British had parachuted him into France. Could I keep him for a day or two? That was all he'd ask. He was desperate. I couldn't refuse. The whole thing was crazy. I'd our son to think of but ... but Janwillem was already in the flat. I did not know who, if anyone, might have noticed him or if, by sending him away, his presence would not be fixed in memory. The concierge ... *Mon Dieu*, that one's a collaborator if ever there was one.' She shrugged. 'You see the dilemma I was in.'

She was all innocence. None of it was her fault. 'So you kept him until...?' asked Kohler, pleasantly enough for Giselle to be startled by his manner.

'Until the late afternoon of the seventeenth.' This wasn't true, of course, thought Nana, but somehow she had to protect the others.

'Then he must have seen your son.'

She would have to smile. 'Yes ... Yes, for the first time. He was very pleased. Our Jani was beside himself with delight. The father he had always heard about had at last come to see him. They played for hours. They ...'

'Forget it,' snorted Kohler impatiently. 'When we took you home from the Avia Club Gym you told my partner to ask De Vries, when we caught him, why he had tried to kill the son he had never seen.'

She touched her chest. 'Did I?'

Kohler nodded curtly towards a far table she could see well enough. 'Were those two couples at the dinner party the SS and their friends threw in your former villa on the night of the eleventh?'

He would only ask it of them if she didn't tell him. 'Yes.'

'And you still don't know who they are?'

'Should I?'

Oona was staring at her wine and keeping very still; Giselle had swallowed tightly.

'Then listen,' said Kohler sadly. 'The one with the cigarette in its ivory holder, the polished jackboots and the blue-eyed blonde with the overhang is Oberstleutnant Willi Löwenstein, head of Funkabwehr Paris and France; that's radio counter-espionage in case you're interested.'

'And the one with the brunette?' she managed, her voice faint.

'Horst Uhrig, his Gestapo counterpart. They're sizing you up, Mademoiselle Thélème, and that can only mean one thing. They've buried their petty jealousies and have agreed to work together. Now you tell me why?'

'I . . . I don't know.'

'I think you do.'

The fire had long since gone to dust. At 4.40 a.m. and out of tobacco, St-Cyr quietly pulled on his overcoat and found his scarf and gloves.

Suzanne-Cécilia Lemaire slept in her chair with arms folded beneath her head on the table. Had she been emptied of her secrets? he wondered, and thought it far too unlikely.

But she had revealed that the house on the rue Poliveau had been essential for its closeness to the Jardin des Plantes, and had told him of the wireless transceiver she had built and had kept hidden in the zebra house.

Two messages had come in from London at 1.50 a.m. on the fifteenth. The first had dealt with the parents of Nanette Vernet, the child-heiress who had lost her friends in the Sandman murders. The second had dealt with the parachuting of the Gypsy into France near Tours on the night of the thirteenth, an untruth she was not yet aware of. But it was the delay between the messages – several seconds – and the signature of the sender that had troubled her enough to confess.

'The first was very clear, fast and sure,' she had said. 'It was what I had become accustomed to, but the second was hesitant, then fast, then surer, the touch firmer at the last, you understand, but it left me thinking . . . ah! what can I say when they are only faint signals in the darkness of the night? I felt it different but the news it brought had to be conveyed to the others at once.'

127

She had packed everything away and had braved the curfew, had cycled to the Club Mirage to inform Gabrielle who had contacted Nana Thélème later that day, but by then, of course, all of them must have known De Vries was in town. Even now they were each hedging their bets and revealing only so much.

Three women and by association, Hermann and himself and, yes, Oona and Giselle. It was not good. Indeed, it was a disaster.

'*London*' had used the code name of Zebra. A coincidence perhaps, if one believed in such things.

Fate if one did not.

At 5 a.m. twenty-five degrees of frost was unkind, the rue Laurence-Savart glacial in its darkness. Kohler let the Citroën's engine idle. Far up the street a faint blue pinprick revealed the workaday world had begun.

Verdammt! what was he to do? Disassociate himself from Louis? Sever a friendship that had begun in the late summer of 1940? Take the side of the Occupier no matter how wrong it felt?

'Get out before it's too late,' he said, echoing the thoughts of many no doubt, for the war news wasn't good. 'Try for Spain. Giselle and Oona first and then myself. False papers, good ones. Money . . .?' He had none but what was in his pocket. Like gypsies the world over, he had always spent when he had had it to spend.

'Expenses,' he said and thought to light up a last cigarette cadged from Nana, deciding instead to break it in half. 'Louis will want a smoke. He always does. First thing.'

In spite of being from opposite sides of the war and old enemies at that, they *had* got on and they *did* work well together.

'Too well,' he confessed. 'It has to end. Berlin are telling me this. Boemelburg too. To them, it's time for me to stand up and be counted.'

Like a cold wind from the Russian steppes, Herr Max had been sent to bring home the point, though it had yet to be stated. 'It's been a set-up ever since that son of a bitch let the Gypsy out of jail. He was aware the Gestapo had bugged Gabrielle's dressing-room. He knew there was a clandestine wireless set sending signals from Paris and that the Gestapo's Radio Listeners and the Abwehr's had located it. What better, then, than to sweep them all into the net by playing a little *Funkspiel*? A radio game. Answer the signals by feeding in a message the terrorists would want clearly to accept. But now Berlin must be crying for Engelmann's head if he doesn't get the bastard back and fast! And now the *réseau* must be tearing their collective hair and wondering what to do.'

8,600,000 francs in cash from the office safe at Cartier's and never mind that it had been Gabrielle's money; 682,000 francs from the Gare Saint-Lazare, to say nothing of what the General-major Wehrle had had in his safe at the Ritz and all the rest. It was enough to tempt a poor detective and to tear him from friendship. Giselle and Oona could buy a villa on the Costa del Sol. There'd be no need for that little shop or bar he'd been thinking about. Giselle could have her babies, Oona too, if she wanted. None of them need work another day. Diamonds and sapphires, gold coins and old stamps.

When Louis joined him, the Sûreté's first words were, 'Don't even think of it, Hermann. Things have gone too far this time. They won't let you escape to Spain.'

'I didn't think they would.'

'Good. Boemelburg wants to see us at first light.'

'That's hours away. Hey, we can be in Tours by then if we hurry.'

'The roads . . .'

'Fuck the roads. There's no traffic anyway. Hang on.'

At noon a wet snow clung to everything and the black overcoats of forty years ago were as glued to it in misery. The heart of Tours, its life, its beauty, its charm had been charred and gutted. Down by the Paris-Bordeaux bridge, the white-stone, blackened wall of a sixteenth-century mansion still retained the sumptuous foliage of Renaissance carvers. Gallo-Roman walls and medieval graveyards had been thrown up as by the hand of a demented archaeologist. Twelfth-, fourteenth- and fifteenth-century half-timbered houses had simply been consumed.

'Incendiaries,' breathed Kohler sadly. 'Stukas.'

Düsseldorf, London, Abbeville, Köln and many more cities and towns had had their firestorms of varying severity. It was still happening. Gone were the quaint little crooked streets where a person could delight in echoes of the past. For three days and nights the city had burned. On 21 June 1940 the provisional government which had fled to here, journeyed to Compiègne to sign the Armistice in the very same railway coach that, twenty-two years earlier, had seen Germany surrender.

'Marianne loved this city. To her, our short honeymoon was the one great adventure of her life.'

It would do no good to remind Louis of the Hauptmann Steiner. War was war. Lovers came and went. Friendships were instant, seldom lasting. 'Cheer up, eh? We got here.'

'*Grâce à Dieu*. Oh *bien sûr*, the Occupation has cleared the roads of traffic – you have said so yourself – but at 120 kilometres an hour, while passing a convoy in blinding snow, was it necessary to lean on the horn?'

'There were only two convoys.'

'*Seven*! Can you not count?'

'Hey, relax, eh? I'll make it right. I'll buy you a pastis as soon as we can find a trough.'

'It's another of your alcohol-free days or had you forgotten that as well?'

'I'll use my Gestapo shield. I'll threaten them.'

It would do no good to argue. Hermann always had to have the last word. They turned left off the rue Nationale, passing through more devastation. Here the Wehrmacht had simply bulldozed the rubble aside and had dynamited the shakiest of walls. There were no glimpses of the Loire. It would be grey in any case. Marianne had loved bathing in it. She had laughed, had smiled at him and had said, 'Tonight, Jean-Louis, we shall make us a baby.'

It hadn't happened then. He'd been summoned back to Paris and had been sent to the south, to Perpignan and yet another murder, the hatchet slayings of wild goats and equally wild women. 'Ever since then I have ceased to trust shepherds,' he said aloud, baffling his partner and causing Hermann to toss his head in alarm.

'You think it too,' said the Kripo. 'They damned well lied, didn't they – Nana Thélème and the Generalmajor Wehrle? There's no prospector, nothing, Louis. That house he lived in was destroyed during the blitzkrieg!'

Not so. On place Plumereau the ancient houses crowded close

as if in defiance of centuries of human idiocy. Some were half-timbered, others faced with the white tufa common to Touraine. Beneath an unwelcoming sky, their dizzily pitched roofs fell to attic dormers above two storeys and ground-floor shops.

The feet of nervous pigeons too hungry to escape were mired in wet snow. An old woman in black trickled scant crumbs she could not spare from a withered hand.

Other people were about but tried to take no notice of the Citroën and its two occupants. A *gazogène* lorry perfumed the dank air with the pungency of green willow, the warren of tubes and cylinders on its roof banging and clanging as it farted its way across the square to disappear up a street.

Timidly St-Cyr approached the woman. The Sûreté . . . Paris . . . she'd have noted both even though her back was still turned to them. 'Madame . . .?'

'*Oui?*' she snapped, letting the last of the crumbs fall.

'A Monsieur Jacqmain . . .'

'*What's he done?*'

'Nothing.'

'Women. Fancy women. Late comings and goings. Whores if you ask me.'

Ah *merde* . . . 'We only want to know where he lives.'

She jerked her head. 'Above the Boucherie Leplat. Next to Au Petit Moka which has, alas, been closed for the Duration due to the extreme shortage of coffee for those of us who haven't the money to afford it.'

'What fancy women?'

'Two from Paris. *Très belles, très gentilles.* The blonde went in at noon. The raven-haired one came by train and followed later. Then that one went out and into the *marchand de couleurs* of Monsieur Gabon.'

It was too much to resist, and he sighed. 'What did the raven-haired one buy?'

Ah! she had their interest at last. 'Flypapers in winter? Sufficient for six summers of infestation? And what, please, are decent citizens to do when the flies visit us again?'

'Flypapers?'

'Is that not just what I said?' Madame Horleau waited for a suitable apology and when one didn't arrive, she let the two of them have the last from her lips. 'Monsieur Jacqmain has not left

131

the house since the newspapers arrived from Paris, so I ask again, what has he done?'

They started out. The pigeons scattered. People took notice but tried not to let on. Everywhere the air was suddenly of trouble.

The house had a white, cut-stone façade, with its entry to the right. Directly above the butcher's shop, there was a wrought-iron Louis Philippe railing that enclosed a narrow balcony behind which there were two tall, tightly shuttered French windows. On the floor above, there were equal but unshuttered windows. Then, as the roof climbed to its peak, there were two large attic dormers, side by side and also tightly shuttered.

Beyond the hardware store next door, there was a hat factory with little business.

'Louis, the flypapers . . . is it what I think?'

'Perhaps but then . . . ah *mais alors, alors, mon vieux*, isn't it a little too early to say?'

'Not if he's up and died of strychnine poisoning.' An agony if true.

Flypapers, the half-metre long pull-out coils of sticky brown celluloid which were hung from kitchen ceilings in summer, offered the greedy, the calloused, the intransigent and the jilted lover a ready means to an end. Boiled in water until it was all but dry, their last few remaining droplets were deadly.

'Let's ask Jacqmain,' said St-Cyr. Hermann banged on the door but of course, there could be no answer, not after such thoughts.

The *flic* on the beat was swift. They'd need the magistrate's order. Kohler flashed his Gestapo shield and was about to kick the door in when the butcher came huffing out with a spare key.

All others were prevented from entering. 'We'll be certain to consult you,' soothed the Sûreté. '*Certain!*' He slammed the door and locked it.

Then they stood a moment in the entrance before the dished and hollowed steps of the staircase. Neither knew, really, what to expect.

'The newspapers from Paris, Louis,' said Hermann as he started up. 'News of the Gypsy, the Ritz, the safe of Hans-Albrecht Wehrle, diamond buyer for the Reich.'

'Nana Thélème and Gabrielle ... both have not confided everything in us.'

'Since when would women ever do that?'

He was sitting in his study, had been looking fondly through a photo album but had set this carefully aside on top of the Paris papers. A much-used pair of field glasses, a water bottle, compass, loupe on its lanyard, sheath knife, match tin and cigarette case were also there.

It was Louis who said, 'Hermann, please go into the salon and have a little look around. Take no more of that benzedrine – I've been warning you it's addictive and that your heart will pack it in when I need you most. You're not flying a nightfighter over Stalingrad.'

Always it was blitzkrieg for them, thought Kohler. 'Why couldn't the son of a bitch have been tidier?'

St-Cyr could hear his partner throwing up into the kitchen sink. Hermann was just too tired of the sight of death. Afraid of it, haunted by it, the bodies of his two sons now frozen in the clay of Russia but still a constant nightmare.

The twin barrels of an old-fashioned Paradox elephant gun had discharged their number 4 calibre shots into the roof of Jacqmain's mouth after which the head had simply disintegrated.

The gun, which must weigh nearly ten kilos, had been propped against a partially opened upper drawer, Jacqmain holding the muzzle in his mouth.

Recoil had splintered the wood and had caused the gun to hit a framed wall map of the Congo, shattering its glass and breaking a lamp.

A single length of string was tied to the left trigger – Jacqmain had known from experience that cocking both hammers, though pulling only one trigger, would discharge the two. He must have run the string behind a front leg of the desk to give purchase.

Powder smoke would have filled the air, the sound deafening – had no one heard it?

Blood and brains had been sprayed across the wall behind the chair and on the ceiling too. An eagle, a honey guide, a francolin, stork and marabou all stared at the carnage through glass eyes.

A grey parrot roosted on a perch above the desk, a former camp-friend no doubt.

The soft-nosed slugs, each weighing more than a hundred grams, had embedded themselves in the ceiling timbers which were now exposed and freed of their centuries of plaster. There were patches of scalp whose short, iron-grey hair looked like some strange sort of fungal growth. There were teeth, bits of bone ... The eye of the cinematographer in St-Cyr recorded everything. It helped. It gave distance. It fed that curiosity which was so necessary.

'The Generalmajor Wehrle ... his presence here, monsieur, it frightened you, did it not?' he asked aloud. Always he had found talking to the victim and to himself helped. 'You had had the assurances not just of Mademoiselle Thélème but of Gabrielle Arcuri. Two beautiful women. Both chanteuses. What, please, did you do with the money the Generalmajor paid you? You could not have deposited it all at once. There would have been far too many raised eyebrows. Ah! the neighbours – one of them at least – watched your every move.'

It was now Wednesday the twentieth. The money had been paid out, and the diamonds collected, on Tuesday the twelfth.

'850,000 francs,' he muttered. 'About one-tenth of the value. Among them there were 657 carats of *Jagers*, Top Capes and Capes. "An excellent haul," the Generalmajor said.'

The Paris papers were yesterday's, and he must have got them in the late afternoon or early evening.

Rigor had set in, and from the presence of the newspapers, it was clear enough Jacqmain had been dead for less than twenty-four hours. 'Last night, then. A small supper, a glass of wine. Perhaps a brandy or two afterwards,' he muttered, 'but Dutch courage would not have been needed. Many times you had faced the charging lion or tiger, the elephant too.'

Yet he had been afraid of arrest.

The money ... a good portion of it ... had still to be in the house, but where? Neither Nana Thélème nor Gabrielle could have taken it, could they? since the Generalmajor had come at 7 p.m. and at so late a time, he had been forced to spend the night in a hotel room, he'd said.

But, had Gabrielle returned? Vouvray was near; the château of her mother-in-law, the Countess Thériault, a little closer. She could have come back easily, and would at least have called in to see René Yvon-Paul, her son.

But had she come back here to take the money into safe-keeping for Monsieur Jacqmain, and why, please, would he have entrusted it to her? Had he known her that well?

Questions ... there were always questions. Hermann could help with the search. 'But I cannot ask him to enter this room again.'

The figurine in the bell jar was of a classical nude, seated not on a stone bench but on some sort of creature, half lion, half hound. She was gazing questioningly to her left and rested that elbow on the creature's head whose fangs were bared so that the snarl it gave was directed at the viewer.

Executed in a fine, white alabaster, and perhaps in 1810, the piece was not valuable as such but curious only in that Monsieur Jacqmain had quite obviously admired it.

The thing was on the satinwood writing-table in his bedroom and beneath a portrait of his mother. This young woman's auburn hair was fashioned into a diadem from which silken wisps escaped. Her dress was of the *belle époque*. The ruffled neckline was low, the expression introspective, she was seated in a straight-backed chair that was all but hidden by the soft pink folds of her dress.

There were other sketches, all of women, all clothed. Indeed, even with the figurine, Jacqmain's bedroom could well have been that of his mother, of a woman of refinement. There was a dressing screen decorated with needlepoint vines and tropical birds on a black matt background. There was a sewing basket ... no cosmetics, a hand mirror, no necklaces, rings or pins – Ah! he had not liked to dress up as his mother or as any other woman. There was nothing to suggest it.

And still there was no sign of the money.

There had been nothing in his bank book to record even a modest deposit. Simply the biweekly withdrawals of 350 francs in cash, a frugal life. Nor would the cash have been placed in a safe-deposit box – that would have been far too risky and by law, such a sum would have had to have been declared.

Jacqmain had kept the diamonds in the house and must simply have put the money in the same place.

When Hermann called down from the attic, St-Cyr went up

with him to find those two rooms jammed with the still crated kit of a prospector whose safaris had been ended by the war.

'Ah *merde*, where did he hide that money?'

'Maybe he never had it, Louis. Maybe our Generalmajor promised to pay it but conveniently forgot, though he told us otherwise.'

'Herr Max was a witness to what he said. Have you forgotten this?'

'Not for a moment. Something's not right. This thing is beginning to smell even worse than we thought.'

'Happy hunting then.'

'We'll be here all night, have you thought of that?'

'Of course. It's all in a day's work. When one finds the indicator minerals, one must search for the diamonds, isn't that so?'

'Piss off. Go on back to his bedroom but *don't* take too long!'

In a bedside table drawer there were two small albums of photographs. The first was of Nana Thélème as chanteuse and dance instructress or caught on the street with a friend or in some café, and it was obvious Jacqmain had been infatuated by her, for the album had been well thumbed. The second was far newer and of Tshaya, of Madame Lucie-Marie Doucette, wife of the Spade. All of the photographs revealed her without a stitch. Back and front, but there were more shots of the back. They were brutal photographs in the coldness of their portrayal which she had fiercely defied when facing the camera.

'The house on the rue de la Bourde,' breathed Kohler, having given up the search.

'You go. I'll continue looking.'

'Not at those. Gabi might not like it.'

'Then take them with you. They might help loosen a tongue since they could not have been taken without the madam of that place having agreed.'

'And for payment, eh?'

'Surely not 850,000 francs!'

When he found a bullwhip made out of the grey and plaited hide from the belly of a 'white' rhino, St-Cyr began to think he understood the prospector's secret desires.

*

The *chambre de divertissements détachés* of the house of the hesitant touch held a carpet and a well-padded, ancient armchair. An ashtray and champagne bucket were provided, as were a few cushions should the viewer need them to glue himself better to the eyepiece in the wall.

A *Défense de parler* notice warned the client or clients to control any such urges. Kohler had seen it elsewhere on numerous occasions. A student of the *maisons de tolérance,* he looked only for what was unique.

Madame de Bonnevies ... 'Madame Charlotte' to her girls ... was not happy. This perfumed battleship of fortitude was in trouble and knew it. She had broken the law on two counts and he'd told her this straight off so as to level the playing field and save time.

'Monsieur l'inspecteur,' she huffed and whispered, teasing dyed red curls. 'Lucie-Marie Doucette – this "Tshaya" you speak of – was intransigent and known to us by another name and with good papers. *Mon Dieu,* what was a poor, delicate creature such as myself to do with that one? She was rebellious, moody, deceitful, silent, wicked, cunning and utterly uncontrollable. Many times she had to be held down or tied so that the client could have the little moment he had paid for and not suffer the indignities of rejection and her fingernails.'

'Or her teeth,' breathed Kohler softly, causing Madame de Bonnevies to jerk her head as if struck.

The ruby lips were pursed in defiance. Rouge rained from quivering cheeks. 'The teeth, of course.'

She was superb! Big, tough, all business and not in the least about to back down even if in trouble. 'So Tshaya came to you in the summer of 1941 and on the run from deportation?'

It had been and still was a criminal offence to hide such people. 'In late August, or was it in the first week of September?' she asked herself. 'I ... I did not know she was on the run. Her papers were perfect. Her name was ...'

'Yes, yes, but you saw profit in her ass.'

Must he be so crude? 'I saw profit in her body, yes.'

'And Monsieur Jacqmain ... we'll get to why you allowed him into a *lupanar* that was reserved for the Reich, so don't hold your breath. What was his reaction?'

Even with the need to whisper this one was formidable. The scar down the left cheek from eye to chin was the mark of a duelling foil, or was it, perhaps, that of a rawhide whip? 'All men have their *bêtes noires*, is that not so?'

Their pet hates. 'Mine's not women who I feel need to be whipped.'

'He . . . he liked to watch. He . . . he always said the scars, they . . . they relieved him of the agonies he felt towards his mother.'

'Pardon?'

'Ah! Inspector, is it that you also have visited such foreign parts and have become accustomed to tastes a mother would not wish to hear of her son?'

She was roasting him now with those swift brown eyes of hers. 'Explain yourself,' he managed.

She would shrug and say, 'It was nothing to me, you understand, but Madam Jacqmain had disowned her son for living in sin with the blacks and the coffee-coloureds. That poor man had pleaded with her for forgiveness in his letters home. He said he had scourged the girls most completely but . . . but then had succumbed to base desires and had had his way with them.'

Verdammt! 'So you let Jacqmain come in here even though the house was off-limits, and *nur für Deutsche*?'

And only for Germans.

'Well?' he demanded, startling her for he'd raised his voice.

'I . . . I had known him from before the Defeat. A regular, you understand. From time to time, after the war had ended for us, he would inquire if we had anyone suitable and if I would let him in but this . . . this was not possible.'

Kohler waited while she fingered her lace blouse in thought. 'Then this . . . this Lucie-Marie arrived and I . . . I knew at once how relieved Monsieur Jacqmain would be. The stress in a man, you cannot imagine. . . . I let him watch her.'

'And broke the rules.'

'Was it such a crime? He did not touch her or any of the other girls. He only watched. One night a week . . . Two nights occasionally, when things were very bad with him. He paid well and it . . . it was good for business.'

'But you worried about it. There could be problems. She was intransigent – you've said so yourself. Her papers might have been good enough to let her walk freely about town but her skin

138

was too dark, right? yet she hungered for a little freedom. Oh *bien sûr*, you had paid off the *préfet* and probably even the Kommandant but it couldn't last, so you informed the authorities in Paris. There was the reward of 100,000 francs to consider, eh? And they, realizing what you had, came at once to put her to use.'

Kohler set the album of photographs Louis had given him into her hands. Some showed Tshaya with her wrists tightly tied and roped to an eye-bolt in a ceiling timber, the girl objecting until told what would happen to her if she refused. The back, the buttocks, the body extended. Defiance when forced to face the camera.

'I . . . I was ordered to feed this . . . this strange desire of his by . . . by letting him watch her and then to let him talk to her, and to photograph her.'

'Ordered by whom?'

The lights were dimmed, a first warning that things were about to begin in the adjacent room. 'By Henri Doucette, her husband, the *pugiliste*. Gestapo of the rue Lauriston in Paris came with that one, and some of the SS also. They . . . they were interested in her, but . . . but also in Monsieur Jacqmain.'

'Just why were the French Gestapo and the SS interested in the prospector?'

May God forgive her. 'The diamonds some said he kept in secret.'

Diamonds that would have to be sold so as to be finally free of their threat or else face arrest and their outright theft.

'When, exactly, did Henri Doucette and his friends come to see you?'

When had she informed on Tshaya? 'Not until the late summer of last year. Inspector, I would have let the girl stay. I did not want to turn her in but the times, they are difficult, isn't that so?'

'Save the tears. Was there anything else that led them to take an interest in the prospector?'

'They . . . they were watching a friend of his, a chanteuse and dance instructress he often spoke very highly of.'

Nana Thélème . . . 'So, two things came about. Tshaya was here from late August 1941 until September of 1942, and the prospector visited her, and then you informed on her and Paris took a decided interest in the diamonds and immediately saw a way of finding out a little more about this friend of his, this other woman, by using Tshaya.'

'She agreed to work for her husband. She had no other choice, nor did I.'

Again the lights were dimmed, this time urgently and repeatedly as a warning to keep silent.

Madame de Bonnevies indicated the eyepiece. 'This girl is one we keep because the one you call Tshaya had to be replaced and there are those among you who desire that which is forbidden to them by their Nazi laws.'

When he did not respond to the rebuke, she softly added, 'Besides the colour of the skin, the marks of the whip also excite others, Inspector. Some of those choose to come to this chamber first before taking the one you are about to see, as they did this Tshaya. It's a spectacle. Nothing else. All is in the eye of the beholder and quite innocent.'

Still lost in thought and worried, for it was obvious the rue Lauriston had been interested in Nana Thélème for some time but for purposes of their own, namely loot, Kohler hesitated. Madame de Bonnevies motioned to the chair and softly crooned, 'It's begun. Please avail yourself of the pleasure. I will send Malou to you with a little wine, and Brigitte will come to pour it.'

'A *marc*.'

A brandy. 'As you wish. Both will, of course, be free to love you for ever tonight – it's on the house – but if it is your wish, you may have the slave, though I must tell you that one has no faith in her fidelity and there are many who want her.'

A top earner.

'Monsieur Jacqmain hated what she represented, as he did that of the girl Tshaya. To him, both represented the evil in all women, especially that of a hypocritical mother who constantly preached piety and self-denial, with the reward of everlasting life in the hereafter among the choirs of angels.'

The girl behind the amber latticework of the screen was a coal-black Senegalese with short-cropped, crinkly black hair and when her eyes flashed whitely in that finely boned and beautifully aristocratic face, they did so with an intensity Kohler found disturbing.

From time to time she turned to cross her wrists high above

her head as if strung up taut. Light played softly on her back and buttocks. There were whip marks, the scars some slaver must have left. The blue-black, dusty-grey to red marks of his shackles were around her wrists, ankles and neck.

Often she clung to the latticework, seeking to join the copulating couple on the bed. At such times her pink tongue would wet her lips in hesitation. The firm dark breasts would be caught, the rosy dark nipples held.

When she began to do the only thing that was left to her, this trapped little fly in amber watched the bed with an intensity that haunted.

The couple took no notice of her for they were far too busy and the client totally unware of her in any case – he could not have seen her at all. The blonde on her hands and knees on the bed was thick-thighed and as strong as a plough-horse; the Oberfeldwebel in his undershirt, swarthy and pockmarked with old bullet wounds. The deepness of the blonde's sighs and groans soon filled the room, the grunts of him as he stolidly rutted at her.

Canopies of heavy, wine-red velvet were draped about the headboard of the bed. The coverlet beneath the couple was armorial with fleurs de lis and fringed with tassels. The Oberfeldwebel had pushed the blonde down so that her head was well over the edge of the bed just like Marianne St-Cyr's had been in the films ... the films ... 'In ... in ...' she cried. 'Oh *mon Dieu, mon Dieu*, your shaft, it is so big and strong. I must come ... I must!'

A tall, leaded glass terrarium on a bureau held dead branches to which iridescent sunbursts of butterflies clung as it shook. Orange on black, indigo on amber, gold on emerald green, a soft, soft lavender, all entombed.

When the slave threw her head back and gave her body to ecstasy, as did the blonde, both quivered. The scars glistened. The blonde's naked back held none of them. Breasts, shoulders and arms throbbed until again the wrists were pressed together high above the slave's head, and again her body felt the lash of an imaginary whip and all but buckled under each blow.

A regular circus but, 'Ah Christ!' breathed Kohler sadly. Had she really been beaten like that and so savagely?

The blonde was disinterestedly washing herself. The sergeant wasn't pulling off his regulation issue rubber boot. Having paid extra not to use it, he had gambled on the bimonthly medical checks every licensed house had to have, and against the infirmary, loss of rank and the guardhouse for himself if wrong.

'Monsieur, is it that you wish to see more?' hazarded a sweet and hesitant voice.

Kohler felt the glass of brandy in his hand but had no recollection of either of them having put it there. The one who had spoken was a sturdy little brunette with a self-conscious smile. The raven-haired one behind her was taller, bolder and more pronounced in every way.

Neither of them wore a thing. 'Which of you is Malou?' he asked, 'and which is Brigitte?'

His grin was nice and the look in his eyes one of warm appreciation. A gentleman for one so big and frightening. Would he take both of them or only the slave?

Kohler downed the brandy and patted each of them on the rump. 'Another time,' he sighed. '*Merde*, the life a poor detective leads. I want to stay but duty calls.'

He kissed them both and held them a moment so that neither would feel slighted and the house could rest in peace.

A last look revealed that the girl behind the lattice had vanished and that the lights there had been switched off. Had they done it with mirrors? he wondered.

The sergeant was doing up his boots, the blonde was smoking a cigarette and fixing her nails, having forgotten all about the 'lover' who had just 'possessed' her.

He'd had his moment, and it would soon be time for the next one.

The Paradox gun had been considered too old to confiscate and the authorities had unwittingly let the prospector keep it as a curiosity. Sometimes such things happened in the provinces, but seldom if ever in Paris. Each lead ball was nearly two and a half centimetres in diameter – enough to drop an elephant at one hundred metres. Each cartridge held nearly thirty grams of black powder. A hero's gun.

Pocketing two of the lead shot for the library of the curious one always tried to build, St-Cyr went through to the sitting-

142

room. Both Gabrielle and Nana Thélème had come here on that Tuesday. Jacqmain had needed Mademoiselle Thélème's continued reassurances that it would indeed be safe for him to sell the diamonds to her friend.

Yet the 850,000 francs were nowhere to be found.

The Generalmajor Wehrle had come at 7 p.m. that night. The woman feeding the pigeons in the square had complained of late comings and goings. 'Whores if you ask me,' she had said.

Enough flypapers to kill an elephant had been purchased by Mademoiselle Thélème.

Vouvray and the Château Thériault were quite close and it would have been easy enough for Gabrielle to have returned after Wehrle had departed.

The *boucherie* was closed, as was the *marchand de couleurs*, but banging hard enough brought the owner of this last, and it was from him that the woman's address was obtained.

She lived directly above the shop but on the third floor.

'Madame Horleau, a few small questions. Nothing difficult, I assure you.'

In the faded light of the landing, the rheumy grey eyes were suspicious, the door all but closed. 'What's happened to him?' she asked. 'I heard a dreadful bang.'

'It would be best, madame, if you simply answered my questions and did not attempt to ask any of your own.'

'Did he shoot himself with that blunderbuss the Kommandant was fool enough to have let him keep for the memories it held?'

'Please, the blonde you said had arrived on that Tuesday morning a week ago. Did she return later that evening?'

'A week ago . . . Why, please, did they come?'

He sighed. He retrenched and asked if she wished arrest for withholding information.

'Arrest would be perfect for such as myself. Is it that you are unaware the Vichy Government *and* the police must feed their prisoners under the conditions of the Geneva Convention?'

He'd best not ask why she would consider herself a prisoner of war! 'The soup is water, and unclean, madame. The bread, if they get any, is grey and full of harmful things your old insides could not withstand but, please, let me help with the war effort.'

A wallet was found, but its state was such that she had to say, 'It needs remending. Have you no wife to call your own? Fishing line . . . *Pah*! men know nothing of such things and should all be raised in skirts for the first ten years!'

He grimaced. He said silently, Sometimes dealing with the provincials could be so very difficult.

He handed over 50 francs which she took and waited for more. 'The pigeons,' she said.

'You can't buy bread on the black market. No one can. It's one of the few things which are, by some unwritten rule, forbidden by all, both buyer and seller.'

She snapped arthritic fingers and he handed over another 50. 'Does the blonde from Paris drive a small Peugeot?' she asked.

'It's dark blue.'

'The same as arrived early that morning. That one returned at eight o'clock in the evening, the new time, but stayed no more than five minutes.'

'And?' he asked.

Did he always suspect there must be more? 'She left with a small suitcase.'

'But . . . but it was dark outside?'

'Dark enough for an old woman to hear her bang it against the car as she opened the door. She said, "*Merde alors*, my nerves. I *can't* drop it! Everything will be all right. We'll soon get him on his way."'

'Was Monsieur Jacqmain going for a trip?'

'The other one, I think. The one who came with the small suitcase at seven that night and left before this woman returned.'

The Generalmajor Wehrle. 'How can you be sure it was the same suitcase?'

'I can't, but I can tell you the first was a brown alligator bag from Louis Vuitton in Paris. As the *vélo-taxi* driver handed it to the man, he let a sliver of light fall on it. I have always wanted to possess such a bag.'

'Your eyesight must be excellent.'

'That's because I don't waste it reading books and newspapers like Monsieur Jacqmain did. Is she known to you, this one who returned?'

What could he say? 'She was known to me, yes, but now I'm not so sure of it.'

The alligator bag had not been in the house – he was certain of this, certain too, that Gabrielle must have come back for it.

'Madame, are you sure she said, "I *can't* drop it?"'

'*Positive*! She was terrified of doing so and gingerly put the bag on the seat beside her. Then the car she allowed only to creep away until, reassured perhaps, she finally gave the accelerator pedal the tiny push.'

'And you're certain she said, "We'll soon get him on his way?"'

'Must I repeat everything for you?'

'Egg white,' breathed Kohler, marvelling at it as he ran his fingers delicately over the scars on the black girl's shoulders. 'Who would have believed it?'

Madame de Bonnevies was firm. 'You did. Monsieur Jacqmain did and so have all others. It is allowed to dry and then is sprayed with artist's fixative before oiling.'

Exhausted, depressed and afraid perhaps, the Senegalese slept flat on her stomach in an untidy attic room. A well-squeezed tube of Veronal was nearby. Had she taken too much?

A half-bottle of cognac had been downed in an instant. The barbitone before the 'performance', the cognac right afterwards.

'She was afraid you would ask for her and had prepared herself.'

'Me?' he managed.

'The scar. The others too, that accompany it on your face.'

'Shrapnel nicks from the Great War, and a bullet graze that's too fresh not to remind me of the bastard who fired the slug that did it. That's the one across the brow. You should have told her she need not have feared me.'

He was still looking at the *négresse's* buttocks. Was he tempted perhaps? 'She was afraid of Monsieur Jacqmain also, and of the others who took her.'

'You said he never touched any of your girls.'

'*Yes*! but this one "felt" his breath on her skin all the same.'

The girls would know everything that went on in the house. When awaiting a client, they would often spy on the entrance so as to get a little preview. She'd have seen him, then, talking to Madame.

Kohler turned to look at the woman. 'Did Tshaya "prepare" herself?'

145

'In such a way?'

Most girls were drunk half the time, some on dope, too, if they could get it in these hard times. 'In any way.'

'That one's defence was her hatred. She despised the profession and rejected all attempts at compromise. She was taken to Paris many times to be used in other ways, perhaps, but when brought back, was simply more sullen and determined.'

'Did she ever go to Jacqmain's house?'

'After dark?'

The woman had held her breath. 'You know that's what I meant.'

'Then I must tell you that she did on three occasions, each of which was after a session such as you have just seen.'

'You were told to let her do this?'

Must he constantly push the matter? 'We were ordered to by that husband of hers. Ah! there was nothing either of us could have done. Monsieur Jacqmain did not beat her, if that is what you are thinking. He merely trailed the bullwhip he had brought from Africa across her flesh. An hour . . . two hours, little more.'

'Was she tied up?'

'Yes.'

She'd have been terrified. 'And how did he pay her – and yourself?'

There would be trouble if she did not answer truthfully. 'In diamonds. He made us swear to say nothing of them and we agreed, of course, to do as he wished.'

The fool!

The Auberge of the Priest Who Travelled With Full Saddlebags served crayfish in white wine, pork stuffed with prunes, pike *au beurre blanc*, Saint-Martin duckling, hare *à la chinonaise, touraine de pêches à la royale, le Lochois* cakes and macaroons, cheese, wine and cognac. Absolutely no ration tickets were required – one didn't even discuss such things. There was hardly a Frenchman in the place and though the hour was late, practically all of the tables were in use but Hermann, being Hermann, had managed a quiet corner.

'Louis, we have to talk.'

146

The *chèvre crottin* before the Sûreté had come dusted with dill and chives as requested; the *baguette* was broken.

'Agreed.'

Disconsolately, Kohler dug his fork into the *saucisson de Lyon* with the hot potato salad. Louis wasn't eating, a bad sign. The Frog was simply staring at his monk's repast as if lost in thought and wounded to the quick.

'Do you remember the Reverend Father of the Abbey of Saint Gregory the Great, Hermann?'

Vouvray, then, and that murder in Fontainebleau Forest. 'How could I ever forget a thing like that?'

Good! The SS had used a bullwhip on Hermann because he had insisted the truth be told. 'The Abbot said the wine owed its flavour to the *aubuis*, the clay with much limestone.'

The snort was harsh, the words bitter. 'It was the boulder of flint you picked up that settled things.'

'Ah yes, but Gabrielle got the drop on me in that abandoned grist mill down by the river. She and I then shared a simple meal such as this and at the time, I wished her rucksack had held a bottle of their wine. With the goat's cheese and the bread, it would, I thought, have been superb.'

So much for the travelogue of memories. The Vouvray *moelleux* was of Sauterne sweetness. For well over a thousand years there had been vineyards along the Loire. The wine was clear and crisp, robust and fruity – '*piquant*' the Abbot had said, and 'a good keeper'.

'The 1934 Clos de l'Oiseau de la Brume, Hermann, the Château Thériault,' he said, showing him the label. 'An extraordinary year.'

'The Countess isn't mixed up in things, is she?'

Hermann still held a fondness for that one. 'Let us hope not because if she is, this time for certain René Yvon-Paul will inherit nothing.'

'Why don't you tell me what's bugging you?'

With great deliberation St-Cyr sampled the cheese, the bread and the wine, nodding from time to time as if well satisfied that his initial thoughts had been correct. 'But have I been so wrong about Gabrielle, *mon ami*?'

'Wrong in what way?'

It was now or never if they were to remain friends and partners. 'Gabrielle collected the money, Hermann, and took it with her but may also have had the nitroglycerine the Gypsy used at the Ritz in that suitcase, cushioned no doubt by the banknotes.'

'Ah Christ . . .'

'Jacqmain may have had a flask of nitro in his prospecting kit and not have turned it in. He'd have *wanted* to be rid of it. An extra condition, then, of his letting Wehrle have the diamonds.'

'And?'

Hermann wasn't looking well. 'The matter is even deeper. That crone I spoke to thought the Generalmajor would soon be on his way. A little trip.'

'To Berlin, idiot, with the contents of his safe. He wouldn't have known the Gypsy was to empty it on the eighteenth.'

'Perhaps but then . . . ah *mais alors, alors*, what if not to Berlin but to Spain? A major coup for a tiny *réseau*, a fund of exceedingly valuable information for the Allies.'

'And what if not the Generalmajor but the Gypsy, eh? What if *that's* who Gabrielle meant?'

'An operation, code-named *Zèbre*, Hermann.'

'A *Funkspiel*, Louis.'

'The Resistance are desperate for funds. Those three women knew this and asked London for help. They set up those robberies and Herr Max, not London, obliged by sending them the Gypsy. Nana knew all about this safe-cracker and that he was one of the best, so perhaps they asked London to send him – this we may never know – but Suzanne-Cécilia detected a different signature at the end of London's last reply. She's convinced of it.'

'Then it's true . . .' Kohler shoved his plate aside. 'God help us now. There'll be no way out of this for Giselle and Oona short of my turning you all over to the Gestapo and Herr Max.'

'But will you, Hermann? That is the question only you can answer.'

6

At dawn the Château Thériault's five towers were shrouded in snow. Off to the right, and away from the river, vineyards occupied the lower slopes, climbing gently until they met those of the Abbey of Saint Gregory the Great in territory that had been disputed for centuries until at last the land claim had been settled not two months ago.

'Louis, go and talk to the Countess, eh? Tell her I'll be along in a little while.'

Hermann had slept badly and, contrary to his usual self, had not driven the car but had lamely wanted to 'look' at the countryside.

That big Bavarian was sick at heart. Moundlike, the shapes of box, yew and hawthorn stood nearest the arched stone entrance which was set in the base of one of the towers. Ivy climbed the walls. Immediately inside the gates, the courtyard of lawns and formal gardens held mothballed fountains and statues.

The château was huge and Hermann had often said it must be a bugger to heat, but now this conscience-ridden Kripo looked away to the centre of the courtyard to where stone greyhounds leapt at a cornered stag and the nothing murder of Fontainebleau Forest had finally come to an end.

It hadn't been easy. It had been a very close thing, and when Louis let him out of the car, Kohler simply asked, 'You haven't got a cigarette, have you?'

He went on then towards the stables which were on the far side. He paused to open the great doors to let the light in, then searched his pockets desperately yet again for tobacco.

'Let him be, Jean-Louis. Give him time.'

'Countess . . .'

'Please wait for us in the kitchens. This frost . . . will it kill the vines? I had thought to burn fires throughout the night but new restrictions have been placed on such things, so I have spent the hours in walking the rows and fretting. It was silly of me, but when one loves a place so much and there is no other recourse, what else can one do but pray?'

'Countess, Hermann needs to be alone.'

'I think he needs to be reminded. Now go. If René Yvon-Paul should come down, tell him he's not to worry about his mother and me arguing. It happens all the time. Tell him also that the life of a detective is *not* a life to aspire to, and please ask him to let the dogs come to me. There will be coffee and croissants for the help, so feel free to partake of them even though the croissants are illegal. My cook will give you brandy. It's rough, but at the moment it's all that is left.'

'The caves were emptied?'

His alarm was gratifying. 'Emptied of every bottle.'

There were no horses in the stables, all had been taken. And when the far doors were also opened, Kohler found himself alone in the pearly light, the breath billowing from him.

Panic came – for just a second it was absolute. He reached out to steady himself. There were splintered bullet holes in the ancient boards. A mare had been wounded and had screamed as she had tried to free herself. Another had been killed. All thirty-two rounds from the drum clip of a Luger had been sprayed about but first there had been the lesson of a rawhide whip.

For pointing the finger of truth, the SS had roped him by the wrists to both sides of the corridor. Blood had welled up along the wound – surprising that, for he'd felt no pain, had still been in shock and staring dumbly down at his parted shirt. From the right shoulder to the left hip had been opened as if by the sudden exercise of a mad tailor's shears. The pain had hit him but by then the left side of his face had been torn from eye to chin.

A hell of a mess. Gabrielle's son had cut him free but the SS had come back. In the ensuing fight, the Luger had been emptied and the boy had driven a pitchfork into the back of one of them. Had killed the son of a bitch. *Killed him*, ah *Jésus-Christ!*

The other one had been killed by the shots. Kohler remembered telling René Yvon-Paul to beat it, to hide in the abandoned mill and had said he'd take the blame himself. Hell, the kid had only been ten years old.

'But now it's different,' he said. 'Now it's far worse.'

'You'll think of something. I've every confidence.'

The Countess Jeanne-Marie Thériault spoke softly to the five greyhounds that had come to her. She still looked the same in that dark blue woollen overcoat, trousers and riding boots, though he felt a thousand years must have passed since he'd seen her last. 'Countess, Berlin are very much involved in this matter of your daughter-in-law's. We were lucky here before, but now . . .?'

'You're not like the others. With you that inherent sense of common decency and humanity has survived.'

She was laying it on the line. Pushing the hood back, she removed the scarf that had been tied over her ears and hair. The dark eyes were very clear and searching. The high forehead was smooth, the pale cheeks reddened by a night in the cold.

At the time of the nothing murder he had had the idea there were carefully arranged rings of defence around the château and that she had a network of informants all too loyal to her. 'The Resistance . . .?' she had said then. 'Oh, we've some of them about here too.'

But did it go much deeper than that? The château could be useful to the Resistance, the hills and caves too. She and Gabrielle had hidden things before, could the two of them not be at it again?

She sent the dogs away and closed the distance. 'A cigarette, I think,' she said. 'Here, let me offer one of Gabrielle's. They're Russian, and given to her by a general on leave.'

And on the run, eh – was this what he was thinking? The very mention of a general on leave brought anxiety and fear, ah so many things to those pale blue eyes of his. 'You're well?' she asked.

He knew she was toying with him and said harshly, 'Countess, why not tell me what that daughter-in-law of yours has been up to?'

Her hair was jet black and had been tied behind but now she shook it out and let it fall loosely about her shoulders, not a touch of grey though she was in her sixties. A timeless and still fantastic-looking woman.

'What has she been up to, do you think?'

The tobacco was black and rough. He coughed and inhaled, forcing himself to become accustomed to it. 'Let me put things this way, then,' he said sharply. 'My confrères in the SS and Gestapo Paris-Central – Berlin, damn it – are about to use that *réseau* your daughter-in-law's mixed up in to sweep Louis and me into the bag along with the rest of them.'

'They want, once and for all, for you to prove that you are really one of them.'

'And if I don't, Countess? Giselle and Oona and the child will have to go too.'

'The child? Is Oona . . .?'

'Giselle is. Look, Gabrielle brought a suitcase here from Tours on the twelfth, at night.'

'If she did, I have no knowledge of it.'

He threw his head back as if struck and clenched a fist. 'Countess, don't trifle. There were 850,000 francs in that bag.'

'And?' she asked, giving him that searching look of hers.

'And a flask or dropper-bottle of nitroglycerine. It ... it belonged to a prospector who has just removed himself from this world.'

Cigarette ash was tapped into a palm. Even when carrying on such a conversation, a part of her mind could still concern itself with the fire hazards of careless smoking.

'Gabrielle tells me nothing, as you well know from past experience.'

'Did he kill himself because he knew too much, Countess?'

'Are you certain she brought such a thing?'

'As certain as you must be. What'd she do? Park that little car of hers outside the walls?'

'She came and she went.'

'She didn't stay the night?'

'She couldn't.'

'She'd have needed a *laissez-passer* to be on the roads. Who the hell provided it? The Generalmajor Wehrle?'

Was this Wehrle on the run – she could see him thinking this.

He asked again. She said, 'That I can't say. Gabrielle is of independent means and has a mind of her own. René Yvon-Paul and I are left to tend this ... this old fortress and to see that somehow it earns sufficient to keep it going.'

'They've taken the last of the horses.'

'They took the wine and five of my best workers. The *Service de Travail Obligatoire.* The district Kommandant is proving difficult.'

'Did you warn Gabrielle to stay away? Is that why she didn't hang around?'

'I told her that to oppose the Occupier was both foolish and inopportune.'

At last they were getting somewhere! 'What did she want you to do? Hide someone? Was that it, eh?'

Why hadn't he just said, Damn you? 'A package. That was all she said.'

'*When?*'

'I can't tell you because I simply don't know. A week, a month ... She was uncertain.'

'So, did the "package" have two legs?'

'Come and see the pigs. We've been fattening them up for the Kommandant's table and for the boys in Russia but when they take our Judith, we'll be left with empty pens. That's how it is and now I trust you understand why we couldn't accept any such packages and why I must ask you to help us.'

Far from the kitchens, St-Cyr let his gaze pass slowly down over the lower vineyards. He'd had no idea they could be seen from Gabrielle's window. She had led him to this room, off in another wing of the château, lost even among those of the servants' quarters. She and the Countess hadn't got along – the Countess had felt her only son had married beneath himself. Her own husband had been killed in the Great War, their son in this one. There'd been friction with Gabrielle, and the loss of two loved ones, which should have brought them closer, hadn't helped.

The single iron bed with its flaking white paint had lent a flea-market desperation to the room and still did. A bureau, a mirror that was none too big and mounted awkwardly for a woman as tall as Gabrielle, an armoire and a chair were about all there was. Country scenes cut from magazines had been pasted into rescued frames. A simple crucifix had been nailed to the wall at the head of the bed.

It was at once the room of a chamber-maid or scullery girl. Gabrielle had deliberately chosen to make her statement that this

153

was how she was perceived by the Countess and therefore this was how it should be.

Since the murder in Fontainebleau Forest, things had improved but still there would be reservations on both sides, old insults and opinions. For those, they needed time.

A soft brown velvet bag with a drawstring of twisted gold thread had held eighteen uncut diamonds, each of five or six carats. Emerald green, yellow, a soft and frosted pink, a blue, some clear white stones ... Russian diamonds Gabrielle had brought from Leningrad as a girl of fourteen and had kept no matter what and always in the hope her family would have survived to be reunited with her.

Diamonds then, and diamonds now.

There were some newspapers on the bed and he wondered at them for they were new. The *Völkischer Beobachter*, the *Pariser Zeitung* and a copy of *Signal*, the picture magazine – the January 1943 issue and photos of Gabrielle at the Club Mirage, entertaining the troops. There were shots of her with laughing soldier boys on leave or boarding the train back to the front, others of her with generals. A collage of her with von Ribbentrop and with the General Heinrich von Stülpnagel, the Military Governor of France, occupied a centrefold.

A smiling, cigar-smoking Otto Abetz, the ambassador, had his arm about her waist, she laughing. Dr Karl Epting, the Director of the *Deutsche Institut* was more staid, as was the General Ernst von Schaumburg, Old Shatter Hand, the Kommandant von Gross Paris.

In page after page she was seen with the high and mighty of the Third Reich. There were bits and pieces of her private life both in Paris and here on the Loire. Shots of the château showed her with her son.

Lying under the newspapers, there was a letter of commendation signed by Hitler himself, 10 January 1943. She had brought the newspapers and the magazine with her on the twelfth to show the Countess but had left them here.

'*Sonderbehandlung*,' Herr Max had warned. He must have known the article had already been published and the magazine distributed not just in France but in every occupied country and wherever the troops were fighting.

She was revered by thousands. Front-line soldiers heard her singing via broadcasts that were picked up live from the club. There had been several requests for her to visit the troops but so far she had been able to put these off.

The Resistance ... a *réseau* ... She had said she'd join up, and he had agreed and had included himself but why had she let the Occupier do this to her unless desperate and thinking it would protect the *réseau*? Every hot-headed *résistant* in the country would be after her.

When René Yvon-Paul came to find him, the boy, who looked a lot like his mother but had the dark brown eyes and hair of his father, gravely said, 'You must tell *maman* we cannot possibly accept any packages at this time. Things are far too difficult for us. She must listen to *grand-mère* in the matter and not argue with those who love her.'

'What sort of packages?'

The boy burst into tears. 'Was it a suitcase?' asked St-Cyr gently.

'*No!* It ... it was someone she wanted us to hide for a few days, just until things could be finalized.'

'*Who*? René, you must tell me if I'm to help her.'

'A *gitan*, a *nomade*. She said he had some work to do for them in Paris and then they ... they would send him to us for "delivery" to others.'

'And were these others to help him on from here?'

'*Yes!*'

Longing for a cigarette, they drove in silence. St-Cyr shut his eyes. He wished he could peacefully gaze at the countryside, but the roads ... '*There's a convoy up ahead, Hermann!*'

'Where? There's no convoy.'

'*Ah nom de Jésus-Christ, idiot, trust me!*'

Trust ... wasn't that what this whole affair was all about? wondered Kohler uncomfortably. Trust between friends and partners, trust between a man and his *Vaterland*, and trust between the members of a *réseau* and two detectives who should have known better than to have meddled with them in the first place but had been ordered to!

155

The brakes were hit. The Citroën slewed sideways. At about 90 kilometres an hour, it sped broadside towards the rear lorry. They did a complete circle. Another and another . . . 'Hermann!'

The car pulled out of its spin and they found themselves at the side of the road.

'So, Louis, why not tell me what you found out, eh? Why keep me in suspense?'

'The Resistance in Vouvray were to pass the Gypsy on to others once he had finished his work in Paris. De Vries will know of this, Hermann. Gabrielle will have told him of it.'

'Then it's even worse than we thought. The son of a bitch will turn them all in if he has to.'

'And if not him, then Tshaya.'

At Beaugency they stopped for the *prix fixe* of watery soup, sour wine, stuffed cabbage leaves but stuffed with what – more of the infamous 'mystery' meat? – and *prunes aux vinaigre*. There wasn't a single one of the Occupier in the restaurant except for Hermann and there were stares from all others.

At Orléans they headed north towards Paris, the meal not sitting well. Neither of them had any tobacco. Even their *mégot* tins, where all cigarette butts, found or otherwise were kept, held only ashes.

At a control, the car was flagged down and they had to go through the motions. *Cartes d'identité* were handed over, their *laissez-passers* and *sauf-conduits*. Cold stares from the burly Feldwebel in charge were received by the Sûreté. Always there was this little panic, this fluttering of the heart only more so now.

But it didn't happen. Louis wasn't asked to get out, and soon they were on their way again, Kohler heaving a sigh of relief. 'Berlin must be tearing their hair,' he said.

'Himmler's, I think, and Herr Max's.'

'Boemelburg's too.' Kohler floored the car as they passed a farm wagon that was driven by an old woman whose black shawl was suddenly caught by the wind. 'Nana must have hoped and prayed De Vries had escaped to England in 1940, Louis. The Norwegians let a lot of prisoners go just before the Defeat. She would have been ready to believe he'd been parachuted into France, but even so, would have been surprised to learn he had arrived on her doorstep to do the very thing they wanted.'

156

Had they asked specifically for him? they both wondered, but thought it doubtful if for no other reason than security. Instead, they must have asked simply for help and then found an expert had been sent.

Wind-drift was carrying the snow across a ploughed field. Sunlight, rare for this time of year, was breaking through the clouds to be caught among the crystals . . .

'If De Vries is now having to get his nitro from dynamite, Louis, then how much of it did those three women find for him? Berlin and Herr Max wouldn't have given him any, no matter what they fed them by wireless, so don't start thinking they did.'

'But does Herr Max know for certain it's them, Hermann, or does he only suspect it is?'

The airwaves, the distance factor, the difficulties of pinning a transceiver down. Was there still a particle of hope or was all lost?

Built on the right bank of the Nonette and surrounded by a plain that was bordered by forests now shrouded in snow, Senlis was about fifty kilometres to the north-north-east beyond Paris. It was a quiet provincial town whose soft grey limestone walls and substantial houses had lasting charm. But it was from this southernmost apex that the triangle known as the Devastated Region began.

To the north, at Péronne in 1917, the British had found on the blackened shell of the *mairie* a signboard left by the Kaiser's retreating army. *Nicht ärgern, nur wundern.* Do not be enraged, only wonder.

The devastation had been deliberate and terrible. Thousands and thousands of fruit trees had been hacked off at exactly waist height and felled so that their crowns all pointed with mathematical preciseness along the path of the retreating army.

The same had happened to the poplars and buttonwoods which had once beautified the lanes and roads. From Senlis to Saint Quentin in the north and to Albert in the west, had been affected but in reality the ruination of that war had been much greater. About fourteen hundred villages and towns had all but been obliterated.

And in Senlis? It had been occupied from 2 September 1914

157

until the eleventh, during the initial push to the Marne. Here the invader had trodden relatively lightly, one might suppose, looting, burning and destroying all but four of the houses along the fabled rue du la République. Its mayor and six others had been executed, but fortunately much of the town had been spared.

During the retreat, all wells and springs had been polluted with the carcasses of dead animals and latrine excrement, the farm buildings either burned or blown up and the roads dynamited.

'It's a wonder you speak to me at all,' muttered Kohler, still behind the wheel.

'Ah! it wasn't of your doing.' Hermann had been taken prisoner in 1916.

'Right after the Armistice we were marched north and through Jussy, Louis. Not a Kaiser's shell or one of yours had hit it but not a wall, a bush, flower or blade of grass had been left. Hell, it was only a little place. Why'd they do a thing like that?'

Hermann must have seen the remains of the orchards, the farmboy in him overwhelmed. 'In war all things are possible. Come on, let's find the house of Monsieur Jacqmain's mother. Let's not dwell on ancient history.'

'It was only twenty-five years ago and now we're right back in the shit again.'

The grey-stone house, with mullioned windows and white trim, was just off the rue de la Treille in the oldest part of town. Built largely in the eighteenth century, it was part seventeenth-century priory, part thirteenth-century chapel, and the two long storeys of it exuded tranquillity, substance and stability. But it was from the back that the treasure of the house was best seen even in winter. Here ivy-covered, high and ancient walls enclosed a large garden with sturdy walnut trees and several venerable apple trees. The remains of the chapel were at the rear of the house where moss-covered stone steps led steeply up from beneath the apple bows, a good six metres to the top of the Gallo-Roman wall that had once surrounded the town.

'Silvanectum, Hermann. Home of the Silvanectes. There were

once twenty-eight towers along this wall, but now only sixteen are left.'

Trying to momentarily forget their problems, Louis added, 'If ever I could move out of that house of my mother's, this is what I would aspire to.'

Kohler had heard it all before. The little retirement with government pension, the farm in Provence where vegetables might be harvested if sufficient water could possibly be secured; the orchard in Normandy not ravaged by cutworms, blight, frost, starlings, war or thieves, namely tax collectors. 'It doesn't look as if there's anyone around.'

They descended the steps. Louis slipped and nearly went down. Kohler cursed the impulse that had led them to explore the place from such an entrance. At the back door, repeated banging brought no answer. All the curtains were drawn. '*Merde*, what now?' muttered Louis.

'We open it up. We have to. Look, for all we know Boemelburg and Herr Max could have had everyone arrested and be only waiting for us to return to Paris.'

'Idiot, they'd have stopped us on the road. You're forgetting the controls.'

Kohler tried to force the lock. 'Messieurs . . .'

The voice had about it a breathless urgency. At the far corner of the garden, a top step was hesitantly negotiated by a wooden-clogged, tall, thin woman in black with a shopping hamper. A hand was thrown up. They held their breaths. 'Madame Jacqmain is in her grave these fifteen days,' she cried out. 'The Mademoiselle has gone to Paris. You . . . *why would such as you demand such as this effort from one such as myself?*'

They recrossed the garden at a run and when these two from Paris who had come in the shiny black car that had been left outside the *mairie* and Kommandantur stood below her on the steps, Madame Augustine Moreel faced them from above, thus blocking their way and putting even the giant at a disadvantage. 'Messieurs, must I notify the préfet himself? You were tampering with the locks.'

A Belgian, a Walloon . . . 'Madame, could we not discuss things on more stable ground?'

Suspicion raked him. 'Please state your business.'

Her purse was black and gripped as a weapon. 'Sûreté and Kripo. He's the Sûreté, I'm the . . .'

Her grey-blue eyes flashed impatience. 'What's the son done this time? Violated another poor young thing? Flayed her to satiate his base desires and then wept on his knees before that portrait of his dear mother, a saint?'

They waited. They swallowed this outburst, these two detectives who clung to the icy ascent beneath her.

'*Well*?' she demanded.

Louis was about to say, A few small questions. Kohler shushed him by gripping him by the elbow and nearly sending the two of them to the bottom. 'You mentioned a mademoiselle, madame?'

'Perhaps I did.'

'There were two ladies who came from Paris. Did they have a suitcase with them?' tried Louis.

'When, exactly, did they come?' she asked.

'That's what we'd like to know,' managed Kohler.

'A suitcase,' she said, the breath held back. 'Travellers always have such things.'

Merde! they were getting nowhere. 'Madame, please step aside and accompany us into the house.'

'I'll do no such thing. Madame trusted me implicitly and carried her confidence in that trust to her grave.'

A treasure, then, if the key to part this one's lips could ever be found. 'The two who came here, did they take Monsieur Jacqmain's daughter to Paris with them?' It was a complete shot in the dark.

'Sylvianne was beside herself with grief, monsieur. The child has lived all her tender life with the grandmother she adored. They were the greatest of companions. No matter was too difficult for either to accomplish for the other. Reading, sketching, piano lessons . . . Night after night exquisite concerts, the singing . . . Though she's only twelve years old, the daughter has the sound of angels in her voice and fingers, but also the great goodness of God in her heart, thanks be to Him who has made us all in spite of accidents of birth.'

'You must be freezing,' said Kohler. 'Here, let's go round and into the house by its proper entrance. It was stupid of us to have come this way. Undignified of police officers.'

160

Suspicion registered but she held her tongue. An eighteenth-century iron railing ran atop the wall. There were the usual 'tourists' about, members, also, of the Wehrmacht's local detachment, but the lack of schoolboys throwing snowballs at schoolgirls reminded one that the light of day was, alas, fast fading. Soon the kids would be let out of school.

'Messieurs, why have you come?'

It was Louis who said, 'He has killed himself.'

She drew in a breath. 'Then you will want to know where his daughter is. Two deaths in such a short time . . . It will be hard for Sylvianne to bear. In spite of everything, that goodness of heart included the father she had never seen except in photographs faded by the rays of the tropical sun.'

'Who was the mother?'

Why were they so anxious? 'One whose skin was that of a mulatto. A gypsy. A "virgin" he took repeatedly in a brothel in Bruges and once beat so terribly with his whip, it brought the police, thereby disgracing his mother in the eyes of her family and friends, while leaving her with the constant reminder of the child that was given to her at birth by the madam of that house.'

Tshaya's child . . . 'A saint, you said,' offered St-Cyr kindly.

'Now, please, let us go in before the neighbours think I've been arrested and that the house will fall into the hands of the son they know nothing of but whispers.'

The house was pleasant, the kitchen spacious beneath a wealth of ancient beams from which, by some avoidance of the ordinance for copper, scrap and otherwise, the pots still hung. There was a large and blackened, grey, cut-stone fireplace in which a small fire soon burned. Clearly Jacqmain's daughter had been in charge of collecting twigs and branches, but it was when he went to get some of the fist-sized balls of drying papier-mâché she had made, that St-Cyr found the half used-up novel.

'*Nana*,' he said. 'Why did I not think of it?'

Zola's novel of the courtesan, 'actress' and 'singer' of no talent but one, had captured readers ever since its publication in 1880. A tall and stunningly curvaceous creature with reddish-blonde hair. Nana had suddenly appeared on stage at the Variétés in the operetta, *La Vénus blonde*. At the age of eighteen she had had no

161

qualms. Her breasts had been firm, the nipples erect beneath the flimsy, diaphanous veil she had worn with nothing else. In triumph, she had lain in the grotto of the silver mine on Mount Etna, its walls serving as polished mirrors to her nakedness. Through their opera glasses, the bankers, financiers, stock brokers and *demi-mondaines* of fashionable Paris had even seen the tawny hair of her armpits and her radiant, if wickedly lecherous smile.

She had known all about men and had known exactly what they had wanted of her. But her young life, after unbelievable riches had been heaped upon her, had ended in smallpox and he could still recall the scent of carbolic that had permeated the death-bed room at the Hôtel Grand on her return from Russia. Only her hair had retained its radiance but Zola had given a last glimpse of it in candlelight. Touched by a chance gust, some strands had fallen forward to be glued to the sores.

Within six months of the novel's end, Bismark's Prussians had marched into Paris. The Franco-Prussian War of 1870–71 had ended and the German state had begun.

'Nana Thélème,' he said when Hermann came to find out what was delaying him. 'It's the stage name our Nana chose and the daughter here must have known of it. Hence her reading the novel, in secret no doubt.'

'I made her burn that book,' said Madame Moreel. 'The child adored Mademoiselle Thélème who, before the Defeat, would come to visit us as often as she could and delighted in this house and in the child. It was through her that Sylvianne took up the piano, the singing and dancing.'

'Is Sylvianne the reason Monsieur Jacqmain sold his diamonds and sent that suitcase?' asked Kohler only to hear Louis interjecting. 'A moment, *mon vieux*.

'Madame, this friend of the child's father, did she sometimes bring along another? A Dutchman? Tall, thin, about . . .'

'Why is it, please, that you ask, Inspector?'

The coldness of suspicion had leapt into her eyes. 'Only to give us background. It's always best to explore all avenues.'

All branches of the tree – was this what he was implying? she wondered anxiously. 'They adored Sylvianne. The child was very fond of Mademoiselle Thélème's friend, but he did not come here often, nor did she explain his long absences beyond

162

that she did not know where he was. What passed between our Nana and her "Jani", Inspector? Love – ah! even an old widow such as myself could see it. But why did he not marry her?'

'The suitcase,' said Kohler brusquely.

'The money was to ensure that Sylvianne and her grandmother should want for nothing, but I couldn't have that father of hers suddenly coming into her life. It was Madame Jacqmain's most fervent wish that her son never see his daughter or take any part in her life. When she died, after a long illness, I had to see that these wishes were carried out and let them take the child and the suitcase to Paris, but now that he is dead, Sylvianne can return. His suicide is as if God had answered all our prayers.'

Fearing she had said too much, the woman gathered an apronful of the papier-mâché balls and, clutching the last of the novel, went back to the fire.

'Was the daughter even Jacqmain's?' grunted Kohler, pulling down a lower eyelid at the vagaries of whorehouses and the paternity of such offspring.

'Tshaya must have been banished from the *kumpania* and from the Rom for ever, Hermann. She'd have left the child with them otherwise. But if De Vries was the father, that could well be why he came here and why Nana took such an interest in the child.'

'What about the nitro? Could he have come to tap a little of it from time to time in the thirties?'

'Perhaps – its certainly worth considering.'

'And the Thélème part of her stage name?' asked Kohler, his mind still on the explosives.

'It's from Rabelais's magnificent satire of 1534. He believed that humanity held within itself a basic instinct to do what was right, if all his conditions of being free and well-bred, properly educated and of good company were met. There was a war in which all the priests but one sought refuge in prayer while their lonely brother took on all comers in the abbey close and drove the enemy from it. To celebrate the victory, an abbey was built whose only rule was "Do what thou wilt". *L'Abbaye de Thélème.*'

'Another *maison de tolérance*!' snorted Kohler.

'Not so. A place where all good things might be enjoyed, *yes!* but goodness being defined and governed by that fundamental instinct in us all. You should read more, Hermann. You really must introduce yourself to our literature.'

163

'Okay, I get the message. Hey, I would never have let you down. You know that, Louis. We're in this together.'

They had no tobacco. They could only share a handshake.

'Madame,' said Louis gently when they had returned to the kitchen, 'was Sylvianne's mother Lucie-Marie Doucette?'

The woman was instantly suspicious. 'If so, she did not call herself that. Her name, and the only one she went by, was Tshaya. Myself, I saw her only once and what I saw, I did not trust, but Madame was determined to make amends by adopting the child, and I am for ever grateful that she did.'

Louis nodded sagaciously. Onions were being peeled for the soup that would be her supper. 'And was Mademoiselle Thélème aware of the mother's name?'

Was she familiar with Tshaya – is this what they were after, these two? 'Madame confided it to her just as Mademoiselle Thélème brought news of Madame's son she then imparted in confidence.'

'And when, please, did these visits begin?' said St-Cyr.

'Inspector, you ask too many questions. I'm an old woman.'

'Then I'll ask it again.'

She shrugged in reproof. 'The Mademoiselle Thélème first came to us almost as soon as we had moved in. The child was about a year old.'

'In 1931, then.'

'Yes, but her "Jani" did not come with her until the summer of 1934.'

'And did she use the name of Thélème at that time?' persisted Louis.

The slicing stopped. Tears began to form. 'Inspector, have I been wrong to entrust Sylvianne to her?'

'No. No, of course not. Please, you mustn't worry. The girl will soon return.'

'Then why did you ask that about Nana? What else would she have called herself?'

It would do no good to avoid the issue, but Nana had obviously come gradually to understand who the child's real father was. 'We only thought it might be a stage name, as is the Mademoiselle Arcuri's, whose real name is Natal'ya Kulakov-Myshkin.'

'A Russian!'

164

'But widowed. Her married name is Thériault.'

Louis was just digging a hole for himself. 'When did they arrive to take the girl?' asked Kohler.

Her look was cold, but she knew she'd have to answer. 'A week ago yesterday. They came, they said, only to deliver the suitcase but when she learned of Madame's death, Mademoiselle Thélème agreed to take Sylvianne with her even though they would have to seek residence and travel papers for her. The Mademoiselle Arcuri was convinced she could take care of the matter and that there would be no problem. "The Kommandant von Gross Paris is an old friend," she said. "He'll understand the need and that there is nothing untoward in our request."'

Old Shatter Hand wasn't going to like it when he learned the truth, thought Kohler but said pleasantly enough, 'They went to a quarry.'

'Yes. Monsieur Jacqmain had told Mademoiselle Thélème of the *pierre fine* from which the Château de Versailles was constructed. This limestone came from quarries nearby.'

Building at Versailles had begun in 1624, recalled St-Cyr. Louis XIII had wanted a small hunting pavilion, but it was the Sun King, Louis XIV, who, from 1661 to 1681, had built on an impressively grand scale and in 1682 had made Versailles the official residence and seat of government.

'Monsieur Jacqmain did come to Senlis occasionally, Inspectors, but never to this house. It was his intention to reopen one of the old quarries but not for cut stone, you understand. For road metal. He invested substantially but was thwarted. No one wanted the noise of the blasting. Several were afraid the vibrations would disturb their livestock, even the honeybees in the orchards. There is also a small and very old chapel near the quarry. A beautiful little church the workers used to be blessed in each day before work began. The resident father was most concerned about the ancient stained glass which is said to be some of the finest in . . .'

'Yes, yes,' said St-Cyr, 'but when, please, did Monsieur Jacqmain invest in the project?'

'During the rainy season in Africa he would return to France. It was in 1936 but if you ask me, Inspector, I believe, as did Madame, that his sole object was to find an excuse to be close to his daughter. We . . . we could not let that happen and . . . and lent our voices to those of the others. Since then, we have not seen him.'

De Vries could not have known then, in 1934, of the explosives and could only have learned of them much later. 'And those two *Parisiennes* wanted to see an ancient quarry just so that they could tell others they'd been there?' asked Kohler.

Was the Bavarian a disbeliever of everything? 'Nana said Monsieur Jacqmain had given her something that had to be returned to the magazine. He was most insistent.'

'The nitroglycerine in the suitcase,' interjected St-Cyr.

'Yes. A flask that was kept in its special box. He had taken it away just before the war stopped him from going back to his savages. You see, I have the keys to the gates and to the magazines. The quarry is just to the east of Aumont-en-Halatte, in the escarpment, but the roads ... this weather ... the darkness. They went in daylight. Surely you're not ...'

'No problem,' said Kohler. 'All we need are the keys. We'll see that they're returned with Sylvianne.'

When they reached the car and were letting its engine warm, Kohler said, 'The kid's the Gypsy's, Louis, and Nana soon figured it out.'

'But was Tshaya aware of Nana's continued interest in the child or of Jacqmain's interest in Nana?'

'She must have been. When faced with deportation in 1941, she fled to Tours to be close to the one man she knew would help her because she had what he wanted, the scars, and his mother had what was hers. Is she the reason Nana bought the flypapers?'

'Strychnine is most unpleasant, Hermann. The body convulses. The face grows livid, the eyes bulge until death intervenes, then ...'

'*Ja, ja, mein lieber Detektiv,* just answer the question, eh?'

Kohler got out to rip the black-out tape from the headlamps. 'It's an emergency,' he said. 'Gabrielle and Nana and Suzanne-Cécilia each must know it's only a matter of time until they're picked up, if they haven't already been.'

Louis sighed heavily. 'Then perhaps that is why Nana wanted the strychnine and it is only a matter of time until they take it.'

*

166

The forest was close, the road winding. Ahead of them the *garde champêtre* of Aumont-en-Halatte pushed his sturdy bicycle, cursing the snow, the lateness of the hour and themselves most especially.

Beyond a wooden bridge across a frozen stream, tall and rusting gates bore a last vestige of the Sun King's coat of arms and the faded notice *Défense d'entrer*.

'I will wait here, Inspectors,' grumbled the village cop. 'That way, if there is trouble, some warning may be given.'

A wise man, was that it? wondered Kohler, squinting down through the driving snow at this father of seven children, all of whom had been under the age of five. 'You do that, Henri, but make sure the tombstones are of granite, eh? and not of limestone. It lasts a hell of a lot longer.'

The bushy eyebrows knitted themselves, the grizzled mooncheeks tightened. Paris would have to be told how things were. Paris must be forced to listen! 'Inspector, no one has been here for years. The magazines are isolated – ah! *certainement*, Monsieur Jacqmain has obeyed all the regulations to the letter. Distance from the working face. Protection in case of accident. Two timbered walls with sand packed between in case some idiot with a rifle should have target practice. A double roof *aussi*, and sufficient ventilation. But . . .' He paused. He gave these two time to reconsider their little adventure. 'But the dynamite should have been taken away long ago. It smells. The heat in summer has not been good for it, the dampness in springtime also.'

'Anything else?' asked the giant, grinning down at him from under a beaver hat with full earflaps that were tied beneath the chin.

'*Oui*. Many times I have notified the authorities in your army to send a disposal crew but without success.'

'We only want to have a look.'

The chubby lips were pursed in exasperation. 'That is what I am afraid of.'

A wise man again.

'Inspectors, there are two magazines and they are well off to your left some 600 metres once you enter the property. They are behind a remnant of the original escarpment, a boss of rock that was not mined out. First comes the powder magazine and then, some fifty paces further, that of the blasting caps.'

Companionably Kohler clapped a hand on his shoulder. 'Give us a fag, eh? For the war effort. Hey, make it two.'

'Hermann, if he has any, they will have to be hand rolled. It will take all night in this wind!'

Woefully the dark brown eyes caught the light from the headlamps. 'I have none,' lamented the village *flic*. 'Now even the tobacco ration has been cut in half, nor can I take one stick of wood from the forest to warm the toes.'

Hard times.

'Inspectors, please watch your step. With the snow, the crevasses in the floor will be hidden. Those, that is, which do not have the cedars sprouting from them.'

The big one switched off the headlamps and the engine and pocketed the keys only to take them out to lock all doors. 'Our guns,' he said. 'I'm the one who's responsible for them. They're under the driver's seat, so keep an eye on the car.'

'*Thieves in this weather*?' came the startled retort but by then the two were negotiating the gates, and soon, even the light of their torches had been swallowed up.

Isolated the quarry was, and huge. Though they would see little, would they not perhaps feel the size of it? he wondered. The utter emptiness? Versailles was a palace but there had been other and more recent demands. As a result, a lot of stone had been removed, the face of the escarpment having been eaten away until it was now indented nearly one kilometre.

Far from flat, the floor was often stepped. There were ledges. There were still places where, in summer one could see the lines of holes, each hole two metres from all others in the line and perhaps thirty centimetres deep. These holes had been drilled by hand using hardened iron chisels and wooden mallets. The lines followed the grain of the rock so that it could be 'feathered' out by pounding hardwood pegs into the holes. The rock was then split along the lines of pegs and along the bedding surface below, a time-honoured method but one which had left the debris of some carelessness for those who would venture in at night, and in winter, to stumble over.

When the beams of their torches found the powder magazine, it stared out of the blizzard at them from under a sloping roof whose tar paper was buffeted by the wind.

The door was solid, the padlock big and tight. And the bare, unpainted boards were weathered beneath the alarmingly bullet-riddled signboard of *Explosifs. Danger, Défense d'entrer.*

'That sand in the walls must be full of lead, Louis.'

'Gabrielle and Nana came here, Hermann. How could they have done such a thing?'

They had come on the thirteenth, in preparation for the Gypsy's arrival. 'They even thought to oil the lock. Look, it's still sticky.'

The powerful stench of bitter almonds came to them. Hermann gagged and tossed his head. Hesitating, he stared at the lock in alarm, then at the key in his hand. He tried to cram his torch under an arm and get it to shine fully on the damned thing. 'Here, Louis. You hold it.'

The key went in. He bit his lower lip. He said, 'Is it really oil, or has that son of a bitch beaten us here and left us another surprise?'

Leaving the key in the lock, Hermann began to search for footprints other than their own, but it was no use. 'They couldn't have had an oil can with them, could they?' he bleated in despair, only to add, 'Beat it, eh? Go on. Take cover.'

St-Cyr reached out and, saying, 'We're in this together,' turned the key and removed the lock.

The door opened easily enough but not before Hermann had gone over and around it carefully. Light shone feebly in on wooden cases, each of which carried embossed words of *Dynamite, 25 kilos. Fifty per cent, 110 sticks.*

Each stick would be twenty centimetres in length by two and a half in diameter, and there were plenty enough of them lying in recently opened cases for one to see that the years and the heat and the humidity had been most unkind.

There were slats of wood under the tiers of cases, and straw beneath these and around them, and this straw had received the seepage.

'Louis . . .'

'Hermann . . .'

Both were speechless. It was eerie, it was terrible. Gabrielle and Nana Thélème and perhaps the Gypsy too, but later . . . later, had used a *screwdriver* to open the cases. They had actually taken handfuls of sticks, had braved the fumes, the dizziness and had been oblivious to the danger.

'Hermann . . .'

'Well, what is it?'

'Flasks of nitroglycerine, but the case is empty.'

Oh-oh. 'How many?'

'A dozen. Each of one hundred cubic centimetres.'

They stared at the flat case whose square compartments were cushioned with rubber and had each held its little wooden box. They tried to comprehend how those two women could possibly have transported such things to Paris without accident. They worried about Janwillem De Vries.

'The house on the rue Poliveau,' blurted Hermann. 'He needed nitro then.'

'But is it that he now has more than enough or is it that they held back on him and gave him only the first flask and not the others?'

Had he been here since, or had only Gabrielle and Nana paid a visit?

Braving the fumes, weeping, gagging constantly, they searched as best they could. Perhaps the freezing temperatures helped to hold off an explosion, perhaps God simply looked down on them and took pity.

The magazine was not large by such standards, and when he found a woman's handkerchief, St-Cyr knew that one of them must have dropped it by accident.

Coughing, choking, they went outside for air. Both were bent double. The fumes burned.

Weeping, they huddled over the handkerchief. 'How many cases are gone in addition to the nitroglycerine?' managed St-Cyr.

'Two, I think, and . . . and some coils of safety fuse.'

The magazine for the detonators was much smaller and was free of fumes. Here there was shelving but broken-open cardboard packets revealed blasting caps so corroded, their copper tubes, each of pencil-size in diameter and no more than three and a half centimetres in length, were encrusted with verdigris. The ones that were used with safety fuse were often stuck together. The ones that were used for electrical blasting had two thin wires protruding from the base of each cap, and often these wires were corroded at their ends.

170

It was clear that Gabrielle and Nana Thélème had searched for the best of them, clear also that they had taken sufficient.

But had the Gypsy been here since to help himself?

At 5 a.m. those who started for work in Paris did not lift their heads. The iron-hard frost of the Occupation's most hungry winter was crushing. They coughed, they wheezed painfully. Steps squeaked. The smoke from the firefly glows of occasional cigarettes did not rise, and everyone, it seemed, had the flu.

Remi Rivard let the last of the Wehrmacht's soldier boys out of the Club Mirage and began to bolt the doors.

'A moment, Remi,' hazarded a frozen voice in pitch darkness. 'Are things clear?'

Of the Gestapo? 'Perhaps.'

The Corsicans, the club's owners, were ever-wary. 'Where is Gabrielle? Her car . . .'

'It was stolen. She has had to file a *procès-verbal* and is not here. Some idiots in the Resistance took it.'

'*Pardon?*'

'You don't listen, do you? The Gypsy, you idiot. The Resistance! Now ask that frozen gumshoe brain of yours what was in her car.'

'Explosives.'

'You said it. I didn't.'

7

From the quai de Tournelle, at first light, the spires of the Church of Saint-Gervais-et-Saint-Protais were hardly visible, and the jumble of rooftops St-Cyr loved so much was a leaden, bluish-grey through which the faded green of copper sheathing made a tracery among the slate and tile.

Hermann and he had been through a lot since September 1940, but this . . . this was not even a nothing murder in which they had had to cross the SS. It was a catastrophe and no amount of fitting the pieces together could solve the thing because they had been pitted against friend and loved one and she had not confided in them.

Gabrielle had driven the Gypsy to the quarry on the very morning of the day they had gone there but had had no need of the keys. They had not even noticed the tyre marks of her car!

He thought back to that nothing murder in the first week of December last. He recalled how, at its conclusion, she had sought him out and had found him staring at the Loire as he was now staring at the Seine. He had just learned of the deaths of Marianne and Philippe. She had offered solicitude and comfort, a room in her flat, since the front of his house had been destroyed. She had wanted to get to know him better and had taken that supreme step of putting her life in his hands by confiding she would join the Resistance, but must already have been in the *réseau* and even then had hidden it from him. Ah *nom de Dieu*, what were they to do?

She had given a signed statement to the police.

The Seine seemed not to care about his or anyone else's troubles. When Kohler found him not in the nearby café as agreed but staring bleakly at the river, he steeled himself and, putting an arm about Louis's shoulders, said, 'They're holding her in a cell at the rue des Saussaies. Boemelburg is saying that since she's the only one who has had recent contact with De Vries, her life is in danger.'

That was simply Gestapo jargon for polite arrest. *Sonderbehandlung.* 'And the other two?' asked St-Cyr, not looking up from the river.

'Now under constant surveillance in hopes they'll lead them to him.'

'But . . . but they'd have been under surveillance anyway?'

'Not entirely. Not by far. Some idiot got slack, but now it's round the clock.'

Fortunately Hermann still had his inside sources at Gestapo Paris-Central, but must have paid dearly for the information. And what price exactly had he paid? His undying loyalty? His renewed oath of allegiance to those monsters? 'What of Tshaya?'

'No one knows. She's probably with De Vries. Everyone's asking what they'll do next, where they're hiding, and who's helping them.'

'And Gabrielle's car, what of it?'

'The Wehrmacht and the préfet's boys are doing another sweep of the city. All courtyards, passages, garages et cetera. She gave them a detailed list of the explosives.'

'*Freely*?' demanded Louis, his eyes full of tears.

'Freely. No torture. Not yet.'

'And who did she say the *résistants* who stole it were? She must have described them. She did, didn't she?'

'Easy, eh? Easy, *mon vieux*. The car was stopped at a road-block on their way out from the quarry. She was blindfolded. She had a pistol pointed at the back of her head. All six of them wore bandannas over their faces and carried rifles.'

'*And rucksacks too*?'

Louis was really upset. 'Look, the six of them didn't pile into that little car of hers. Only three of them did. The others stayed behind to remove the road-block. She and De Vries were driven right into the city where she alone was let out at the *métro*, at the Saint-François-Xavier station.'

'It's closed. Did they not know that? The Mabillon, Chambre des Députés, Solférino – every second station has been closed to save electricity. If you had to take the trains, you'd know!'

When Kohler didn't say anything, Louis blurted, 'Did she try to warn us, Hermann? Was that why she dropped that handkerchief?'

Was it proof she'd been there with De Vries and against her will? 'She had no choice but to take him there, Louis. He still had enough nitro with him to fragment that little car of hers.'

'And Boemelburg believed this? And Herr Max?'

'I ... I don't know. I wish I did.'

'And what about the controls? Surely they must have been stopped? Their papers ... their *laissez-passers* ...?'

'You're forgetting De Vries wore uniform. A Hauptmann ... He'd have done the talking.'

Kohler fished about in his pockets and, finding a mangled cigarette he had cadged from Giselle, broke it in two, lit up and passed one half over. 'Don't draw on it too hard, eh? Give it time. Slowly, Louis. Make it last.'

They could have been back in the front lines waiting for each other's artillery barrage to begin at dawn. 'This is what happens when those in authority decide to let criminals out of jail for purposes of their own, but you're holding back on me, Hermann. Like the river, you're keeping the corpse I need from rising.'

'They're to raid the zebra house. It's to be a combined Abwehr-Gestapo operation to show the Führer that those two organizations really can work in harmony. They'll find that wireless set.'

'Suzanne-Cécilia will be arrested, and since I have been fool enough to share my mother's house with her, I, too, will be arrested.'

A *fait accompli.*

'Giselle says she's going to kill herself and the baby by leaping from the belfries of the Notre-Dame. Oh *bien sûr*, it's the notion you'd expect from an hysterical *lorette*, not a sensible, practical girl like her, but Oona says she means it.'

The last of Louis's half of the cigarette was not saved for another time but crumbled to dust and given to the river as the offering of the desperate. 'And herself?' he asked.

'The Seine, I think. I don't know. There's another thing, Louis. Boemelburg's out for our blood. He hasn't slept, hasn't eaten. Berlin have been dinging his ears with our disloyalty. There's more talk of his being "retired" early.'

'And Herr Max?'

'Hides behind the flak knowing he's the son of a bitch who took it upon himself to let that bastard out of jail in the first place. We're what he has to have out of this, and all the rest.'

'The loot.'

'That car full of explosives. The wireless transceiver. Those three women ... What's to happen to their children, to the Countess?'

'*Why did Gabrielle not confide in us?*'

'Because I'm one of them and suspect though a friend.'

'What else is there? Come on, Hermann, give it to me.'

'Then read the headlines. Our boy's been busy in our absence.'

Kohler showed him Wednesday evening's *Paris Soir*. GYPSY STRIKES AGAIN. WEHRMACHT PAY TRAIN PLUNDERED IN THE SMALL HOURS.

Thursday's *Pariser Zeitung* hit with their own little lament but not as a headline, as an article tucked away on the back page. *Late-night break-in at villa in Saint-Cloud nets gold bars, jewels, cash, identity cards and passports.*

Both robberies had been committed on Wednesday. It was now Friday the twenty-second.

St-Cyr thrust the papers back at him. 'Like you said, he's been busy.'

'Read further. That villa was Nana Thélème's.'

'The party. Tshaya was there.'

'And must have found out where the safe was and its combination.'

'*Cyanide, dummköpfe!*' hissed Boemelburg, purple with rage. 'One hundred capsules, and now the terrorists are in possession of them!'

'The villa robbery . . .' croaked Kohler, only to be silenced by the savage lift of a fist.

'But how many are to be poisoned? All officers at the Ritz? All those at the Claridge? Who, please, is to receive one-half to one-third of a capsule?'

Never mind the threat of explosives or the loss of so much loot. Like cancer, syphilis and tuberculosis, the Occupier most feared poison, and Paris was his playground. Berlin must really be tearing their hair. 'We'll get on to it, Sturmbannführer. We'll find them.'

'Passports,' breathed Boemelburg. 'Identity cards – *Ausweise*, you idiots – and all necessary franking stamps to make the forgeries appear genuine to the most careful scrutiny. Four British Webley revolvers also, and eighty rounds – yes, eighty!'

Ah *merde* . . .

The Webley, along with the Lebel, was the Resistance's weapon. During the Defeat of 1940 God alone knew how many of them had been quickly passed from hand to hand. But the presence of the Webleys in that safe confirmed beyond doubt that the SS of Nana's villa in Saint-Cloud had been equipped for counter-subversion – for infiltrating *réseaux* by providing their infiltrators with high-quality documents and a suitable British weapon. A *Sonderkommando*, then, a special unit. Had they been helping Herr Max in this little venture? Of course they had.

Kohler had worked it all out and so had St-Cyr. Boemelburg told himself again that he had had need of these two in the past, but now? he demanded. Now what was he to do with them?

St-Cyr had taken up with the chanteuse they had put in the cellars so that she might prepare herself for honest answers. He had allowed her friend to stay in his house until the veterinary surgeon and zoo-keeper could find new accommodation.

Clandestine wireless signals had been coming from the Jardin des Plantes whose zebra house and paddock were that one's responsibility.

'Walter . . .'

'It's Sturmbannführer, damn you!'

'Forgive me. If . . . if the Gypsy had agreed to work with those of the villa in Saint-Cloud, why did he not go directly to them from Tours? Surely he had been told by Herr Max to check in with them first before he did anything?'

'That whore he's with must have let him know what happened at the party those idiots threw to kick off this insane operation. They felt its outcome a foregone conclusion but she must have told De Vries how the Spade had been using her.'

'So the couple went out on their own and began a series of robberies – is this how it was?' asked St-Cyr.

Is this what Gestapo Paris-Central believe – wasn't *that* really what Louis was asking? wondered Boemelburg. There had still been no mention of the *réseau* De Vries was to have made contact with, no confession of their knowing anything untoward had been done by those three women.

'The SS and Herr Max, the Abwehr and the Gestapo Listeners have been running a *Funkspiel*, Sturmbannführer,' said Kohler levelly. 'The Gypsy was released and probably "dropped" near Tours on the night of the thirteenth. He was then met at the railway station on the fourteenth by Tshaya because the Spade had told her to keep an eye on De Vries and to report everything he did, and everyone he met, but instead of his infiltrating the *réseau* Paris-Central and Abwehr-Paris had thought they had fingered, the two of them decided to do what they knew best and buggered off on everyone.'

'Herr Max should have confided fully in us,' said St-Cyr, grimly shaking his head. 'It's unfortunate he failed to.'

'He didn't trust us,' said Kohler accusingly. 'How could he not have told us everything, Chief?'

'Explosives,' grunted Boemelburg. 'We'll get to them in time but first, the bimonthly pay-train. 2,587,000 *Reichskassenscheine*, all in pay packets with unit designations and the names of every German officer and man in Paris and its environs. A *perfect* documentation of the whereabouts and movements of our troops here and the sizes of our garrisons!'

And at the twenty-to-one exchange rate, a further 51,740,000 francs had been stolen.

'What more valuable information to send the British by wireless?' demanded Boemelburg, toying with a pencil only to snap it in half and throw it into the metal waste basket.

'Have the Listeners had any evidence of renewed signals?' asked St-Cyr, far too quickly to hide his alarm.

A mint was found and carefully unwrapped. The question would deliberately be left unanswered. 'There were six of those grey, wooden boxes, each weighing fifty kilos and with rope handles. All had been stamped with Paymaster Kliest's insignia and padlocked by him personally in Berlin. The guards ... *Verdammt!*' Angrily Boemelburg gripped his broad forehead as if he was catching the flu. 'Those idiots left their positions to go to one of the Army's mobile soup kitchens for the midnight meal they had missed but are now digging latrines in Russia.'

When St-Cyr asked again if the wireless listeners had had any evidence of this new information having been relayed to London, Boemelburg glanced at his wrist-watch as if checking on the time of the raid on the zebra house, but continued talking of the robbery. 'That railway truck had only a simple padlock, easily broken with a hammer and chisel. All of those boxes were ready and waiting just inside the sliding door, and were quickly loaded into an ambulance. We really do not know for certain yet, but a nurse was seen – this has definitely been confirmed.'

Nurses were as common as dust in train stations these days, what with all the wounded on rest and recuperation. 'The robbery took place between 0330 and 0500 hours,' said Kohler, 'and about two hours after the explosion I accidentally set off at the Gare Saint-Lazare. He must have borrowed one of the ambulances from there.'

'He had to have had help. A great deal of help,' seethed Boemelburg. 'Now perhaps you'd both be good enough to tell me why you left Paris without my authority, to say nothing of that of Herr Max?'

'The explosives ... that blast on the rue Poliveau,' said Kohler quickly. 'We went to Tours to question the prospector about them.'

There was a sigh. 'But what led you to suspect Jacqmain knew anything of them?'

'The Gypsy had to have got them from somewhere,' said Kohler. 'He had met up with Tshaya who knew the prospector intimately. Prospectors are known to dabble with explosives, aren't they? We also thought to question Jacqmain about his dealings with the Generalmajor Wehrle, but . . .'

'Yes, yes, the prospector had shot himself which would indicate what, Hermann? What, exactly, do you think?'

Ah *Gott im Himmel*! 'That . . . that he was more deeply involved in things than we had surmised.'

'But just how deeply, Louis?'

'This we do not know, Walter. He might simply have been afraid he'd be connected to the diamonds and thus sent into forced labour or worse.'

A cautious answer. 'And what else did you uncover?'

The truth, the whole truth and nothing but it? The flypapers? The suitcase with its banknotes and flask of nitroglycerine? Gabrielle's taking it to Château Thériault and then on to Senlis with Nana and back to Paris, the two of them getting explosives for De Vries, a first visit to the powder magazines?

'A fondness for the gypsy woman, Tshaya,' said Kohler, 'and that she worked for the Spade who was after the diamonds the prospector had illegally kept.'

'As was Nana Thélème, but for the Generalmajor and the Reich,' said St-Cyr.

'The Generalmajor . . .' breathed Boemelburg.

'*What about him*?' leapt Louis, alarmed.

The Sturmbannführer studied these two in whom he had invested such patience. Louis and he had worked together with the IKPK before the war but old alliances and friendships could count for nothing. 'I want him questioned thoroughly. I want no more surprises. I want the location of those explosives and the names of the terrorists who took them. I want the cyanide capsules returned in total, and I want the hiding place of this Tshaya and her safe-cracker, and I want, yes, all those who have helped them in the slightest even though misguided they might have been.'

Gabrielle and Nana and Suzanne-Cécilia ... 'And your sense of things, Walter?'

'Is that now he'll go underground and make us wait for his next surprise.'

'Louis, why doesn't he just have us arrested and put an end to it?'

'Because he knows we're his only chance of getting the Gypsy, and because he has trusted us in the past. If he admits to having been wrong, he condemns himself. Now leave me. Let me do this myself. Please. It's for the best. We'll meet up later.'

Beneath the rue des Saussaies there was a vault, and within its sturdy iron grille, a solidly bolted door.

'St-Cyr, Sûreté, to see the prisoner Arcuri.'

The guard took his time. Ah! it was a distraction and everyone knew this Sûreté and his partner were for it. Key by key the search went on, the suit ill-fitting, the cheeks unshaven, the greeny-brown deceitful eyes full of mischief. 'Open it.'

'That is what I am trying to do. There is no hurry.'

Reluctantly the key grated in the lock, the hinges squeaked. Repeatedly a boy, a young man, cried out from somewhere until there was the sound of a wooden stave solidly cracking a tibia or femur.

'*Talk!*' came the shriek. '*Tell us where your friends are?*'

The stones were yellowish-grey, the light dim. Fresh vomit lay pooled on the steps, blood also. In a cell whose door was wide open, a skinny, rib-showing, naked human being with dark curly hair was suspended by the thumbs from a meat-hook. He had pissed himself, had shat himself, and the bastards who were his interrogators, their breath billowing in the frigid air, were stripped to the waist and *sweating*!

The guard paid the prisoner no notice, but as they passed the cell, he hawked up phlegm which he spat against the wall down which bloodied, now frozen pus had run. More steps led to another iron grille, beyond which sat one of the *Blitzmädels* from the Reich, the 'grey mice' who had come in their droves to catch a man and help out as secretaries, telegraphists and prison warders, ah so many things.

Sucking on a tooth, she surveyed the visitor with disdain. Had she seen the films of Marianne and the Hauptmann Steiner? wondered St-Cyr in dismay. Had she seen his wife fornicating with that one and crying out for more?

The laughter in the *Blitzmädel's* blue eyes reinforced his thoughts. The warder's baton indicated he was to follow. It beat upon the doors. It slammed them, and when the woman came to the far end of a corridor, she shrieked, '*Achtung, Hure. Schnell! Schnell! Aufstehen!*'

The palliasse was filthy, the cell no more than the length of the iron bed. In *deutsch* St-Cyr said, 'Leave us.'

'*Das ist verboten.*'

'Get out!'

He heard her lock the door. 'Ah *merde*,' he said and began immediately to pull off his overcoat. Tearing the filthy blanket from Gabrielle's shoulders, he wrapped the coat about her, pulled off his scarf and gloves, and made her take them. 'Forgive me,' he said, 'but I've come to take you upstairs. A few questions.'

'Nothing difficult?' she croaked but seemed to imply, You're one of them, aren't you?

A tin pail served all needs. There was 'coffee' in the morning at 5 a.m. Soup followed at noon, with perhaps fifty grams of soggy, mouldy black bread and a piece of gristle floating in the watery broth among the shredded cabbage leaves. Then at 8 p.m. there was more 'coffee', nothing else.

Seepage had formed oozing runnels of badly stained ice on the walls. High up, and with a pin or secreted carpenter's nail, someone had scratched the warning, *Silence á tout prix*. Silence at all cost.

'Jean-Louis, I've given them my statement. I don't know anything else. I was abducted. I was forced to drive him to Senlis, to a quarry nearby. It's crazy of them to keep me here. My voice . . . I've a radio broadcast tonight – it is Friday, isn't it?'

And then, a moment later when he could find no answer for her, 'They'll cancel it.'

She bowed her head to indicate the door and he turned to see the *Blitzmädel* watching their every move through the slot.

It was slammed shut as he approached it. He said aloud, '*Grâce à Dieu*,' and when he went over to sit on the edge of the bed, he pulled Gabrielle to him and let her weep. '*Courage,*' he said. 'You must have courage.'

'Walter, forgive me for intruding, but isn't it a little unwise to leave Paris's *première* chanteuse in the cellars? The General von Schaumburg, the General von Stülpnagel and yes, even the General von Paulus at Stalingrad, will all be most upset if she should lose her voice and fail to sing for the men.'

Boemelburg took his time. 'What would you suggest?' he asked warily.

'The villa at Neuilly. You keep it for your most distinguished guests. At least let her go there.'

'Then she's a suspect and you're convinced of this?'

'I . . . I'm not sure. Not yet. We need more time.'

'Those three women have been up to no good, Louis. Please don't try to shield them.'

'We don't know what, if anything, they've been up to, Walter. Is it that you *want* the whole of the OKW down on your neck?'

'The Oberkommando der Wehrmacht . . .? *Verdammt!* would you go to them? *Would you?*'

Ah *merde* . . . 'Stalingrad is all but lost, Walter. The morale of the front-line troops not only in Russia, but in North Africa, Sicily, Greece, Italy – wherever there is fighting of any kind – needs bolstering. Do you want the rage of their officers and men by *silencing* the Songbird of Montparnasse at such a time? *Certainement, mon vieux,* we've a terrible crisis on our hands but why make it greater than need be? Von Schaumburg and von Stülpnagel will know you have been telling Berlin you hold them both responsible for the explosives. The one for not finding them yet, the other for not having had them destroyed in the first place and for patently ignoring the repeated warnings of the *garde champêtre* of a little village.'

How could he say this to him? How could he? demanded Boemelburg silently. With great deliberation the quartier de l'Europe was outlined in more red crayon on the wall map behind the desk. Sector by sector the city was being searched.

'Very well, see that it's taken care of but first, Herr Max would like to sit in while you question the Arcuri woman.'

'Then let us do that at the villa. Let her have some clean clothes and a little warmth.'

'Don't try to save her, Louis. You do that and you and Kohler will go down with her.'

It was the end for them. Kohler saw Louis bring Gabrielle up from the cellars. Christ! what had they done to her? He hurried along the corridor to catch up with them but Louis signalled otherwise and soon Herr Max had joined them and they were getting into a car.

There was no hope. They were for it. Abwehr and Gestapo Paris listeners would raid the zebra house and find the wireless set and that would be it. Proof positive.

He took a breath. He tried to still his racing pulse. He said, 'At least I can tidy things up here. At least I can do that for Louis.'

The sound room was unattended. Pick-up spools turned constantly but there were no films here now, no projectors . . .

Kohler ran up the stairs and along a corridor. He took another set of stairs, sent a shower of reports from the arms of a *Blitzmädel*, and barged through the door whose hammered Gothic letters told the world this was the ARCHIV of Gestapo Paris-Central.

Morning coffee and a little tête-à-tête were disturbed. A hand was glued to a silk-stockinged knee . . .

'The films of Marianne St-Cyr and the Hauptmann Steiner. *Vite, vite, imbécile.* Von Schaumburg is demanding them again and this time it's final.'

The parasite behind the desk removed his hand. The secretary, all of forty-seven and straight from the cowsheds of Saxony, hesitantly tidied her bleached blonde hair and grey skirt.

'It's all right, Ursula. Leave me to deal with this one. Come back later and we'll finish our conference.'

'*Conference* . . .? Verdammt! *The Chief had better clean up this little nest. Fornicating, were you, behind the shelves?*'

Her cheeks grew red, her painted lips began to quiver.

Kohler ignored her and leaned on the desk she had vacated. 'Your boss is becoming too territorial,' he said darkly of Turcotte in Records. 'This used to be Glotz's domain until he was sent to

Kiev to face the partisans, at Old Shatter Hand's insistence. Now give me the films, all six copies, and all others.' Fingers were snapped.

This was Kohler of the Kripo, Kohler of the whip-scars, the prostitute Giselle le Roy and the Dutch alien, Oona van der Lynn. Two superb pieces of ass and one of them up the stump. 'Copies, Inspector? What copies, please?'

'I'm waiting,' breathed Kohler.

'Then wait. Produce the pink slip signed by Directeur Turcotte and I will carry out his instructions to the letter!'

Ah *Gott im Himmel*, this idiot was but one of the occupied!

The Walther P38 was taken out and lain on the desk with its muzzle pointing the right way.

'Accidents . . .' managed the custodian, swallowing tightly as he stared at that thing.

'They happen all too often in wartime. I've tried my damnedest to get our armourer to fix the safety on that weapon but you know how things are.'

A *Gauloise bleue* was hesitantly fingered but quickly set aside. 'Two copies were sent to Berlin. Don't ask me to whom. It was before my time.'

The lying son of a bitch! 'Hey, Gaspard – that is your name in bronze, isn't it, and bronze is needed in the Reich? – you'd better tell me or I'll help myself to your cigarettes and say the accident happened as you were taking them out of your jacket pocket. Everyone here knows too much benzedrine has made me jumpy. Everyone will tell that to your wife and kids at the funeral.'

'Herr Goebbels. He and . . . and Herr Himmler expressed an interest in viewing the films, as did Gestapo Mueller.'

Pour Louis, poor Marianne. Nothing could be done about the copies in Berlin. Uncoiling canister after canister, Kohler struck a match. '*Idiot!*' cried the custodian, darting for the metal waste basket in which to catch the ashes, such as they were.

'Now get me the negative, or whatever it's called. We wouldn't want to leave temptation up there on that shelf.'

Marianne had been a Breton. Blonde, blue-eyed and a lot younger than Louis, she'd had a gorgeous figure and yes, she had succumbed to that little love affair, had been so lonely. But all such things must come to an end. Even Giselle and Oona? he

183

asked himself, and yanking a final spool from a waiting projector, pulled out its leader to hold the film to the light and sadly shake his head. 'Gaspard, what's become of this once proud nation of yours? Such dishonesty can only bring its own reward.'

He made the bastard torch the last copy and, with the pistol pointed at his head, swear there were no others. It felt good to burn the bridges down behind himself, terrific to be rid of those films. Everyone would be thoroughly pissed off but now if only he could find Louis a bottle of pastis, a last present before the firing squad, a tin of pipe tobacco too . . .

'Oeufs à la Duchesse,' whispered Gabrielle, tears starting from her for it was the simple things in life one valued most and this . . . why this meal had far exceeded her modest request. 'Poached eggs on little rafts of potato cakes which have been baked a golden brown,' she said in fluent *deutsch*. 'The whole to receive its delicate rain of veal stock and butter. Oh *Mein Gott*, Jean-Louis, I . . .'

Bathed and wearing pyjamas and a pale blue silk dressing-down, her hair put up in a towel, she looked much better, thought St-Cyr. But at no time could he warn her that Herr Max had let the Gypsy out of jail and that what she and the others had thought was London answering at the last, had also been a *Funkspiel*, a Gestapo *Mausefalle*, a *souricière*. 'Eat,' he urged. 'The questions can wait.'

'No they can't! snapped Herr Max. Boemelburg had obviously been afraid of offending too many, and Berlin, who should have known better, had reluctantly agreed that she should be brought here. 'We haven't time. Too much is at stake.'

'Of course, but as one experienced detective to another, might I not gauge when the moment to begin is appropriate?'

'Gestapo Mueller will hear of this! I've got you and Kohler pegged, so don't forget it!'

'We could hardly do so.'

Jean-Louis sat down and took up the *procès-verbal* she had given and had signed on Thursday afternoon at the Invalides Commissariat de police on the rue de Bourgogne. Gabrielle started to eat – she would have to, she told herself. The room grew quiet. The one from Berlin lighted a cheroot but did not take his eyes from her. What was he thinking? she wondered. How much does he really know?

The Neuilly villa at the corner of the avenue Victor Hugo and the rue de Rouvray was reserved only for the most special of suspects. Surrounded by a tall fence of Louis XIV ironwork, and behind a façade of substantial pillars, its ten bedrooms, three salons, library, office, billiards- and dining-rooms came complete with a cook and his two daughters who doubled as kitchen help and chamber-maids.

A kitchen garden behind the house and a spacious lawn, with chestnut, lime and fruit trees and shrubs all round, gave ample privacy even in winter. There were guards but these were unobtrusive. 'Guests' were allowed an hour's walk out of doors and at times could even meet informally. Like the eggs, thought Engelmann bitterly, they were treated with the greatest of respect so as not to offend their respective powers that be but would such a courtesy make any difference to this one who so delicately sipped her *Moselblümchen*?

He thought not. 'Berlin are demanding answers,' he said, curtly flicking ash aside.

She set her knife and fork down and dabbed at her lips with the napkin. 'I would not have willingly reported the theft of those explosives had I been a terrorist. My car, yes – yes, of course I could have told the police only that it had been stolen. But I didn't, did I, Herr Engelmann? And I can assure you, I thought most definitely I would soon be dead.'

'A pretty speech. The Gypsy tries to kill Kohler and St-Cyr. He leaves their booby-trapped auto directly below your friend's flat yet he *lets* you go?'

'Herr Max . . .'

'VERDAMMT! *How dare you interrupt me?*'

'He . . . he said he had no quarrel with me, that I . . . I had been of great service to the . . . the cause.'

'*The cause?*'

'That . . . that is correct.'

Fists were clenched. The grey-blue little eyes darted hatred at her. 'Herr Max,' interjected St-Cyr. 'Her statement of the twenty-first is very clear on the matter. Six terrorists . . .'

'Then *bitte, meine französische Büroklammer*, ask her how the hell she knew of the quarry's location in the first place?'

185

'*I didn't*! He told me where it was. I'd never been there before. *Me*? How could you even *think* a woman such as myself would visit a place like that or even know of it?'

Verdammt, the bitch! 'He came to the Club Mirage and entered via the courtyard?' seethed Engelmann.

She swallowed hard. 'Yes, at just after the curfew had ended. I . . . I was preparing to leave for home. It's all in my statement.'

'*Mein Schatz*, I want what isn't in your statement.'

A little too quickly Gabrielle said, 'Someone must have told him where I worked and that I had the use of a car.'

Not the Thélème woman and not the veterinary surgeon, but some as yet unknown person! snorted Engelmann inwardly.

His tie was yanked down. The buttons of his blue serge waistcoat were undone, the jacket removed. Ah *nom de Jésus-Christ*! thought St-Cyr.

'So,' breathed Engelmann softly, 'a man who can steal an ambulance at will, and who can move from robbery to robbery with complete assurance, suddenly finds it necessary to have you as a driver? Surely, Fräulein, it was the Thélème woman who told him of you? At least let us have the benefit of knowing that much?'

'She . . . she hasn't seen him since before the birth of their son. You . . . you must know this as well as myself. You have questioned her, haven't you?'

Alarmed, Jean-Louis was about to intervene. Was there no way she could stop him?

'And Tshaya, his woman?' breathed Engelmann. 'Was she not with him when you drove the Gypsy to Senlis to get the explosives?'

She would have to eat a little to calm Jean-Louis. 'Blame me if you wish, but I will not hide the truth. He said she was not well. The flu, I think.' She took another bite.

'And he forced you to drive him at what? Gunpoint?'

'Yes. Tshaya had told him of the quarry. A client of hers, a prospector, had told her where his explosives were kept.'

It was all lies, thought St-Cyr. More and more of them were being piled up yet she seemed unaware of this.

She was tall and statuesque, said Engelmann to himself, and at the Club Mirage the troops avidly listened to her, but that

186

could so easily be a screen behind which to hide a *Terroristin*. 'Was that where he got the dynamite he boiled at the house on the rue Poliveau?'

Her lovely eyes widened with innocence. 'It must have been.'

'But you didn't drive him to the quarry that time.'

'No. No, I didn't.'

'Yet he must have got at least a case of dynamite then.'

She shrugged. Her napkin fell to the floor and as she bent to retrieve it, she said, 'Perhaps, but I really wouldn't know.'

Ah *mon Dieu, mon Dieu* . . . swore St-Cyr silently, it was coming now. Herr Max would grab her by the hair. He'd bring the glowing end of that cheroot to her face and what will I do? he demanded. Kill him quickly. I'll have to.

'Senlis,' muttered Engelmann. 'You and Nana Thélème went there on the thirteenth, a day before De Vries arrived in Paris. You dropped into the Luftwaffe base near Conflans-Sainte-Honorine for lunch – it's all on record – and were given a tour of the clubhouse and aerodrome.'

Ah *non!* panicked St-Cyr. Gabrielle said nothing. She just seemed to tighten up. A hand was lightly pressed to her stomach. 'A concert,' she said at last but it was clear she was afraid. 'A benefit Nana and I are to give on the thirtieth. We . . . we were asked there by the commanding officer of the base, the Oberstleutnant Ritter Koenen. Could we have refused his very kind invitation?'

Paris's venerable yacht club, the Cercle Violier, had a rambling old clubhouse, some eighty guest cabins and a fabulous collection of wooden scale models, the original mock-ups of famous racing yachts, and a fortune in silver cups. But had Suzanne-Cécilia sent over information of that base to London? worried St-Cyr, concluding sadly that she must have and that Herr Max had simply been confirming what the Gestapo's and the Abwehr's listeners had told him.

'We went on to Senlis to visit the mother of Monsieur Jacqmain, only to find she had passed away. On our return, we brought the prospector's daughter to Paris. She's staying with Nana while we see if it is possible for her to remain in the city. The General von Schaumburg has most kindly agreed to intercede on her behalf.'

187

'So, two trips to Senlis after all,' grunted Engelmann. 'One with the Fräulein Thélème on the thirteenth, and the other with the Gypsy yesterday morning.'

'Yes.'

'And you knew nothing of Janwillem De Vries until he forced you to drive him to that quarry?'

'No, that is incorrect. Nana had told me of him but I had not met him until then.'

More lies, thought St-Cyr grimly. Gabrielle *had* to have met De Vries when he arrived in Paris on the fourteenth. She *must* have given him details of Cartier's for the robbery on the night of the eighteenth. And what of the schedule at the Gare Saint-Lazare's ticket office? he wondered bleakly. She must have stood in line to get details of that safe and the deposits, or had it been Suzanne-Cécilia or Nana, or all three of them? The same, too, for the pay-train.

Herr Max continued to study her in silence, she to resist all urge to move only to suddenly break and abruptly get up to look out of the windows and down into the kitchen garden.

Jean-Louis will die, she said to herself. Hermann will die – all of us – but I cannot give in. I must not break. Everything had seemed so straightforward. The Gypsy was to have been taken to Château Thériault once he had finished the targets they had lined up for him in Paris, but the *réseau* had been plunged into something they had not anticipated in the slightest and Janwillem De Vries had left them totally out in the cold.

'Reinforced interrogations, Fräulein,' said Herr Max. 'Those are used only when all else fails.'

She didn't flinch.

'Herr Max, a moment,' interjected St-Cyr. 'A handkerchief was dropped in the powder magazine as a warning to us. Clearly Fräulein Arcuri felt she would not survive the trip.'

'The Gypsy's mad – insane,' she said, turning to angrily face them. 'He said he was going to leave me *there* for Jean-Louis and Hermann to find, that he *wanted* to kill them. "Those two," he said. "They're the only ones I have to fear. The others are nothing." He ... he had been told to be especially wary of them, I think, and ... and yes, to kill them.'

Her eyes were wiped with the corner of a sleeve. 'Forgive me,' she said. 'You see the state I'm in. He was very definite about

188

what he wanted and, in spite of the powerful smell from the dynamite – I was soon sick at my stomach and had to go outside – he *forced* me to help him. *Explosives*, Herr Engelmann! *Nitroglycerine*! A *woman*!'

'Yes, yes, but did he give any hint of his plans?'

'His plans?' she shrilled in despair and tossed her hands. 'The Kommandantur perhaps? The Opéra during a performance, since so many of the seats are taken up by members of the Reich. The rue des Saussaies itself ... Who knows really what he and his friends will do?'

'The "friends". Describe them please.'

'It's ... it's all written down there, is it not?' She pointed to her statement only to hear him snort and brutally say, 'Just tell us.'

Momentarily she shut her eyes to squeeze the tears from them, then blurted, 'All right. Though they wore bandannas, I ... I did see something I forgot to write down. They were swarthy. Their skin was like those of the Midi so at the time I thought nothing of it, you understand, but now must think they ... they were gypsies.'

'There aren't any of them left. They've all been deported.'

'Not all. Tshaya wasn't. There ... there is another thing, though I'm certain he told them not to speak Romani, one let slip the word *Gaje*.'

'Six terrorists,' muttered Engelmann.

'But others, perhaps. Ah! I had forgotten. They did speak of piano concerts and that they would have to move their piano to another location and quickly. This has puzzled me greatly, as a singer, you understand.'

'Their piano,' said Engelmann darkly, and getting up, he started for her.

'Their wireless transceiver!' interjected St-Cyr. 'It's terrorist talk. We ... we had best warn the Sturmbannführer, otherwise the ...'

The raid, Jean-Louis? Is this what you were about to say? wondered Gabrielle, sickened by the thought.

'The telephone?' demanded Engelmann.

'Downstairs in the Sturmbannführer's study,' said St-Cyr. 'There's another in the corridor.'

Engelmann motioned for Jean-Louis to leave and once the two

189

of them were out in the hall, he closed the door and Gabrielle heard him lock it.

A raid . . . Suzanne-Cécilia, she silently pleaded, be brave, *ma chère*. Do it because you have to! You must!

And biting her knuckles to stop herself from completely going to pieces, sat down heavily to await the end.

The raid on the wireless set had been moved up. Kohler had been taken along. Helplessly he watched as Suzanne-Cécilia Lemaire tried to make a run for it. Others scattered in the Jardin des Plantes, others shrieked. Shots were fired.

She hit the ground, was dragged up, cried out, *'No . . . No, you don't understand!'* and was thrown against the bandstand, was pinned to the wall below its railing – was slammed, hit hard. Blood poured from her nose and broken lips. Shock registered in her dark brown eyes.

'Hure!' shrieked the SS-Untersturmführer in charge. *'Terroristin!'*

Bang, bang, her head hit the wall. *'Cochon!'* she spat, only to be struck again. *'I've done nothing but what I should have. Nothing!'*

Ah *merde* . . . 'A moment . . .' managed Kohler.

'READ IT!' shrieked the Untersturmführer, his pistol drawn.

Her white surgical smock had been torn open. Blood was spattered down it. There was more blood on the cable-knit, grey-blue sweater. The white Peter Pan collar of the blouse she wore had flecks of it too.

'Okay, okay, I'm reading,' he said. Ah *Gott im Himmel* the racket was really something. Every animal and bird was terrified, every person. Another burst from a Schmeisser was followed by pistol shots and screams. An old man with a beard and briefcase had been hit. Jewish . . . was he Jewish? Had he been in hiding?

Suzanne-Cécilia caught a breath. Frantically her eyes searched for escape. *'Don't even think of it,'* he shouted at her. 'They've surrounded the Jardin and have sealed it off.'

The directive from Section IVF, the Gestapo's wireless listeners in France, was damning.

GEHEIM

ACHTUNG! RUNDFUNKSENDER ZEBRA GESENDET FOLGENDES 1310 PARIS JARDIN DES PLANTES UBER 6754 KILOCYCLES. (Attention!

190

Wireless sender Zebra sends following 1310 hours ... transmitting at ...)

MOST URGENT. REPEAT URGENT, MUST BREAK OFF ALL CONTACT.

Merde! why had she done it? Why hadn't she simply left the set silent?

Kohler looked up to see her struggling to get free of two Waffen-SS twice her size. The zebra paddock was just to the north of the bandstand, the jackals and hyenas to his right. Wehrmacht lorries and half-tracks, Gestapo cars and SS vehicles were scattered about. An MG42 had been set up. Twelve hundred rounds a minute and for what, for one defiant woman with thick shoulder-length auburn hair that was now gripped so hard in the fist of the Occupier, she winced in pain?

Rapidly her chest rose and fell. Suddenly she tried to get away again. One of the Waffen-SS drove a fist into her diaphragm so hard, she dropped to her knees in panic at the sudden loss of breath. The butt of his Schmeisser was raised. Kohler cried out, 'AUFHÖREN, IDIOT. *Stop! She may be able to tell us what we need.*'

They dragged her up. Her chest heaved. She glared at the Untersturmführer with nothing but hatred. A fierce little *résistant*. A bantam, a terrorist who, at the house on the rue Poliveau, had blurted, 'No one told me this would happen.' No one ... Not Gabrielle and not Nana Thélème.

The Untersturmführer Schacht cocked his pistol and pressed its muzzle to her forehead. Her bloodied lips began to move in silent prayer. The greatcoat and cap, with silver skull and crossbones, were immaculate. Schacht was clean-cut, blond, blue-eyed and all the rest, the giver of that drunken party at Nana Thélème's former villa in Saint-Cloud, the head of the *Sonderkommando* Herr Max had used to set up this whole bastard operation. Everything about him said she'd suffer. Afraid for her, terrified for her, Kohler dropped his eyes to the remainder of the directive and began, again, to silently read it.

THIS WIRELESS MESSAGE WAS PRECEDED AT 1257 HOURS BY AN URGENT TELEPHONE CALL TO THE COMMISSARIAT DE POLICE ON THE AVENUE GEOFFROY-SAINT-HILAIRE, SAID REQUEST BEING IMMEDIATELY RELAYED TO THE WEHRMACHT BOMB-DISPOSAL UNIT AT CHARENTON.

A suburb about four kilometres upriver, but why had she called them? *Why?*

The contents of the telephone call followed: COULD SOMEONE PLEASE COME? I THINK THERE IS A BOMB IN MY ZEBRA HOUSE. THE ANIMALS ARE VERY RESTLESS AND THE GATE IS WIRED SHUT IN THE STRANGEST WAY.

Another bomb . . .

The jackals grinned, the hyenas skulked. Heavily armed troops and SS were mopping up – herding everyone not of the Occupier to the amphitheatre where all papers would be thoroughly checked and the sieve shaken so hard, they'd soon sort things out.

'She usually transmits at 0150 hours and now only on Fridays,' said Schacht, having left off his pistol-pointing but not having holstered the weapon.

'What makes you think it was her?'

The grin the Untersturmführer gave reminded Kohler of the jackals.

'We've been on to the slut since November and now our little mouse has made her final move.'

'She breaks off contact but first rings in an alarm? Is that what this thing is saying?' He shook the directive.

Kohler was a part of it. Kohler and that partner of his would try everything they could to shield the terrorists. Their arrests were imminent.

Schacht tapped him on the chest with the pistol's muzzle. 'It proves the Gypsy and the Tshaya woman are still working with the female terrorists and not independently as you and that partner of yours claim.'

There wasn't any sense in arguing. De Vries must have forced her to make the telephone call and then to send the wireless message as he set the charges. The son of a bitch was still playing with them. Two flasks of nitro . . . had he used that much, or was the timer wired to a case of that leaky dynamite? The blasting cap would be so corroded in any case, it would go off at the heat of probing fingers, ah damn.

A copper wire could be seen cutting across the paddock at shoulder height from the gate to the zebra house, a distance of about twenty metres. Had De Vries *wanted* them to see it?

'We'd better look for what else he's left,' breathed Kohler.

'That's already been done.'

'Then why did he leave us a warning if not to slow us down so that he could make his getaway?'

'All surrounding streets are being watched. If he makes a break for it, he'll be caught and killed.'

'*Killed*? But what about the loot, what about the cyanide, the dynamite, the nitro . . .?'

Berlin had ordered it – Kohler could see this in the bastard's eyes. 'What about the other terrorists then?' he demanded.

'We'll get them. Now go in there and defuse that bomb for us. That also is an order from Berlin.'

There was a signboard on the wall of the bandstand where, in summer, concerts were given *Courtesy of the Society for the Prevention of Cruelty to the Beasts of the Wild. Concerts! Der Westen Wald?* he wondered. *Deutschland Über Alles . . .* or Wagner from Wehrmacht brasses to soothe the lions and tigers?

'*My zebras?*' cried out Suzanne-Cécilia Lemaire, struggling to get free. '*They will be blown to pieces, messieurs!*'

The stench of urine-soaked straw and zebra dung was pungent. Trampled snow covered the ground. The copper wire was looped around the gate, and as he tried to get a focus on it, Koher realized it had to have been her aerial. At least twenty-five metres would have been needed. She must have strung it from the zebra house to the fence every Friday at just before 0150 hours. London . . . Calling London . . .

The Laboratory of Physiology was a shambles. Displays which had once illustrated the life cycles of newts, worms, ants and tropical fish et cetera, had all been wrecked in the search for her wireless. Pale and shaken, Suzanne-Cécilia stood with her back to tall windows, between cages of snakes too poisonous for the searchers to touch.

But had she chosen that place by design? wondered St-Cyr and thought it likely. Specimens from Australia of the taipan, *Oxyuranus scutellatus,* and of the death adder, *Acanthophis antarcticus,* lay immediately to her right; that of the water moccasin of Louisiana and the Mississippi Delta to her left – the cottonmouth, *Agkistrodon piscivorus.*

The cages had but simple catches. Here the public would have been kept at distance for there was a bronze railing which separated the displays from the visitors' area but allowed her, or an assistant, to give illustrated talks.

Dragonflies and moths had all been trampled. Their glass display cases were shattered, their fragile wings torn to pieces.

Among the wreckage, a large praying mantis, still with its silver-headed mounting pin, waited as if for a meal. A mouse of some kind suddenly darted by it. When a python appeared, there was a little cry from Suzanne-Cécilia. Gently she gathered the snake in and let it drape about her neck and shoulders.

'They will find nothing, Inspector. Why will they not believe me? It's crazy this talk of my sending secret messages to London. How could I have done such a thing?'

He didn't answer. What could he have said since they both knew it was a lie?

Herr Max had joined Boemelburg and the SS-Untersturm-führer Schacht in urgent discussion. Walter was aware that Hermann had gone into the zebra house some time ago – everyone was acutely aware the bomb had yet to go off and that Hermann must still be fiddling with it.

A timer? wondered St-Cyr. Hidden tripwires among the hooves of restless beasts? Hermann knew and loved horses but would zebras respond to those same calming words, that same touch? A farmboy always. Ah *merde alors*, be careful, he said silently. Giselle and Oona need you and so do I.

A spider monkey flitted about. As it avoided the brutality of the searchers, it would leap from wreckage to wreckage, chatter-ing excitedly at each new onslaught of debris, bitching, screech-ing as floorboards were probed and sometimes ripped up.

'I would call it to me, Inspector,' said Suzanne-Cécilia, the concern in her voice all too evident, 'but must comfort Caesar. Joujou can't stand to be near Caesar. It's understandable.'

'*Joujou*' he blurted. 'Not *the* Joujou from the carousel in the Parc des Buttes Chaumont?'

'The same. Its former owner was arrested for murder, I think.'

There was a nod, the quivering of memories too painful to bear. 'The Gestapo of the rue Lauriston and the SS of the avenue Foch were involved in that affair also.'

Was it a warning of things to come? 'Then you're old friends,' she said, resigned to despair.

194

She stroked the python. It welcomed the warmth of her body, and when she laid it on the radiator that was beneath the windows, the thing languidly stretched out and she was again free to snatch a viper from one of the cages. 'Please don't,' he begged and heard her say, 'I will if I have to.'

The flask of nitroglycerine was delicately balanced on a board that rested loosely between two cross-beams some five metres above the tethered zebras. When Kohler finally reached it, his fingers trembled so much, he didn't dare try to remove it.

The Gypsy had run the wire from the board to, and over, a nail high in the wall. From there, it ran down the wall but out from this by about ten centimetres and to another nail. When fully and sharply opened, the door was to suddenly have struck the wire which would have yanked the board away and allowed the flask to hit the paving stones below.

He shut his eyes and said, 'Ah *Gott im Himmel*, I can't take much more of this.' He was all alone up in the gods and freezing under the thatch roof. Unused to being constrained, the zebras were highly nervous and yes, they had had to be tethered. Otherwise the Gypsy couldn't have put the nitro where he had.

Gingerly Kohler lifted the flask away and when he had it tightly in hand, he began to ease himself downwards, but hooves struck the floor, hindquarters were squeezed and rubbed against the ladder. He felt the damned thing being tilted beyond control and cried out, '*Easy*, my honeys. Easy, eh?'

In unison all fourteen of them swung sharply to the right. In panic, he shoved the flask into a pocket only to think better of this as the ladder began to tilt a little more . . . a little more.

The book was among the references in the surgery. From where he stood, St-Cyr could see Suzanne-Cécilia in the other room. With the python draped behind her, she was like a goddess torn from the pages of Greek mythology. She was under guard, but the young Gefreiter was afraid of snakes and did not know, really, what to make of her.

She had refused to 'witness' the destruction of a surgery that could, if necessary, attend wounded German soldiers. 'That bomb, messieurs,' she had said. 'Have you forgotten it? Please do not rip up the floorboards of what you may well need. You will find nothing, I assure you.'

Nothing . . . But she, too, could see him, and he knew then that she had so positioned herself not simply because of the snakes. The book had been left high on a shelf above her desk, a tragic oversight in the rush of all the things she must have had to do.

In 1893, Félix-Marie Delastelle had published *La Cryptographie Nouvelle*, his new system of cryptography which was, at the beginning of this war, still far superior to the Playfair system of the British. It took the Playfair square of the alphabet, which was arranged five letters by five and with the I and the J both falling in the same place, but added the numbers 1 and 5 along the top and left-hand side of the square so that co-ordinates could be assigned to each letter.

The message was then written out in plain text and broken into groups of five letters whose co-ordinates were written down vertically under each of the letters.

To encode a message, these co-ordinates were then read horizontally which gave different letters and different groups of five letters, which were then sent in Morse.

To decode a message one simply reversed the operation.

Two men were searching the text. They were being very thorough but impatient, Boemelburg having told them the Reich would have to compensate the City of Paris for the damages if nothing untoward was found.

Frantically St-Cyr looked about the surgery. One of the Waffen-SS was going through her thin stock of medicines. Another was reaching into a cabinet where surgical gauzes and bandages were kept. A bottle of disinfectant fell over. *'Be careful, idiot!'* shouted the SS-Untersturmführer Schacht.

The book remained on its shelf. If only there was some way of getting it out of sight . . .

When next he looked, Suzanne-Cécilia had again taken up the python. She was going to use it to distract her guard so that she could reach into one of the cages. She knew how afraid the boy was of snakes. She was letting him see her cradle the python's head, was stroking it, was now holding it out to him as he backed away . . .

'RAUS! RAUS! *Get out! Get out! Clear the area! Nitro!'*

196

Hermann had a flask in hand, Ah *merde*, he looked old and grey and badly shaken.

The others ran. They left the surgery. Quickly St-Cyr snatched the book from the shelf and tucked it into a pocket. Hurriedly rejoining her, he said gently, 'Come. Please come. Leave that death adder alone, eh?' And letting her put the python back on the radiator, took her firmly by the arm. 'It's not necessary you kill yourself. Not yet, but where, exactly, have you hidden it?'

'Hidden *what*, please?' she asked with complete candour. 'My life is an open book, Inspector, as you can well see.'

Outside the Laboratory of Physiology, Hermann was putting the flask into the Untersturmführer's hands. None of the others had stayed around.

8

At 6 p.m. the distant tolling of the Bibliothèque Nationale's bell thudded on the cold, hard air in darkness. Strains of Greta Keller singing *'Eine Kleine Reise'* – 'Just a Little Ramble' – filtered out on to the rue du Faubourg-Saint-Honoré. A staff car drew up. A quiet, 'Later, Friedrich. An hour,' was given, and the car, like a wraith, pulled softly away and into the *vélo*-crowded, pedestrian-filled night.

Others came. The traffic in and out was intermittent. Most arrived on foot to slip as unobtrusively as possible through the darkened entrance above whose double doors a faint blue light shone.

Studio Pleyel No. 6. Tango, waltz, etc., and all the latest ballroom dances. Madame Jeséquel, Professeur Diplômé et Mademoiselle Nana Thélème, danseuse électrique de flamenco.

Edith Piaf sang *'Parlez-moi d'amour'*, a recording, and then, as Kohler went up the stairs ahead of Louis, *'L'Étranger'*, a song about a man with dreamy eyes who was very gentle and with gold in his hair and the smile of an angel! *Verdammt!* no Schmeissers, eh? No jackboots? he snorted inwardly. No Gypsy either!

Round and round the dance floor the couples circled. Stiff-

197

backed Prussian generals with monocles, colonels, majors, Luftwaffe fighter pilots, Kriegsmarine U-boat captains; corporals, sergeants and noncoms, all looking painfully uncomfortable and very out of place. *Mein Gott*, it was a cross-section. Franz Breker of the Deutsche Institut was here, also Hugo Krause of the Militärbefehlshaber in Frankreich, Weber of the Kommandantur and Ilse Unger of the Propaganda Staffel. Wealthy industrialists and big black marketeers had joined them, minor Vichy politicians too, and financiers.

There were perhaps sixty students, mostly male but with a sprinkling of *Blitzmädels* and other females of the Occupier. Not nearly enough instructresses were available. Some of the clients did have to wait in the wings and dutifully watch as Nana Thélème and Madame Jeséquel gracefully moved among the dancers, getting those big Boches' feet right, male or female.

The old, the grey, the fat, the thin – most were a head and shoulders above the *petites Parisiennes* with the flashing dark brown eyes who wore woollen frocks and double sweaters, thick woollen stockings under ankle socks and the ever-present wooden-soled high-heels with their imitation leather uppers.

The hands of the instructresses were clad in fingerless gloves because, even with all the exercise, the studio was freezing.

'Inspectors, to what do I owe this intrusion?'

Madame Jeséquel was in her late forties. Tall, thin and supple, and with her greying jet black hair pinned into a tight chignon, she was made-up, and the dark brown, olive eyes were hard in resolve but wary.

Nana had stopped to look across the floor at them. Her height, her shoulders, eyes and jet black hair – the very way she stood – were the same.

'Inspectors, am I not to be granted an answer or are you so struck by my daughter's likeness to me, you have lost the power of speech?'

A tough one, she had once been a promising ballet dancer but the former child out on the floor had ended that career. A 'bayonet divorce' had come early in 1914 and ever since then she had run this studio.

'Your daughter,' said Kohler. 'We have to talk to her.'

'Then wait. Don't embarrass us. Hang up your coats and hats. Take a girl. Learn a little so as to silence all questions.'

They've come for me, said Nana Thélème to herself in despair. It's over. 'Loosen up a little, Colonel. Try not to cling so much.'

Somehow she managed to smile and to laugh a little, but had they finally met her in all of her guises? wondered St-Cyr. Gypsy singer, mother of the son of Janwillem De Vries, finder of diamonds for the Reich, hauler of explosives, purchaser of flypapers and member of a *réseau*, two of whom were now incarcerated in the Neuilly villa of Gestapo Boemelburg.

Foster mother to the daughter of Tshaya and the Gypsy.

Nana was nearly as tall as her partner and, as the couple circled about the floor, she did it effortlessly but what, really, was running through her mind?

My purse, she said to herself, passing near to them. Will they search it and find the revolver, or can I get to it before they do?

Suzanne-Cécilia had been taken this afternoon. Gabrielle had been arrested yesterday. Everything was falling in on them. They had not realized what had really been going on. They had stupidly thought they could pull it off. Idiots that they had been, they had not thought Janwillem would go against them, but had thought only of what they could contribute to the cause.

'Inspectors, what is it you want of me?'

She had broken off her dancing to stride through the couples. In rapid Spanish she said, 'Mother, *don't*! You're not involved. Stay out of it. We'll go into the office.'

'What have you done, Isabella?'

'*Nothing*, idiot! Stay here and teach. Do what you've always done. *Don't* interfere.'

'You fool. I warned you to stay away from Janwillem but you wouldn't listen. He's never been any good for you and now . . . now what am I supposed to do? Bury the daughter I sacrificed my life for and raise your son as I raised you?'

Nana stamped a foot. 'Mother, *please*, I'm begging you. Leave it. You've already said too much.'

In French the woman said, 'When my daughter was nine, I sent her to live with my father and my brothers in Córdoba so that she could learn to dance and sing. Now look how she repays me!'

The recording changed. Maurice Chevalier sang '*Boum!*'. Nana closed the door to the tiny, cluttered office where billboard posters and press photographs announced her début at the Schéhérazade in 1924.

'Inspectors, what am I supposed to do? Lead you to Janwillem when I don't even know where he is and he won't have anything to do with me?'

Was she still being evasive, or had Gestapo Paris bugged the room? 'You're our only link,' said Kohler.

'We have to find him,' pleaded St-Cyr. 'Someone has to be helping him, not just Tshaya.'

They had come for her and she could see it in their eyes. 'And you think it's me?'

'Exactly how much did the Generalmajor Wehrle tell you of the Reich's need for diamonds?' sighed St-Cyr.

'*Nothing*! How could he have? Hans had security clearances you'd be *proud* to carry.'

Seizing a scrap of paper, he scribbled, *Did you relay even that information to London?*

Her eyes leapt. '*How could I have? Merde*, you're fools! We had a working relationship, that was all. Hans paid me to help him buy diamonds from those who had hidden them away.'

Even this would have been intelligence the British could have used. Kohler hauled her out of the office and into the music. 'He knew everything about our needs for diamonds. That's one of the reasons Berlin are so concerned. Now give, before it's too late.'

'Then why not ask him? Why not bring us face to face and let him tell you how wrong you are!'

She would get her scarf and coat. She would tell them nothing further since they looked as if ready to arrest her.

She would try to reach the revolver in her purse.

When she went to get her handbag, Kohler was ahead of her and picked it up. '*Merci*,' she said as she snatched it from him, but had he felt the weight of it, had he realized what it must contain? 'Now, please, a moment to say goodbye to that kindest and wisest of women. The bane of my existence, but the heart and soul of my life.'

The caviar and the champagne, the Taittinger 1934, were the same: untouched as if waiting yet again for the couple to get together. But a celebration for what reason this time? wondered Engelmann.

Seen from the balcony, the surface of the Ritz's swimming pool was mirror calm. Wehrle's body, clad in navy blue bathing trunks, floated face down in the centre to throw its darkened shadow on the decorative tiles below.

'So, Fräulein Thélème, perhaps you would be good enough to explain this sudden turn of events.'

Engelmann was going to kill her. He knew she was hiding things he had to have. 'Did he take a cramp?' she asked, her voice barely audible. 'He was a strong swimmer. I . . . I have no idea why he should have drowned.' Dear God, please help her . . .

Lies . . . it was all lies, he thought. Kohler and St-Cyr stood warily on either side of the woman, each trying to anticipate what must happen and what the other would do to prevent it. Kohler had her by the left arm. Her hands were deep in the pockets of that fancy overcoat of hers. The collar was up. There was no hat this time. Her handbag was clamped under the left arm.

St-Cyr had taken a step away from her so as to be free and ready should the need arise, and it would. *Büroklammern*, both of them. *Klötze* who should by rights be redeeming themselves by shoving that pretty head of hers under water to make her talk.

'Berlin,' he mused, fingering the table settings to see that everything was exactly in its place, and wasn't that what was needed? he wondered. An order to things. 'Fräulein, he had been recalled. The telex . . . Ah! I have it here. He left it beside the pool with the wineglass he used. "Suspected terrorists . . . an association with one of them. Possible breaches of security . . . *Questions*" your Generalmajor could not bring himself to face.'

Ah Christ! swore Kohler silently.

'*Why did he order this little repast*?' shrieked Engelmann, filling the air with the sound of his voice.

In panic, she blurted, 'I . . . I've no idea. We were not supposed to meet. I . . . I haven't seen Hans since . . . since the night of the robbery.'

There had to be a gun in that purse of hers, thought Kohler. *Don't*! he silently prayed. Engelmann will have brought help.

'"You haven't seen him,"' said Herr Max. 'A correction is

201

necessary, Fräulein. You have not seen him since the night you gave Janwillem De Vries the key to the suite and told him where to find the combination.'

'No! Why are you still trying to accuse me of such a thing?'

She was quivering. 'Then why did you say, "Not supposed to meet?" Please explain this.'

She must try to kill herself. She *couldn't* let him force her to tell them the truth. 'I meant only that we had not arranged a meeting. I thought Hans had returned to the Reich.'

'To see his wife and children.'

'Yes.'

Below them, around the pool and under subdued lighting, there were deck chairs among the Grecian columns. The wineglass Wehrle had drunk from was with his towel at the poolside, the Beaujolais half gone. 'I'm going to ask you once more. Why would he have ordered this only to leave it untouched to take his life?'

The grip she had on her handbag tightened.

'Herr Max, shouldn't we examine the body?' asked St-Cyr anxiously.

'Was it strychnine that killed him, or was it potassium cyanide?' demanded Engelmann swiftly of the Sûreté.

Merde . . . 'Cyanide is very rapid. Strychnine would have taken longer – from five to twenty minutes on average, sometimes an hour or two or even more,' said St-Cyr, watching him closely.

'There'd have been time enough for the attendant to have pulled him out,' interjected Kohler hurriedly. 'A doctor could have been summoned.'

The champagne bottle was removed from its ice-bucket. 'But one wasn't,' sighed Engelmann as he began to untwist the wire that held the cork in. 'Instead, there was an agony so great, Fräulein, it shot needles through his heart. He panicked – anyone would have. Repeated seizures were so violent, he thrashed about and frequently went under.'

Please, she silently begged. Let me kill myself and take you with me.

'His eyes bulged,' went on Engelmann, his thumbs easing the cork out. 'He tried to scream but took in water. He did not know what was happening to him.'

'*All right, all right! He had fallen in love with me!*'

The cork flew into the pool. Champagne foamed down over Engelmann's hands. 'You betrayed him.'

'I *didn't*! I tried my best to avoid his advances. I meet many men, some of whom become infatuated with me. They're lonely. It's only natural but . . .'

'But he was different. He was the target.'

'*No! There was none of that!*'

She was frantic. 'Please remove your coat and gloves. Take off your shoes and sweater.'

'Herr Max, a moment,' interjected St-Cyr. 'De Vries has had no contact with her. He blames her for putting him in the Mollergaten-19 in '38.'

'Janwillem was very angry,' she cried. 'He wanted revenge and you . . . you . . .'

'Ah! And what did I do, Fräulein? I who know so little of him?'

As champagne filled a glass, her dark eyes glistened with tears. Her handbag was now on top of her coat and accessible.

'Drink this,' he said.

Sickened, she frantically glanced about for escape. 'I . . . I don't know why Hans would do this to me,' she said of the champagne and the caviar. 'Was he trying to implicate me in something?'

'How cheated he must have felt,' breathed Engelmann. 'Just like Janwillem De Vries.'

Swiftly she smashed the glass he had handed her. Blood ran from her fingers as she clutched the stem and used it to keep him away. Desperately she tried to get at her purse but others ran up the stairs from the poolside, others crowded in on them, tearing Kohler from her, slamming her against a pillar.

St-Cyr fought to get clear of them. A table collapsed beneath him, a chair went over. Seized, yanked up from the floor, his revolver was torn from him and he was held at gunpoint.

She wept as her purse was opened. Frantically she shrilled, '*Janwillem sent that to me! It's one of those he took from the Gare Saint-Lazare.*'

'And the others? Where are they?' shrieked Engelmann.

'*I don't know. I really don't! Can't you see he was trying to implicate me too? Ah damn him, damn him! Why must he hate me so?*'

*

The leg of venison had been laced with salt pork and marinated in dry white wine with bay leaves, peppercorns, savory and onions. Drained, it had been roasted for an hour at a medium heat and then for fifteen minutes at a high heat, after which brandy had been poured over it and set aflame.

Brandy as if at a dinner party! and here they were, the two of them, dining with Gestapo Boemelburg in his villa as though nothing had happened and their lives were not in jeopardy. And what was to become of them? fretted Gabrielle anxiously. Suzanne-Cécilia, her nose all but broken and her lips split and swollen, sat across the table from her. Dressed in borrowed evening gowns and wearing diamonds that had, no doubt, been stolen from deported Jews, did they appear to him to be defenceless, demure, sophisticated, poised or just so damned afraid, they could hardly bring themselves to face him?

The Sturmbannführer had come to the château to witness the conclusion of that nothing murder which had brought Jean-Louis and her together. But now, she asked as her plate was set before her, now what was to happen to them all?

'Enjoy,' said Boemelburg, gruffly indicating the roast. 'Try the sauce. You'll find it superb.'

Furious with them and with how things had gone, he had to ask himself what he was to make of these two? Von Schaumburg and von Stülpnagel were yelling their heads off about the dynamite and the cyanide capsules; Oberg, Head of the SS in France, was demanding an immediate end to things, as was Gestapo Mueller in Berlin. Everyone wanted the loot. Everyone was being greedy. He'd be the laughing stock of Paris and of Berlin if the débâcle continued and the Gypsy escaped.

'One would have thought you would have left well enough alone and kept out of trouble,' he grumbled, referring to the murder.

'But I *have*, Sturmbannführer,' replied Gabrielle earnestly. 'Every night until five o'clock in the morning I sing for your troops. I do it out of loyalty and the goodness of my heart. They'll have missed me. Personally I hope they will not be too upset and that their morale will still be cheered on by my recordings.'

Verdammt! how could she persist? 'Don't tamper with me,

Mademoiselle Arcuri. It's serious. You've been under surveillance for some time.'

What did he want from her? A full confession over dinner with her throwing up all over the place? 'It wasn't right of your people to have bugged my dressing-room at the club.' They hadn't been following her, too, had they?

Sauce dribbled from his fork. 'Wireless signals were being picked up repeatedly and not just by Gestapo Paris.'

'*Pouf!*' exclaimed Suzanne-Cécilia. '*Quelle folie*, Sturmbann-führer! They found nothing – *nothing*, you understand, and yet they still persist in accusing me? Why did they not ask of the comings and goings I and our gatekeeper have heard at night? Oh *bien sûr*, some do try to find a place to bed down. Are we to have thrown those poor unfortunates out at such an hour and in such terrible weather?'

'Transients?' he asked, bemused.

'*Exactement!*' she exclaimed, blood trickling from her broken lips as she cut into her venison. 'Sometimes I have to remain in my surgery overnight. A zebra with bronchitis, a wart hog with appendicitis but is this a reason to accuse me of terrorism?' She used her napkin to staunch the bleeding.

'Those transients . . .'

'How were we to know they had a wireless set? Ah *maudit*, Sturmbannführer, please ask how many of your soldiers I have given conducted tours to? And then . . . why then . . .' She caught a breath. 'Ask, please, would I *knowingly* have taken them into a place where there was a hidden wireless set?'

'Would I have reported the theft of my car and the presence of those explosives had I been a terrorist?' asked Gabrielle earnestly. 'The ones who stole my car must have been the same as had the wireless set.'

He ate in silence and he could see that they were worried they had offended him. He had to go carefully. Sympathies were running high, what with the constant attention of the press. Gabrielle Arcuri, particularly, had a tremendous following and not just here in Paris but all over the Axis world. Three women. *Verdammt*! what was he to do?

At least one of them had to be broken. That would then cause the other two to confess. With full confessions there could be no questions from von Schaumburg or any of the others. Short of this, the whole affair would have to be handled very carefully. *Sonderbehandlung.* Berlin would demand no less. An end to them.

He set his knife and fork down and took a sip of the Vouvray *demi-sec* that had been taken from the cellars of the Château Thériault not two weeks ago. 'These days people are dropping out of sight all the time. Everyone questions where they've gone but no one dares to ask.'

He'd arrange it – was this what he was telling them? wondered Suzanne-Cécilia. Letting her anger get the better of her, she said bitterly, 'Is it true what people say about Marguerite Vilmorin?'

More sauce was taken. Potato cakes were a side dish and he took another of these and some carrots and peas. 'And what, precisely, do they say of that one?' he asked and there was a lifelessness in his voice which made her shudder.

'That . . . that when presented with what they were about to do, she bared her breasts herself and that her interrogator then talked of philosophy and music while he burned her breasts and ribs and then her vertebrae with a red-hot poker and questioned her for hours. That . . . that he then served her real coffee which she could neither taste nor feel since he had also torn out all her fingernails.'

Boemelburg threw down his knife and fork. *'How dare you? Now either you co-operate or you go to Buchenwald where the axe will take that silly head of yours from your shoulders!'*

She ducked. She cringed. She blurted, 'Forgive me. I . . . I'm so ashamed. The meal . . .'

'Quit being a faux jeton, *madame! Use that brain of yours which is so capable.'*

He was going to kill her.

'Now have a little wine. Drink it down and Georges, here, will refill your glass.'

Dear Jesus help them.

Boemelburg oversaw the Bickler Unit, a school which trained informers and infiltrators who then penetrated the Resistance. Tshaya? wondered Gabrielle. Had Henri Doucette sent her to such a school or had he simply put her to work, she needing no training in those arts whatsoever?

And what of Nana? she asked herself. Could Nana hold out

long enough to say the right things? Everything depended on her doing so. Everything ...

'Now look, you two, I'm giving you both the opportunity to avoid such treatment,' said Boemelburg. 'If we could trap the Gypsy perhaps things would be better for you.'

Berlin would be appeased – was this what he was saying? 'Are you offering us a deal?' managed Gabrielle.

'Betray the Gypsy and you will let us go free?' asked Suzanne-Cécilia. 'But ... but how could we possibly do such a thing when we do not even know him and have had no contact with him other than for me to be tied up in bed – yes, *bed*, Sturmbannführer – while he *boiled* dynamite the terrorists had given him? *The terrorists!*'

She burst into tears and, shoving her plate aside, put her head down on her arms and wept.

He was having none of it. 'Think of your Marguerite Vilmorin if you wish. Think of baring your own breasts. Those robberies were all targeted, madame, and well beforehand. He had help. Your friends can be connected to at least two of the robberies. More, if persuaded.'

There was silence from him. He took up the carving knife and fork. He ... 'They did say something about a meeting-place, Sturmbannführer,' blurted Gabrielle. 'Those terrorists who stole my car talked of it with De Vries. A place where gypsies used to camp. A ruin near a forest, I think, but it's all so hazy. I was terrified, you understand, and thought they were going to kill me.'

Tears streamed from her. Had he finally broken the two of them? 'A ruin ... A forest ...' he said.

'Near Paris, I think.'

'And what of your friend, Nana Thélème? Would she know of this meeting-place?'

'Tshaya would,' blurted Suzanne-Cécilia. 'Ask her, why don't you? Perhaps *then* you will find what you're looking for!'

The stench of bitter almonds, of potassium cyanide, emanated from the corpse, from its folds and creases, its cavities especially. The skin was lividly pink and cold, the fingernails a midnight blue. *'I didn't poison him! I didn't!'*

The sound of Nana Thélème's shrieks reverberated about the swimming pool. Gripped by the back of her neck and by the hair – drenched repeatedly and still on her hands and knees at the side of the pool – she tried to hold herself away from that thing but Herr Max was too strong for her. Her lips touched Hans's chest. Her face was crammed into an armpit. *'You betrayed him!'* shrieked Engelmann. *'He knew you had betrayed him!'*

She vomited, jerked, coughed and panicked as he yanked her up to shove her head under water again.

Hermann cried out, *'Dead she's useless, damn you!'*

'You ... you ...' The echoes rang as bubbles burst from her nostrils and mouth and her eyes began to widen again in terror.

Others helped. Others held her under too. *'She'll drown this time,'* cried St-Cyr. *'Idiot, why must you do this when she may not even be involved?'*

Held back, restrained and at gunpoint, all he and Hermann could do was to object. Suddenly her legs began to thrash, her arms to give those final spasms. Evacuating herself, the stench of this was mingled with that of the cyanide and the pool's chlorine. Yanked up and out, she tried to breathe but couldn't seem to and began to black out only to be hit hard on the back.

Vomiting water, choking, coughing, she lay in her swill, fighting desperately for air.

Engelmann screamed at her to tell him everything.

'Herr Max ...' began Louis only to see rage cloud the visitor's eyes as he flung the woman down to charge at him.

'Bastard!' shrieked Kohler.

Ah *nom de Jésus-Christ!* Engelmann had torn a pistol from one of the SS. He was going to shoot Hermann ...

'Put that down.'

Jackboots came together at attention, here, there and all along and around the pool.

'General, this is idiocy. That woman knows nothing,' seethed Kohler, straining at those who held him.

St-Cyr ... St-Cyr and Kohler again. Must they always bring trouble? wondered von Schaumburg. 'There are rumours, whispers, Herr Engelmann, that the city's drinking-water supplies are to be poisoned and if not those, then the food that is being rationed and that, also, of every officer under my command and that of the General von Stülpnagel.'

'General, this woman knows everything!'

'And you?' asked the Kommandant von Gross Paris icily. 'What of yourself who let the Gypsy out of jail and who is still responsible for him?'

'Herr Himmler will hear of this!'

'He already has. Not fifteen minutes ago I spoke with the Führer.'

The greatcoat's shoulders and back betrayed none of von Schaumburg's advanced years. Taller, bigger even than Hermann, he looked at Engelmann with scorn. 'Gestapo,' he said scathingly. 'SS idiots. What did you think you were doing by releasing a man like that? Safe-cracking is a criminal offence and Paris is not your jurisdiction. Let these two handle it and then ask the questions of them if any are left.'

Himmler would be furious. A Prussian of the old school, a pious bachelor and hypocrite, von Schaumburg was still a power to be reckoned with, and through him, the High Command.

Engelmann wiped water from his face. Released, Louis reached Nana even as Kohler did, and together they helped her to a *chaise*.

Though it took her time to find her voice, and she was still in agony and very weak, she managed to say, 'General, let me have some dry clothes. I will tell you everything.'

Coffee came with little white tablets Gabrielle and Suzanne-Cécilia thought at first were saccharin but then as Gestapo Boemelburg, still watching them, held his breath, they hesitated and thought the worst. Each of them set the tablet carefully aside with a spoon. They both said a faint, '*Merci*,' to Georges who had served them and turned to gaze emptily into the fire which threw its heat at them in the *grand salon*.

Georges thrust the poker more deeply into the coals. Georges tidied things. Boemelburg swirled cognac. A cigar was brought and lighted for him using the poker.

The veterinary surgeon shuddered at the sight of that thing. 'Cigarettes?' asked Georges, his voice startling them both. The chanteuse quickly shook her head, the other one quavered, 'No . . . No, I . . . I had to give them up due to the shortages and . . . and do not wish to start again.'

'Why not be reasonable?' chided Boemelburg gregariously. 'No one will ever hear of it, I assure you. Help me and, in turn, I will help you both. You have my word.'

How kind of him. 'If we can, we will,' said Suzanne-Cécilia, setting her coffee aside untouched. 'But you might as well consult the pages of *Je suis partout* for their address. Neither of us know where the Gypsy and his woman are hiding.'

'But . . . but Mademoiselle Arcuri said they could be holed up in some ruins, in a forest near Paris? A former encampment of the gypsies?'

Georges had not left the room. Georges stood with his back to the innermost wall, the ever-present but 'unseen' butler.

An Alsatian, Gabrielle told herself. Somehow she found her voice. '*Je suis partout* publishes the whereabouts of those the authorities are looking for. That was all she meant, and you must know of it in any case.'

The brandy glass was lifted in signal. Georges immediately disappeared. Flames curled about the poker. Scales of iron were flaking from its cherry red surface. A cup rattled, a saucer fell, Suzanne-Cécilia crying out, 'Ah no . . .' as it struck the carpet and bounced, but did not break.

'Now listen, you two, my patience is gone,' said Boemelburg.

'It is to be the poker now?' shrilled Suzanne-Cécilia in despair. 'Is this what you want?'

She ripped open the front of her dress and pulled down the brassière. Angrily Boemelburg shrieked at her to cover herself. 'Don't be such an idiot! Just give me answers!'

Georges came back to say, 'She was right, Sturmbannführer.'

Boemelburg snatched the newspaper from him and when he had read the notice, he thrust it at Gabrielle.

'*Those wishing to find Tshaya, companion and accomplice of the safe-cracker known as the Gypsy, need* . . . She paused to look up at them. '*Need hunt no further than the garret at the head of the stairs in the house at 15 rue Nollet.*'

The newspaper was a weekly but published on Fridays, today then, the twenty-second.

'Henri Doucette will have seen this by now,' she said, dismayed by the thought. 'If he should get to her before you do, Sturmbannführer, what will he do to her for disobeying him?

210

Will she be alive long enough to tell you where Janwillem De Vries is?'

'Tshaya,' said Nana Thélème, her jet black hair now braided, her voice still far from strong. 'I first met her in 1914. I met Janwillem then, too, General. The *kumpania* of her father was at a bend in the Guadalquivir among the cork oaks and junipers. There were some sheep – merinos of ours – and my uncle had ridden out with my cousins and some others to settle the matter.'

She was clutching at straws, thought Engelmann. She coughed. Her throat was sore. Her lips and the left side of her face were badly swollen. 'Forgive me,' she said.

They waited. Von Schaumburg had insisted she be allowed to speak. Louis was grim and clearly felt she would have to tell them everything. She had that look about her and stood facing Old Shatter Hand, her eyes never once leaving him.

'Even at the age of nine I recognized the hold Tshaya had on Janwillem but I wanted him too, and I told myself I would take him from her.'

'How old was Tshaya?' asked St-Cyr.

Stung by the interruption, she glared at him, her eyes smarting. 'Seven, I think, but one can never tell with those people because they live entirely in the present.'

'And this incident?' asked von Schaumburg.

Again she lost herself in memory. 'To understand what happened, General, is to understand the harshness of Córdoba. The heat is so great, the sun refuses to relinquish its hold on life. Distant among the foothills of the Sierra Morena a bluish haze remains. The olive groves seem everywhere, and there is the soft but heady scent of them and of juniper and sage, of sheep and horses, too, and it mingles with the heat to sharpen the silence.'

'*You're a terrorist, damn you!*' seethed Engelmann. '*We have the proof!*'

'The *what*?' she countered sharply, not turning to face him but painfully choking. 'General, your people don't really know if I'm a terrorist or not. Janwillem sends me a gun to implicate me further and succeeds with this one because, when I bring it to

211

him, he doesn't give me a chance to tell him. He just shoves my head under water and tries to drown me!'

Engelmann leapt from his chair. A hand was raised to stop him. 'General . . .' he began, only to hear von Schaumburg saying, '*Sit down*! Don't make an even bigger fool of yourself than you already have.'

Again she was given a moment to compose herself.

'The gypsies were very poor and in rags, as was Janwillem, who was a boy of eleven, yet they had a resilience and love of life which transcended their poverty. My uncle . . .' She tried to ease her throat. 'He let them stay and help with the olive harvest and gave them the sheep, knowing they would steal no more from him because that is the gypsy way. For them he became a protector, a benefactor who soon found himself taking up their cause with the *guardia*. A *Gajo*, yes, but kind and useful, and one whom they came to respect greatly.'

Still she hadn't taken her eyes from von Schaumburg except for that momentary lapse to glare at Louis. From somewhere a white cashmere throw had been found, but it was in the way she had wrapped this about her throat to hide the marks, and in the way she stood that one saw how fiercely proud and defiant she was.

'Some years they came to our hacienda to help with the harvest, some years they didn't, but I never forgot Janwillem or Tshaya. You see, it was through her and others of the *kumpania*, and at my uncle's insistence, that I really learned to dance and sing, though she relished the opportunity to show me she could still do so far better than I.'

'The party on the night of the eleventh at your former villa,' said St-Cyr.

Though she didn't look at him this time, she said, 'Yes. Under gypsy law, she could never marry a non-gypsy.'

'When she was fifteen,' said St-Cyr, 'she ran off to Paris but couldn't find De Vries and married Henri Doucette instead.'

'The boxer,' murmured von Schaumburg. 'One of that gang over on the rue Lauriston.'

The French Gestapo.

'Her family took her back that first time but he came after her and beat her terribly, General. Janwillem had by then started in on the life he was to lead. He's very cool-headed and is fascinated, not just by locks, but by explosives. He is at heart a

212

true gypsy. This is what you must realize. He believes himself one of them and that there is nothing wrong with his robbing the *Gaje* or of his lying to them or cheating them if . . .' She paused to gaze at Herr Max with contempt. 'If in the end it will give him what he so desperately craves, his freedom.'

'*Where is he? Where have you been hiding him?*' demanded Engelmann fiercely.

'General, if the story is not told, the answer cannot be given.'

Ah *merde*, thought St-Cyr, try not to be so swift to anger.

'Janwillem came into contact with *kumpaniyi* all over Europe – remember, please, that he speaks their language fluently which very few non-gypsies do. Everywhere he went he behaved as one of them. He shared completely and freely the loot he had stolen, buying food, wine, whatever was needed, and became very close to them and loved as one of their own.' Again she paused to moisten her throat. 'So he knows, General, all the ways they would use to mark a trail, all the safe havens, the protectors too, like my uncle, who serve as letter boxes and listening posts. A brief telegraph or telephone call, a word passed from one caravan to another and a haven is ready with whatever it will take to hide him for as long as he wishes.'

It was von Schaumburg who asked if she was suggesting the terrorists who had stolen Gabrielle's car had been in contact with De Vries from the moment he had arrived in Tours.

'From well before that. Probably right from the night he was arrested in Oslo in 1938. Prison is death to a gypsy. Tshaya betrayed him – she's exceedingly jealous of me and very possessive of him but he still doesn't see this. I had him, General. He was mine! We were to have a son in a few more months. I had the villa in Saint-Cloud. Everything was waiting for him to . . .' She ducked her head a little in acknowledgement of her own folly. 'To give up the life he had led and live the one I wanted. We had agreed to marry.'

But he had lied even to you, thought St-Cyr, and asked, 'Did he finance the purchase of the villa?'

'What would you have me say?' she countered hotly. 'That it was bought with stolen money? Ah! you do not understand us Andalusians, Inspector, and I pity you. I bought it myself with funds borrowed from my uncle and with those gained from my work!'

213

'Forgive me,' he said, mollified but very conscious of that temper of hers.

She did not toss her head. 'For Gabrielle's sake I will. This whole affair is rubbish, General. Of course I wanted to see Janwillem when he dropped in so unexpectedly from Tours but he stayed less than an hour and as I stand before you, I have not seen him since.'

'She's lying,' said Herr Max.

'*I'm not!*' she countered swiftly. Again she choked and had to force herself to swallow. 'He's ... he's completely under Tshaya's spell. If you want him, then find her. *Her!* They will not be staying together – have you even considered this? Ah! I see that you haven't. *Think* as a gypsy. Stop *being* the son of some *Gaje* ... *Bitte, bitte*, what was your father?' She snapped her fingers.

'A woodcutter.'

Verdammt! but she was magnificent, swore Kohler. A natural. A gypsy herself in many ways. Louis could see it too.

'Tshaya will be separate from Janwillem because if the one is taken, the other will be ready to bring freedom or revenge. And please don't forget she's not alone but has others to help. Gypsies who know their lives count as nothing, so what, please, is there for them to lose?'

Uncomfortable at the thought, von Schaumburg asked, 'What will they do next?' and she said, 'General, this is a confusion of his, a flimflam, a sleight of hand, a typical gypsy ruse that is guaranteed to bewilder the *Gaje*. Tshaya and he will have it all planned. The lure is your recovering the loot, the cyanide and explosives and in silencing a press which continues to laud him. These temptations will drive you to allow him to accomplish what he wants.'

'Which is?'

'Something so shocking it will show you all up for what they think you really are.'

'And where might he be hiding?' asked Herr Max acidly. He'd had enough of her.

'Please just tell us what you think possible,' said von Schaumburg.

'A place known only to gypsies and that is why you must find Tshaya but remember he's one of them if not by birth, then by all the rest. He'll be ready to disappear at a moment's notice.'

214

She let the silence hang in the room, then told them exactly how it would be. 'Tshaya will have remained in the city. She'll be co-ordinating things with the others. That husband of hers will be looking for her – he is, isn't he? but she'll be waiting for him too, to rid her life of him. Go carefully. She'll have explosives because, as Janwillem's accomplice from time to time over the years, she, too, has learned their use.'

Ah no!

'And then?' asked von Schaumburg.

'Either you will take Janwillem, General, or he will vanish without a trace until he's ready to surface again.'

'And the loot?' asked someone.

'Will go with him, of course.'

'He has blank papers,' said Kohler. '*Ausweise*, identity cards, ration tickets . . .'

'And all the franking stamps that are necessary,' said von Schaumburg, scowling at the incompetence of the SS, the Gestapo and Herr Max. 'Berlin are too far removed from us. See that this Tshaya is found and then convince her to tell us where he is.'

Only Herr Max breathed a little easier, for in those last few words room had been cautiously made for him to proceed. Von Schaumburg was only covering his own ass. These days everyone did so if possible.

Had it been daylight, Hermann would have said he didn't like the look of things. At six minutes to curfew, and with the rue Nollet in utter darkness and its tardy citizens prevented from hastily entering or leaving the area, he said nothing, a sure sign he was deeply troubled.

All attempts to find Henri Doucette had failed. Boemelburg's Daimler, with the General's Mercedes in front of it, was parked just ahead of the Citroën. All engines were silent. Wehrmacht lorries had sealed off each end of the street. Troops were deployed, some to the rooftops, others to watch the adjacent streets.

Searchlights would be used, torches too, and headlamps. If Tshaya tried to make a run for it, she would be stopped.

'But is she alive, Louis? Has the Spade already taught her a little lesson in obedience?'

'He has a temper,' sighed St-Cyr. 'If she's dead, he will simply have left her for us to find and will claim he knows nothing of it.'

The rue Nollet was perfect. Les Batignolles was in the seventeenth arrondissement and largely industrial. One of the city's garment districts, it had formerly been a quiet little village but had suffered repeated incursions of slum-housing.

The huge railway depot and switching yard that serviced the whole of the Occupied North was but a street away and offered unparalleled chances for escape. Not far to the south, and in line with the yards, were those of the Gare Saint-Lazare. The quartier de l'Europe was to the east; the Club Monseigneur not far.

'The citizens of this district have a total allergy to authority and a complete aversion to the police,' sighed St-Cyr. 'That is why all attempts have failed to find her.'

Even the reward of 100,000 francs hadn't been claimed. *Je suis partout* were co-operating but could only say that they had received the news by telephone.

'He knocks off the Ritz on the night of the eighteenth, then fades up the rue de la Paix to Cartier's where Tshaya is waiting for him,' snorted Kohler. 'Then the two of them knock it off and hit the ticket office of the Gare Saint-Lazare.'

'After which they simply fade away to here and let the police and everyone else hunt for them.'

'Then the son of a bitch boldly hangs around the Gare Saint-Lazare waiting for me to blow myself up!'

That had been in the small hours of Wednesday, and afterwards the Gypsy had gone on to the Gare de l'Est to knock off the pay-train before the curfew had ended.

Fifteen or so hours later, they had emptied the wall safe of the villa in Saint-Cloud.

'Their timing's perfect, Hermann.'

'And they still have plenty of explosives.'

'I'll come with you.'

'No you won't. You'll try to look after Giselle and Oona if anything happens.'

A knock on the windscreen was soft, though it had the sound of finality about it.

'*Au revoir, mon vieux,*' breathed Kohler.

216

Hermann's grip was far from firm. '*À bientôt, mon ami. Bonne chance.*'

St-Cyr got out of the car to silently close its door. Standing in the darkness and the freezing cold, he looked up at the house and wondered what awaited his partner. Another tripwire, another bomb?

Gabrielle and Nana and Suzanne-Cécilia were now all being held at the Neuilly villa. They would not be allowed to talk to one another and would be kept completely separate.

'But will they try to escape?' he said quietly to the night. 'If so, Herr Max will be waiting for just such a thing.'

From where she stood behind her door, Gabrielle could see the head of the main staircase. The corridor was well lit. There were lights on in the foyer below. Apparently the house slept, but she could not understand why she hadn't been locked in.

It was suicidal to try to escape, suicidal to stay. Jean-Louis and Hermann would find the house at 15 rue Nollet. Both would be only too aware of what Henri Doucette would do to Tshaya. And then? she asked, and closed the door to let its bolt click softly back in place. 'And then they will find the truth but will they accept it?'

Henri Doucette would want Tshaya to tell him where the Gypsy was hiding, but more than this, he would want her to tell him where the loot was hidden. And Tshaya, Jean-Louis? she asked. What will Tshaya do if she wants to get back at that husband of hers before she and the Gypsy vanish into thin air?

Would she not have notified *Je suis partout*, knowing such a notice would be certain to bring him to her and that he would have been forewarned of it by one of the reporters and would tell no one of it until he had had a chance to get to her?

The house at number 15 had been condemned, the notice on the door was all too clear. *For the acts of terrorism committed by the son, André Lemercier, in place Bellecour on 14 and 17 October in the city of Lyon* ... All members of the boy's immediate family had been taken. The house had been sealed, and so much for the folly of committing terrorism.

There was no mention of what the boy had actually done. Kohler tried the door and found it opened easily. Nudging it, he stepped inside.

Freezing, the place smelled of mould and dampness. All the furnishings had been taken. The bastards had even unscrewed and removed the coat-rack in the foyer and the light fixture. A door led straight ahead, another to his left, a third opened on to a staircase whose steps, when he shone the torch up them, looked uninviting.

He searched the wainscoting for tripwires, searched for steps whose boards had been pulled loose and put back, turned the torchlight so that it shone up at the ceiling above himself. There was nothing up there . . . not a damned thing that he could see, ah *merde* . . .

The first step was solid but deeply worn. The faded wallpaper was peeling. The second step was as solid as a rock, and so was the third one. Confident, he found the fourth step suddenly giving way beneath his weight. He was caught and dropped the torch, cried out softly, '*Verdammt!*'

No bomb exploded. Apprehensively he looked up the stairwell, thinking Tshaya or Doucette would be up there but no one came. No one.

The door up there was still closed, half lost in the gloom.

He ran his fingers over the next step, felt the nails in place and chanced it. Progress was painfully slow. No flask of nitro dangled from the ceiling of the stairwell. No detonator had been wired to sticks of leaking dynamite. There wasn't the smell of it. Was the place clean of explosives?

The Lemercier family had occupied the first storey. Making his way from room to room, Kohler picked out those in which they had eaten, slept or relaxed. He could imagine the heavy, stuffed armchairs with their lace antimacassars, the ashtrays. The outlines of the pictures that had hung on the walls were there, those of the crucifixes too. The water closet was nothing but a bucket under the kitchen sink. Ah Christ!

There was a second and a third storey which had been let to others and in their rooms the smells were different.

Now only the garrets remained. Louis, he said silently to himself. Louis, I don't like this.

He heard a noise below him. He thought that it must be his

218

partner but neither of them had a gun. Those had been taken from them at the Ritz's swimming pool.

The garret at the head of the stairs, he told himself and, looking up at the attic's door, shone the torch fully on it. But was there a bomb? Had she wired herself in? And who the hell had let *Je suis partout* know about her hiding here? Who unless . . . Ah *maudit*! had it been herself who had told them?

St-Cyr could hear nothing. The darkness was absolute. The fronts of opposing houses on either side of the street tended to shut one in. No stars shone from above.

'Louis . . .'

A side window of the Daimler had been rolled down a fraction. 'Yes, Walter?'

'Get in there and see what's taking that partner of yours so long.'

The stairs were steep. One of the steps had been broken. Hermann had never let anyone hear him if he hadn't wanted them to. Had he been so nervous he had become careless?

When he reached the garret, St-Cyr switched off his torch in alarm. Drunkenly the beam of Hermann's torch shone across a barren floor. There was no sound, only the smell of charred wood and burnt flesh. Ah *nom de Dieu* . . .

Hermann was on his hands and knees. He had tried to vomit but had had nothing to throw up. His hat had fallen off. The collar of his greatcoat was up.

'*Merde, mon vieux*, you have given me a scare,' said St-Cyr gently as he took his friend by the shoulders and felt the splash of tears.

'In . . . in the next room. I can't take any more of this, Louis. I want out. I want to take Giselle and Oona to Spain, to live like decent human beings.'

'Stay here – here, sit with your back to the wall. Switch off your torch. Save the batteries. You know how difficult it is for us to get replacements.'

Frisking him, and himself, St-Cyr at last found what was needed, and lighting the bent and crumbling cigarette, placed it between his partner's lips.

'You've been holding out on me,' came the complaint, a good sign.

'Only for the emergency of emergencies. You're having a breakdown. You know that, don't you? Try to be calm.'

Kohler motioned with a hand and gasped, 'In there, like I told you. Look for yourself. It's . . . it's been cleaned.'

There were no bombs – Hermann had forced himself to check it out thoroughly. The garret was the equal of the other one but when the beam of the torch fled from the window to the floor, rats scurried away. 'Ah *merde!*' exclaimed St-Cyr as the sickly sweetness hit him. Henri Doucette was spread-eagled on the floor. His wrists and ankles were tied to ringbolts. The light fled over a patchwork of horribly charred and blistered skin where fluid-filled encrustations had become glued to the tatters of clothing and then frozen.

Rigor had set in. He'd been dead at least a day. Lengths of a rawhide whip had been used to tie him down. Anointed with cognac, he had been set afire and had been allowed to scream.

But not to see.

'A skewer,' St-Cyr heard himself saying, detached and remote, for this was murder. 'His killer used a skewer to blind him, Hermann. Is this what caused you to be so ill?'

From the darkened corridor came the broken response. 'That and . . . and the rats.'

The cognac bottle had been left near the corpse. It was empty and one look at the blistered, encrusted face with its gaping mouth and eye sockets, told St-Cyr the killer had forced Doucette to drink.

Then she – had it really been Tshaya? he asked, for he had always to question such things – had found a match and had sat back to look at the victim before striking it. Had he been tormented first with the skewer? Had the killer then provided another mouthful of cognac? The Gypsy . . . had it been De Vries who had done it?

Revenge.

The skewer had been stabbed into the floor next the head. No attempt had been made to hide the thing. It was simply from a kitchen and would have been readily available in most households. 'But why put out his eyes, Hermann? Did hatred run so deep, or did the killer not want him to see something should death fail?'

'Don't they skewer the eyes of live rabbits in the markets of

220

the Loire?' blurted Kohler shrilly from the darkness of the corridor. 'Don't the peasants *swear* it makes the poor things taste better?'

How could you French do such a thing? – the accusation was very clear. Hermann had a file as big as a mountain in that brain of his about all things French and the curious. In 1850 a law had been passed forbidding such cruelty but it had been found unenforceable.

'*Well?*' he demanded.

Tshaya had worked in a brothel in Tours and would have seen or heard of such a thing. 'Yes. Yes, they still do it but now, of course, rabbits are so very hard to come by.'

'But do they taste better?'

'Did she tell the Spade she was doing it for the sake of the rats?'

'*You know that's what she'd have said!*'

'Go downstairs, Hermann. Immediately! Tell Boemelburg we've got a murder on our hands and that I will have to go over this place thoroughly.'

'She did it, Louis. Don't get to thinking otherwise. We haven't time.'

'Of course, but then ... ah *mais alors, alors, mon vieux*, the cognac.'

'*What the hell's the matter with the cognac?*'

'Nothing. It must have been superb. A Bisquit *Vieille Réserve*, VVSOP and fifty or more years in the cask for the youngest of its *crus*, the *youngest*, Hermann.'

'So, what's the problem?'

'Tshaya. Wouldn't any *marc* have done as well? Why choose something so fine and rare? Why not use something cheap and rough and easily obtainable, since it would burn just as well and for just as long?'

'Are you trying to tell me Tshaya had expensive tastes?'

'No. I am simply saying that not everything is as one would think it should be.'

9

The last of the papier-mâché balls went into the kitchen stove. Alone, cold and deeply troubled – afraid, yes – St-Cyr brought the lighted taper to the bowl of his pipe, but chopped blotting paper, sun-dried herbs, sawdust, carrot tops and beet greens were no substitute for tobacco.

'*Diable!*' he cried, and spitting furiously several times, cleaned out the pipe and laid it on the table, another failed experiment in what the Occupation had produced, a nation of experimenters.

The house, he had to admit, was lonely without the veterinary surgeon and zoo-keeper who could, in moments, bubble with laughter or play the imp only to become serious. A terrorist, a *résistant*.

Suddenly he remembered the book he had taken from her shelf and cursed himself for having carried it all this time. Page by page he burned it, watching the flames but seeing her standing between the cages of poisonous snakes, ready to kill herself.

Three women, all very intelligent and resourceful but desperate and driven to extremes – each asking what they could possibly do to save themselves when ... when, really, nothing could be possible.

That business in the house on the rue Nollet was not right. Oh for sure Tshaya would hate the Spade and would want to kill him but would she have taken such a risk as to notify *Je suis partout* ahead of time, knowing only he would come and not with others? At the least, she would have requested a private meeting there ahead of time and would have notified the paper later. And where, please, had the Gypsy been? In hiding, in a forest somewhere, among old ruins and in an encampment known only to other gypsies who were now with him, or in Paris at the killing with Tshaya? It must have taken at least two persons to have forced Doucette to lie on the floor like that and then to have tied him to the ringbolts. A gun would have been necessary also.

The leather binding of *La Cryptographie Nouvelle* refused to burn – the fire was simply not hot enough. The gilded letters on the spine remained, a damning indictment should they be found.

Cutting them off the charred leather, he ate them – it was the only thing to do. The ground outside was frozen solid, the drains could be opened and searched . . .

'We were in Tours,' he said so silently no Gestapo bug could have picked it up. 'On Wednesday the twentieth we were away from Paris and on Thursday also, until 0500 hours Friday.'

Early on that Wednesday, before the curfew had ended, the Gypsy and Tshaya had robbed the pay-train at the Gare de l'Est. Then on the night of that same Wednesday or early on the Thursday they had cleaned out the wall safe of Nana's former villa.

After the Gare de l'Est robbery, Tshaya and the Gypsy could have lain up in the house on the rue Nollet but search as he had, there had been no conclusive evidence of this.

Fighting sleep, he sat down at the table to strip the leather from the boards and to cut it into digestible shreds. 'I can't be the cause of her arrest,' he said, but wondered how she had hidden the wireless set so well, no one had been able to find it.

And what of Gabrielle? he asked. A handkerchief had been dropped in the powder magazine at the quarry but this could just as easily have been done by accident on the first visit, on the thirteenth. On Thursday, the twenty-first, she had been returned to Paris by the Gypsy and the *résistants* who had taken her car and had immediately informed the police of what had happened. As much as twelve flasks of nitroglycerine and at least two cases of dynamite were missing but how much had been taken on her first visit with Nana? One flask and a few sticks, or all the rest as well?

The Gypsy had run out of nitro by the time they had encountered him at the house on the rue Poliveau. Nitro was far more portable and therefore preferred but now . . . did he have all he needed or had she lied to the police? Had there never been a second trip? Had they simply held back on the explosives, storing them for De Vries? Hermann and he had seen no tyre tracks, no evidence of that second visit, but, yes, the Gypsy could easily have come and gone. Then why had he not left a surprise for them, especially since he had been trying to kill them?

And what of Nana? he asked. Nana had had one of the

revolvers from the Gare Saint-Lazare in her purse but had claimed she'd not been given a chance to tell Herr Max about it. Another good citizen unjustly wronged, but where, please, were the other two Lebels that had been taken during that robbery?

None of them had confided much. Indeed, the lies and half-lies had been piling up to screen the whole thing. Henri Doucette would have been a threat to them. He'd have held back from letting Herr Max know everything. Tshaya could well have told the Spade things Nana and the others couldn't have him repeating.

Certainly the murder implicated Tshaya. Certainly it would send a definite message to the Gestapo of the rue Lauriston and to all such types. It would say exactly how great had become the hatred of them. But had it been Tshaya who had killed him?

Still deeply disturbed by the murder and by the horror of it, he sadly shook his head but spoke aloud and softly. 'Tshaya must have obtained the cognac during the villa robbery while with De Vries. The SS always drink the most expensive stuff since they don't have to pay for it.'

From the rue Nollet to Saint-Cloud was half-way and some across the city, easy enough if the Gypsy had had a car and had been able to hide it safely. But in her statement to the police Gabrielle had sworn that just after curfew on Thursday morning she had been forced to drive De Vries to the quarry. They had used *her* car. Tshaya had had the flu and had not been able to go with them.

Only the coroner could give a reliable estimate of the time of the Spade's murder, but had Doucette been killed when Hermann and himself had been in Tours on Wednesday?

By then Nana had come face to face with Doucette not only at the Avia Club but at the party in her former villa on the eleventh. She had also talked to the Spade's latest pigeon who must have been at the party too.

Tshaya had been at that affair. The cognac could have been taken then, her mind set in its intention to kill.

He knew he was arguing with himself, knew also that Boemelburg would have his own suspicions. Walter would have sensed doubt in him. Walter would have begun to question the murder.

*

224

Subdued, terrified – pulled from a fitful sleep at 0347 hours – Gabrielle stared emptily at the cognac in her glass. She knew she must say something, that they had to have answers.

'*Drink it!*' said Boemelburg using French.

Anger flared. 'Why should I? I *don't* want it! I want a robe – something to cover these ... these pyjamas which are not my own.'

A hand was raised. She wouldn't duck. She would take the blow and rebound from it.

The hand was halted in mid-air.

'Now drink it,' grunted Boemelburg.

The cognac was the *Vieille Réserve*. Was he certain it would make her sick? 'We didn't kill the Spade, if that's what you're thinking,' she said ashenly. 'We had no reason to. I've never met him. Tshaya ...'

'*How could she have tied him down like that if alone?*' demanded Engelmann in *deutsch*.

An irritated shrug was all she would offer.

'The Gypsy wasn't with her. He was in hiding, was he not?' said Boemelburg quietly.

Ah damn him. '*I don't* know. How could I?' she winced.

Her throat constricted. 'The Spade was useful to us,' said Boemelburg, reverting to French, 'but now that he's gone, you and the others are our only leads.'

'Then bring us all together, Sturmbannführer. Let us tell you what we know. We'll help you in any way we can,' she pleaded.

'Where were you last Wednesday night?' he asked flatly.

Herr Engelmann was incensed at the continued use of French. 'I ... I was at the Club Mirage.'

'And during your breaks?' asked Boemelburg.

'In my dressing-room. Your ... your Listeners should have a record of it.'

'Those tapes are mostly silent.'

'Then please ask the Rivard brothers, the owners. I did not leave until after the curfew had ended at five on Thursday morning as you well know.'

'The explosives ...'

'She's lying,' said Engelmann in *deutsch*. 'There were no other terrorists. She went willingly with De Vries to the quarry.'

225

'*Bitte, ja*? Herr Max. I wish to get a sense of things. You will have your chance with her, never fear.'

'There ... there were six of them, Sturmbannführer, and I am certain one of the three who came with us mentioned a campsite in a forest, at some ruins. I swear it. I wouldn't lie to you. There ... there is too much for me to lose.'

'The Château Thériault and your son.'

'Yes.'

More cognac was called for and again she found herself staring at it and unable to lift her eyes to him.

'Did he scream?' asked Boemelburg.

She leapt. Her drink was spilled. 'He ... he must have,' she blurted, forcing herself not to burst into tears. 'The ... the rabbits shriek when blinded. It's a despicable practice and, yes, I've seen it done.'

Ah Sweet *Jésus*, save her now, she thought, quickly draining the refill he had given her.

'Why will you not co-operate?' he asked. 'I don't want to see you hurt, Mademoiselle Arcuri. The people who do those things are not nice.'

She tried to speak but couldn't. Furious with her, he told Engelmann to bring the veterinarian. '*You*, go and sit on the bed and keep silent.'

Pale and badly shaken, Suzanne-Cécilia was hustled into the room and thrown into the chair. Terrified, she tried to make herself as small as possible but they shone the light on her. The nightgown she wore was thin and someone else's. Wounded, her dark brown eyes lifted furtively to them only to duck away as she was struck once, twice, three times, not knowing what had been said to them, not even knowing if she had been betrayed.

The thick auburn hair was dishevelled. The long lashes and perfect eyebrows were knitted as she cringed in pain, Gabrielle realizing in that moment that Céci had earlier worn Marianne St-Cyr's clothes and that they had fitted her perfectly.

It was a silly thought and such jealousy had no meaning here.

'*Je suit partout*, madame,' said Boemelburg quietly.

'*Oui*?' she blurted, blood trickling down her chin, the fear in her wounded eyes all too clear.

'At 1630 hours Thursday a woman telephoned them to report

226

that she had "information on the whereabouts of the estranged wife of Henri Doucette".'

'And?' she asked, biting off the word.

'Did you or did you not give them the address they then printed?'

She sucked in a breath and wiped the tears from her eyes. '"Estranged", it's a big word for an anonymous informer to use.'

Verdammt! he'd have to cut to where it would hurt. 'Your husband, madame?'

'My dead husband, yes?' she blurted in tears.

'Your wireless code was similar to that of his unit during the invasion. It was modified but followed the pattern of those advocated by Delastelle.'

Ah no, the book ... 'Honoré told me very little about his life in the army. If his code, or one like it was being used by whomever hid that wireless set in my zebra house – and I'm not saying there was a wireless set there – I ... why I know nothing of it. How could I?' She wiped blood from her lips and nose with the back of a hand that trembled. Smarting, she blinked her eyes to clear them but could not seem to stop herself from shaking.

Engelmann passed in front of the lamp to throw his shadow over her. Then he stepped behind her and she had to ask herself what was he going to do now?

'Your student days,' breathed Boemelburg. 'One of your professors mentions "a remarkable ability with electronics".'

'I ...' she began, only to flinch as she felt Herr Engelmann's hands brush the back of her neck. 'I was young. I was interested in everything. It ... it was just something to do.' She shook him off.

'But when asked, the professor was quite convinced you could have built a wireless set and would have had no trouble in operating it. "As a student, Madame Lemaire belonged to a group we called the Cricket Talkers, the Society for the Improvement of Wireless Transmission."'

'But ... but why would he have referred to me as Madame when I was to him unmarried at the time?'

Tears were blinked away. *Verdammt*! why would she not confess without the use of reinforced interrogation? 'The questioner gave him your married name,' snapped Boemelburg gruffly.

'Then he should have used Carrière, Sturmbannführer. My father is a pharmacist, a gold medallist, as is my mother. This professor you speak of did not know me. If he had, he would have shaken his head in despair at the memory of all my questions, and would have referred to me as Céci or *la petite espiègle.*'

The little imp! Furious with her, Boemelburg grabbed the front of her nightgown and, bunching it up, shoved his fist under her chin so that she was pushed back into Herr Engelmann. '*Bring the other one!*' he shrieked.

The left side of Nana's face was very red and swollen. Her lips were bleeding again. The bruises on her neck were darker, bigger. Violently she was thrown into the light. The nightgown had been torn and hung by a single shoulder strap. She'd been banged up against a wall and had been struck repeatedly.

'*I'm your only link,*' she hissed, yanking herself free of Engelmann. '*I may even know where Janwillem is hiding, but as long as I live I will tell you nothing!*'

Ah *nom de Dieu*, winced Gabrielle.

'*Leave us. Get out!*' he shouted in *deutsch* at Engelmann, and when the door was closed, took a moment to study these three. Everything in him said that things were not as they should be. The wireless signals, the Gypsy, the robberies, each of which must have been well surveyed beforehand. The murder of the Spade ... the death of Hans Wehrle ... Berlin were demanding an end to things. Himmler had taken a personal interest and had been shrieking for blood.

Calming himself, Boemelburg indicated they should sit together on one of the couches. Cursing them silently, he gave them each some of the cognac. 'Now tell me', he breathed, 'where Dr Vries and his woman are hiding. Do it, damn you, or I swear I will have you taken from this house and given over to those who would like nothing better than to strip you naked and beat you until the answers gurgle from your battered lips and punctured lungs.'

Ah *Jésus* ... 'If ... if we knew ...' began Suzanne-Cécilia only to feel Gabrielle's warning hand on her arm.

'Nana ...' Gabrielle tried to find her voice. 'When ... when Janwillem left you in the spring of 1938 you had just discovered you were pregnant. Do you remember we met at the Café de la

Paix? You were so upset, *chérie*. You thought Tshaya must have come back into his life and that he was staying with her father's *kumpania*. A woods to the west of Paris, some ruins – I think you said it was at an old monastery, or what was left of one.'

Nana stared at her cognac and tilted the glass to let some of it run over her fingers, but if she thought the *Vieille Réserve* a deliberate reminder of the Spade's murder, she gave no indication of this.

She bathed her lips and indicated Céci should do the same.

'That . . . that was all I knew at the time,' she said. 'A place the gypsies had been going to for centuries but one, yes, that the *Deuxième bureau des nomades* knew nothing of.'

There, she would let this Gestapo pig digest the crumb she had given him.

His watery blue eyes sought her out. 'Are we to search every woods to the west of the city?' he asked blandly.

'Only those with ruins,' she countered swiftly. 'I *don't* like being hit, Sturmbannführer, nor having my nightclothes ripped from me, nor do I like being nearly drowned when a few sensible questions calmly given are all that is necessary. Janwillem is not himself, not any more, but your people and the Norwegians before them kept him in prison so long he can only think of himself as a gypsy and therefore at complete odds with the rest of us. Get that into your head. You're a *Gajo*; he's now of the Rom completely.'

'Versailles,' hazarded Boemelburg only to see her vehemently shake her head and hear her acidly toss the words at him. 'It's too popular, too fashionable, particularly these days.'

'Then try to think. Try to give us a little more.'

'So that the guillotine or the axe might fall on a neck whose head was empty?'

He sighed. 'That temper of yours is far too swift for your own good. If you and your friends are innocent, I will personally see that you are cleared of all charges. You have my word on it.'

Is it as good as your Führer's? she silently asked. Will you apologize for what you've done to us? 'Agreed,' she said but did not try to smile.

He gave her a moment. Gabrielle took her by the hand. 'A monastery . . . You told me the gypsies always marked the way they had travelled by using special signs. You wanted us to look

229

for Janwillem, Nana. You were certain that together we could find him.'

'The *patterans*,' she said. 'The trident, the cross – heaps of leaves or grass at a corner of a crossroads, branches piled up in winter.'

'The swastika,' said Suzanne-Cécilia. 'I remember once reading of it. An ancient symbol from India which was adopted and used by the gypsies in their wanderings. The gypsies ...'

'Don't you *dare* taunt me, madame. And as for you.' He looked at Nana. 'De Vries would not have marked his trail this time.'

'Not unless he wanted other gypsies to follow and to gather,' said Nana softly.

'For what purpose?' he asked.

She let him have it. 'Sabotage, since the times are no longer ordinary and there are so few of their people left. He has everything he needs, hasn't he?'

'*Think*, Nana,' urged Gabrielle quickly interceding. 'A conservatory – didn't he once tell you of one?'

'A house that had been fashionable in its day,' added Suzanne-Cécilia, 'but one which, on the death of its owner, had been left to a religious order.'

'An arcade,' said Nana. 'An inner courtyard. Janwillem ... I once overheard him saying to someone on the telephone that they should meet in the conservatory where ... where the Prussian general had established his personal latrine during the war of 1870–71. The house is a former villa, Sturmbannführer, within whose stairwells the ceilings are still decorated with the same paintings of swallows that were there in the fourteenth century. There is a chapel. A maze of corridors connect innumerable bedchambers, since cut up into the more recent cells of the monks who have now long departed. Above the rooms and corridors there are gaping holes in the roof.'

'Would it be in or near the Forêt de Marly-le-Roi, Nana?' asked Gabrielle.

She didn't look at any of them but said faintly, 'Yes, that is where it is. L'*Abbaye des frères bienveillants*.'

The Abbey of the Benevolent Friars. 'Were you ever there?' asked Boemelburg.

Her gaze met his fully and she had to ask herself, Does he know of it after all? Has he suddenly remembered it?

'Once and now . . . now I have given him to you and may my son and God Himself forgive me.'

In the pitch darkness before dawn, Hermann was silent. The rue Laurence-Savart had barely awakened. The Citroën was freezing. 'Didn't you sleep at all?' asked St-Cyr.

'A couple of hours.'

'And Giselle, is she still determined to throw herself from the belfries of the Notre-Dame?'

'*What* . . .? Oh, Giselle. A false alarm. Cramps, all that sort of thing. Her cycle's way out of tune, but she's still determined to kill herself, though she says she'll wait to see if we return.'

'And Oona?' asked St-Cyr sadly.

'Still thinks she'll drown herself but admits it will be difficult cutting a hole through the ice without an axe.'

'*Bon*! That should slow her up. Now why don't you tell me what's really bothering you? No baby on the way? I would have thought you'd be . . .'

'*Celebrating*? Then read this. I got it from a friend of a friend at Gestapo Central but had to pay the lousy son of a bitch 10,000 for it.'

'Francs?'

'*Idiot! Reichskassenscheine.* Suddenly nobody wants francs any more, not since von Paulus stopped being supplied. There's a rumour he told the Führer he was going to have to throw in the towel.'

Stalingrad . . . The Sixth Army . . . A hundred thousand men at least and had the pendulum finally begun to swing the other way? Berlin would be enraged.

The flimsy slip of paper was a copy of a telex from Himmler to Boemelburg and it had come in at 0530 hours, not ten minutes ago. SETTLE IT – that was all there was to the message, but the intended inference was *Befehl ist Befehl*, an order is an order.

'Jacqmain blows his head off. The Spade is torched. Wehrle takes cyanide. Death follows on death but all Gestapo Paris-Central and the SS over in Saint-Cloud have to show for it is a shortage of at least 100,000,000 francs, an obvious absence of cyanide and explosives, and three women in their nightgowns, each of whom steadfastly claims her innocence! The Chief hasn't

231

any other choice. I'm telling you, Louis, it's us or them. They're terrorists.'

'We can't turn them in!' It was a cry.

'Look, I know that. I just had to get it clear with you because now it'll have to be the five of us against all of them.'

'Snipers?'

'Or grenades but, yes, it's the thought of snipers that worries me the most. *Killed while attempting to apprehend the Gypsy*! You, me, the three of them and it's . . . why then it's all settled and no one has to fuss about us any more. Hell, we only look after common crime. No one cares about that, not with all the really big crime that's going on!'

'And we've crossed the SS once too often.'

St-Cyr wet his lips in uncertainty as he searched the darkness ahead. 'What did Boemelburg send the Reichsminister to engender such a response?'

'That he wasn't sure of our loyalties, nor those of the three suspects.'

There was a sigh. 'Then they really do intend to kill us. It's to be a classic Gestapo-SS ploy.'

Kohler tossed his hands in despair. *'And we're going to have to go in there after the Gypsy knowing there's a gun at our backs and that the trigger will be pulled!'*

Or the grenade thrown . . .

It wasn't fair. It was criminal! but there was nothing they could do. 'We're already as good as dead. There will be mountains of white silk lilies and carnations for Gabrielle and her friends. Their coffins will be draped with swastikas. Tears will be shed wherever soldiers wait, and Goebbels will have a field day with it. Loyal French women *killed* in the act of *assisting* the Reich!'

Snow-covered, the lane passed through magnificent stands of oak and beech whose trunks stood tall and sentinel in the hushed and frozen air. The ruins were not within the Forêt de Marly-le-Roi, but were just on its outskirts and well to the north-west of the Joyenval crossroads.

From where he stood beside Boemelburg's car, St-Cyr could not yet see them. Silently, as before an assault, heavily armed

232

troops in their white, padded parkas, hoods and overtrousers fanned out to take up positions. Perhaps a platoon in number, perhaps two squads and some.

Uncertain of what lay ahead, Gabrielle looked steadily at him from the other side of the car; Suzanne-Cécilia also. From the north, another approach was being made. But there, the troops would have to pass through several hectares where willow shoots had been harvested down through the centuries for basket-making and other wickerwork. There, with backs to the thickets, Nana Thélème and Hermann would have to cross a frozen brook and fields and then make their way uphill through the abbey's former gardens to the ruins.

The Forêt occupied a low and hilly plateau which had once bordered the ancestral Seine; the ruins were downhill of it on a lesser rise. Beyond them, in the lowlands, there was a brook and, beyond this, the willow shoots. It was, for De Vries and Tshaya and, in the past, the gypsy caravans, a perfect location. Isolated yet within twenty-five kilometres of Paris and all but surrounded by forest, copse or low-lying field and farm.

Boemelburg didn't even bother to get out of the car. 'Louis, we'll give you two hours before we move in. Warn us if he's wired it. Enough good men have already been lost. Berlin are adamant. We can't spare any more.'

'But there are at least three others with them, Walter?'

'Talk to them. Convince them to come out. If they throw down their arms, they'll be deported. That's the best I can do.'

'And if they refuse?'

'We'll come in and get you.'

'*Am I not even to be allowed my gun?*'

'We want to talk to them, Louis. I'm sorry.'

'And Hermann?' The bags below Walter's eyes seemed bigger, sadder, more jaundiced in the grey light.

'No weapon either. Signal twice with the white flag when you've contacted De Vries, and three times when you're ready to bring him and the others out. If they try to make a break for it, we'll get them.'

'There's no need for Gabrielle and Madame Lemaire to come with me. Why not keep them here?'

Must Louis make things difficult? 'They'll soften them. Their presence will make De Vries less cautious and more open to talking.' Twice now Louis had noticed the rifles the snipers would use and had frantically torn his gaze from them. Had he realized what was to happen?

'And if he's not there? If there's no one?' leapt St-Cyr.

'We'll deal with that when we come to it.'

'Then it's *au revoir*,' he said, dismayed.

'*Bonne chance.*'

Sickened by what was to happen – betrayed, angry – he took Gabrielle and Suzanne-Cécilia by an arm. As they picked their way among the trees and underbrush, his spine was tense. If he could he would shove each of them aside and try to cover for them as they scrambled away.

But it would do no good. They'd all be taken. 'Did you kill the Spade?' he asked. There was a shallow ravine they had to cross and he was helping them into this. Gabrielle met his gaze.

'Why do you ask? Why do you doubt me so?'

Suzanne-Cécilia said, 'There is no way we could have, Inspector.'

'It's Chief Inspector,' he replied impatiently. 'Gestapo surveillance on you both was not in any way complete until after you had turned yourself in, Gabrielle. Not until Thursday afternoon. Did you pierce his eyes?'

'Is this what you believe of me, Jean-Louis?'

They would tell him nothing. They would each be shot – would he hear the sniper's gun? he wondered. Would he see them throw up their arms and open their mouths to cry out silently in shocked surprise even as they crumpled to the ground, or would they die from a grenade?

'I need to know. I cannot find it in me to believe any of you capable of such cruelty but the detective in me says I could be wrong.'

Silence followed the outburst. Gabrielle was a good head taller than either of them and easily pulled herself out of the ravine. Suzanne-Cécilia remained behind and when the two of them waited, looking down at her, Céci, disheartened and afraid, looked up to say, 'They're going to kill us, aren't they, Jean-Louis?'

In despair he looked away to where the men could no longer be seen. 'Yes.'

Hurriedly she crossed herself and kissed her fingertips, having pulled off Marianne's mitten to do so. 'I've not killed anyone,' she said, 'but since it seems a time for confessions, I would have slept with you willingly in that house of your mother's we shared so briefly.'

'*I knew it!*' said Gabrielle. 'You can't be trusted, can you, Céci?'

'Then the sous-directeur of Cartier's was not your lover?'

'*M. Laviolette*? Me? I simply rented the house from him to be closer to the wireless. He was tempted to believe an affair possible. He was always prepared and would try to press the issue but . . . Ah! what can a woman say?'

Kneeling, reaching out to her, he wrapped a hand about her arm and pulled her up, and for a moment the two of them knelt facing each other, Gabrielle looking uncertainly towards the troops, then to them and then towards the ruins which could not yet be seen. 'Have I lost you, Jean-Louis?' she asked, but heard no answer, simply his, 'Where, then, did you hide the wireless set?'

His eyes were so large and deeply brown, soft, warm, full of concern and compassion for them, and for herself, thought Suzanne-Cécilia. 'In the holding tanks below the pens of the wild pigs. They are not to be emptied until spring but by then it won't matter will it?'

He pulled off a glove to gently touch her swollen cheek and to refix the sticking plaster which had come loose over the bridge of her nose. 'I enjoyed our moment, even as I have enjoyed those I have shared with your *amie de guerre*. Now, please, let us go forward. To stay here is to invite the bullet or the grenade. Hermann and Nana may already have been killed.'

'*But . . . but we have heard nothing? No shots . . . ?*' blurted Suzanne-Cécilia.

'She's right, Jean-Louis,' said Gabrielle more harshly than she wanted, for this was love she was seeing before her and she knew she could not fight it but must let it happen.

The willows had been a bugger to get through. Not copsed since before the Defeat, they offered superb cover. But now there was open space, now snow-covered fields of stubble sloped down to the brook in its swale before rising gently up to the ruins.

Perhaps eight hectares had been enclosed by the abbey's outer walls, perhaps a little more. It was hard to tell, for the walls had fallen in several places offering perfect defensive and sentry positions. Forest and brush had long ago encroached on an orchard that could now hold terrorists. Ah *Gott im Himmel*!

Desperately looking for a way out, Kohler stood beside Nana Thélème. The men, supremely confident and thoroughly experienced, had taken up their positions. The dogs they had brought with them were muzzled but intently searched the lie of the land as he did.

There wasn't a sound. Breath steamed in the air.

'At least let us have a look, eh?' he said to the lieutenant in charge. Under the padded white parka, the bastard wore the ribbon of the *Winterschlacht im Osten* 1941/42, the 'Frozen Meat Medal'. He had lost his right leg to the Russians but had got through the willow shoots easily enough on that prosthesis of his.

The silver wound badge and both the EK2 and EK1 were pinned to that same tunic, the *Eiserne Kreuz*, the Iron Cross.

Max Engelmann and the SS-Untersturmführer Schacht had chosen to wait in the Citroën. Schacht had even asked for the keys 'in case of problems'. Goodbye car, goodbye trouble.

Given the field glasses, Kohler searched the ruins for any sign of life.

'Janwillem and Tshaya won't have built up the fire during the day,' confided Nana sadly.

The belfry of the chapel dominated everything. From there, the abbey's walls enclosed a substantial inner courtyard in which there were now large trees. He could make out nothing of the arcades at ground level, could get only glimpses of gaping windows and holes in the roof above them. Once stuccoed, the thick grey limestone of the walls was often exposed in ragged patches and where not, the yellowness of age and dampness remained.

A lane, unused in today's approaches, could just be made out leading in from a gap in the forest to the west. Men would be covering it, should De Vries and his band attempt a break-out.

'That is enough, *ja*?' said the lieutenant.

Kohler handed the glasses back to him. 'Your rifle's Russian. Hey, my boys were both killed at Stalingrad. I wonder if it was with one of those?'

'A lady's gun. The Soviets always make a big thing of their women snipers but the truth is, the weapon doesn't stand up to field use.'

'May I?' asked Kohler, and not waiting for an answer, took the rifle from him to examine its telescopic sight. 'What's it set for?'

'1300 metres,' came the grim and wary answer.

The distance from here to the outer walls? wondered Kohler. The SVT40, the self-loading Tokarev, had a ten-round detachable box and used 7.62 mm cartridges. To the sniper, its semi-automatic action's main advantage was that a second shot could be rapidly got off without moving the cheek from the stock to reload. 'It seems we can't make anything ourselves any more,' he grumbled. 'Our *Gewehr* 41s are simply copies of this.'

'But better. Now give it back to me, *ja? und* go. Already we are a little behind schedule.'

'Just let me tie my shoelace. Here, Nana, would you hold this?'

Swiftly Kohler turned aside to give the rifle to her. The lieutenant made a move to get round him, but the muzzle of a 9 mm Beretta was pushing his chin up.

The gun had been strapped to a leg . . .

'Say nothing, my friend,' breathed Kohler. 'Just walk out there as if there's been a little change of plan and you're going to check out the ruins with us. Nana, put the rifle under your coat, the muzzle down. Leave only one button done up so that you can hand it to me quickly.'

'*You won't get away with this*!' seethed the lieutenant.

'Hey, relax. We already have.'

Where the forest ended, the walls began. Trapped, St-Cyr looked anxiously back towards the troops and Boemelburg's car, but there was no sign of anyone, so well were the men hidden.

Then he realized tears were misting his eyes and lamely said to the others, 'This way, I think.'

Merde, it was terrible knowing the shots could come at any moment. Why do they not get it over with then? he demanded. Why must they torment us like this?

'Janwillem De Vries was the "package", wasn't he?' he said bitterly to Gabrielle who was in front of him. Suzanne-Cécilia had fallen back a little. 'When I talked to René Yvon-Paul, he told me things were far too difficult for them. After De Vries had done all the robberies you had arranged for him, he was to have been taken to Château Thériault to meet up with the local Resistance. From there, what was it to have been?'

Neither of them replied. Gabrielle pulled off one of her mittens to break a small icicle from the lip of a rocky ledge. It was so beautiful.

'Your Vouvray people were to have taken the Gyspy where?' he demanded. 'Was he to meet his next contact under the tail of the bronze horse?'

Lyon was a centre of the Resistance and one of their meeting-places, known just as he had given it, was near the equestrian statue of Louis XIV in place Bellecour, but how had Jean-Louis learned of it? 'Lyon is far too dangerous now,' she said. 'Our contacts in Vouvray had agreed to take him through Château-roux to Limoges, Toulouse and Narbonne.'

'And then?' he asked, subdued.

It was Suzanne-Cécilia who said, 'Perpignan and then into Andorra.'

'Via the tobacco smugglers of Las Escalades?' he asked.

'And from there into Spain to Seo de Urgel and Córdoba.'

The truth at last. 'Then Gibralter,' he sighed. 'The diamonds would have been proof enough of the Reich's desperate need for them. It's a tragedy it went so badly, but what I cannot forgive is that you didn't take Hermann and myself into your confidence. We could have helped!'

He was really upset and was needing answers. 'I tried to keep you both out of it,' said Gabrielle sadly. 'I knew that Hermann would be placed in an untenable position, and with him, Giselle and Oona. Oh for sure, I had faith in him but even so, it was not simply up to me. The decision had to come from all of us.'

'We were striking a fantastic blow for France, Jean-Louis,' said Suzanne-Cécilia earnestly.

'And the money the Gypsy stole? Was it to have funded the Resistance?'

Must he press so hard? wondered Gabrielle, dismayed to be facing him like this. 'They were to have taken it south. Eventually it was to have reached the *maquis* of the Auvergne and those in the Haute Savoie.'

238

'They are desperate for funds,' confided Suzanne-Cécilia, hesitantly reaching out to him. 'We . . . we had worked it all out. At least 100,000,000. It's a lot, but . . .' Hastily she wiped away her tears. 'But it wasn't to be.'

'Did the Spade learn of your plans?' he asked.

'Why must you keep harping about that one?' demanded Gabrielle, in tears herself.

'Did Tshaya tell him of what Janwillem De Vries knew of us – is this what you're thinking?' blurted Suzanne-Cécilia.

'You know that is what I wondering. *Mon Dieu*, why must you both be so stubborn? Why can you not tell me everything now? The Gypsy is in there among the ruins with others. He'll have wired the place, will have created a last refuge, lines of defence, escape routes most certainly.'

'Perhaps, then, you had best ask him when we find him,' said Gabrielle. 'Perhaps either he or Tshaya will tell you so that you . . . you will not believe us guilty of such a sadistic murder!'

'The Generalmajor Wehrle had no choice but to kill himself,' interjected Suzanne-Cécilia earnestly. 'Once he learned Nana was seriously under suspicion, and then of Gabrielle's arrest and the raid on my wireless set, he knew precisely what awaited him at the hands of his fellow Nazis.'

Swiftly he asked which of them had given Wehrle the cyanide. 'Answer me, damn you. Men like Wehrle wouldn't have been issued such a thing.'

They said no more, these two *résistants*. Taking each other by the hand, they walked on ahead of him until coming to a gap in the wall. Then they were lost to view and he was left to face the forest and his doubts, to search, to try to find the rifle that had marked him down.

When no shot was fired, he made his way along to the gap and stepped through it to find them waiting for him. Both were desperately afraid of what must lie ahead. Both anxiously swept their eyes over the trees and brush that lay before them until the ruins were reached.

'Wehrle had ordered caviar and champagne again,' he said, 'but Nana couldn't understand his having done since it automatically implicated her in his death and in everything else. Perhaps he blamed her for betraying him and helping the Gypsy, perhaps he merely wished to atone for the mistake he had made and was thinking of the well-being of loved ones in the Reich, but someone had to have given him the cyanide.'

'And?' asked Gabrielle sharply.

He shrugged. He said, 'That leaves only the two of you.'

'Which implies we robbed Nana's former villa in Saint-Cloud – is this what you are thinking, Jean-Louis? A stronghold of the SS. The headquarters of their *Sonderkommando*?'

'Didn't Janwillem and Tshaya rob it?' demanded Suzanne-Cécilia.

'They wouldn't have given Wehrle the cyanide. They had no reason to do so. Having robbed him, what more need of him had they?'

It was Gabrielle who said, 'The SS could have taken him aside and given it to him with an ultimatum.'

'But . . . but they showed no signs of having done so?' he said, looking earnestly from one to the other of them.

'He doesn't realize we're in a war,' blurted Suzanne-Cécilia. 'He has failed entirely to understand us!'

'Then perhaps he had best talk to Nana. Perhaps Nana can tell him the things he so desperately wants to know.'

Two shots rang out. Two more soon followed but by then they were running towards the sounds only to now hear the fierce barking of dogs. 'Hermann . . .' began St-Cyr. '*H . . . e . . . r . . . mann!*'

Widely spaced from one another across the open expanse of fields, three of the dogs lay dead in the snow.

Kohler waited for the others to be released. Lying flat on his stomach, his legs spread, he held the rifle ready. 'Let the lieutenant go,' he said, not looking back to where Nana kept the Beretta on the man. 'Take his ammunition pouch. Hey, *mein Kamerad*, we want no trouble with any of you. This is between Herr Engelmann, myself and the SS-Untersturmführer Schacht. Tell your men to hold the rest of the dogs and to send those two up to us.'

'You are to be allowed to enter the ruins alone. No one else is to go with you. I have my orders.'

'Fuck your orders. We've now warned the sons of bitches we're here and they're surrounded, eh? The Gypsy will have wired those ruins so well we can't have the dogs setting them off. I'll need the extra hands and eyes.'

'The dogs were let go because you took me hostage. They were not to have been released unless all else had failed and you hadn't been able to bring the Gypsy and his woman out.'

'And if we had?' asked Kohler, taking aim again. 'You'd have dropped each of us, eh? and would have left De Vries to the last.'

'And then released the dogs to stop him from running,' said Nana in *deutsch*. '*Bitte*, Herr Leutnant, I do not want to kill you or anyone. This whole thing is a tragic mistake. Herr Engelmann and the Untersturmführer are very wrong about us and are the ones to blame for what the Gypsy has done.'

The pistol was too tightly gripped. Kohler was pinned down . . .

'I will shoot you if I have to,' she said. 'You see, they have left us no choice. Now go, please, before I do.'

Engelmann had come to the edge of the willows. One of the dogs strained at the leash he held.

With a single shot, Kohler hit the animal in the chest, causing it to rear up suddenly on its hind legs and to fall back. Herr Max scrambled for cover.

'Tell Gestapo Boemelburg I could have dropped that man had I wanted to. The rifle's good but it pulls a little towards the top left quadrant. Hey, tell the boys I *like* dogs and hated to shoot them. They were beautiful animals.'

'I'll tell him and I'll try to keep the other two back.'

'Good.'

They watched as he walked down towards the brook. He held up his arms and spread them widely to signal that no one should do anything until he got there. Without a word, Kohler got up and together with Nana ran for cover behind the wall.

'Now start filling me in on De Vries,' he said, not letting her get free of him. 'And *don't* stop until I know how the son of a bitch will think and what he'll do and have done.'

'And Tshaya?' she asked, her dark eyes registering dismay as he took the pistol from her. 'She hates me. She'll try to kill me.

241

She can use explosives just as well as Janwillem but is of the Rom and knows their ways and these ruins, so will have the others at her beck and call.'

'Look, just fill me in on the two of them and on this place.'

'But ... but I haven't been here in years. I wouldn't know where to begin. He's *crazy*. There are so many places ... He's *not* the same as the man I once knew. He's ...'

She felt Kohler's fingers gently touch her lips; his thumb, her tears. '*Listen*,' he whispered.

It was Louis. Louis was calling to him. Louis sounded trapped and in despair but was a long way off.

'He's inside the ruins, in the great hall,' said Nana sadly. 'That is where the gypsies gathered to hold their feasts and the *Kris Romani*, the trials at which all serious offences and conflicts within the *kumpania* were settled by the elders. He's found something and is trying to warn you of it.'

A trial ... Ah, Christ!

The hall, where the monks had once dined, was long and huge, its ceiling high. And from where there had been leaded glass in more recent years, the grey light of day entered under the arcade outside to throw pale shafts across the littered floor.

Snow had been swept in by the wind. Rags, cushions, blankets, bits of tattered, faded carpet lay among scattered eiderdowns whose feathers were teased by the wind and whose carmine, beige or white silk coverlets, with a black embroidery of flowered designs, had been torn.

Overturned cooking cauldrons were beside the fourteenth-century fireplace. An iron tripod still stood over long-dead ashes. There was broken furniture, some of it still bearing ancient fabrics and leaking horsehair. There were carved oak chairs with no legs, chairs with two or three ... Benches, a narrow wooden bed, a wicker *chaise-longue*, a broken card table ... Scatterings of dresses, the skirts wine purple, deep red and brown, all voluminous, the blouses once white and loose and low-cut.

A faded yellow kerchief that would have been tied around a boy's neck lay next to the *diklo*, the headscarf in magenta which had once covered the long and braided, glossy, blue-black hair of his mother.

242

There were broken wine bottles, kicked-over wooden water buckets, battered fedoras, old suit jackets, horseshoes, horse harness, tarpaulins, anvils, the leather bellows of a simple but effective forge ...

Jars of pickled cucumbers, those of hot red peppers in vinegar.

'August 1941 ...' St-Cyr heard himself sadly exhaling the words. 'Tshaya, daughter of the horse trader Tshurkina la Marako who was deported to Buchenwald 14 September of that year with all members of his *kumpania* except herself.'

'Jean-Louis ...' began Gabrielle only to hear him caution her with, 'Wait, please. What have we come upon?'

The ancient leather trunks and suitcases, the wooden boxes, had all been opened and dumped in a mad search for gold coins. The men would have been herded to one end of the hall, the women and children to the other. Sandals, broken shoes, sabots, old rubber boots – all of it was here.

Stripped of their gold, the gypsies had been loaded on to lorries and taken from this place.

And now? he asked himself.

He picked up a photograph from among the scattered hundreds. The long, drooping moustache, heavy gold rings, gold coins hanging from the watch chain across the waistcoat, fedora, crumpled dark suit jacket, wide corduroy trousers and riding boots were those of a *Rom Baro*. 'Tshaya's father,' he said. A sweat-stained silk kerchief of dark colour was knotted around the neck.

'Did she turn them all in?' he asked of Tshaya. 'Did that husband of hers force her to tell him where her family was in hiding? Is this why the Spade was murdered in such a horrible fashion?'

He took a moment and then told them the worst of his thoughts. 'Boemelburg must have known of the round-up and yet has said nothing of it to us.' Instead, Walter had let him and Hermann believe the Gestapo and the SS had had no prior knowledge of this place or of what had happened here.

Some granular snow struck the shattered remains of a window, startling them. Suzanne-Cécilia found his hand to grip it tightly. Gabrielle moved closer.

'There are no recent tracks,' he said emptily. 'Has no one been in here since it happened?'

'The chapel then,' said Gabrielle in a whisper. 'Perhaps they are using it.'

'*For what*?' he asked, alarmed.

'For her trial and . . . and as a last redoubt.'

'But . . . but how is it that you know of this?' he bleated.

'I don't. I'm only suggesting it.'

For two days he and Hermann had been absent from Paris. Gestapo surveillance of the *réseau* had been slack and had only been stepped up on their return. Had this given Gabrielle and the others an opportunity to travel unnoticed?

The Spade had been murdered; the Generalmajor had been given a cyanide capsule and told *what*? he wondered. *The truth*?

'Where is the chapel?' he asked, sickened by his thoughts. 'Show me, please.'

Neither of these two *résistants* argued with him. In single file, with Gabrielle leading, they picked their way among the rubbish to a far portal. He did not know if Hermann and Nana had been killed, only that the shots they had heard had come from a rifle.

And now? he asked himself. What will we find?

Half hidden among the barren branches and undergrowth, and at a distance of perhaps 200 metres, the bleached grey ribs of six large caravans stared emptily at the sky. Tensely Kohler let his gaze sift questioningly over them, understanding only too well what must have happened. There had been no recent tracks in the overgrown orchard and gardens, no tripwires, not even snares for rabbits or signs of wood-gathering.

The ruins just beyond the caravans were quiet. The air was clean and sharp – there wasn't a hint of hastily extinguished cooking fires nor of tethered horses.

Nana Thélème could not seem to take her eyes from the caravans. 'There is scattered clothing,' she said hesitantly.

They could go round the carvans, they could head for them. The belfry of the chapel was some distance to their right. She started for it. He heard her suck in a startled breath when held back by him.

'Were the girls and young women raped?' he asked.

Stiffening, she answered fiercely, '*How could I possibly know*?'

'Let's have a look at what's left. Now start telling me about De Vries, like I asked. I want everything.'

'He . . . he was always gentle and kind and had such a sense of humour but was mischievous. He . . . he loved Tshaya's father as his own and was adopted by him.'

'And Tshaya – how did he feel towards her?'

'She was forbidden. She was not for him. When she was fourteen her father agreed to marry her off to someone younger from a neighbouring *kumpania*. They were third cousins, I think. Tshaya wanted no part of the boy but the bride-price had been paid and was soon spent lavishly on drink and food to celebrate.'

Kohler helped her over some fallen branches. 'So she ran off to Paris after Janwillem.'

'At the age of fifteen, and has been running after him ever since.'

Kohler pulled her to a stop. 'She disgraced her family yet they took her back when the Spade came for her?'

Nana's head was shaken. 'She was considered *marhime*, as was her family.'

'So her father let the Spade beat her?'

Why must he demand answers now? 'Janwillem wasn't there to stop it, nor do I think he could have, though he always regretted his not having done so.'

A sigh was given. 'The *kumpaniyi* gathered and had a trial,' said Kohler. 'Her father was a *Rom Baro*. They threw her out. They banished her but De Vries still loved her.'

'Not in that way. To him she was like a sister. It was she who wanted him as a woman wants a man.'

'You're only saying that because he left you for her.'

'To commit a robbery, yes, but has he now discovered the truth about her? *Has he*?' she demanded.

'And what of the others who are supposed to be with them? What of the three who went from the quarry to Paris in Gabrielle's car?'

What of the car and of the explosives? 'I . . . I don't know. I . . . I wish I did.'

Once among the caravans, it was easy to see what had happened. There were human remains among the bloodstained, torn and rodent-infested eiderdowns and dresses. Some of the braids had come undone, others were tied together . . .

'Come on, let's find Louis and get this over with.'

'Look, I'm ... I'm sorry I spoke out like that. All I want is to see Janwillem a last time. When he hears what I have to tell him, he'll understand I didn't betray him, nor would I ever have done such a thing.'

Oslo, 20 April 1938, then the Mollergaten-19, prisoner 3266, cell D2 and cell C27. Well over four years until Herr Max paid visit after visit to finally offer a *Gaje* deal that couldn't be refused.

'He must have told Tshaya we were to have a child and be married. This ... this she could not allow.'

With the stirring of the wind, the snow was gently swept across the floor of the arcade. Depressions were soon filled; others uncovered. Footprints led down the length of it to a staircase. St-Cyr hesitated. Alarmed, he strained to listen. There were at least two sets of footprints. Were De Vries and Tshaya waiting for them in the chapel? The others? he asked. Were there tripwires?

Gabrielle's eyes, of the softest shade of violet, were full of apprehension. Suzanne-Cécilia gazed warily at him, searching for the slightest sign of *what*? he demanded and wished again that they had confided fully in him and Hermann. Was it doubt she sought? he wondered.

He went on. They had to follow. And when he crouched to pass exploring fingers over one of the footprints, he looked up first to Gabrielle and then to Suzanne-Cécilia with only the heartfelt sadness of a detective doing his job.

'These are at least two days old,' he said. Whispering to themselves, they trailed behind – he could hear them doing so. Are there no guns? he cried out silently to them. No other gypsies? Ah damn you, damn you. I thought you were my friends.

Light bathed the little chapel, passing through a ragged hole in its once eloquently decorated ceiling where faint black swallows still flew in premonkish paint.

The rope was coarse, the trailing *diklo* crimson. The benches were ancient, grey and heavy – carved and covered with dust and rubble. A handprint was here, a gap was there. Some of the chairs had had to be moved.

Tshaya stirred but slightly in the softly eddying wind which carried the granules of snow down from the belfry above to pass them over her body. Her hair was long and braided and blue-black but not glossy in this light. Her face was slightly puffed, the expression placid, the brow wide and strong, the jet black eyebrows fierce perhaps but not now, the eyes dark and wide and bulging only slightly, the lips a dark blue. Frozen ... the corpse was frozen.

The rope had been thrown up and over a sturdy yet worm-eaten timber. It had been knotted about her throat, the knot placed on the right side so that the head was crooked to the left and the *diklo* trailed that way and would have caught the saliva as it drained from her mouth.

Thursday ... had it been done then? he asked himself.

Her bare feet were together. The ankles had not been tied. Though her wrists had been secured behind her back, it seemed she had put up little if any struggle. Had there been three or more of them and she with no chance of doing so, or had she simply defied them to the last?

There were bloodspots, the petechiae that were caused by ruptured blood vessels immediately below the skin. He looked for mucus which should have issued from her nose, for signs of saliva draining from her mouth – for urine and faeces. Had they all been washed away?

Rigor had set in. Two days at least, he thought. The dark brown skin of her back and buttocks, and of her bare arms and shoulders was blotched and covered with a mass of glistening scars.

'Help me,' he said. 'We must cut her down.'

'Louis, don't! Leave her for the Chief. It can't matter now.'

St-Cyr reached out to him. '*Merde*, I thought you had gone from me. She had had the flu, Hermann. She had not been able to go with Gabrielle and De Vries to the quarry.'

Turning, he said swiftly to Nana, 'What did you do with the flypapers you bought in Tours? Damn it, you tell me!'

She threw Gabrielle a desperate look. 'They ... they were for the school of dance,' she tried. 'Mother ... mother wanted them. We can't get them in Paris any more. I ... I bought all I could, thinking I could sell what we didn't need.'

'Oh yes, oh yes.'

'De Vries, Louis. The belfry. We'd better find him and quickly.'

But was the Gypsy still playing with them? wondered St-Cyr sadly. And why had he tried to make it look as if he had hanged Tshaya if not to hide her having first been poisoned, and to indicate she had been punished for betraying her family and himself?

From the belfry there was a clear view of the surrounding countryside. Down from the forest, up from the willows, the men advanced. There was no way of stopping them. If De Vries and the others had rigged the place, several were bound to be killed.

'*Killed*, do you understand?' swore St-Cyr, still demanding answers.

Gabrielle shouted, '*Don't you dare talk to me like that!*' Suzanne-Céclia said, 'Look.'

'Look *where*?' swore Kohler.

'The inner courtyard. Under the arcade at the far corner.'

Ah *nom de Dieu*.

Hermann used the telescopic sight. Thinking he was about to shoot at them, the men threw themselves to the ground. Schmeissers opened up. Bullets struck the stone tower. They ducked. They cringed. One of the women shrieked, 'I've been hit!'

Fresh blood spattered the timbered floor next to her. '*Ah Christ, cut it out!*' cried Kohler, waving the white flag desperately. '*It's wired! Stay back!*'

Sniper fire singled him out. He ducked. Stone splinters flew. Hesitantly Louis raised the white flag above the lip of the ruined wall. There were gaps through which they could be easily hit.

'Hermann . . . Hermann, I think there is a lull.'

Hermann was staring down through the hole in the floor at the corpse. Louis shook him. 'Here, give me the rifle,' he said.

'No. No, I'm better at it than you, eh? Hey, I've already had to use it.'

Cautiously he got to his feet, was soon too exposed. At least three of them would have him in their sights. The lieutenant . . . Herr Max . . . the SS-Untersturmführer Schacht. Ah bastards . . . bastards . . .

Putting the rifle to his shoulder, wrapping the sling around his left arm, he sighted down into the courtyard. Slowly he moved

248

the sight along inside the south arcade until he came to Gabrielle's car. It was parked in a far corner, tucked beyond brush and tree limbs, and he could just make out De Vries sitting behind the wheel.

'Kill him,' swore Louis. 'You're going to have to.'

'There's a flask of nitro hanging from a cord about his neck. The . . . the rest of it's in his lap and on the seat beside him.'

'Are there others with him?'

'None that I can see.'

'Is he going to drive the car along the arcade and into the wall?'

Kohler thumbed the rear lens to clear it of the fog the closeness to his eye had caused. 'He's not moving, Louis. Maybe the battery's dead.'

'Maybe he's dead – is this what you're really saying? Maybe there was no second trip to the quarry. Maybe there were no other "terrorists" to apprehend the car and hitch a ride back to Paris but merely a trip to here . . . to *here*, Hermann.'

'Hang on. Get down.'

There was a blinding flash, a rush of air. Stones, timbers and earth flew up and outwards. The dust was thick. A timber fell, another and another. Someone screamed as she dropped through the floor, someone else cried out, *'Don't try to move! I've got you!'*

It was Gabrielle and she dangled by her coat and scarf and was hanging on to the rope beside Tshaya.

Louis scrambled over to the gap in the floor. Leaning down, flattening himself next to Suzanne-Cécilia, he gasped, 'Grab me by the ankles. *Hermann, help!*'

Slowly, gradually Gabrielle was pulled from the corpse and when they had her safely on the floor, he held her tightly and rocked her gently back and forth, saying, 'Forgive me. Murder is only murder when one is not at war. You had no other choice but to kill or be killed.'

Tears streamed from her. 'I didn't want to pierce his eyes, Jean-Louis. I will hate myself for the rest of my days but we *had* to make it look as though Tshaya had done it. We *had* to make it look as if Janwillem had tried and convicted her for what she had done.'

Startled, Kohler looked from one to the other of them and then to Suzanne-Cécilia and finally to Nana.

'My arm,' she said. 'It's shattered. I can't feel any pain but am so cold.'

For a moment her eyes were clear. 'The cellars,' she said and softly smiled at them. 'The cellars.'

'Ah *merde*, Louis, she's gone.'

There was blood on the snow where Nana lay, and all around her soldiers came and went without regard for her body. They were hurrying to recover the loot from the cellars. Flames towered beyond them. The abbey's roof and floors threw pillars of smoke and glowing ash high into the winter's sky.

Kohler put an arm about Suzanne-Cécilia's and Gabrielle's shoulders and pulled them close. 'Hey, hang on, eh? We're not done yet.'

Tallying the loot, Herr Max had to crouch to thumb through the bundles of banknotes and the jewellery or examine the leather bags and small cardboard boxes in which Wehrle had kept the diamonds. Nearby, the Untersturmführer Schacht stood at the ready with pencil and paper. Both of them were only too anxious to save their own lives.

Boemelburg had given himself distance and had taken Louis with him to hear the Sûreté's side of the affair.

'Jean-Louis doesn't love me any more,' said Gabrielle woodenly.

'Now, now, it's not like that.'

'We're all to be shot in any case so why, please, make such a crisis of it?' snapped Suzanne-Cécilia. 'Could we not *both* have shared him?'

Merde, what had happened to the women of France that they would even *think* of such a thing? Too few men, he said sadly to himself. Too few opportunities for a little happiness.

'Well, Louis, tell me what went on here,' asked Boemelburg, offering a cigarette to fingers so desperate they shook.

St-Cyr inhaled deeply and paused to hold the smoke in. Flames had reached the belfry. No attempt had been made to recover Tshaya's body. 'When they got here, De Vries saw the caravans and the littered rubbish of the *kumpania* and realized his companion had betrayed her family. For a time, I think, he said nothing, Walter. She danced for him and the other terrorists in the cellars. They slept and ate down there. Then at the height of a dance or at its conclusion, she was accused and taken up to the chapel. This, perhaps, was when he found out that Nana Théléme had not been the cause of his going to prison.'

'Tshaya did not resist being hanged?'

'The others must have been with him but left De Vries afterwards, perhaps to seek escape routes. They'll see the fire or will be told of it. They won't come back.'

'So we've no hope of finding them?'

'Not here. Not in Paris either. It will simply be too dangerous for them. No, I think they will head south, perhaps to the Camargue, to Les Baux and Les Saintes-Maries-de-la-Mer.'

A gathering ground and holy place of the *nomades* before the war. 'Will there be others of their kind for them to take refuge with?'

'This I really cannot say. I've no knowledge of how effective the deportations have been.'

Was St-Cyr simply guarding that tongue of his, or had he finally seen the light and would now no longer be so difficult? 'What went on with the Spade?'

'Tshaya lured him to the house on the rue Nollet. Together, she and De Vries murdered him.'

'You're certain of this?'

Had an autospy been done? Had they found something? he worried but would have to take the chance. 'Yes. Yes, I'm certain of it.'

'And the robberies?'

'The loot will, I think, be totally recovered, the cyanide capsules as well.'

For a time they smoked their cigarettes in silence. The remains of the belfry's roof were collapsing. The men were now watching the fire. The two women knelt beside the body of their friend, with Kohler standing near them, looking lost and alone. 'Herr Max returns to Berlin with the diamonds, Louis. The Untersturm-führer and the rest of his *Sonderkommando* will go with him as security. The villa in Saint-Cloud will be occupied by others. It's much-needed accommodation.'

'And the banknotes?' asked St-Cyr. 'The jewellery, the sapphires ...?'

'Will go up in smoke. Tell Kohler to see that they are loaded into my car. Go with him to make certain none are stolen.'

'And Nana Thélème?'

'A small funeral, a quiet burial in the Père-Lachaise. No members of the press. This matter is closed. See that your little songbird sings her heart out. Understand that even the Führer listens to her when not attentive to his Wagner.'

Understand that this is a final warning.

They would walk in the Bois de Boulogne as they had before the problem of the Gypsy had begun. They would each in their own way try to find that moment to settle things between themselves but would Jean-Louis understand and forgive?

'I could sleep like a dormouse,' said Gabrielle sadly. 'Never have I been so exhausted.'

In Provence, in the late fall of each year, the dormice come indoors to find themselves a hole in which to sleep until spring.

'Nana's death couldn't have been helped,' he said. 'None of us, not you, not Hermann, nor I or Suzanne-Cécilia could have prevented it.'

'Two shots. One in the left arm; the other in the abdomen.'

'I've seen it happen too many times and so has Hermann.'

'We could have done something! We could have . . .'

Gabrielle burst into tears and he had to hold her tightly. 'We *couldn't* have done anything,' he pleaded with her. 'We were *trapped*! Things simply happened too quickly.'

She bowed her head and tried to stop herself, blurted, 'At first, when he arrived in Paris, the Gypsy led us to believe he was on our side and that he would pull off the robberies we had lined up for him. We would get the funds to the Resistance. We would see that he got safely back to the British, but then . . .'

'He turned against you as he fully intended. He and Tshaya went out on their own determined to cause trouble and to take advantage of the situation.'

She took the proffered handkerchief. 'We had to stop him before it was too late. We *had* to!'

'He and Tshaya robbed the pay-train.'

'It . . . it had all been looked over – arranged, you understand, well ahead of time. By then we thought it the end for us but later that day he and Tshaya paid Nana a visit. They wanted me to take them to the ruins. They . . . they wanted out of Paris.'

252

'But Nana had prepared a little something for yourselves should things go wrong.'

Gabrielle ducked her head away. 'She ... she gave them each a glass of the *eau de vie de cassis* she had made herself from grain alcohol, saccharin, artificial blackcurrant flavouring and colour.'

Lots of people made such things these days. They were invariably dreadful and horribly sweet. 'Strychnine is very bitter. How long did it take?'

He was so grim and sad. She wanted desperately for him to take her in his arms and to tell her things were well between them. 'Seven minutes for Janwillem; ten for Tshaya. Nana ... Nana did it on Wednesday at about two thirty in the afternoon. They ... they had told her where they had left the loot.'

'In the house on the rue Nollet.'

'Yes.'

'Who telephoned the Spade at the Avia Club Gym?'

'I did.'

'And he came running all by himself.'

'Yes! We were desperate, Jean-Louis. Frantic. You and Hermann were not around. We felt you must have gone to Tours and then to Senlis, to the quarry. What, *please*, were we to have done?'

They had reached a copse of birch trees. Leading her among them, he asked, 'Was it you who lit the match that set the Spade afire?'

She blinked her tears away. 'Will you despise me now?' she asked. 'Will you turn your back on me if I tell you I did it?'

'You pierced his eyes.'

Only Suzanne-Cécilia had been with her, but Céci had already told him she hadn't killed anyone, so it was no use avoiding the truth and she had best get it over with. 'Yes, I did it. There, does that sanctify your self-righteousness, Monsieur l'Inspecteur principal? I am a *résistant*. We had each to make terrible sacrifices and we had, Céci and I, drawn straws to see who would do it.'

When he said nothing but simply fiddled with a tiny shred of bark, she said, 'We had to make it appear as though Tshaya had done it, otherwise those of the rue Lauriston and the Gestapo would have done the same to us or worse. Besides, he knew too much and we couldn't have that.'

Was the war within France to become one of outright savagery? he wondered.

253

'Later that night we ... we robbed the villa in Saint-Cloud. We had to make it appear as if ...'

'Yes, yes, as if De Vries and Tshaya were still alive. Which of you gave the Generalmajor Wehrle the cyanide?'

He would hate her now. He would never be able to find it within himself to sleep with her for fear of ... 'I did. I know a lot of those at the Ritz, so it was no problem my going there to leave a little envelope for him when I got back to Paris. I went there first before giving my statement to the police. Wehrle ...' She shrugged. 'He must have seen he had no other choice but ... but as to his having ordered caviar and champagne for Nana, that can only have been a parting gesture, his little revenge.'

'But he didn't kill himself until Friday.'

'He waited to see what would happen.'

'Only to find he had been recalled to Berlin.'

A tiny shred of the paperbark was pulled from the tree and examined. 'The bomb in the zebra house,' he said, and she told him Suzanne-Cécilia had put it there. 'Only Nana and I went to the ruins with the bodies of Tshaya and Janwillem, the loot and the explosives. We started out soon after the villa robbery. It was very dark and bitterly cold. Perhaps this is what saved us, who's to say? And yes, I was supposed to have been at the club and I worried all the time that the Gestapo would come looking for me there or to Monseigneur for Nana, or to the Schéhérazade. The car ... would the engine seize up? The snow ... We ... we were stopped only once. I ... I simply told the Feldwebel the Hauptmann and his lady friend were asleep and not feeling well, and that we were driving them to their country house. It worked. Don't ask me why. Fear of the flu perhaps.'

'And on the return?'

Must he have everything? 'We each went our separate ways. I stole a bicycle but then managed a lift to Les Halles in a *gazogène* lorry full of rutabagas. Nana walked until able to catch a lift in a Wehrmacht lorry full of troops. They were coming into the city to help search for the Gypsy.'

The risks they had taken, the chances ... 'Suzanne-Cécilia is being transferred to Lyon, to a private zoo.'

'But ... but the Untersturmführer Klaus Barbie is head of Section IV there? He'll ... he'll have her constantly watched.'

'It's his little zoo. We could do nothing. She's Boemelburg's insurance that we behave and say nothing further of the loot. It simply had to be.'

'Ah no . . .'

'Please don't do anything more, not for a good while. Lie low, Gabrielle. Keep out of it. Let others take up the sword.'

'She's in love with you. I saw it happen. It . . . it was quite beautiful, but . . . but it made me hate her for a brief moment.'

'Love has no place in war. It can only intrude.'

They walked in silence through a frozen land where those who were in uniform enjoyed themselves on skis, sleighs or on horseback. When asked what was to become of Nana's little boy and the daughter of Janwillem and Tshaya, she told him that she'd already asked the General von Schaumburg to allow the children *laissez-passers* to Vouvray and Château Thériault. 'Nana's mother agrees and so does Madame Moreel in Senlis.'

They had reached the Carrefour de Longchamp. 'And now we must part,' she said. 'Please don't hate me. What was done had to be done.'

Hermann had caught up with them in the Citroën. 'Avignon, Louis. Something about a madrigal singer who suddenly lost his or her voice. I can't quite make out the telex Boemelburg handed me. It's blurred. He wants us to get out of town for a bit. Hop in.'

'A moment, then.' Turning to Gabrielle, St-Cyr took hold of her mittened hands, saying earnestly, 'Give me time. Let us speak of things when I get back.'

'Kiss her, Louis. Ah! you French. The Italians could teach you plenty!'

'And the Boches?' came the swift retort as Louis got into the car.

'More again if you'd only listen. Hey, there's a bottle of pastis and a tin of pipe tobacco on the seat.'

Kohler got out of the car to take Gabrielle in his arms, to kiss her on each cheek and draw in the faint scent of that fabulous perfume, and to tell her to stop worrying. 'He's just being self-righteous. He'll be okay. I'll straighten him out.'

'Even though detectives make such lousy lovers?'

'Hey, ask Oona and Giselle about that. They'll give you an earful. Ah! would you see that they get this? I forgot.'

The roll of banknotes was bigger than needed to choke a zebra.

Thousands ... ten thousands ... He peeled off 100,000 at least. 'Expenses,' he said. 'Boemelburg will never miss it. Oh, I forgot these too.'

In the palm of his hand were the sapphire ear-rings from the jewellery she had ordered at Cartier's. 'Keep them out of sight until spring comes, eh? They're from Louis but he's just too shy to give them to you.'

Alone, she watched the car cause the snow to swirl and billow until she could see them no more and they were gone from her.

'Au revoir, mon cher vieux,' she said. *'Alles ist Schicksal.* All is fate.